Memoirs of Hecate County

BOOKS BY EDMUND WILSON

I THOUGHT OF DAISY

POETS, FAREWELL!

AXEL'S CASTLE

THE TRIPLE THINKERS

TO THE FINLAND STATION

THE WOUND AND THE BOW

NOTE-BOOKS OF NIGHT

THE SHOCK OF RECOGNITION

MEMOIRS OF HECATE COUNTY

EUROPE WITHOUT BAEDEKER

CLASSICS AND COMMERCIALS

THE SHORES OF LIGHT

FIVE PLAYS

THE SCROLLS FROM THE DEAD SEA

RED, BLACK, BLOND AND OLIVE

A PIECE OF MY MIND

THE AMERICAN EARTHQUAKE

Memoirs
of Hecate County

by

EDMUND WILSON

L. C. PAGE & COMPANY
NEW YORK

ACKNOWLEDGMENTS are due the *Atlantic Monthly, Partisan Review* and *Town and Country,* in whose pages, respectively, the first three of these stories appeared.

For this new edition of *Memoirs of Hecate County* I have made a revised text, which differs in many passages from the version originally published. *Hecate County* is my favorite among my books—I have never understood why the people who interest themselves in my work never pay any attention to it—and I am glad to have been able to improve it a little.

E. W.

Of a sudden . . . in the midst of the silence . . . the iron lid of the coffin burst open with a crash, and the corpse of the dead girl sat up. Even more frightful was she now than the first time. Frightfully her teeth rattled, convulsively her lips twitched, wildly she screamed incantations. A whirlwind swept through the church; the icons fell on their faces; the smashed panes flew out the windows. The doors were torn from their hinges, and an innumerable horde of horrors swept into the holy church. The whole place was filled with a terrible sound of the scratching of claws and the swishing of wings. In a flock, they swooped and wheeled, searching everywhere to find the philosopher.

NIKOLAI GOGOL: Viy

Contents

I.

The Man Who Shot Snapping Turtles

IN THE DAYS when I lived in Hecate County, I had an uncomfortable neighbor, a man named Asa M. Stryker. He had at one time, he told me, taught chemistry in some sooty-sounding college in Pennsylvania, but he now lived on a little money which he had been "lucky enough to inherit." I had the feeling about him that somewhere in the background was defeat or frustration or disgrace. He was a bachelor and kept house with two servants—a cook and a man around the place. I never knew anyone to visit him, though he would occasionally go away for short periods—when, he would tell me, he was visiting his relatives.

Mr. Stryker had a small pond on his place, and from the very first time I met him, his chief topic of conversation was the wild ducks that used to come to this pond. In his insensitive-sounding way he admired them, minutely observing their markings, and he cherished and protected them like pets. Several pairs, in fact, which he fed all the year round, settled permanently on the pond. He would call my attention in his hard accent to the richness of their chestnut browns; the ruddiness of their backs or breasts; their sharp contrasts of light with dark, and their white neck-rings and purple wing-bars, like

3

the decorative liveries and insignia of some exalted order; the cupreous greens and blues that gave them the look of being expensively dressed.

Mr. Stryker was particularly struck by the idea that there was something princely about them—something which, as he used to say, Frick or Charlie Schwab couldn't buy; and he would point out to me their majesty as they swam, cocking their heads with such dignity and nonchalantly wagging their tails. He was much troubled by the depredations of snapping turtles, which made terrible ravages on the ducklings. He would sit on his porch, he said, and see the little ducks disappear, as the turtles grabbed their feet and dragged them under, and feel sore at his helplessness to prevent it.

As he lost brood after brood in this way, the subject came, in fact, to obsess him. He had apparently hoped that his pond might be made a sort of paradise for ducks, in which they could breed without danger: he never shot them even in season and did not approve of their being shot at all. But sometimes not one survived the age when it was little enough to fall victim to the turtles.

These turtles he fought in a curious fashion. He would stand on the bank with a rifle and pot them when they stuck up their heads, sometimes hitting a duck by mistake. Only the ducks that were thus killed accidentally did he think it right to eat. One night when he had invited me to dine with him on one of them, I asked him why he did not protect the ducklings by shutting them up in a wire pen and providing them with a small pool to swim in. He told me that he had already decided to try this, and the next time I saw him he reported that the ducklings were doing finely.

Yet the pen, as it turned out later, did not permanently solve the problem, for the wild ducks, when they got old enough, flew out of it, and they were still young enough to be caught by the turtles. Mr. Stryker could not, as he said, keep them captive all their lives. The thing was rather, he finally concluded, to try to get rid of the turtles, against which he was coming, I noted, to display a slightly morbid animosity, and, after a good deal of serious thought, he fixed upon an heroic method.

He had just come into a new inheritance, which, he told me, made him pretty well off; and he decided to drain the pond. The operation took the whole of one summer: it horribly disfigured his place, and it afflicted the neighborhood with the stench of the slime that was now laid bare. One family whose place adjoined Stryker's were obliged to go away for weeks during the heaviest days of August, when the draining had become complete. Stryker, however, stayed and personally attended to the turtles, cutting off their heads himself; and he had men posted day and night at the places where they went to lay their eggs. At last someone complained to the Board of Health, and they made him fill up his pond. He was indignant with the town authorities and declared that he had not yet got all the turtles, some of which were still hiding in the mud; and he and his crew put in a mad last day combing the bottom with giant rakes.

The next spring the turtles reappeared, though at first there were only a few. Stryker came over to see me and told me a harrowing story. He described how he had been sitting on his porch watching "my finest pair of mallard, out with their new brood of young ones. They were still just little fluffy balls, but they sailed along with that air they have of knowing that they're somebody special. From the moment that they can catch a water bug for themselves, they know that they're the lords of the pond. And I was just thinking how damn glad I was that no goblins were going to git them any more. Well, the phone rang and I went in to answer it, and when I came out again I distinctly had the impression that there were fewer ducks on the pond. So I counted them, and, sure enough, there was one duckling shy!" The next day another had vanished, and he had hired a man to watch the pond. Several snapping turtles were seen, but he had not succeeded in catching them. By the middle of the summer the casualties seemed almost as bad as before.

This time Mr. Stryker decided to do a better job. He came to see me again and startled me by holding forth in a vein that recalled the pulpit. "If God has created the mallard," he said, "a thing of beauty and grace, how can He allow these dirty filthy mud-turtles to prey upon His handiwork and destroy it?" "He created the mud-turtles first," I said. "The reptiles came before the birds. And they survive with the strength God gave them. There is no instance on record of God's intervention in the affairs of any animal species lower in the scale than man." "But if the Evil triumphs there," said Stryker, "it may triumph everywhere, and we must fight it with every weapon in our power!" "That's the Manichaean heresy," I replied. "It is an error to assume that the Devil is contending on equal terms with God and that the fate of the world is in doubt." "I'm not sure of that sometimes," said Stryker, and I noticed that his little bright eyes seemed to dim in a curious way as if he were drawing into himself to commune with some private fear. "How do we know that some of His lowest creations aren't beginning to get out of hand and clean up on the higher ones?"

He decided to poison the turtles, and he brushed up, as he told me, on his chemistry. The result, however, was all too devastating. The chemicals he put into the water wiped out not only the turtles, but also all the other animals and most of the vegetation in the pond. When his chemical analysis showed that the water was no longer tainted, he put back the ducks again, but they found so little to eat that they presently flew away and ceased to frequent the place. In the meantime, some new ones that had come there had died from the poisoned water. One day, as Asa M. Stryker was walking around his estate, he encountered a female snapping turtle unashamedly crawling in the direction of the pond. She had obviously just been laying her eggs. He had had the whole of his place closed in with a fence of thick-meshed wire which went down a foot into the ground (I had asked him why he didn't have the pond rather than the whole estate thus enclosed, and he had explained that this would have made it impossible for him to look at the ducks from the porch) ; but turtles must have got in through the gate when it was open or they must have been in hiding all the time. Stryker was, as the English say, livid, and people became a little afraid of him because they thought he was getting cracked.

II

That afternoon he paid a visit to a man named Clarence Latouche, whose place was just behind Stryker's. Latouche was a native of New Orleans, and he worked in the advertising business. When Asa Stryker arrived, he was consuming a tall Scotch highball, unquestionably not his first; and he tried to make Stryker have a drink in the hope that it would relieve his tension. But "I don't use it, thanks," said Stryker, and he started his theological line about the ducks and the snapping turtles. Clarence Latouche, while Stryker was talking, dropped his eyes for a moment to the wing collar and the large satin cravat which his neighbor always wore in the country and which were evidently associated in his mind with some idea, acquired in a provincial past, of the way for a "man of means" to dress. It seemed to him almost indecent that this desperate moral anxiety should agitate a being like Stryker.

"Well," he commented in his easy way when he had listened for a few minutes, "if the good God can't run the universe, where He's supposed to be the supreme authority, without letting in the forces of Evil, I don't see how we poor humans in our weakness can expect to do any better with a few acres of Hecate County, where we're at the mercy of all the rest of creation." "It *ought* to be possible," said Stryker. "And I say it damn well *shall* be possible!" "As I see it," said Clarence Latouche —again, and again unsuccessfully, offering Stryker a drink—"you're faced with a double problem. On the one hand, you've got to get rid of the snappers; and, on the other hand, you've got to keep the ducks. So far you haven't been able to do either. Whatever measures you take, you lose the ducks and you can't kill the snappers. Now it seems to me, if you'll pardon my saying so, that you've overlooked the real solution—the only and, if you don't mind my saying so, the obvious way to deal with the matter." "I've been over the whole ground," said Stryker, growing more tense and turning slightly hostile under pressure of his pent-up passion, "and I doubt whether there's any method that I haven't considered with the utmost care." "It seems to me," said Clarence Latouche in his gentle Louisiana voice, "that, going about the thing as you have been, you've arrived at a virtual *impasse* and that you ought to approach the problem from a totally different angle. If you do that, you'll find it perfectly simple"—Stryker seemed about to protest fiercely, but Clarence continued in a vein of mellow alcoholic explaining: "The trouble is, as I see it, that up to now you've been going on the assumption that you ought to preserve the birds at the expense of getting rid of the turtles. Why not go on the opposite assumption: that you ought to work at cultivating the snappers? Shoot the ducks when they come around, and eat them—that is, when the law permits it"—Mr. Stryker raised a clenched fist and started up in inarticulate anger—"or if you don't want to do that, shoo them off. Then feed up the snappers on raw meat. Snappers are right good eating, too. We make soup out of 'em down in my part of the country."

Mr. Stryker stood speechless for such a long moment that Clarence was afraid, he said afterwards, that his neighbor would fall down in a fit; and he got up and patted him on the shoulder and exerted all his tact and charm. "All I can say," said Stryker, as he was going out the door, "is that I can't understand your attitude. Right is Right and Wrong is Wrong, and you have to choose between them!"

"I've never been much of a moralist," said Clarence, "and I dare say my whole point of view is a low and pragmatical one."

III

Stryker spent a troubled and restless night—so he afterwards told Clarence Latouche; but he got up very early, as he always did, to go hunting for breakfasting turtles, which he lured with pieces of steak. He would scoop them up with a net, and this morning he paused over the first one he caught before he cut off its head. He scrutinized it with a new curiosity, and its appearance enraged him afresh: he detested its blunt sullen visage, its thick legs with their outspread claws, and its thick and thorny-toothed tail that it could not even pull into its shell as other turtles did. It was not even a genuine turtle: *Chelydra serpentina* they called it, because it resembled a snake, and it crawled like a huge lizard. He baited it with a stick: it snapped with a sharp popping sound. As he held the beast up in his net, in the limpid morning air which was brimming the world like a tide, it looked, with its feet dripping slime, its dull shell that resembled a sunken log, as fetid, as cold and as dark as the bottom of the pond itself; and he was almost surprised at the gush of blood when he sawed away the head. What good purpose, he asked himself in horror, could such a creature serve? Subterranean, ugly and brutal—with only one idea in its head, or rather one instinct in its nature: to seize and hold down its prey. The turtle had snapped at the hoop of the net, and even now that its head was severed, its jaws were still holding on.

Stryker pried the head off the net and tossed it into the water; another turtle rose to snatch it. Then why not turn the tables on Nature? Why not prey on what preyed on us? Why not exploit the hideous mud-turtle, as his friend from the South had suggested? Why not devour him daily in the form of turtle soup? And if one could not eat soup every day, why not turn him into an object of commerce? Why not make the public eat him? Let the turtles create economic, instead of killing aesthetic, value! He snickered at what seemed to him a fantasy; but he returned to Clarence Latouche's that day in one of his expansive moods that rather gave Clarence the creeps.

"Nothing easier!" cried Latouche, much amused— his advertizing copy irked him, and he enjoyed an opportunity to burlesque it. "You know, the truth is that a great big proportion of the canned turtle soup that's sold is made out of snapping turtles, but that isn't the way they advertize it. If you advertize it frankly as snapper, it will look like something brand-new, and all you'll need is the snob appeal to put it over on the can-opening public. There's a man canning rattlesnakes in Florida, and it ought to be a lot easier to sell snappers. All you've got to do up here in the North to persuade people to buy a product is to convince them that there's some kind of social prestige attached to it—and all you'd have to do with your snappers would be to create the impression that a good ole white-haired darky with a beaming smile used to serve turtle soup to Old Massa. All you need is a little smart advertizing and you can have as many people eating snapper as are eating [he named a popular canned salmon], which isn't even nutritious like snapper is—they make it out of the sweepings from a tire factory. —I tell you what I'll do," he said, carried away by eloquence and whisky, "you organize a turtle farm and I'll write you some copy free. You can pay me when and if you make money."

Mr. Stryker went back to his pond, scooped out two of the largest snappers, and that evening tried some snapping-turtle soup, which seemed to him surprisingly savory. Then he looked up the breeding of turtles, about which, in the course of his war with them, he had already come to know a good deal. He replenished his depleted pond with turtles brought from other ponds, for which he paid the country boys a dime apiece, and at the end of a couple of years he had such a population of snappers that he had to stock the pond with more frogs.

Clarence Latouche helped him launch his campaign and, as he had promised, wrote the copy for it. There had already appeared at that time a new device, of which Clarence had been one of the originators, for putting over the products of the meat-packers. The animals were represented as gratified and even gleeful at the idea of being eaten. You saw pictures of manicured and beribboned porkers capering and smirking at the prospect of being put up in glass jars as sausages, and of steers in white aprons and chefs' hats that offered you their own sizzling beefsteaks. Clarence Latouche converted the snapping turtle into a genial and lovable creature, who became a familiar character to the readers of magazines and the passengers on subway trains. He was pictured as always smiling, with a twinkle in his wise old eye, and he had always some pungent saying which smacked of the Southern backwoods, and which Clarence had great fun writing. As for the plantation angle, that was handled in a novel fashion. By this time the public had been oversold on Old Massa with the white mustaches, so Clarence invented a lady, lovely, highbred and languid like Mrs. St. Clare in *Uncle Tom's Cabin,* who had to be revived by turtle soup. "Social historians tell us," one of the advertizements ran, "that more than 70 per cent of the women of the Old South suffered from anemia or phthisis [here there was an asterisk referring to a note, which said 'Tuberculosis']. Turtle soup saved the sweethearts and mothers of a proud and gallant race. The rich juices of the Alabama snapping turtle, fed on a special diet handed down from the time of Jefferson and raised on immaculate turtle farms famous for a century in the Deep South, provide the vital calories so often lacking in the modern meal." The feminine public were led to identify themselves with the lady and to feel that they could enjoy a rich soup and yet remain slender and snooty. The advertizement went on to explain that many women still suffered, without knowing it, from anemia and t.b., and that a regular consumption of turtle soup could cure or ward off these diseases.

Deep South Snapper Soup became an immense success; and the demand was presently stimulated by putting three kinds on the market: Deep South Snapper Consommé, Deep South Snapper Tureen (Extra Thick), and Deep South Snapper Medium Thick, with Alabama Whole-Flour Noodles.

Stryker had to employ more helpers, and he eventually built a small cannery, out of sight of the house, on his place. The turtles were raised in shallow tanks, in which they were easier to catch and control.

IV

Mr. Stryker, who had not worked for years at anything but his struggle with the turtles, turned out to be startlingly able as a businessman and industrial organizer. He kept down his working crew, handled his correspondence himself, browbeat a small corps of salesmen, and managed to make a very large profit. He went himself to the city relief bureaus and unerringly picked out men who were capable and willing to work but not too independent or intelligent, and he put over them his gardener as foreman. He would begin by lending these employees money, and he boarded and fed them on the place—so that they found themselves perpetually in debt to him. He took on as a secretary a school-teacher who had lost her job. A plain woman of middle age, she had suddenly had a baby by a middle-aged Italian mechanic who worked in a crossroads garage. Asa Stryker boarded the mother and agreed to pay board for the baby at a place he selected himself. As the business began to prosper, this secretary came to handle an immense amount of correspondence and other matters, but Stryker always criticized her severely and never let her feel she was important.

He had managed to accomplish all this without ever giving people the impression that he was particularly interested in the business; yet he had always followed everything done with a keen and remorseless attention that masked itself under an appearance of impassivity. Every break for a market was seized at once; every laxity of his working staff was pounced on. And his attitude toward the turtles themselves had now changed in a fundamental fashion. He had come to admire their alertness and toughness; and when he took me on a tour of his tanks, he would prod them and make them grip his stick, and then laugh proudly when they would not let go as he banged them against the concrete.

Clarence Latouche himself, who had invented Snapper Tureen, presently began to believe that he was a victim of Stryker's sharp dealing. At the time when the business was beginning to prosper, they had signed an agreement which provided that Clarence should get 10 per cent; and he now felt that he ought to have a bigger share—all the more since his casual habits were proving fatal to his job at the agency. He had been kept for the brilliant ideas which he was sometimes able to contribute, but he had lately been drinking more heavily and it had been hinted that he might be fired. He was the kind of New Orleans man who, extraordinarily charming in youth, becomes rather overripe in his twenties and goes to pieces with an astonishing rapidity. In New Orleans this would not have been noticed; but in the North he had never been quite in key and he was now feeling more ill at ease and more hostile to his adopted environment. He had been carrying on an affair with a married woman, whom he had expected to divorce her husband and marry him; but he had become rather peevish with waiting, and she had decided that a divorce was a good deal of trouble, and that it was perhaps not entirely true that his drinking was due to her failure to marry him. Lately Clarence had taken to brooding on Stryker, whom he had been finding it rather difficult to see, and he had come to the conclusion that the latter was devious as well as sordid, and that he had been misrepresenting to Clarence the amount of profit he made.

One Sunday afternoon, at last, when Clarence had been sitting alone with a succession of tall gin fizzes, he jumped up suddenly, strode out the door, cut straight through his grounds to the fence which divided his property from Stryker's, climbed over it with inspired agility, and made a beeline for Stryker's house, purposely failing to follow the drive and stepping through the flower-beds. Stryker came himself to the door with a look that, if Clarence had been sober, he would have realized was apprehensive; but when he saw who the visitor was, he greeted him with a special cordiality, and ushered him into his study. With his highly developed awareness, he had known at once what was coming.

This study, which Clarence had never seen, as he rarely went to Stryker's house, was a disorderly and dark-ish place. It was characteristic of Stryker that his desk should seem littered and neglected, as if he were not really in touch with his affairs; and there was dust on the books in his bookcase, drably bound and unappetizing volumes on zoölogical and chemical subjects. Though it was daytime, the yellow-brown shades were pulled three-quarters down. On the desk and on the top of the bookcase stood a number of handsome stuffed ducks that Stryker had wished to preserve.

Stryker sat down at his desk and offered Clarence a cigarette. Instead of protesting at once that Clarence's demands were impossible, as he had done on previous occasions, he listened with amiable patience. "I'm going to go into the whole problem and put things on a different basis as soon as business slackens up in the spring. So I'd rather you'd wait till then, if you don't mind. We had a hard time filling the orders even before this strike began, and now I can hardly get the work done at all. They beat up two of my men yesterday, and they're threatening to make a raid on the factory. I've had to have the whole place guarded." (The breeding ponds and the factory, which were situated half a mile away, had been enclosed by a wire fence.) Clarence had forgotten the strike, and he realized that he *had* perhaps come at a rather inopportune time. "I can't attend to a reorganization," Stryker went on to explain—"which is what we've got to have at this point—till our labor troubles are settled and things have slowed up a bit. There ought to be more in this business for both of us," he concluded, with a businessman's smile, "and I won't forget your coöperative attitude when we make a new arrangement in the spring."

The tension was thus relaxed, and Stryker went on to address Clarence with something like friendly concern. "Why don't you have yourself a vacation?" he suggested. "I've noticed you were looking run-down. Why don't you go South for the winter? Go to Florida or someplace like that. It must be tough for a Southerner like you to spend this nasty part of the year in the North. I'll advance you the money, if you need it." Clarence was half tempted, and he began to talk to Stryker rather freely about the idiocies of the advertizing agency and about the two aunts and a sister whom he had to support in Baton Rouge. But in the course of the conversation, as his eye escaped from Stryker's gaze, which he felt as uncomfortably intent in the gaps between sympathetic smiles, it lit on some old chemical apparatus, a row of glass test-tubes and jars, which had presumably been carried along from Stryker's early career as a teacher;

and he remembered—though the steps of his reasoning may have been guided, as he afterwards sometimes thought, by a delusion of persecution that had been growing on him in recent months—he remembered the deaths, at intervals, of Stryker's well-to-do relatives. His eye moved on to the mounted ducks, with their rich but rather lusterless colors. He had always been half-conscious with the other of his own superior grace of appearance and manner and speech, and had sometimes felt that Stryker admired it; and now as he contemplated Stryker, at ease in his turbid room, upended, as it were, behind his desk, with a broad expanse of plastron and a rubbery craning neck, regarding him with small bright eyes set back in the brownish skin beyond a prominent snoutlike formation of which the nostrils were sharply in evidence—as Clarence confronted Stryker, he felt first a fantastic suspicion, then a sudden unnerving certainty.

Unhurriedly he got up to go and brushed away Stryker's regret that—since it was Sunday and the cook's day out—he was unable to ask him to dinner. But his nonchalance now disguised panic: it was hideously clear to him why Stryker had suggested his taking this trip. He wouldn't go, of course, but what then? Stryker would be sure to get him if he didn't take some prompt action. In his emotion, he forgot his hat and did not discover it till they had reached the porch. He stepped back into the study alone, and on an impulse took down from its rack on the wall the rifle with which Stryker, in the earlier days, had gone gunning for snapping turtles. He opened the screen door. Stryker was standing on the porch. As he looked around, Clarence shot him.

The cook was out; only the gates were guarded; and Clarence had arrived at Stryker's by taking the back cut through the grounds. Nobody heard the shot. The suspicion all fell on the foreman, who had his own long-standing grievances and had organized the current strike. He had already had to go into hiding to escape from his boss's thugs, and after the murder he disappeared.

Clarence decided soon that he would sell his Hecate County place and travel for a year in Europe, which he had always wanted to see. But just after he had bought his passage, the war with Hitler started, and prevented him from getting off—an ironic disappointment he said, for a smart advertizing man who had been speculating in snapping turtles.

He had dissociated himself from the soup business, and he went to live in southern California, where, on his very much dwindled income, he is said to be drinking himself to death. He lives under the constant apprehension that the foreman may be found by the police, and that he will then have to confess his own guilt in order to save an innocent man—because Clarence is the soul of honor—so that Stryker may get him yet.

2.

Ellen Terhune

I ALWAYS FELT, when I went to the Terhune house, that I was getting back into the past—or rather, perhaps, that an atmosphere which had first been established at the beginning of the eighties, when the house in which she lived had been built, had been preserved there as a vital medium down into the nineteen twenties. Most of the places in Hecate County seemed either newer or older—modern households or old-fashioned farms; but the moment I entered the gate in the high green picket-fence, which was matted with honeysuckle in summer, and caught sight of the white obelisk of the windmill, dismantled though it was of its sails, towering behind the trees, I felt that I had come back into something which had definitely vanished with the war but which was perfectly familiar from my childhood.

There was a drive, always covered with gravel, that swept around in a beautiful curve and brought you up under a big porte-cochère, which reminded you of horses with fly-nets, and shiny and black closed carriages; and the house, which was yellow and covered with shingles that overlapped with rounded ends like scales, was an impressive though rather formless mass of cupolas with foolscap tops, dormers with diamond panes, balconies with little white railings and porches with Ionic columns, all pointing in different directions. It had been built or bought by Ellen Terhune's grandfather, a brilliant and highly successful doctor. Dr. Bristead, even in that period when doctors were more "humanistic" and had wider interests than now, had been a man of remarkable cultivation, and the house was richly lined with the evidences of his pastimes, his studies and his travels. One found in the downstairs rooms such treasures and curiosities as signed photographs of or framed letters from Theodore Roosevelt, Kipling, Pierre Loti, Mark Twain, Adelina Patti, Paderewski, Mechnikov and Pasteur, all of whom had been patients or correspondents of his; a statue of Hebe by Canova, a Daubigny and a couple of Corots; a hookah, which Ellen told me her grandfather had actually smoked; a group of Chinese gongs, with which dinner was still announced; a regal set of carved ivory chessmen, brought back from a trip to the Orient, which had elephants instead of bishops; an Australian bushman's boomerang; a Stradivarius and an eighteenth-century clavichord.

The Bristeads had especially been musical. The doctor had mastered several instruments; and he had organized a family trio in which he had played the cello, his daughter the violin, and Mrs. Bristead the piano. Later, when the doctor's wife had died and his daughter had come with Ellen to live with them, they had had the trio again, with Ellen, at the age of twelve, taking over the cello. When her mother had died a few years later and she was living there alone with her grandfather, they had played an immense amount of music; they had gone right through Beethoven and Brahms, both of whom her grandfather had ended by detesting; had then escaped backward into the eighteenth century, with Ellen learning Boccherini's cello sonatas and the doctor getting special transcriptions made of Pergolesi's trios for violins and bass; and had from there, in obedience to one of her grandfather's peculiarly indomitable manias, gone right back through the history of music. Ellen had been forced to retrace the elegance and restraint of Corelli at an age when she would much rather, she told me, have been pounding out Schubert and Schumann; and the doctor had had a small organ installed and relentlessly insisted on their deciphering the intricate masses of Palestrina, thence exploring mediaeval motets, troubadour songs and Gregorian chants, and, finally, reconstructing ancient Greek modes.

Ellen had thus had the advantage of an exceptional musical training, and she had begun to compose early. By the time she got out of the Conservatoire, where she had started in at eighteen, she was producing work of real merit. She had been influenced in Paris by Debussy; but, working with the whole-tone scale, she had developed an impressionism distinctly her own. She was, in fact, probably the first woman composer who had ever contributed to music anything of authentic value. It is strange that, though women have excelled as novelists and lyric poets, and though there are a few women painters of interest, there should be no important music by women. That is, unless Ellen Terhune be an exception, and I have always thought her work first-rate, though it somehow seems incommensurable with masculine compositions of even the same school. It would be foolish to compare her with Chaminade, with whom she has nothing in common; but, on the other hand, even Ravel and Debussy were builders on a bigger scale than Ellen. Her talent in the best of her work, her songs and piano pieces, is as personal as Georgia O'Keeffe's pictures or Marianne Moore's poems: a woman's sharp and ready reactions to people and things encountered and a woman's emotions of quick challenge, of a kind of dark resigned despair or of a clear and rapt exaltation.

I called on Ellen one afternoon in the summer of 1926. It was August, and I had assumed she was in Maine, where she usually went at that time of year; but I ran into her one day at the post office and she asked me to come to see her. I was delighted, because I always liked to talk to her—her comment on the musical world was wonderful—and, though some considered her arrogant and forbidding, I found her personality sympathetic. It would be especially a relief to get away from the Hecate County summer life, which had involved a great many parties with people who were only made tolerable by summer sports and drinking. I went to see her that same afternoon.

But I found her much disturbed and distressed. She had three highballs in rapid succession, which I had never known her to do before, and which made me a little disappointed, as it associated her to my mind with the summer people, great publishers of their emotions over drinks, so that her house seemed less the haven I had hoped for.

It turned out that Ellen like everyone else was going through a domestic crisis. She had married a man somewhat younger than herself, the conductor Sigismund Soblianski. He had genuinely admired her abilities, had done more perhaps than anyone else to have her work performed; and he had profoundly respected her character as only the matriarchal Jew can respect the austerity of a woman who is set firmly on her own moral base; but the fact that she was also an artist—she had married too late to have children, which might have done something to fuse them—had stimulated a fatal competition. Sigismund, before he married, had worked rather seriously at composing, but Ellen was so much better than he was that he must have become ashamed of his productions, for he ceased to write anything at all. Instead, he had begun to develop a hair-raising professional exhibitionism. A brilliant and resourceful musician with a special gift for dramatizing effects, he had gradually come to abandon the playing of new or native music, which, partly at the instance of Ellen, he had originally attempted to encourage, and to go in for great quantities of Chaikovsky and Strauss, Sibelius, Beethoven and Wagner, overcoloring and overacting, and posing to a public who adored him while the serious musicians gave him up.

It was a long time, however, since Ellen and he had seemed to be living together—though I did still run into him sometimes in the country. He had always had his rehearsals in town and Ellen did not like the city; and he had had, also, during the last two or three years, a whole series of love affairs which everybody knew about and which Ellen appeared to accept. He had even adopted the practice of bringing out his protégé of the moment—serious-minded little Russian dancer or black-eyed Hungarian violinist—to spend the day with Ellen; but this, though she took it coolly, I am sure Ellen did not like. The truth was, I always thought, that they were still much involved with one another, and that Sigismund did such things in a kind of defiance of Ellen for making him feel second-rate.

But he now, she told me, wanted a divorce: he wanted to get married again. And I could see that Ellen was profoundly upset—through she ascribed her reluctance to the fear that he was making a fool of himself. The woman that he proposed to marry was a much- and long-publicized actress, and Ellen was inclined to believe that Sigismund's interest in her was merely a part of his own self-publicizing activity. Frances Fielding was one

of those figures who took the place, during the twenties
and thirties, of the old-fashioned male matinee idol. She
was adored by a following mainly feminine, and she
was supposed not to care much about men. But in her
pictures and plays she was invariably subdued, at the
end of much high-spirited rebellion, by a stubborn and
combative lover; and it was obvious that there would be
for the public a wonderful double story about Frances'
at last meeting her fate at the same time that Sigismund
Soblianski had found a creature as dashing as himself.
It was particularly disturbing to Ellen, who had toler-
ated the little protégés, because she was herself the type
of the serious professional woman of an earlier generation and was losing to a formidable competitor.

"I always thought she was hard as nails," she said,
"but she does have a certain—shall I say, style and brilliance?—I can't bear to call it glamor. She and Sigismund are both what the Russians call 'firebirds,' I suppose—they like to show their plumage in an atmosphere
of bright lights and admiration. They're only able really
to express themselves by creating for themselves characters that are two-thirds fictitious. And I don't shine
in that way—I'm naturally quiet and drab. I can't bear
to go to night clubs and places, and I long ago ceased
to enjoy staying up all night over musical suppers where
people get intoxicated and take off Shalyapin and play
Viennese waltzes. I'd rather be home in bed reading. I
don't like to travel the way Sigismund does, and I hate
triumphant tours. I'd rather stay right here with my
house and my piano and my furniture and my daily routine. Sigismund is younger than I am and he's temperamentally quite different. I suppose I was always a wet
blanket for him, and I can't blame him if he wants
somebody gayer. Only I'd like him to have somebody

who would be good for him. I can't imagine she really cares about him. I'm afraid he'll end up in Hollywood."

Ellen was, of course, not drab, but there *was* something in her that didn't give. As I looked around the room, I reflected that, though Sigismund had spent much of his time here during the early years of their marriage, though the house had been supposed to be *their* house, he had left little or no imprint upon it. Dr. Bristead and his daughter and Ellen—both Ellen and her mother were only children—had assembled the things in that room. The low couch on which I was sitting was comfortable but there was something rather stale about it. It had been ministering for too many years to the comfort of too much the same people; the upholstery and the cushions had become almost as personal as a bed, and the pattern of flowers was faded. The effect of the whole room, in fact, seemed somehow a little tinged with the yellow of the discoloring photographs; and, though there were beautiful old dark cabinets and tip-top tables and one of the finest of those convex mirrors, with a still glowing round gold frame and an American eagle on top, the room had never quite been purged of the bad taste of preceding generations; and the delicate crepuscular paintings were thrown into deeper shadow by larger canvases, also French, of picturesque Moorish scenes that made patches of rather messy color, just as the orange-pink gladioluses and the deep maroon double dahlias had, the former a touch of Victorian china, the latter a touch of upholstery. Still there was something about it I liked, and I was glad it had remained the same.

And now Ellen was telling me about her girlhood. She had been terribly homely, she said, and she had had an awful time at dances: she always knew that, if a boy asked her to dance, it was only because his mother had made him. "I was a sight," she said. "I had crooked teeth and my head was too big for my body. Even Mother was discouraged about me." She was certainly not bad-looking now and she could never have been so homely as she imagined; but she was short and did have rather a large square head on a neck that was a little too small for it—physically, she resembled the doctor—and I could see that, with her precocious intelligence, she might not have been a belle. But her magnificent agate-green eyes must at any age have been arresting: they seemed to concentrate the light of the intellect as a powerful lens does the sun, and in this intellectual quality they suggested the eyes of a remarkable man; yet they were also extremely feminine and responded to everything that met them as the eyes of men seldom do. The rest of Ellen's features were neither so striking nor so mobile: her mouth was small and her nose a little owl-like, and her face with its square jawbones was too broad for them. But the effect of her eyes was mesmeric.

She involved you in her concentration, and as she went on describing her childhood, I was forced to see it all as she did. Her parents should never have married, she said—though I tried to point out that it was silly to imply that she should never have existed. They had never had anything in common. Her father, before his marriage, had been a man about town and a sportsman—she showed me a photograph with a handsome mustache, hair amiably parted in the middle, and some kind of small chrysanthemum in the buttonhole. He had done a great deal of drinking, and they had belonged, in the first years of their marriage, to a rich and rather fast set. He had had no intellectual or artistic tastes, and for her mother, brought up by Dr. Bristead, this life must have been deeply uncongenial, even, she thought, disgusting. Ellen's father, a Wall Street man with a seat on the

Stock Exchange, had been ruined, the year before Ellen was born, by the crash of 1884; and after that he had always done badly. They had gone to live with Ellen's grandfather, and her father was always in town. Sometimes he was brought home in very bad shape—which she gradually learned was due to drinking—and had to stay in bed for weeks. He had killed himself when Ellen was eleven in a cheap little New York hotel, of which he had been ashamed to let her mother know the address.

Those tragedies of the turn of the century! I thought; it was one thing to die or be broken for a political ideal or a social order as had happened to both Southerners and Northerners in the years of the Civil War; but to die, to be crushed, to be shattered, through the overpowering progress of big business, through the unrestrained greed of speculation, seemed hard on those men and women whom we remember as gentle and bright and who look at us, in such photographs as those which Ellen produced from a drawer, with the American friendliness and candor.

She could hardly remember anything pleasant in the relations between her father and mother. Her mother had studied violin and had wanted a professional career; her marrying Ellen's father had put an end to this, and she had never forgiven him for it. She would complain that she had given up her music and then been left without resources for the social life in which he had involved her. "She might have had," said Ellen, "a quite different life. Technically, she was very good. I don't think she was meant for marriage." They had used to have long dreadful controlled quarrels, which Ellen would sometimes overhear: her mother's cold voice would go on and on, pretending to appeal to him in a reasonable way—What was she to think? What was she to expect? when he didn't keep his promises to her,

when he didn't even care any more whether he humiliated her in public or not. He would be sorry, try to
reassure her about his conduct and prospects for the
future. It was heartbreaking, Ellen said: though not at
all intellectual, he had really been a lovable man, and he
had a distinction of feeling quite different from her
mother's hard dignity. After he had lost his money, he
had never been willing to borrow from friends—though
there were plenty who would have been glad to help him.
But he had never had to work before, and he had never
in his career as a ladies' man been up against anyone
like Ellen's mother. "It must have been wretched beyond
words," she said. "You say that I ought to be glad I
came out of it—but, even assuming that I'm worth anything, how does that make it better for Mother and
Father, who died without getting what they wanted
themselves when I was still an ugly little girl?"

"They must have been happier than you think," I said.
"All married people have those conversations, and then
they go to bed and forget it."—"There was something
about Mother that chilled people," she went on, disregarding my attempt to be helpful and forcing me to
follow her vision of the unrelieved hopelessness of her
parents' situation. "She was sensitive on her musical
side, but I suppose that what she presented to Father
was a surface of solid whalebone.—And I do the same
thing!—I know it. I chill people and put them in the
wrong. That's what I did with Sigismund. He always
said I made him feel guilty. But it's really because *I*
always feel guilty. Mother made *me* feel guilty, too. I
can't help thinking that I oughtn't to make claims on
people, that I oughn't to expect them to care about me.
I behave as if I took this for granted, and then I reproach them for neglecting me. I know myself all too
well!"

"You can't still think you're not good-looking," I said. "It isn't merely a question of that: Mother had a special and distressing reason for not liking the way I looked. It seems that she had a terribly bad time when I was born on account of my head's being so big, and I don't think she ever really recovered from it. I suppose it was what she died of. She used to talk about it sometimes in my presence. She may have thought I didn't understand, but she must have wanted people to pity her for having produced such a little monstrosity, and I think she also wanted me to feel that she had suffered and sacrificed herself for me." She was casual enough in tone; she was not herself laying it on; but, under the compulsion of her serious eyes, I felt the pain of the situation penetrate me and pin me to the spot. "I imagine, though, that she didn't exaggerate," she relentlessly and steadily went on. "I'm not sure I can't remember it myself. I've been subject all my life to peculiar spells when I think that I can't move or do anything. . . . I get it when I'm nervously exhausted," she explained in reply to my question, "and sometimes in my sleep. It's a perfectly horrible feeling—it's a kind of overpowering inertia that seems all to be located in my head—as if I were weighed down by a millstone, as if my head were a great stone ball. I suppose, though, that it's only an intensified form of a tendency I have all the time—I'm an extremely inert person. I think my difficulties in getting born may have made it more difficult for me to live. I hate so to move or make serious changes. That's one reason I'm so tiresome for Sigismund." "I've always thought of you, Ellen," I said, "as a very dynamic person." "Some of the most dynamic people," she insisted, "can't move at all, you know. They try to make up by a lot of loud talking and rushing around from place to place for their fear that they're really static." "You don't

do that," I assured her. "No: I sit like a fire hydrant—
that can always be tapped for cold water.—I've been
trying to face my immobility lately and to do something
with it in music. I've always been a little bit scared by
these states that I was telling you about, and I thought it
might be a good thing to take hold of them and deliberately exploit them—to try to put them outside myself."

I was afraid that she had been suffering from them
lately: there were circles about her eyes, and her face,
even for her, seemed pale. I thought the drinks were
making her run on in a way that was not characteristic
of her and that I probably oughtn't to encourage, and I
was glad to shift the conversation from her parents to
her artistic problems. "What are you working on now?"
I asked. "I've been trying to do a sonata," she said, "just
an old-fashioned sonata." Was any of it in shape to
play? "I've been having rather a struggle with it," she
said, "but I'll play you the part I mean." She put out
her cigarette, and we went into the next room to the
piano.

There were no leaves to turn—she had it in her head
—and I sat in a low carved armchair which reminded
me vaguely of Abbotsford, and contemplated the curious
shape of a "nun's trumpet" or *tromba marina* which was
hung on the opposite wall. This obsolete instrument,
which the doctor had acquired and even more or less
managed to play, producing, as Ellen had told me, rather
unpleasant hoarse and squawking sounds, looked more
like an oar or a cricket bat than a member of the violin
family, whose curves it completely lacked. It seemed to
me pathetically mistaken; and so did Ellen's music. This
piece, which she said was the second movement, began
with a four-note theme that sounded simple and conventional enough, and I was prepared for something genu-
inely classic; but the theme was not given the de-

velopment one expects in the sonata form nor did it even get the kind of variation that one finds in a passacaglia. She did not even retard or speed it up: she simply played it over and over. It was as if she did not know what to do with it, and the listener was constantly subjected to the embarrassment of fearing that the pianist had got stuck like a phonograph which stutters. There was at moments a suggestion of a second theme that seemed to play about the first in a flimsy and trivial manner, but this would fade off in atmospheric chords and leave the field to the original four notes, as boring and inexpressive as ever. It was like a perverse child, compelled to practice on a summer day, and deliberately annoying the household. At the end, the ghost of a second theme limped off and dropped away in irremediable speciousness and impotence, and we were back with the same confounded phrase, which was never satisfactorily resolved, but simply repeated eight times at precisely the same loudness and tempo.

It sounded a little insane; I felt more worried about Ellen than before. I sat constrained, almost scared, when she stopped, and did not know what to say. Of course it was rather remarkable to have carried off this monotony musically—if she had done so, of which I was not very sure—and that was the line that I took with her. I saw that she was vibrating with tension, that the music had excited her in a way which seemed to be almost unbearable for her and was rather embarrassing for me. She was perspiring in the August heat, and I began to perspire, too. "I'm afraid you're not well," I said.

I remembered with uneasiness that she had sometimes been subject to a kind of epileptic seizure, which was preceded by nervous headaches. I had seen her in one of these fits one evening when I had taken her to a concert where a concerto of hers was to be done and where Sigismund had to conduct. She had usually played her own things; but she was not a very accomplished pianist, and on this occasion Sigismund had believed that it would be better to get a pianist who was accustomed to playing with orchestra. This performer had, however, not much liked the piece and had been antagonized by Sigismund's vehement coaching, and, in spite of a house packed with friends and admirers, who gave it the expected ovation, Ellen knew that it had not been right. I do not think, as a matter of fact, that it was one of her good things, and I imagine that the dutiful applause made her feel worse about it. At any rate, she withdrew to the ladies' room and stayed there so long that I was worried. I went in and found her rigid on a couch, with an anxious attendant bending over her and trying to get her to speak. As soon as the concert was finished, her husband and I took her back to the hotel. He told me that she had had such fits before, and that they sometimes lasted for hours. On this occasion, however, she came to and got into a cab, though I did not hear her speak again.

I was afraid this afternoon that the question of divorce might be bringing on another such seizure. But she smiled and tried to reassure me. "It makes me nervous to play that thing," she said. "I wish I could get it finished. The last part has been driving me crazy, and even this part isn't right yet.—I can see that you're thoroughly depressed by it." "Oh, no," I untruthfully answered: "I think it's remarkably interesting." She smiled at the conventional evasion, and I disliked having to talk so to Ellen.

I asked her before I left whether there was somebody there in the house with her, and she told me that she had a maid. I didn't like to remind her of the concert: she was the kind of self-managing woman that it is hard to do anything for. I told her that she must let me know if there was any way in which I could help her; and she apologized for boring me with her own affairs—"But you're one of the few people I can talk to. Out here you're the only one—I don't really know any more even who the people are who live here, though we used to know everybody."

It was all pretty awful, I thought, as I walked along the drive toward the gate, between the lawns which the late sun was gilding and the magnificent collection of trees (a true collection, planted by the doctor and including many exotics and rarities), with the vision of Ellen's wide sweating forehead under her none-too-abundant brown hair and of her eyes which I had thought, toward the end of my visit, were beginning to get a little out of touch with me till, at the moment when I was saying good-by, they had come back to responsive life. She did not know even who lived about here; and there had been a few seconds just now, while I was talking about her music and she had seemed to hesitate in replying and to stare and go into herself, when I had not been quite sure she knew *me*.

I turned away my mind, I confess, with a certain complacent relief to a big party I looked forward to that evening: one of those gatherings where great quantities of tan-backed girls and scarlet-faced men, with highballs fizzing in their hands, lift laughing and strident voices among glass-topped cocktail tables and lamps that give indirect lighting.

II

I dropped in on her again in September when I came back from a short summer trip. I noticed that Ellen's place showed signs of restoration and refreshment. The honeysuckle on the fence had been trimmed, and the name on the gates, "Vallombrosa," had evidently been recently repainted. I had the impression that the trees and the shrubbery had also been lately pruned; and the sails had been put back on the windmill, which was turning in a chilly wind that came up suddenly as I entered the driveway.

Ellen herself I found rejuvenated in a most surprising way. She no longer had rings under her eyes, and she displayed a kind of nervous vitality which I thought at first was overwrought but which I presently came to feel as natural. The rather recessive attitude which had grown on her with her alienation from Sigismund seemed to have given way to a readiness to meet and taste life. It seemed to me that the definite break with him, which I noticed she never mentioned, had had the effect of releasing her to revert to her own personality, which, I thought, must have suffered and shrunk in the course of her relationship with Sigismund; and it seemed to be a symbol of this that she had completely changed her style of dressing and her way of doing her hair. The last time I had seen her she had been wearing the short skirt of 1926, and she had at one time bobbed her hair, which had made her head a little too mannish; but now she had been letting it grow, and, parting it in the middle and brushing it over her ears, had coiled it at the back of her head and stuck a comb at an angle behind it, and she was wearing a white shirt-waist with full sleeves and a long green-and-black plaid skirt, which were old-fashioned but very becoming to her. She looked somehow smarter than she had before. I complimented her on her appearance, but said nothing about the antiquity of the costume. I thought at first that she had got it out of some trunk and that it must be at least twenty years old; but as I looked at it, it seemed to me new, and I concluded that she had had it made to order. It was an affectation, of course, perhaps a self-conscious protest against Sigismund; but I rather enjoyed it for the emphasis it gave to the non-fashionable character of her work: it was a joke on the cult of jazz and the professional lost generation that one of the most original of American artists should have the aspect of a period piece.

My relation with Ellen today seemed somehow a little less intimate. She was not alienated as I had felt her to be at the end of my last visit, as if she were losing the outside world; but her perceptions appeared to have been dimmed by her intentness on her musical interests. She looked at me for a moment when I first came in as if she were not quite sure that she recognized me, replying rather formally to my greeting; and at one point she seemed to assume that I had personally known Dr. Bristead. She was more obviously excited about her music than I had ever seen her before and talked as if she had been composing with a new gust of creative energy. She told me about playing some piano pieces—a suite which she had just written—at the invitation of Arthur Whiting, at an informal concert in his studio, at which the Schirmers and the Damrosches had been present, and on a program with D'Indy and Loeffler. Though she always maintained the attitude of the advanced and self-confident woman who is not afraid of conventions and who knows that she can compete with men in fields which they have largely monopolized, she was obviously gratified by this; and I was at first a little puzzled at her pleasure in recognition from so stuffy a quarter; but I felt that she was perhaps, as sometimes happens, falling back for reassurance in her new personal loneliness on public appreciation of her work from anywhere and by anybody. "Well, that makes you a classic!"—I smiled. "They don't really approve of me at all," Ellen

said. "They think I'm a freak like Carrie Nation. Arthur
Whiting made one of his sly jokes about my being more
masculine than Debussy. But Whiting at least is no fool.
Some of the people there were still sure that Debussy
was a lunatic, and they thought that my use of the whole-
tone scale had something to do with Max Nordau's
Degeneration—and that the whole thing was mixed up
with woman suffrage. I don't know why American musicians have to be such a lot of old women!"

Yet she seemed to me herself today unmistakably and
agreeably feminine. The very outspokenness and challenge to men which the young ladies of that generation
had cultivated when they set out on professional careers
characterized her as a woman more vividly than the
sexually neutralized role of the business girl or bar companion did the women of my own generation; and she
had also a pretty keen instinct to make her attractiveness
felt: she talked with a certain flashing play of her proud
and arresting eyes. So she must have appeared, I imagined, in the days when she had been wholly independent and after her grandfather's death.

By this time our old understanding had completely
been reëstablished, and she was letting herself go. She
was very amusing and ruthless about the older American
composers—the fancy-dress costumes from Italy and
France and the mythological insipidities which played so
large a part in their work: the reveries at Carcassonne
and the tone poems on *Pippa Passes,* the Icaruses and
Daphnes and Psyches, the sarabands of satyrs and
nymphs. "David Emery Nickerson's *Semiramis,*" she
said, "is simply Mrs. Wentworth of Boston. In the first
part you see her in her Brookline house surrounded by
obedient Nubians; in the second, she has a conversation
with David Emery Nickerson and he reads her some
sonnets by Rossetti; in the third, she regrets that she

can never be married to David Emery Nickerson and goes in for social work."

I was rather surprised, however, when she told me that the pieces of her own which she had played at the Whiting concert had titles that seemed to connect them with the impressionism of an earlier period and that did not seem characteristic of the harder and more formal style in which she had been lately working. They were *Gulls off the Coast of Nantucket, The Lighthouse,* and *The Island Cemetery*—the products, she said, of her vacation. I forbore to ask about the sonata which had seemed to worry her so. She had evidently been to Nantucket since the time when I had seen her in August, and managed to come back refreshed.

I begged her to play her new suite, and she consented with a frankness and grace which seemed youthful and contrasted with the professional matter-of-factness, that matter-of-factness of the middle-aged artist that has almost become grim, with which she had taken me into her workshop before. We went again into the adjoining music room, where the cellos and violins, even the old dark cracked box of the clavichord, looked ripe in the September light, which made things inside seem the ruddier for the turn for the colder outside. It was pleasant to watch Ellen's straight back, her sure and energetic features, as she took command of the keyboard. And the pieces were lucid and lovely—at moments they were even thrilling. They did seem to me a lapse into the past: they were so much like other things she had written in a vein I thought she had put behind her. But then, why shouldn't she escape into the past? It was better than going to pieces. I noticed, however, in the last one an insistent reiterated phrase which recalled the obsessive monotony of the movement from the sonata she had played me. "I like the one about the cemetery particularly," I said, wanting to reassure her after our rather painful conversation in connection with the other piece. "I think you've handled that heavy recurrent effect perfectly successfully there." "It returns to solemnity and deadness," she said, playing the last bars again. "I wanted to give the effect of the whole thing being anchored by the graveyard. In a place like that, it's the dead, the men who have died at sea, that give life its price, its importance. You feel them under the ground, just lying there and never moving. The cemetery doesn't speak aloud, but everybody knows what it means. Even the lighthouse implies the cemetery—and the gulls can fly around above the graves, they can fly ever so high up above them—but the gulls are just light irresponsible spirits that haven't anything to lose from the sea—the thing that's really serious is the human dead, and the living who are pledged to the dead. The islanders who are dead are lying there like the part of the island that's submerged—all the part that's above water is based on them.—You see I've got suggestions of the same effect in the other pieces, too." She showed me how the flight of the gulls would fall back into the shadow of the earth and how the graveyard returned a deep echo to the pealing of the Lisbon bell.

"Are you sure that that belongs with the gulls and the bell?" I felt that it tarnished the clearness. "No: it *doesn't* belong with them, of course: it's supposed *not* to belong—but it has to be there just the same.—Oh, I know it: it's flat, flat, flat!" she said suddenly, flinging over the leaf and getting up from the piano. "It's the David Emery Nickerson in all of us—or should I say, the Mrs. Wentworth of Brookline?" She smiled and was amusing again.

She had said it as the French would say, *"C'est plat, plat, plat!"* and I had noticed during our conversation

an addiction to French gestures and phrases. She had
had *"toute une histoire"* over a manuscript which she
had sent to a music competition, and she had shrugged
over the inefficiency of the old fuddiduds who made the
awards. There was a certain fluidity and elegance that
might have been brought back from Paris about her hair
and the green silk bow that she wore in her starched
white collar and that softened the squareness of her face.
That was one curious thing, I reflected as I was walking
away from the house, about the effect on American artists
of going to study abroad. They got in Europe a kind of
inoculation with the cultures of alien races which might
give them the illusion for a time that they were part of
European culture, that, carried along by its current, they
had actually been merged in its waters. But in ninety-nine
cases this had never affected in any at all vital way the
native American base. If this base had no principle of
growth of its own, the inoculation simply wore off and
left something that was flat, flat, flat.

I found that I was thinking of Ellen as if she had
just come back from Paris. In her case, of course, when
France had worn off, she *had* had a base that sent up
shoots. Yet there was something about those iterated
phrases—which suggested a stubborn child's question or
the insurmountable image of a mad person—that wasn't
right, wasn't good.

I thought about Ellen often; I hoped she wasn't herself going mad. I tried to call her a few weeks later,
and they told me the phone was out of order.

I walked over that afternoon. The trees of Vallombrosa were quite transformed with reds that were blazing
or paling, deep orange or lemon-yellow, made richer by
a slight autumn mist; and they were so much in advance
of the trees outside, which were only just beginning to

turn, that I wondered whether the doctor's rare species were particularly sensitive to frost.

When I had almost arrived at the house, a girl on a bicycle shot by me, coasting along the drive. She looked toward me when she had set her bicycle against the latticed base of the piazza, and I felt that she expected me to speak to her. But something in her face disconcerted me, and, instead of inquiring for Mrs. Soblianski, I asked—perhaps because Sigismund seemed now so remote from that house in the presence of what I took to be a relative and because at the same time it was incorrect to refer to Ellen as "Miss"—whether "Mrs. Terhune" were at home. "Mrs. Terhune is in the city," said the girl. She had green eyes that reminded me of Ellen's and a rather pale indoor face. She wore a bang over her forehead and short hair fluffed out behind, and she had on a white dress with a long skirt and long sleeves and an enormous folded-over collar that completely enveloped her shoulders. I had been startled to note as she rode by me that she was also wearing long black stockings. Just the wrong thing for bike-riding— what an archaizing family they were! (I assumed this was some cousin of Ellen's): it made me a little impatient.

"Won't you come in?" she said, as I stood searching her face rather queerly. It was a serious intelligent face, and her manner was so mature that it was difficult to tell her age, though she could not have been more than thirteen or fourteen. I replied that I wouldn't come in but would sit down on the porch for a moment. There were a pair of white wicker-backed rockers, and we settled ourselves in them side by side. "How has Mrs. Terhune been?" I inquired, conscious that I had said it again. "She had to go to the hospital," replied the girl. "Grandfather took her up today." I was startled and

troubled to hear it; I hoped it wasn't anything serious.
"Grandfather says it isn't serious." I was glad that there
had been someone to take care of her. "She may have
to have a slight operation—they won't be able to decide
for a few days." She had a reasonable and earnest tone
and the language of an experienced head nurse; but I
saw that she was distressed and keyed up: she had a
nervous little trick like a tic of tossing her bang aside. I
wondered about the operation and asked for the name of
the hospital, which turned out to be, not, as I expected,
the Neurological Institute or anything of the sort, but a
gynecological place.

I didn't want to inquire further and presently remarked on the beauty of the trees. She explained to me
the different species, of which she knew all the Latin
names, with the same peculiar poise and precision, which
seemed to mask an uncomfortable tenseness. "Haven't
you been doing a lot to the place lately?" I asked. She
thought a moment and tossed her bang: "We've planted
a new copper beech. It was almost the only thing we
didn't have. I hope it gets to be as gorgeous as the ones
on the place across the road. They look as if they were
made of bronze. You could play them on the cello." She
did not smile and was not trying to be clever: that was
the way they evidently talked in that family. "We have
a new birdhouse, too." "Have you really?" I expressed
an interest. "It's a summer hotel for martins. Would
you like to see it?" she asked.

She led me by steps down a terrace that smelt rankly
of grass in the autumn damp and past large symmetrical
maples that had dropped their leaves in round golden
rugs, to a cluster of cedars and firs where I did not remember to have been. I noticed that Sigismund's studio,
which ought to have been visible from there, had been
taken down since summer. There was not a trace of it

left; and I was shocked at the thought that Ellen had had it removed out of bitterness. I was amused, when we came to the birdhouse, to see that it had been designed in the same ornamental and obsolete style as Dr. Bristead's house itself. There were three stories perforated by windows and numerous cupolas and towers. The young cousin explained to me about purple martins, which, she said, were really steel-blue and opened and shut like scissors. She talked about other birds, too, and I saw that she not only knew their habits and names, but had a kind of poetic perception of their qualities. It occurred to me that Ellen in her girlhood must have perceived things in the same quaint and personal way. She had once composed, I remembered, a whole suite of little pieces on objects and creatures about the place: the cupola, the stained-glass window, the garden, the pedigreed collie—and yes, there had been a birdhouse.

There was a squirrel cage not far away, and I went over to see what was in it. It was built around the trunk of an oak and had one of those wheels that they turn. When we came up, there was a squirrel inside it, madly making it spin. I have always disliked these wheels, which I regard as an imposture on the squirrels. "Do you think they like to do that?" I asked. "I don't know," the girl seriously answered. "They don't have to go in there, you know. But I suppose it must be rather discouraging for them when they stop and the wheel begins to carry them back. It always make them start working again even when they must be tired. They're afraid of going backwards, I guess. Yes: I don't think that can be at all pleasant." She gave her bang a twitch. "Some people are sorry they were born, but everyone has a right to his life, don't you think? People just have to go ahead and realize their own possibilities."

I thought I caught an echo here of old plays by Ber-

nard Shaw or other writings of the live-your-own-life
era, which she must have got hold of in her grandfather's house and which had made an impression on
her. But it reminded me also of Ellen and her talk about
her mother and father. The girl, of course, was perfectly
right: you did have to go ahead and do your best with
whatever you had. I felt a little disgusted at Ellen's attempt to undo her own past by having Sigismund's
studio removed. After all, he had studied and composed
there in the most creditable phase of his career. They
had worked together, been something together, even
though they had later pulled apart. And now she had
struck it out as if it had never been.

As we were watching, the squirrel in the cage stopped
running against its treadmill. But it did not behave as
the girl had described: it allowed itself to be carried
around tail-first for several revolutions, then darted out
of the wheel and began rushing up and down and from
one corner of the cage to the other, as if it were trying
to find a breach.

"Do you like them shut up in cages," I asked as we
were walking away, "or running around wild?" "When
they're wild," she readily answered, "they aren't really
any more free than they are when they're kept in cages,
if you take the different conditions into account. They
can only live in certain places where they can get certain kinds of things to eat, and in the cage they don't
have to worry about food because we give them lots of
nuts and things—and they're safer than they are outside,
because they're protected from the red squirrels. The red
squirrels bite the gray squirrels and try to drive them
out." She was a formidable little pedant—perhaps a little
prig. She could never have been much with other children. It was appalling to think of the figure she would
cut among boys and girls of her own age in that dress

and those long black stockings and with those metal bands on her teeth. I felt, in fact, a certain nervous self-consciousness involved with her precocious complacency.

"I shouldn't mind living in a cage," she went on, "if I were sure I'd get out someday. I *am* in a sort of cage out here." These shifts of hers disconcerted me, and I didn't know how to reply. "Young people often feel they're caged," I said in a tone of lightness and kindness but with a feeling that I was being sententious. "But, as you say, they find the way out." "Grandfather doesn't want me to go away to school, because he says that he and the governess can teach me a great deal better, and when I went to school in New York last winter it did make it rather embarrassing because I was so far ahead of all the other girls. But I think that there are other reasons for a girl's going away to school." "Yes, of course there are," I assented—I found myself siding against her grandfather. "I wish you would tell Grandfather that," she said in her sedate way. She evidently assumed I was a friend of her family's, or was it merely that we had somehow established a sympathetic understanding? "I will if the occasion presents itself," I found myself naturally replying. "Oh, please do! won't you?—It might help, you know,"—she became for a moment quite girlish; then returned to her judicious tone: "Of course, if anything happened to Mother, I'd have to stay here with Grandfather. I shouldn't be justified in going away."

We had reached the front steps, and I said good-by. She invited me to come again in her most mature manner and hoped, with a twitch of her bang, that her mother would soon be back. I hoped—getting the name right with an effort, as if I were obliged to struggle with some false conception that bulked in my mind without my being able to see it—I hoped that Miss Terhune would soon be better. The effect that this had on the girl I was unable to understand and yet it gave me a queer sort of qualm as if I knew that I had said the wrong thing. She suddenly seemed embarrassed, but she handled it with her usual self-possession: "Oh, I'm not really sick. Mother worries about me, but Grandfather says it's not important. It's silly, of course, to have fainting-fits, but I'm not really sick at all!" I saw that she had taken my remark to herself: she must be some sort of niece of Ellen's father. "Well, I hope," I said, "that everybody's better."

As I left her alone on the steps, with the darkened house behind her, in that countryside of deserted residences, the colors of the trees fading in the day-end and the thickening mist, I was visited by a doubt, a pang, by a feeling almost dolorous that lingered, as if I almost knew something about her which I could not remember to have learned, as if I wanted to save her from something. Though I had never quite recognized the fact in the past, I could see now that that house was an unhappy one. I thought about the girl mounting the steps, passing the chairs in which nobody sat, swinging open the large front door with its paneling of varnished oak and its upper and lower parts that were separate—going back into that lampless interior, so full of an American past which I felt to be even at its best rather cluttered, middle-class and banal. I had left the place so quiet and dark that it seemed to me even improbable that anyone would come out of the kitchen to drum on the Chinese gongs and summon her in to dinner.

III

When the summer people in Hecate County go away after the first of September, the people who stay on through the winter are more thrown in on themselves and on one another. New contours of the community emerge; you distinguish a new scale of values. You gradually become interested in neighbors of whom you would never have seen anything at the time when there was more going on; and you meditate on the lives of persons who mean absolutely nothing to you.

I brooded a good deal on Ellen. I sent flowers and a note to the hospital, but I never had any reply. Her phone was still out of order, and I thought I ought to call at her house and find out what had happened to her; yet for days I was inhibited from doing so by the brake of some instinctive reluctance which would divert me into town to buy papers or make me call upon some other neighbor when I had intended to go to Ellen's.

This reluctance was due partly to an unpleasant re-action which I had had after my last two visits. One of the symptoms of certain neurotic states is an irrational drop of morale, a depression that may suddenly descend on you and absolutely flatten you out, from some stimulus that seems irrelevant or trifling—a passing sarcasm in conversation directed at someone else, a child ducking a cat in the gutter, a memory drifting into your head of something clumsy you once did in your child-hood. I had had a touch of this at one time, and I found that my visits to Ellen's renewed it. This was only, I told myself, vicarious: I was merely being affected ac-cidentally by things that in reality were experienced by others; but it was enough to give me disagreeable sink-ings, living as I then did alone, in the evening or even the next afternoon after I had been at Vallombrosa with Ellen. It was a revival of my old morbidity; but it took a peculiar turn. I would feel suddenly after lunch or dinner that living in the country was hopeless, that I had no communication with other people, and that nothing I was doing meant anything; yet on the other hand I could not see any hope in living in the city or traveling: I knew what human beings were—they might be more or less picturesque in their various environments and climates, and to the young this was a source of excitement; but to me, on the verge of thirty, it was desolatingly, incontrovertibly evident that people under any conditions were the same wry pathetic freaks, and why should I go to the trouble of moving about among them in order to observe the shapes which their defects and distortions could take?

I had had something like this feeling before, though the emphasis on deformity, I believed, was new; but in the past it had led to an impulse which was vaguely directed toward suicide. Now the impulse was aimed at an act that would be absolutely immediate and definite: to go back to Ellen's house. This seemed a good deal less serious than suicide; yet there was something about it that scared me. For one thing, it presented itself as a compulsion imposed from outside as to which I had not even the option of yielding on my own terms; and, for another, I had a definite conviction that, in revisiting Ellen's house, I was getting into something very queer that I didn't know how to handle. I did my best to resist this compulsion, and I did not allow myself to go till the impulse was no longer felt as morbid and I could put it to myself that I was merely dropping in to inquire about the illness of a friend. But, nevertheless, I went: I could only choose one way.

I did, however, semi-consciously, make a point of going early in the afternoon so that I should not have to be there at nightfall. I tried to insist to myself that I could not really be afraid because the day itself was overcast and dull. Yet when I entered the gates of Vallombrosa, the sky became suddenly clear. I looked up: it was almost cloudless; before me the thinning branches and the angles of the slate-covered roof were distinct and a little bleak in the emptied October light; and I recognized, against my intelligence, that each of my last entrances there had been marked by some discontinuity of weather or of the appearance of things on the grounds.

Discomfited, I became self-conscious: like an explorer in an unknown terrain, I scanned the place carefully for changes, without, I told myself, noticing any; then I dropped my eyes to the driveway and I saw that the ground was wet: though it had not rained yet outside, it had recently been raining on the Bristead place. There were hoofmarks in the muddy gravel, and what looked like the tracks of a carriage.

I rang the bell at the paneled front door and observed, as I stood on the porch, a croquet set in a long wooden box which I noted that I did not remember. I felt a little dizzy for a moment, but told myself it was perfectly natural that the visiting girl cousin should have brought it out.—Then a brisk and definite step; an accurate hand on the latch; the door opened, and I found myself confronted with a woman I had never seen—the mother of the girl, no doubt. She bore some resemblance to Ellen: her long nose was a little beakish and her jawbones, like Ellen's, stood out; but she was blonder and rather taller. Her sharp eyes were not green but blue-gray, and they were not so intelligent as Ellen's.

"Oh, how do you do," she said in a cordial but formal manner, as if, though she did not know me, she knew about me and had expected my visit. I came into the familiar hallway. "Won't you leave your coat and hat here?" she said. I noticed, as I was taking off my coat, that she gave a keen glance at my clothes—the glance of a woman who is certain that she knows what is correct and what is not, who is severely and unremittingly critical of everyone with whom she has to do and who is not in the habit of hesitating to make her disapproval felt. But any surprise that I may have caused her by the unconventionality of *my* clothes could have been nothing to the shock I received when she turned to lead me into the living room. She was wearing a kind of bustle, a built-out ruffle at the back of her skirt that looked like one of the scalloped crests on that elaborate and poisonous jellyfish called the Portuguese man-of-war. She had also a jacket buttoned closely in front, with two little tails that stuck out above the ruffle; and on her dress, which was silk and mauve, there were several fringes of lace: at the bottom of the skirt, at the throat, and on the sleeves that came just beyond her elbows. It must have been the kind of thing that was in fashion in the middle of the eighties; but the dress was so handsome and so naturally worn that it did not seem obsolete. Her hair was done up high toward the back of her head, and she was wearing black onyx earrings.

The smell of the living room, though this had been different before, seemed curiously natural, too. It emanated from the fumes of a hot coal-grate red-glowing in the white marble fireplace, from the stuff of the garnet curtains muffling the windows with balances and loops, and from the pinkish flowered thick-napped carpeting which I told myself was not really suffocating and which caused me to say to myself "Brussels carpet" in the moment before I sat down. But I had been at first so stunned by the whole situation that I had not been able to look at things calmly, and I subsided into it now in a way that seemed to be depriving me of the power to examine them closely and take account of what had happened to the house.

"It was kind of you to come," she said. "My father

was extremely sorry that he had to go to town today.
They telephoned him this morning that Mr. Schroeder's
condition was worse. It's such a deeply distressing tragedy! He was deceived by the people he trusted, and
my father says the shock has almost killed him." "Yes:
I'm sorry not to see your father," I fell readily into
replying. "He told me to tell you you would hear from
him," she said, and immediately addressed herself to
what was evidently the business before us. "I don't
know how far he has described to you my symptoms"
. . . "Not in any great detail," I answered.

I told myself, suddenly relieved at discovering a clue
to the strange situation, that the woman was obviously
insane and that she was going to tell me about voices
and about people who were working against her as they
had against Mr. Schroeder. But, instead, she began giving me a very precise, a positively clinical, chronicle of
fainting-fits, spells of nausea, and convulsive internal
pains. I presently grasped that she was pregnant and, in
my rather lightheaded embarrassment, I was about to
ask her whether she were the mother of the girl I had
seen the other day, but I pulled myself up at the realization that such a question would be out of character with
the role I was allowing myself to assume—since the physician I was supposed to be would undoubtedly know
about her children and would probably not have been
here when I had. Such a query, in fact, was impossible; I found that I was powerless to put it—I was
powerless to say or do anything which would violate the
logic of the scene. And now, with a beating of the heart,
but inevitably and by clear recognition, I sank into the
consciousness that the woman before me was Ellen's un-
fortunate mother and that her father was old Dr. Bristead; and I knew—had already known?—that it was
Ellen herself in her girlhood whom I had seen on my

previous visit: Ellen as she had been in her girlhood and just before her mother's death; and that the Ellen I had met on the visit before had been Ellen at some time in her twenties when she had just come back from Paris. And now here was her mother, a young woman— I saw it perfectly—just before Ellen's birth. As the picture became clear in my mind, I stiffened and sat perfectly still. I was kept tense by the anxiety to follow her, to say something that played in with the story. The queer thing was that it had now become impossible for me to set myself right with Time, because whenever I summoned to mind the order of my adventures in that house, they seemed to me perfectly normal: looking out on my series of glimpses from the point of my visit today, the first image I saw was of Ellen as a girl, and the next was of Ellen a young woman; further on she was middle-aged—and wasn't this the natural sequence? I beheld her growing older—of course: that was what people did. I had a feeling of unreality, yet I couldn't see it in any other way. Giddily and intently I listened, inquiring, when it seemed necessary for me to say something: "Did your father prescribe anything for that?" or "How often have you been having these attacks?"

But she needed no prompting to talk. I got the impression that she was rather hypochondriac and was gloating over the tale of her symptoms. She was not at all restrained by the prudery which might have gone with the upholstery of her costume: she was the daughter of an enlightened doctor and she had been taught not to shrink from such subjects. Though she was dignified and restrained in the extreme, the very patient objectivity and exactitude with which she described her disorders somehow made demands on the hearer for astonishment and commiseration, and I found myself evincing in my expression and tone a graver and graver concern. "I dare say," she continued, "that my condition has been aggravated by the domestic situation—I suppose my father has spoken to you about it." "A little," I replied: I was remembering what Ellen had told me about her parents. "I don't know," she went on with pretended detachment but deadly masochistic hatefulness, "whether a normal parturition is possible under circumstances of that kind: continual scenes that are deeply disturbing to a person in my condition and the uncertainty every night as to whether my husband is coming home." "Can't you stay down here?" I suggested. "I don't want to stay longer than two or three days: I'm afraid of what might happen to him without me. When one thinks how even men of fine character like Mr. Schroeder and General Grant—I don't mean that my husband isn't a man of fine character, but he is unstable and a little irresponsible—when one thinks how even men like that have been ruined and humiliated!"

She now went on to tell me in detail about a physical examination which had been given her by her regular obstetrician and which had disclosed certain structural conditions that he was afraid might make childbirth difficult. "What does your father say about it?" I asked. "He tells me that he doesn't think it's serious, but he wished to consult you." The idea was somehow conveyed to me that she had called me for the purpose of advising her that it would be dangerous for her to have a baby—not, I thought, that she wouldn't go through with it, but she wanted to make her husband suffer by continual complaint and reproach. I felt that I must bite off the interview and escape from that disquieting house. Ellen's mother's cold eye and her reasonable smile which masked the morbidity of her pregnancy were exercising upon me an influence that I had to struggle to break.

"Everything is so uncertain, isn't it?" Mrs. Terhune was saying—"with all these dreadful disasters. One doesn't know what kind of world one is bringing one's children into. People lose all their resources overnight, and one doesn't want to have one's child not have the things one has had oneself." I answered shortly, and got up brusquely—being a doctor gave me this right— and told her that she must come to my office: I would give her an examination there. She seemed puzzled and a little displeased as if she had imagined that this was what I had called for, and suggested that it would be a good thing if I could examine her right away, since her symptoms were becoming worse. "I'll phone you tomorrow," I said—then feared I had slipped in my role; they had certainly had telephones then—or now, but had they talked about "phoning" people? I was frightened for a second, then fortified by the thought that my instinct had kept me straight—I was still in the actual world. I almost smiled at the joke; but the woman would not allow it. She looked at me gravely, as if she were a trifle dismayed and even not quite sure what I meant; and I saw that she thought I had been speaking of some unfamiliar clinical technique. I seized the occasion to shake hands and say good-by in a reassuring manner, and get out of the house and outside the grounds.

All the way down the drive, however, I had the illusion that her insistence was attached to me, lengthening out like a rubber band, whose pull I felt growing stiffer as it was thinner and thinner drawn. At the gate I hoped the pull would snap, but I awaited the moment with a fear that it might not after all bring relief: it was as if I were cheating on some perverse obligation, leaving unfinished some ugly task. Whatever I was leaving behind me—and I did not quite know what it was—I was definitely involved in that thing.

I woke up in the night in a panic: a seizure of horror and disgust which had projected itself in a nightmare. I had thought I was in the hallway of Ellen's house, struggling with the *tromba marina,* which I was trying to carry upstairs. It would catch in the mahogany-stained banisters in such a way that it was difficult to extricate or it would get between my legs and cause me to fall on all fours on the heavily-carpeted stairs. And this was all bound up in some way with the naked Canova Hebe, which I had noted the day before in the hallway, though Ellen had always kept it in a museum-like reception room. The statue in the dream, I decided, had represented some ideal of nineteenth-century womanhood, symmetrical, smooth and chaste, to which my clumsy mishaps with the obsolete instruments were somehow an impious affront. But then the thing took a sinister turn. I had the bow of the *tromba marina* and I was trying to do something damaging to a modern violin: instead of using it to draw forth music, I was jabbing it into the f-holes; I was compelled to do this, but whenever I did, Mrs. Terhune would shriek out in a way that I felt was overdone and malicious—it was all, as a matter of fact, prearranged—yet which, none the less, convicted me of hideous guilt.

I turned on the light to make sure that that woman was not with me there, and as I looked at my green-stained woodwork and my rough-finished plastered walls, of which the fine leaded folding windows opened right on the trees and the grass, I was aware that a revelation had been pushing to the surface through sleep. In that loneliness of the forest surrounding my house, the meaning pressed in with the night. What the woman really

wished me to do was to declare her unfit to have a baby
and to recommend a legal abortion. She wanted to spite
her husband, the child that was to be, life itself. But
why? I couldn't understand her. Was she human or a
specter of nightmare? She was real in the sense that I
had seen her, with her horrible well-cut mauve dress and
her cold and shallow eyes, and that I could not get her
out of my head; but in the dream there was somebody
behind her, she emanated from somebody else—at the
moment just before she began to scream, it had seemed
to me that her eyes were bright green, alive with intellect, and glaring not in hypocritical agony but in fixed
and unforgiving condemnation.

And now I seemed to see it quite clearly: the appari-
tion had come from Ellen. It was Ellen herself who had
created this monster in the image of her mother, who
was forcing her to get rid of her baby, who was destroy-
ing her own existence before it had come out of the
womb! And she was somehow forcing me to abet
her. . . . I had, I felt, to make a moral effort to free myself from Ellen's influence, and I got myself to sleep
with a book just as the windows were unblotting from
night.

When I woke again, this certainty faded. The sun
was quite brilliant and bracing: it sent a long pane of
light across my breakfast and brought out the whites
and yellows of my eggs with their sprinkling of salt
and pepper; I talked to my soft-spoken colored maid
about the movie she had seen the night before; and I
stood outside for a moment and was delighted by the
deep-orange zinnias, the pompon clusters of little lemon
marigolds, the big scarlet daisies of cosmos on high and
spidery stems that still were bright at the end of October. I decided that my explanation of my visit of the day
before had been simply a part of the nightmare. What

I had seen was not a woman of the eighties but a contemporary relation of Ellen's, completely insane no doubt but an actual human being, and I must not allow myself to be led by her into getting insane myself. I expelled the whole thing from my mind; read the papers, wrote several letters, and contemplated a trip to the city. I needed the city, I felt.

But when I went for a walk that afternoon, the sun had gone out for the day and the whole thing came back on me again. I saw the situation precisely as I had seen it in the middle of the night, and I could not see it in any other way—I could not seem to get outside it. And I now felt not merely an irrational pull toward the house in which Ellen lived; I had a fear it would come to find me—that the past might have its gangsters, too, who could wait for you and meet you on the autumn roads where so little traffic passed. I presently turned back, came home, and lay on a couch and brooded.

Yet I could not go to town, I now told myself: there was something I could not leave unfinished. I had to see it finished, and I had to do my best to see that it was finished as it should be. Precisely what this meant I did not know—except that it imposed upon me a duty to stand up to the Bristead-Terhunes. I must not be afraid to go out, I must not be afraid to pass the place; I must even be not afraid to go back there, but I must not go back in response to that pull which was itself a fear.

All the rest of the week and the week following, then, I took my afternoon walk every day, and I several times glanced in at Vallombrosa, where I could not see that anything was changed—though I believe I did not look very closely. I still had my bad moments at night after the painful importunings of dreams and during stretches of those solitary strolls which had now become daily trials. But by the end of the second week I was imagining that the pressure was lighter. I had had two untormented nights, and I set out on Saturday afternoon with something like ease and indifference.

I walked first along a little back-road that ran parallel with the regular motor-road on which the Bristead house faced: it passed behind the Bristeads', but there was somebody else's place between Ellen and it. Then I turned down a hedge-lined lane that connected with the larger road, admitting to myself humorously as I did so that I had lately never taken these lanes. I heard something drive in behind me and I drew over close to the hedge, but it was something that ran very lightly, and I did not glance round as it passed. A horse stopped in front of me: I looked up and saw a lady in a varnished yellow phaeton, who seemed to be speaking to me. "Oh, how do you do," I replied with an instinctive familiarity that preceded conscious recognition. "You ought to have let us know that you were coming today," she said as she reached down her gloved hand. She was slimmer and brisker and trimmer than when I had seen her before. She was wearing a tight dress of a brown-and-green plaid, with a beautiful hour-glass waist and no bustle or ruffle to encumber the skirt, and a pretty little straw bonnet, which was tied under her chin with a big green bow.

I got in at her invitation, as if it were a matter of course, and she drove on, sitting up very straight between the gracefully scrolling wicker fenders and behind the slim long-lashed whip that stood upright and smart in its socket. I was occupied for the first few minutes in fitting my story to my role. There was a passage in the conversation where she and I almost lost connections when I had to explain that I had walked instead of asking them to meet me at the train because I so much enjoyed walking, then found out that the railroad station was eight or nine miles away. I was forced to confess, laughing nervously, that I had only been boasting before, that a farmer had brought me part way. And I did not notice at first that we were driving through a landscape that seemed new to me. We had turned out of the lane to the right through a gate I had not known was there, and now were trotting along a driveway which should have led to the house next door to the Bristeads'; but, to my surprise, there was no house there: instead of a house, there was a wide expanse of lawn, unbroken by a hedge or fence, through which the long drive made a curve. We approached a yellow new-looking house and drew up under a porte-cochère. I realized suddenly and queerly that we were back at Vallombrosa again. I remarked that I hadn't known about this driveway which connected with the other road. "Yes: the drive runs right through," she replied. It came to me that the place next door was still a part of the Bristead estate: the doctor would later sell it. I had entered into the domain of the Bristeads as soon as I had turned into the lane.

"I don't know why Jerry didn't see me," she said when she had waited hardly a second. "Would you mind going into the house and telling Rosa to call him? —I think he's getting very lax," she said, as I climbed down from the phaeton. I opened the front door and went in. Should I bolt? No, I couldn't do that. I walked resolutely through the hallway—conscious, as I passed the Hebe, that I did not give it a thought. But when I got to the door to the kitchen, I knew there would be nobody there. I opened it, however, and looked in. There was a big black coal-range with a stovepipe, a bare clean wooden floor, a double row of copper pots and pans hanging along the wall. I called out, "Hello . . . Rosa . . ."; but nobody answered. I ought now, I said to myself, to go out the back door to the stable; but I was swayed by a half-dreamlike instinct that I should not find anyone there either; and my sense that I was not going to go there was strengthened by a voice from the hallway which told me that the coachman had come.

I joined her. She was removing her bonnet. "Well, the styles in men's clothes astonish me," she said, as I took off my overcoat. "Is that really what they're wearing now?" "I'm perhaps a little eccentric," I said. "I get to town so seldom," she continued, as we went into the living room, "that I don't even know the fashions—and I believe that the young men I see are rather conservative about their clothes."

The atmosphere, I felt, was relaxed. The room seemed to be largely unchanged. There were the curtains, the grate with its coals, the tables with low-hanging covers, the ornaments on a whatnot in the corner. I noticed a large bronze gas-chandelier with shades of pattern-frosted glass. I must have scrutinized these objects rather curiously because she glanced toward a group of swords and sabers, hung up so as to form a design, at which she evidently thought I was looking, and explained: "Those are oriental weapons. I don't think they have any place here—but Papa seems to consider them decorative. I tell him he ought to build a small armory. —Do sit down: take that comfortable chair."

I questioned her, still standing for a moment, about the various kinds of weapons; but she wasn't quite sure what they were and was obviously impatient with them. There was some matter that she wanted to get on to —so I finally took the comfortable chair. "I should like to talk to you quite frankly about something," she began almost as soon as we were seated, "and I want you to advise me frankly. You're the closest friend now that we have—though it's been such a long time since we've seen you." I was, then, an old family friend. "I have no brothers or uncles to turn to as most women have—I have nobody in the world but Papa, and you know how prejudiced he is about so many things, and how obstinately he sticks to his prejudices. I know that I can say that to you because you know that I love and admire him more than anyone else in the world—but—well, you know how sure he is about everything." I nodded and smiled in concurrence. "Well, I'd like to put my problem before you—if you don't mind being plunged into family affairs just the very minute you come. I know it's not a very cheerful welcome, but I think that if I'm going to talk about it, I'd better do it before Papa gets back. You know that he doesn't give people much chance to express opinions different from his own.—Well, here is my problem quite baldly. A young man has asked me to marry him——" "And your father doesn't approve of him," I put in, a little more at ease in the new situation than I had been in the role of physician. "—And Papa doesn't approve of him at all. In fact, he's violently opposed to my marrying him—and you know how he is when he's opposed to anything. He's even making it difficult now for Fred to come to the house." The young man, then—I half felt I had known it already, was Ellen's father, Fred Terhune, and this was Ellen's mother, younger than when I had seen her before and not yet come to a decision about marrying him.

"Why does he object to this young man?" I asked. "It's simply that he's in Wall Street," she answered. "I think that his attitude is very unreasonable. The financiers have done so much for this country and it's ridiculous to pretend that they're not as good as our best—Mr. Morgan, for example, who has just as much taste as Papa and is making such a wonderful collection. It isn't as if he were in business! Fred's family are Terhune

Brothers, the bankers, and his position is perfectly unexceptionable. I am sure that his character is sound. He was a little wild in his younger days, but now he wants a home and an ordered life. That's hard for Papa to understand, because Papa has always been occupied with intellectual things, and he can't recognize that a man whom he regards as a mere man of fashion can be a proper person to marry. I really think he'd rather I married a musician—someone preferably who played the cello, so that we could have a family trio." I was aware of the prejudice against "business" on the part of the professional classes that had lasted in the United States till long after our national life had been actually dominated by businessmen; but this prejudice, I thought, as a rule, had not been extended to bankers, and I put down the doctor's opposition to distrust of the particular young man or to some special and personal crankiness. But she went on to indicate another cause which I guessed to be fundamental. "Of course, I understand, too, that Papa has been lonely since Mama's death, and that he doesn't want to have me leave him. But, after all, Papa has so many resources—his work and his music and his collections and his chess—and I can't go on like this forever. He doesn't understand that if I don't get married now, I may be left alone myself. And Fred needs me, too—he's told me so with all the feeling of which anyone is capable—and I can see that his bachelor life is beginning to do him harm.—Now please tell me frankly and sincerely what you think I ought to do. Shall I just go ahead and marry Fred in spite of Papa's opposition? I feel that he's perfectly capable of refusing to give me anything and never having anything to do with me again. But if I do as Papa wants, I'll feel that I'm betraying Fred's trust in me. Now how would you advise me to act?"

This, then, was an earlier turning-point, another moment to determine the future; and again there was the curious effort to put off the decision on me.

This plea of Miss Bristead's, who I gathered was now in her latish twenties, reminded me of Ellen's appeal, at the time I had seen her in her girlhood, that I should put in a word with her grandfather to have her sent away to school. And I had now a very clear conviction of something that I had only felt without figuring it to myself before: that Dr. Bristead was an egregious old egoist, selfish in his relations with his family and oppressive in his opinionated omniscience. The daughter, too, in her turn, would want to get away from Dr. Bristead, and she would certainly have sympathized with her mother. I sympathized with her myself. Miss Bristead had a genuine distinction, she was handsome in her glamorless way; above all, as she leaned forward in her modish dress that reminded me of Ellen's plaid skirt when she had just come back from Paris, and threw out her very well-shaped hands that might have been reproduced in china for those vases that hold single flowers—above all, she was an eager young woman who wanted to escape from that house and marry an urgent suitor. Besides, there was a certain authority, a certain force of assertion she commanded, to which I could feel myself yielding. Why shouldn't she, I asked myself, be bored with ministering to her father's hobbies? Why shouldn't she want to live in town? Why shouldn't she yearn for and why shouldn't she share in that codified social life for which she was obviously well adapted and of which her father had undoubtedly skimped her? Why shouldn't she marry Fred? He was doing no one any good—it seemed to me, as if I had known him—as a man about town past his prime. He could at least give her an independent position, help her to found a family. It was as if I could not foresee the future.

"I'm sure that it's right for you to marry him," I replied to her request for advice. "I do wish you would tell Papa that!"—she was grateful to me for recommending the thing that she wanted to do, though she must have been sure all along that I would follow the lead she had given. "If anyone could persuade him, you could. I don't want to do anything without his consent —it would be so distressing for everybody!" "I'll try," I assured her, smiling.

She looked away toward the adjoining music room, the door into which was open, but which I could not see from where I sat, as if she had just heard somebody enter it. Then she was turning to me again as if to go on talking when someone began to play the piano—ringing out, as I imagined at random, the Don Juan theme from Strauss, which had not been quite accurately remembered. Miss Bristead looked up as if uncertain how to deal with the situation; but the music went on consecutively, developing and playing with the theme. We saw that it was an organized piece. "Oh, yes: do play it, dear!"—she looked toward the music room. "This is your new composition, isn't it? I want so very much to hear it!" She leaned over and said to me in a lowered voice, which was, however, it seemed to me, quite loud enough to carry clearly into the next room: "Our guest is playing something of her own. I hope you don't mind. It may not be very wonderful, and I don't think the middle of the afternoon is quite the best time to listen to music, do you?—but I don't want to stop her now that she's started. I wasn't sure whether she was going to be here and I hope she won't be in our way."

I nodded and gestured with my hand so that she

would be still and I could listen to the music. It was amusing and very adroit. The composer had taken an echo of the blare of the Don Juan theme and subjected it to all kinds of transformations. After stating it at first in its full exultation, she had gone on to break its pace and to reduce it to a wavering whimper. Against this appeared a steadier theme, sober, distinct and insistent, which began by going along with Don Juan in a fairly orderly manner but ended by getting at odds with him in a jagged amalgamation that seemed to be jamming the movement. Miss Bristead gave me a look of ironic disapproving amazement when these cacophonies began to sound. She had listened before that rather thoughtfully, as if she did not know quite how to take it, with her cheek leaned against her fine fingers and her face partly turned toward the door; but now, as the music appeared to her to be getting more and more insane, she coughed toward me a dry little laugh as if it might all be supposed to be funny, and slightly shifted her pensive pose, self-consciously and pleasantly smiling. Don Juan had the last word of the contest that went on in the music, but in a triumph that verged, I thought, on the trashy. The whole thing had reminded me of Sigismund, who so loved to exploit the Strauss tone-poem, identifying himself with the hero and bringing down the house. "I *don't* know what you want to do to our ears," said Miss Bristead in the direction of the doorway. "That certainly doesn't lack vivacity—but it does sound a little like a couple of children letting *Chopsticks* run away with them."

There was no answer from the other room: after a moment the piano began again. Miss Bristead faintly raised her eyebrows at the pianist's bizarre rudeness— for this person whom I could not see had offered neither announcement nor excuse—and again became silent.

And now, almost without astonishment, I recognized the slow movement of the sonata that Ellen had played me in August. Yes: I heard unmistakably that theme— that sullen immovable impediment—which had worried me so at the time and of which I had felt a premonition in the music of Ellen's youth. I looked up toward the door with interest, and Miss Bristead shot me a glance and threw out her hands in a gesture of "Well, I give it up!" How horrible Ellen's harmonies must sound to her mother, I thought: they must be forty or fifty years beyond her. I smiled faintly and nodded curtly and thereafter kept clear of her eye. I listened to the music with attention. It was not now so thudding and stunning: she had worked out devices to vary it so that it no longer made one nervous with the fear that she was simply getting stuck, and yet she had kept the effect of monotony. Daring and disconcerting though it was, I saw that it would be ultimately successful. Certainly Ellen was an admirable musician!

When again there was a pause for a moment, Miss Bristead sat and looked at her lap. But quickly she returned to the charge: "I suppose," she said humorously to the doorway, "that the first section represented Baby when he was just beginning to bang and that the second is called *Five-Finger Exercises.*"

The piano picked up when the space had been made. I listened for this movement with excitement. It began with the theme of obstruction again, and, though this had been sharpened and speeded up, I felt at first rather disappointed. In a moment, I was almost terrified. The four notes which had not let her move now in their way became hysterically insistent. The thing seemed to be getting out of hand and was beginning to sound absolutely hellish, a shrieking of desperation; and the horror of the nightmare came back on me. Miss Bristead got up and coughed slightly and went out through the door into the hall as if she had to speak to the maid but at the same time desired definitely to indicate that she was done with the music. I continued to listen, and there crept upon me a dark apprehension like that of those days when I had dreaded to come to the house: the piano seemed to be carrying me, like the panic of my dreams, to some bad unintelligible goal. The awful accelerated movement had passed from the negative of inertia to a frenzied destructive denial. But now it met a new kind of theme, which it seemed to have thrown up itself and which was lifted like the human cry in the slow movement of Beethoven's last string quartet, shuddering and terror-stricken at first as it shrilled from the sinister harping that was beginning to tear like a beast at a carcass, then rising to a plangency, to a clarity, that, passing the conventional limits of this sort of affirmation in music, began to assail one's attention more recklessly, more compellingly, more triumphantly, just as the diabolic yapping of the other theme, becoming fiercer and fiercer, had forced itself beyond all limits. This cry, itself now reiterated, not only wrecked the bounds of the conventional, it seemed even to escape from the probable—anguished, appealing, pitying, recognizing all human discrepancy, debasement, self-disgust and self-accusal of the individual who knows his own nature and who yet cannot undo what he is; but reaching by the voice of music out of the brooding of deformity in solitude to speak to other beings of their solitudes and of the general human fate, declaring by its certainty of pain how much our nature wrongs us. The voice broke away: for that moment, becoming at once more complex and more ordered, it had been freed to a life of its own—something that shone and resounded and yet had a solid wholeness, something that had left all deformity behind and that nothing now could ever violate.

Miss Bristead came back into the room just as the final statement was struck, pulling up perhaps a little short of the development one might have expected and yet perfectly making its point. "That was immensely interesting!" she said to the person in the music room. "It must be extremely fatiguing playing such violent music." She sat down beside me on the couch and remarked in her inadequately lowered voice: "I don't think our friend in the next room has discovered the use of the soft pedal yet—as well as a number of other things! . . . I don't think she's entirely normal—one can see it by her oversized head."

I realized then that it was not only in technique that Ellen's music was beyond Miss Bristead: musically trained though she was, she had no real feeling for music whatever. The daughter had been mistaken in her notion that her mother's marriage had shut her off from a musical career: Miss Bristead was conventional and worldly, she could not conceivably be anything else. And now Ellen, surmounting her own despair, had come back all the way through the years to justify her, to communicate her love, to show her that something fine had come out of her, something that might make all that—the coldness, the sickness, the quarreling, the bad birth and the ugly changeling—something that might make all that right. I wanted to tell Ellen that she had triumphed, that she had perhaps written a masterpiece. I wanted to assure her, confronted as we were by the Gorgon-like incomprehension of her mother, that I at least understood and applauded.

"I liked it very much," I said, and got up quickly and went into the music room. But Ellen had already escaped. There was nobody there: I looked around. Every-

thing seemed perfectly familiar, unexpectedly and yet re-
assuringly: the mask of Beethoven, the old violins, Ellen's silver-framed photograph of Debussy. But the
room, rather queerly, was much darker than the one
from which I had come.

I had an impulse to go after Ellen and call to her that
I was there. I was eager to see her again. But I knew
that it would be better to return to Miss Bristead and ask
her to make Ellen come in. I went back, then, into the
living room; but it was empty: Miss Bristead had gone
out again. This room had darkened, too—the weather
must suddenly have clouded. I turned on the electric
lamp on the little round table by the couch, and saw
that the mahogany of the surface was dimmed by a film
of dust. There was a pile of current magazines, current
for 1926. I picked two or three of them up and noted
the dates on the covers. Then I looked about the room.
There it was just as I had seen it in August. All the
shades were drawn. I picked up from another table a
vase of faded flowers and got a whiff of a foul stink:
they were gladioluses withered to a crisp yellow thin-
ness. On the mantel were the shrunk mummies of dahlias. The house had been shut up in haste: the flowers
had been forgotten.

I found my hat and coat in the hall, but the big front
door was fast locked. I came back into the living room,
threw up one of the front windows, and stepped out
on the dark porch, where I saw that it had just been
raining. I did not fear that Miss Bristead would catch
me—I knew there was nobody there.

The next day I read in the paper that Ellen Terhune
had died. She had gone, it turned out, to the city the
night of my visit in August. She had taken a little suite

—registering under her maiden name—in a little old hotel in the West Fifties which was frequented by musical people and where you could have a piano in your room. She had apparently made efforts to compose during the first two or three weeks she had been there; but later she would be found by the chambermaid lying on the couch or the bed in what seemed to be a kind of stupor, and the management became aware that she was never going out and not eating. They had decided that she was suffering from the sleeping sickness and got a doctor in. But Ellen had then revived and explained that she had come for a rest and did not want to be annoyed, and sent the doctor about his business.

She now reassured the hotel people by directing that a breakfast with two pots of coffee should be brought to her every morning; and she was heard at the piano again, pounding the same thing over and over in a way that made them fear she had gone insane. In the evening she would leave the hotel, but they did not know where she went.

One day, however, she had not got up but had stayed in bed till afternoon, and the maid had not been able to do the rooms. It was the day of my last call in the country, and at what must have been the same hour that I was listening to the playing of the sonata, the maid heard the piano and knocked. She had just started work on the bedroom when Ellen stopped and came in and put on her things to go out. She was tense and her hands, which had been strained over the keys, had difficulty adjusting themselves to manage her coat and hat. The chambermaid tried to help her, but Ellen paid no attention.

She went out quickly and rang for the elevator. On the trip down, the elevator boy said, he had stopped and gone back up a floor to get a passenger who had rung after they passed, and Ellen had "bawled him out," telling him he must never go back once he had passed a floor. This sudden scolding had so flustered the boy, who was new and rather inexpert with the old-fashioned elevator, that he had made the situation worse by stopping below the door and then jerking the car up just as the passenger was stepping down. Then, in an effort to make up for his delay, on the assumption that Ellen was in a hurry, he had shot abruptly down, in a drop which the passenger who had just got in said afterwards had given him an unpleasant shock. It must have shocked Ellen, too, for she was pale when they reached the bottom, and leaned against the side of the elevator for a moment before she got out. The boy was worried and tried to help her; but she stepped out by herself into the lobby, and there she fell dead. It was said that she had had a bad heart.

3.

Glimpses of Wilbur Flick

I FIRST KNEW WILBUR FLICK in college. It was the day of the big freshman rush, in which the sophomores would hold the doors of the gym and try to prevent the freshmen from charging into it. This was the stiffest of the freshman ordeals, and there were legends that men had been killed.

I got into conversation with Wilbur while we were waiting around to start marching. He was a wispy little fellow with small hands and feet, blond hair that was already thinning, and a face which, with its pale green round eyes and what I can only call spatulate nose, looked curiously like a duck's. We found that we had in common that we were both disaffected about the gym rush. Wilbur, who smoked cigarettes with an air and liked to lift his left eyebrow, had the tone of a man of the world with a light and pleasant touch, who had just gone ashore on some island in the course of a yachting trip and had found himself obliged to take part in an outlandish native ceremony. And yet there were moments when his ripe urbanity gave way—it was embarrassing to see it—to uneasiness and apprehension. He complained of the wetness of the day and of the time it took the leaders to get going, as if our class were a

hotel or a theater, where the management was respon-
sible for your comfort; and he hopefully began to wonder whether the delay might not be due to discussions
of the propriety of postponing the rush to some day
when the weather was better.

"I don't really care," I said, "whether we ever get into
the gym, do you? I think it would be marvelous, in fact,
if the sophomores kept us out so that we'd never have
the right to go in and wouldn't be able to take compul-
sory exercise!" "You know," said Wilbur—I had won
his confidence—"it really isn't as hard as all that to get
into the damn place, anyway. After all, you don't have
to go in through the main entrance." I asked him what
he meant. "There's a little door under the steps that goes
down into the basement," he said. "I'm afraid that
would be frowned upon," I answered. "But why
wouldn't it be a perfectly good way to steal a march on
the sophomores? I did a little reconnoitering yesterday,
and that door is going to be open with a clear way
through to the upstairs. The janitor's a friend of mine."

Just then the shout came for us to fall into line, and
our column of fours began moving. Wilbur was next
to me, the outside man. I lost track of him when we
got jammed in the big mêlée at the bottleneck of the
gym door. I squeezed through smoothly enough myself: I was well in the rear of the column, and the resistance of the sophomores had been broken by the football men at the head. Then, sweating and disheveled,
my jersey askew, but relieved and a little exhilarated, I
stood inside the hot crowded entrance hall and watched
the rest of the class push in. They were greeted with
cries of "Attaboy!" and paeans of organized cheering,
which were worked up by cheerleaders with their jerseys
and shirts rather ostentatiously torn. I found Wilbur
standing almost at my side, but just a little behind me, as

if he did not want to impose his companionship. He was smoking a cigarette and his hair was still smoothly brushed back under his little black freshman cap. He had slipped in, I felt perfectly sure, through the janitor's basement door, which had interested him less as a stratagem than as a dodge for self-preservation. He must have been very quick and sly.

"Why not come up to my diggings for a drink?" he suggested, as we walked out of the glaring gym into the muddy autumn gloom of the campus, after decently taking part in the cheering and the singing of the college anthem that wound up the afternoon's ritual. "Why not come up to my diggings?" was not the way we talked at college, but I was curious about him and went.

I was mystified when he took me to the local inn till I found that he actually lived there—in a suite which must have been their most splendid. He was evasive when I expressed surprise and said that he had applied too late to get anything satisfactory in the dormitories. "And one might as well be comfortable, what? I can't stand to use a shower room with other people." It was queer to come into that fancy apartment in the black jerseys and corduroy pants that were then the required costume for freshmen. I had been living in the college microcosm and suffering severely from the strain imposed by the pressure of the social code and my anxiety to distinguish myself; and now suddenly all this seemed lifted; it was as if I had gone to town for vacation.

He phoned downstairs for cocktails, which startled me, since we were not allowed to drink in our rooms; then announced that he was "going to change," and disappeared into the bedroom. I was left to pass the time with the furniture, which he had obviously brought himself and which mixed green silk curtains, good mahogany, large specimens of green and purple Tiffany glass and an enormous silver-mounted humidor, in a way that was not inviting. I examined the books behind the panes of a handsome eighteenth-century escritoire, and saw a *Rubáiyát,* the works of Oscar Wilde in gold and purple morocco, and a complete set of Surtees' hunting books in an almost equally magnificent binding. Wilbur presently came back in a white soft shirt, a blue polka-dotted bow-tie—which he told me had come from Peel's in London—a black velvet smoking jacket, gray trousers and patent-leather pumps. I had wondered whether he were really a sportsman, and asked him about the Surtees. "To tell the truth, I've never read it," he said, "—probably never will"; it had been sent him that fall by an uncle as a going-away-to-college present. "I don't like horses and they don't like me. I don't even like to look at pictures of 'em."

When the shaker of manhattans arrived, he produced a jar of maraschino cherries and insisted on putting an extra one in each of our drinks. He had three with his second cocktail, soaking them one by one and then munching them; and when the cocktails were all gone, he went on eating them out of the jar. "I love 'em, you know," he said.

He told me how he had got into the gym. It was absurdly simple, he said: he was surprised that nobody else had thought of it. "I didn't like the way what's-his-name—that big youth——" "Lem Mitchell?" I prompted him. "Yes, Mitchell. I didn't like the way he spoke to me when we were coming away from there." I asked what he had said. "All he said was, 'Hello, Wilb,' —but I didn't like the way he said it. I've never even met him, mind you, and nobody has ever called me Wilb. I think he must have known about my underground route." "Nonsense: he just wants to be popular," I tried to reassure him—I knew Lem Mitchell from boarding school. "He makes a point of knowing every-body's first name. He's one of those fellows whose great ambition is to be a big man in his class."

"I suppose it wasn't exactly cricket," Wilbur con-tinued his soliloquy—he had not taken in what I said, as he had really no notion of the existence of anyone except himself. "But the whole thing's just too kid-dish. My uncle writes me that he wants me to go in for all the experiences of college life, but I believe in choos-ing your experiences. Experience, as a rule, is just the name that people give their mistakes—what?" He lifted his left eyebrow. I saw that he *had* read the Wilde. "Fencing I don't mind. You have your rules and you don't have to maim one another. I used to fence with a little French kid, and I almost always won. But what sense is there in a brawl like this? What, for heaven's sake, does it prove? Absolutely nothing, what? I went in through the basement; you went in through the door; neither one of us wanted to go to the gym. We're just a couple of damn fools, aren't we?—what?"

I was one of the only people at college who ever saw anything of Wilbur or who ever liked him at all. He was at least outside the college conventions—something for which I sneakingly envied him—and not ashamed of his tastes, and my visits to his sybaritic suite relieved my freshman tension.

His grandfather had been the founder of a big bak-ing-powder fortune, and Wilbur, who was an orphan and an only child, must have been in line for a million. The family seemed to have come from Denver, but were now enjoying their money in the sun of southern California. Wilbur had spent part of his childhood on the ranch of a California uncle, for whom he did not care very much, and most of the rest traveling in Eu-rope with a tutor. He never had any connection with the other rich boys in the class, because he had neither been to their schools nor belonged to their social circles. He was at once given the nickname "Ducky," and it was soon pointed out by someone that he looked more like a decoy than a real duck, so that he was thus not merely consigned to the category of people too queer to know but even excluded from humanity. When Wilbur appeared in the classroom, somebody would usually whisper something like, "Here comes the decoy!"; and as he was always from five to fifteen minutes late, he attracted particular attention and always raised a laugh. This caused him to stay away when he could not get to class on time—with the result that he took too many cuts. When he did come, it was pitiful to see him. He had been taught entirely by tutors, who must have humored him and helped him a good deal, and he was never able to answer a question. He would freeze rigid when his name was called; and then, when the professor passed on, he would flush and whisper loudly to his neighbor: "Damn it, I knew that perfectly well! —he might at least have given me a chance!"

He flunked out at the end of the year. I could not imagine he minded much, because college had never seemed real to him. But he said to me the last time I saw him: "They can't get over the way I beat the gym rush!" The truth was that nobody but me had ever known anything about it.

II

I ran into him again later in New York and used to see him off and on through the twenties. I occasionally went to his parties, and they were among the jumpiest of the period.

You would start out after dinner by going to some

play for which tickets were hard to get and you would
come in just at the end of the first act. During the second act, Wilbur, who was dazed with drinks, would
keep saying: "Talky—it's talky.—Dragged out—it's
draggy!"; and before the curtain had fallen, he would
have us all out of the theater and on our way to a musical show, of which we would catch the last numbers.

When we stayed at his house, he would assail us with
spasms of frantic showing-off, which usually depended
mainly on something he had just acquired. There were
the toucans and gila monsters, with which he would
make very bold—bullying them and calling them "old
dear"—but which were likely to bite him and get away.
And there was also the collection of glassware. I thought
it was characteristic of Wilbur that, in aiming to become a connoisseur, he should have gone in for a kind
of rarity which is not easily distinguishable from rubbish. I didn't mind the carboys so much—they have a
certain heroic amplitude; but the rolling pins made of
glass—that used to be filled with cold water, as Wilbur
would triumphantly explain; the log-cabin whisky bottles which had been given to everybody who voted for
Harrison in the election of 1840; the Indian-shaped
bottles of Indian bitters; the bull's-eyes from old tran-
soms; the pickle jars of Sandwich glass that looked
exactly like the ones at the grocer's—the array of these
objects among white kid poufs, tables with mirror tops,
and artificial gilt and silver flowers, seemed a master-
stroke of dreadful taste. And Wilbur didn't even really
know anything about old American glass himself. It was
all bought for him by an agent.

Then, inevitably, one had to watch films. You would
start off with a Chaplin comedy or some primitive
Western of the silents, at which you were supposed to
laugh; but what, before long, you were in for were

pictures of Wilbur and his wife smirking at the camera over cocktails under a sun umbrella in the Bahamas or ineptly tossing a surf-ball on the beach at Waikiki.

Sometimes he would begin yawning loudly at an early stage of the evening, announce he was going to take a nap, and never be seen again. On such occasions, his rather pale and silly but fairly well-bred little wife would be left to carry on alone, and the evening would crumble or trickle away. May Flick had been married before to someone else and she was afterwards married again. There was supposed to be something queer about her, but I have forgotten what it was.

It was not, however, till after the crash, when he lost a good deal of his money and came to live in Hecate County, that I ever saw much of Wilbur.

I met him one day in the town in a buff overcoat with large pearl buttons and an enormous turned-up collar, into which—he wore no hat—he was shrinking from the February chill, so that his head, which was now nearly bald, looked almost like an egg in an egg-cup. He had a new wife in his car, to whom I was chummily presented. I thought he was glad to find an old acquaintance.

This new wife seemed to me stronger than the previous one. She was a blond Western girl with good square shoulders, who wasn't exactly plain-looking, though her complexion was rather dull and her face, too, was rather square. She must have been well along toward thirty by the time she married Wilbur. He had known her from early visits to Denver. Her family had lost all their money, and Adele, left stranded in the West, had, I gathered, fixed upon Wilbur when he had had to go on to Denver to do something about his

father's estate; she had then managed a trip to New
York; and, as Wilbur had been left rather limp and
bemused by the break-up of his first marriage, had
stepped into the vacancy quickly. Adele had never pretended to be at all in love with Wilbur, and as a result
she made a pretty good job of him. He and May had
quarreled like children; but Adele, when he would start
his hysterical scenes, would manage to remain cool and
brief, like an official taking care of a complaint. She
succeeded to some extent, also, in getting the household
under control. It had never made sense before, since
Wilbur had never been able to keep a servant longer
than a month or two.

Adele would sit at the end of the dinner table, perfectly calm and confident, never embarrassed by Wilbur's absurdities, which she seemed to take for granted.
She had at once assumed the role of a great lady, and
a part of this role was "sophistication." She evidently
supposed that the behavior of Wilbur was simply a
feature of one's life in the East when one occupied a
certain position. She made this position and maintained
it herself independently of social connections. She drank
quite a lot, but slowly, long highball after long highball,
and was one of those people who derive from drink a
kind of intensification of dignity. As a châtelaine of
Hecate County, she gave the Flick household a new
stability and almost a kind of impressiveness.

They inhabited an enormous mansion, which, though
built by a millionaire, appeared to represent to Wilbur
the extreme of depression economy, because the house
was so ugly and so out of date that he had been able to
buy it relatively cheaply. It was all made of some gray
composition that was studded with big round lumps like
pudding-stone, and it was full of arched doorways and
plate-glass windows. "Don't you love it?" Wilbur would

say: "Peanut-brittle rococo!" He seemed to think he had got a rare piece, like an Indian bitters bottle.

I went there quite often that summer and fall. They entertained a strange mixture of people, and it was usually more amusing than elsewhere—though Wilbur still had his hobbies and was still rather annoying about them.

I was not quite prepared, however, for the direction that was given his interests when his income was cut in half. He took me rather mysteriously one day into a room which he was having done over. The walls were being plastered in white, and at one end there was some sort of platform. "Remind you of anything?" he asked me. I knew it couldn't be a schoolroom, because he and Adele had no children. "There's going to be a railing around here," he hinted, flipping his hand at the platform and sketching with gestures some other features which I was evidently supposed to recognize. He compelled me to elicit by cross-questioning his intention of having a Roman Catholic chapel. "Very simple and severe," he said. "You've actually become converted?" I asked him. "What else is there? It's stood the test. Where are we when the bottom falls out of things? We're all just damn sinners in the sight of God." "Do you believe in God?" I pressed him. "You know, I could have the loveliest little choir"—I saw that he was shy of my question—"I'd train boys from the local school.—There's no use thinking about all that, though, till I know what I'm going to have left after my income tax next month." But the room was never finished as a chapel and eventually became an indoor badminton court.

He also went in at this time for magic, and there was a period when he entertained his guests with elaborate escapes and illusions. He had some turn for this kind of thing, and I remembered from his days at college how he had used to collect puzzles and was able to do them all. But he allowed his after-dinner drinking to confuse him in performing his tricks, and on one occasion his valet was obliged to come to the rescue when he had had himself handcuffed and locked in a trunk. He devoted the whole of one evening, when he had invited twelve people to dinner, to working up what they were supposed to accept as an entirely unprepared exhibition of sawing a woman in two. I had agreed to play the role of accomplice and turn the conversation to conjuring and pretend to bet him fifty dollars that he couldn't perform this feat. But a story-telling traveler who was present got to describing a banquet with the head-hunters and so carried away the conversation that I was unable to feed in my cues. When I asked Wilbur after dinner whether he had learned any new magic, the same man began telling at length about witnessing the Indian rope trick and other inexplicable feats. "You people fake your tricks," he said to Wilbur. "You have false bottoms and wires and what not; but those Hindus do things that can't be done!" We got the trick under way rather lamely. The woman who was to be sawed in half had to be a professional contortionist, and in order to make the trick seem spontaneous, she had appeared as a guest at dinner, where her awkwardness and Brooklyn accent had very much puzzled people; and it was, therefore, with enlightenment and relief that they saw her accept Wilbur's invitation to allow him to saw her in half. "You know, I love this!" he said, as he finally stood over the box, flourishing a long saw. The girl gave a none-too-piercing shriek as the saw-blade was supposed to strike her hip. Wilbur finally managed to cut himself when, just as he was executing a last fierce sadistic stroke, the saw ripped through whatever it was that had held the two halves together, and gashed him rather badly in the knee. These accidents almost always occurred; and people found them so amusing that they began to make a practice of clamoring for Wilbur's tricks, and the poor fellow, aware that he was cast as a clown, at last sulkily refused to attempt them.

One evening—the New Deal was well under way— a pretty heavy economic conversation took place after dinner at Wilbur's between a broker, a Broadway producer, the traveler who had sidetracked Wilbur's trick, and Wilbur and myself. The producer, who had been struggling with the stagehands' union, declared that what the country needed was not all this labor legislation, but a spiritual reawakening. "I'm with you a hundred per cent!" said the producer—and told us about a wonderful play that he wanted, he said, to put on more than anything else in the world, though he would probably lose every cent—a play in which there was a mixed lot of people all going somewhere in a train and one of the passengers was a little old man who had a mysterious power over the rest and really represented God. The broker derided the attempt to "repeal" economic laws that no human agency could regulate, and asserted that the so-called unemployed were actually unemployable— half of them were simply hobos and the other half incompetent workmen. The traveler was able to corroborate this by telling about how, somewhere in the West where he had gone on a hunting trip, he had run into the biggest hobo-jungle that he had ever seen in his life—there must have been a hundred people, and they had even made huts for themselves out of all kinds of old junk.

"You know how I'd handle the problem?" said Wilbur, in that bold and authoritative tone with which the rich like to announce their opinions. "I'd take the whole lot of unemployed and I'd put 'em on an old steamer that had been condemned and I'd send 'em out somewhere in the middle of the Atlantic and I'd have the whole outfit sunk! It's absolutely idiotic to try to keep them going, and you might as well get rid of them right away. Otherwise, on the one hand"—he became very cogent and lucid—"you're simply making life goddam well impossible for the rest of us by shooting our standards of living all to hell—and on the other hand, what are you doing? —you're spending the money that you get by taxation to try to produce work artificially when there isn't any work to be done. All right!—and in the meantime what happens to the things that make civilization? They're starved out!—they're damn well destroyed! I could have built up the best collection of Sisleys anywhere in this country if the government hadn't decided to make me pay to keep these morons alive. So I say: Take 'em out and drown 'em!" "We'd have to send you on that ship, Wilbur," I said. "What do you mean?" he asked, exhilarated by his eloquence. "Well, you're unemployed." "Go to hell!" he said. He pretended to accept it as a joke, but his further discussion of the subject flapped with a broken wing. I could see that he was a little hurt, but he was always getting hurt. I lost touch with the conversation and looked around at the high-ceilinged rooms that all opened into one another through enormous doorways of the eighties. These doorways would once have had heavy portières, but now there were no longer any hangings, and the big folding doors were all open. Wilbur and Adele and the rest of us looked too much like sprawling dolls and stuffed animals that children had left strewn on the floor. I soon took my leave and went home.

But two nights later the Flicks' butler called me up and said that Wilbur wanted to see me—could I come

over there right away? It was characteristic of Wilbur
that he should be obviously right by the phone and
shouting things audibly at the butler, but that he did
not do the talking himself. I went over and found a
scene which I did not at first understand. Adele was
sitting alone, playing Canfield; and three guests—a local
married couple and a young man who was staying with
them—seemed completely engrossed in books. The husband and wife, whom I hardly knew, greeted me with
a certain slight constraint and put the books away, but
the young man went on reading. I felt also a certain tension between Wilbur and his guests, and I found out
that he had been trying to entertain them with one of
his silliest amusements—which was to feed into his
record-changing phonograph a series of incongruous
records that mixed fragments of sonatas and symphonies
with dance orchestras and Chinese opera. He was under
the illusion that his arrangement of these gave the pot-
pourri some sort of point, and he would watch his
victims intently for signs of appreciation or shock. On
the evening I speak of, however, the guests were not
musical enough even to be annoyed by the performance;
and, as Wilbur had made the mistake of showing off to
them earlier in the evening a collection of pornographic
literature in elegant morocco bindings, they had taken
out the books and begun to read almost as soon as the
music started, and had completely forgotten Wilbur.
This was something—forgetting Wilbur—which often
happened at the Flicks' parties, but which Wilbur
would never forgive. He had sometimes revenged himself in the case of offending week-end visitors by sending them concocted telegrams insisting on their return
to town. But this evening he had summoned me.

With a pointed disregard of the other guests, he told
me that he wanted to talk to me, and took me at once

to his study. He ensconced me in an immense leather chair of the kind you fall asleep in in clubs, with the apparatus for highballs at my elbow. He began by complaining of the bad taste of the guests. "Mozart doesn't seem to mean a thing to them. Jesus, what an aristocratic soul that is!—and if you sandwich Gershwin in between, you appreciate his infinite good breeding. I go back to the great ones more and more. What else have you got in these times?" He sat down at a flat expansive desk, on which were a silver writing set, a neat little pile of letters and a copy of the *Reader's Digest*. He had the air of staging a serious interview, as gray-mustached middle-aged businessmen are sometimes made to do in the movies. "Look here, old egg," he began: "I've got a bone to pick with you. You socked me the other night. You told me I was a damn loafer. . . . I know that wasn't what you said, but that was what you meant to convey. I resented it at the time, but I couldn't talk it out with you then. Now I know you think I'm brutal as hell because I want to drown a million people—and I would, I'd do it in a minute! That's the trouble with all you liberals: you think that people ought to be kept alive just because they happen to exist. Well, *I* think that's all baloney: you can't even have decent civic conditions with these bums and human dregs around—as it is, you can't go down a street in New York without finding some bedraggled piece of vermin picking in a garbage-pail. Now *I* don't care a curse in hell about all this diseased human rubbish, and that's where I'm different from you—but, damn it, I'm not any better satisfied than you are with the way that things have been going. I frankly believe in rule by the best in the interest of the survival of the best—but that isn't what we've been getting by a damn sight. What we've been getting is a goddam messing-up of our government and our finance by a lot of goddam crackbrained speculators and two-for-a-nickel politicians with no sense of responsibility and not a trace of any kind of background. Now my grandfather there who made the money"—he jerked his head toward a photograph—"was a hard-boiled man of business. From your point of view he was a pirate. But the old buccaneer was a prince—you know!—he was a Yankee *conquistador.* He had a kind of magnificence about him —and, what was more, he knew his stuff: he pulled his company through three reorganizations without the stockholders' losing a penny. I wish he were alive now: there wouldn't be any of this damn nonsense about passing dividends. As it is, the business is sounder than most because we didn't overexpand during the boom— but I was a damn jackass—I thought the old Flick tradition was stuffy, and I invested in a whole lot of things that went pop like so many balloons. And while I was being a playboy, I let these confidence-men get away with my money. Well, we've got to stop now and see where we are—we've got to take in sail. The people who ought to control things have let the game slip out of their hands—and we've goddam well got to check up on them and we've goddam well got to *act!"*

"What are you going to do?" I asked.

He told me he had given some money to a so-called Economic Council, which I knew to be an organization subsidized by the New York manufacturers for purposes of propaganda and lobbying against child labor and the minimum wage. I tried to explain this to Wilbur, but he went back to his Nietzschean line: "From my point of view," he asserted, "they're definitely on the right track." And he went on to talk about fascism, which seemed to him "perfectly sound." I suspected him of having also contributed to one of the American fascist groups. He complained that when one went to the theater, one ran into too many Jews in the lavatory.

But one thing he said rather touched me, as there had always been something about him I liked. "You know," he confessed to me finally, when he had swallowed another drink, "I get nervous as hell nowadays. It was all right while the big circus was on—but now I feel I ought to be doing something and I don't know what the hell to do. *You've* got your schedule—your deadline and all that. But nobody wants anything from me, and there isn't any need for me to do anything. If there *did* happen to be a necessity, I imagine I could function at least as well as most of these bimboes that buy us our pictures and write us our editorials and invest our money in the wrong things for us. But I can't *create* a necessity—so—!" He shrugged, with a gesture of his hand. "Well, someday maybe fate will come to find me."

I wanted to say something encouraging, but I couldn't think of anything to say. I had got up to see the picture of his grandfather, and he did not look in the least like a buccaneer. With his gray business suit, his clipped white mustache and his small eyes protected by glasses, he seemed sober and commonplace, as if he combined only the right amount of ruthlessness with diligence and "business sense." He was the son, as I afterwards learned, of a well-to-do Methodist minister; and poor Wilbur had behind him, I fear, no tradition of reckless adventure: his real heritage was a vague bourgeois feeling that he ought to be busy about something—an impulse which nobody had ever done anything to encourage or train him to satisfy.

Sometime rather early in November, Wilbur suddenly found the country intolerable. He decided just before

dinner one night that they must move to New York at
once; and they skipped dessert and coffee and leapt on
the next express, leaving the servants to pack and close
the house. I happened to be dining there that night, and
Wilbur's frenzied efforts to make the train seemed to
be dictated by so urgent a necessity that one could
hardly even feel he was rude. In giving people orders,
changing his clothes and getting hotel reservations, he
exhibited a quick-thinking resourcefulness and unshak-
able determination which, though exercising themselves
in the void for an aim that was in itself absurd, commanded a kind of respect.

After that, I saw the Flicks less often. This sudden
and rapid moving seemed to become a mania with Wilbur. He had added narcotics to his liquor, and he was
very soon suffering from a delusion that it was utterly
impossible for him to get to sleep—he liked to drama-
tize his insomnia with a kind of diluted *Weltschmerz*
that had a flavor of both Hemingway and Spengler—
without a complicated ritual of drug-taking. The next
afternoon, when he came to, he would have to resort
to benzedrine and other things in order to get himself
going. He loved to say to ladies who had wanted to
write down the name of some sleeping potion of the
effectiveness of which he had been boasting: "You can't
buy it, my dear—you'd better let me give you some.
You can't get it without a prescription, and they don't
pass out many prescriptions!"—or, "I'll give you some,
but not the way I take it. What I take would kill you.
You'll be out with half a grain, but I usually have to
have eight or nine before I even begin to get blurry."

Adele had already, I was told, resorted to paying
nocturnal calls on both the male and the female guests.
And now Wilbur slept in a room by himself and was
always fully doped by midnight. It was said that his

mad dashing about was being stimulated partly by an instinct to get away from Adele's lovers. He would travel to some distant place such as Majorca or Mexico City and then spend only a single night—coming back with a peevish account of the dirtiness and dullness of the country, and especially of the discourtesy of the people.

I heard sometime in the middle thirties that he had been sent to a sanitarium.

III

That autumn Adele called me up and said that she wanted to see me. I arranged to have dinner with her.

She was calm, as she always was, and she didn't seem to worry about Wilbur: she behaved as if his total collapse were a natural incident of one's life, to be quietly accepted like a hangover. But, in spite of her bright vermilion lipstick and the waxen bloom of her "facial," I could see that she was getting rather pouched from many lunches with women friends over cocktails and many evenings of highballs after midnight.

She told me that Wilbur wanted to see me, that he had spoken of me several times, declaring that I was the only person that he had ever been able to talk to seriously. So I stopped off one afternoon, on my way driving out from the city, at the place to which Adele had sent him.

It was an old-fashioned "nerve sanitarium," which still ignored psychoanalysis and which mainly went in for rich patients. They did, however, seem to be doing something for Wilbur—though the treatment was as gradual as possible. He spoke with admiration of the doctor, whose guidance he appeared to have accepted with a passivity surprising in him—though I thought that, with his unschooled youth, he had perhaps an unsatisfied need to be told what to do and when to do it. It had perhaps been behind the attraction he had felt toward the Catholic Church.

In any case, he could now get to sleep on a much diminished dose of narcotics. He looked very smooth and soft, as if he had been bathed in milk and always kept at precisely the right temperature. He had nothing very special to say to me, though he made a few woolly remarks about how utterly impossible it was for all of us to go on as we had been doing. On the whole, I was depressed by my visit. There seemed to be so very little in him when one took him out of his toy palace. He was boring, and he bored himself. I tried to talk to him about people we both knew, but he did not really want to hear about them, and his contemptuousness was tinged with venom. He did not want to believe that anybody was still able to carry on when he, as he said, had been put "in the padded cell." Yet these people *were* mostly worthless, and what he said about them was sometimes acute. I felt either that I couldn't defend them or that to do so would injure an ego that was already rather dangerously weakened. He had got himself into a position where he would not have to compete even with people who mostly did as little as he but who managed to stay out of the hospital.

As I glanced around during a silence into which the conversation had dropped, my eye was caught by a booklet with playing cards and rabbits on the cover. I picked it up: it was a catalogue of magicians' supplies.

"Don't you adore it?" cried Wilbur, immediately taking it from me. "Listen to this!" He read: " 'Boldini's Miracle Mind-Reading Trick. Magician fans a pack of cards and the spectator is asked to mentally think of any card. Card is then produced from behind the back.

It seems unbelievable that the magician should be able to find the card which has been merely mentally thought of. The secret of this trick, invented by me, which has baffled the keenest minds in magic, would previously not have been sold for under $200, but the treachery of a friend, who betrayed it, makes it possible for me to offer it for $1.50.'—Isn't it superb?'' he demanded, and went on to read me further extracts—accounts of doves and ducks, all alive and flapping, produced from empty boxes, goldfish pulled in with fishing-rods that were simply whipped about in the air, panes of glass that could be pierced with rods and then found as amazingly unbroken as if they had been pools of water. One felt oneself a little let down, after the exciting descriptions of these wonders, when one came to the back part of the catalogue and found quotations of prices for false thumb-tips, durable rubber canaries, celluloid goldfish, collapsible carrots and imitation rabbits that really kicked and would "give you a lifetime of satisfaction and service."

"Isn't it a howl?" said Wilbur. "Isn't it the whole of life?—society, love, politics—everything! You pretend you can do the impossible: no elastics, no threads, no gimmicks as they call them, no confederates, no rigged-up table—the spectators can stand all around you! And anybody at all can do it! It used to cost two hundred dollars to learn to perform a miracle, but now it's only a dollar fifty. You can panic your friends, you can get your girl, you can make yourself a big reputation. All you've got to do is to have a rubber canary!"

It *was* funny when you thought about it in this way. I was relieved to be able to laugh, and I perhaps overdid my hilarity because Wilbur became almost hysterical. One of the things that delighted us most was the immediate social success which was promised with the torn-up paper that turns into a pair of ladies' panties or the lighted cigarette that suddenly pops out of one's mouth.

I began to fear, however, that Wilbur was losing control of himself, that his orgiastic laughter would be followed by a slump. The nurse looked in, and I left.

When I dropped in on him again two months later, I saw at once that he was nearly "normal." Normality in persons we have always known in a state of over-stimulation is likely to be disconcerting. We do not seem to recognize our friends in their new and quieter roles, and they themselves have not quite learned how to play them. I was at first rather baffled by Wilbur. He courteously took me for a tour of the grounds and explained the therapeutic methods in use, in a way that was almost professional. His respect for the doctor who had been handling his case seemed to have grown into a deep admiration, and, in discussing the other patients, he would sometimes fall into a tone which suggested that he and the doctor were running the place together.

We strolled back to his room. I looked around and saw a couple of golf-balls on a chair. "You go in for golf?" I asked. "The dullest goddam game in the world!" he declared. He picked up one of the balls and held it between his thumb and first finger. "Watch," he said. A second golf-ball seemed suddenly to appear out of nothing between his first and second fingers. Then a third ball; then a fourth—until his whole hand was full. "Marvelous!" I said. "You do that well." He smirked in self-satisfaction and made them disappear one by one. Then he squeezed the last one up in his fist, appeared to be kneading it like clay—opened his hand, and it was gone. I applauded, but took it for granted that they had been shooting under his coat on elastics. "Listen, old egg," he said. "This is sleight of hand, not elastics!" He took off his coat and rolled up his sleeves and showed me both sides of his hands—then he plucked from the end of his left forefinger a shiny red billiard ball about the same size as the golf-ball, which he tossed to me to show it was solid. He made it split up into two like the cells in biological pictures; turned one of the red ones into a blue one by rubbing it with his palm; and then made the blue one breed blue ones.

It was certainly a triumph for the doctor. Wilbur told me that he practiced every day. He had a magician come out to give him lessons. This was "classical" conjuring, he explained to me, which did not involve apparatus and which actually required skill. "I call it 'classical,'" he said, "because the effects look so simple and chaste, and yet they involve a hell of a lot of calculation."

I was impressed by the steadiness of his nerves, but he finally attempted too much in mixing red, white and blue. He missed a move and lost his handful of balls— though I did not discover the secret. He angrily picked them up and flung them away in a drawer, declaring that he really could do it, in a tone that reminded me of his plaints when the professor, at college, had passed him by. I praised him and tried to reassure him, but he was still rather sunk when I left.

This was winter. Rather late in the spring I was invited by Adele to dinner. She said that Wilbur was out of the sanitarium.

I found him looking so fit and behaving with so much aplomb that my previous respect for his doctor began to extend to Wilbur himself. He had now a kind of positive self-confidence that was different from his mere negative sobriety of the hospital. He drank no cocktails, no wine and no brandy, and did not even seem to find this humiliating, as ex-drinkers are likely to do;

and he did not show off much to the guests, though
when he talked to them about their interests, he made
it clear by the play of his left eyebrow and a certain
slightly mocking tone that he did not take these quite
so seriously as they did. These guests, besides myself,
were the traveler who told about his travels and who
had now got to a point at which his only object was to be
able to absorb enough alcohol so that he would not feel
the normal inhibition against boring people with his
stories; Wilbur's little first wife, who did not seem to
be married at the moment and who had evidently got
somewhat queerer in whatever way it was she was queer
—for she now had a nervous tic of wrinkling her nose
like a rabbit; and one of those ladies with a salon who
wants to admire talent but always cultivates people like
Wilbur and likes to gloat over their absurdities and
weaknesses.

After dinner he took us to a night club, and I was
very much amused by his anxiety to get there in time
for the early show. I wondered whether it indicated a
new regime which involved getting to bed by midnight.

We sat of course right beside the dance-floor. The first
number was a German magician of a more or less commonplace kind. Wilbur watched him with the irony of
an expert. When the man presently came over to our
table and made Wilbur examine a small black velvet
bag from which he had just produced an egg, Wilbur
insisted on taking the egg, and when he opened his
hand, it had vanished. "Wise guy, eh?" said the magician, and, reaching inside Wilbur's tail coat, he brought
forth, first the egg, then a whole handful of eggs, then
an imitation hen, and finally an imitation rooster, which
gave a ventriloquial crow. The magician, with a chicken
in either hand, went back to the center of the stage.

Wilbur got up and followed him. "All right, old chap!" he said, with a smile of appreciation. "Now let's see what *you've* got."

It was embarrassing; Wilbur was incurable. "Oh, don't!" cried Adele. "Let him go on with his act." But Wilbur had seized the magician and was extracting from inside his coat a fantastic succession of objects: first, an enormous green snake; then a very long string of sausages—"I thought you had the accent," he said, "of a delicatessen dealer!"; then a woman's brassière—he stopped and lifted an eyebrow at his victim; and finally a handful of knives and forks, which he threw down with a loud clatter on the floor—setting off a flare of laughter from the audience, who had by this time become aware that the whole scene was part of the show. He gave the man's coat a last shake, and a whole hail of cutlery fell out and was greeted by a general roar. Then he picked up a folding screen and set it around the magician, and clapped his hands in a signal to two waiters who were standing by. The waiters folded up the screen, from which the magician had vanished, and rapidly carried it out. The house broke into applause, and Wilbur bowed ironically but graciously.

"Well, it looks as if Fritz has folded up," he said. "He was a hell of a fake, anyway.—Look at this!" He picked up the snake and showed that it was a spring which collapsed. "That's fakery," he declared,—"that's not magic. Let me show you what magic is!" He took off his dinner coat, rolled up his starched cuffs and showed his empty hands. Then he produced a red ball from one finger and went into the act I had seen. But he performed it now with much more ease and with all kinds of clever variations. The very amateurishness of his manner—he had no real magician's patter but might have been amusing his friends—made his skill all the more impressive; and, though the multiplying balls, I am told, are now a rather well-worn stunt which is included in every child's box of magic, the trick had been worked up by Wilbur into something quite surprising and pretty. He would come down among the tables—for he played a long engagement at the night club—and make the balls hop in and out of sight, blinking brightly between his fingers, right under the spectators' noses. He even introduced an element of poetry by inviting members of the audience to summon the balls and then producing special numbers supposed to be appropriate to the people: for the ladies, gold or silver or polka-dotted pink, or purple mottled with red; for the men, navy blue or mud-color or balls that were under- or oversized. Sometimes a potato would appear; sometimes a gleaming crystal. Since he did not have to worry about expenses, he would always give the crystals away. Some of these features were refinements that he added as his engagement went on; but he was proficient enough that night, and the effect could not have been more dazzling to his friends, who had expected nothing.

As a finish, he went back to the stage and picked up an opera hat and cloak which the stooge had taken off at the beginning of the act. He showed that the hat was empty. "One thing," he announced, "I shall not do—I shall positively not do: I shall not produce a rabbit." He bowed and put on the hat. There was cordial applause; he bowed again, and as he took off the hat with a flourish, a big black ball that looked like a cannon-ball fell out with a thud on the stage. Wilbur set down the hat, got the ball back from a delighted party under whose table it had rolled, and examined it with curiosity. Then he laid it down, put on his hat, bowed in response to the clapping, and took it off again

—and with a bang another bigger ball fell out. Wilbur, amid shrieks from the audience, looked after the cannon-ball and stared into the hat with suspicion. "That's a damn treacherous topper!" he said. He flattened it out with a slam, sent it skimming away over the audience, and took a final bow.

When he returned from backstage to our table, we greeted him with noisy congratulation. It is always a relief when a very rich man who has insisted on having people play up to him exhibits some kind of real competence; and Wilbur had shown positive aptitude. This occasion when he astonished our party must have been the high point of his life. There was that tiresome confounded traveler, who had made him listen to stories about his marksmanship; there was his first wife, who had left him for a bridge expert and who had compelled Wilbur to hear a good deal about her husband's master mind; there was the scintillating lady with the salon, one of whose specialties for years had been telling funny stories about Wilbur and who had come more or less to behave, even when he was actually present, as if he were a creation of hers; and there was I, who had gibed at him for his idleness.

But hadn't he earned his triumph? He had found his necessity in himself: he had learned to do something well, and he had made people recognize his mastery. He had always had the yearning to astonish people, and he was able to astonish them now by real imagination and dexterity, instead of merely by eccentric expenditure.

"What did you think of the G-major scherzo?" he asked. I hadn't particularly noticed the music. "Where they begin coming fast and the color changes. I tried to give the effect of Mozart. I begin with the andante, you see." I told him that the whole thing was beautiful.

"I don't like the clowning at the end," he explained. "But you've got to have something to wow them."

I was delighted by Wilbur the magician, and I used often to take people to see him, because he liked to have a party at his table when his scene with the stooge took place, and he of course always paid the check. It soon got to be the smart thing to sit with him, and he was usually surrounded at the second show on the later evenings of the week by his old crowd of hilarious friends, whose influence, I sometimes thought, was rather demoralizing for him. The lady with the salon upset him by telling him that the objects he produced from inside the stooge's coat were psychoanalytic symbols whose significance was obvious to everyone; and the alcoholic traveler spoiled the start of his act by reaching for the stooge's egg before Wilbur had had a chance to get it, and substituting for it an ostrich egg which Wilbur was unable to manage.

Yet I believe that the poor fellow could have survived all this if he had not had other forces against him. I dropped in one Tuesday night in the early days of summer when the audience was rather slim—people were leaving town—and found Wilbur quite neurotic. He took a drink just before his performance, which I had never seen him do. He complained to me in a virulent whisper about the slowness of the waiter in bringing it and the way he slopped the soda into the glass; and when the stooge pulled the chickens out of his coat, he said hatefully and in none too low a voice: "Look out for my shirt, you damn fool!" He skipped his finale with the cannon-balls; he did not even pick up the hat and cloak, but bowed with an invidious curtness and insolently walked off the stage.

When he sat down at the table again and I asked

him what was the matter, the poisons of fear and resentment spurted out in spasmodic mutterings. The stooge, he said, was sabotaging the act. This man was a professional magician, a German refugee, who had only accepted the job because he could get nothing else to do and who now, according to Wilbur, had become so insanely jealous that he had taken to planting the cannon-balls where it was difficult for Wilbur to get at them. I had noticed, in the searching of the stooge, that Wilbur had introduced a new and rather ugly detail: when he followed the magician to the platform, he would now rip out the whole of his shirt-front, which was the kind you tie around the neck; and I think he was afraid of reprisals.

I asked him why he didn't get rid of the man and hire a more reliable assistant; but this opened a new abyss. "If they don't get me first," said Wilbur. I asked him what he meant. It turned out that he was afraid of being fired himself. He had got the job through Jinx Ames, the daughter of a Morgan partner, who had had some success as a torch singer and had put money into the club. He was convinced that Jinx, too, was jealous—and it was evident that he was jealous of Jinx—though his way of expressing his feeling was to say that she was ruining the show by the way she was mugging her songs. He was also at odds with the headwaiter, whom he was finding it impossible to treat as he had treated headwaiters in the past and who, Wilbur insisted, now regarded him as on a social level not far from his own. At the same time, on an opposite principle, he had worked up a feud with the hat girl, who, he said, had lost his hat on purpose because he didn't give her a tip every night—after all, he was part of the club, and he oughtn't to have to pay like a customer. I could see that his position was confusing.

It was as if I had been holding my breath. The end came inevitably and soon. He sabotaged the piano one night, putting chewing gum on several of the hammers, so as to spoil the accompaniment to Jinx Ames's songs, and then was so furious when she sang alone and went over better than ever that he refused to take part in the second show. He simply handed back the stooge's egg and allowed him to return to the stage—whereupon the professional magician embarked at once on his own line of patter, borrowed a fifty-cent piece from one of the audience, and proceeded to perform, with tremendous success, the perfectly astounding trick in which the coin is made to disappear while the spectator still seems to feel it grasped in his hand.

Afterwards, Wilbur and Jinx had it out in a terrific scene in which each one accused the other of taking dope and letting down the show. Adele had lost her influence over Wilbur since he had made himself a night-club performer, and he threw up his job that night. As he said, he did not have to let the waiters ride him and be insulted by Jinx Ames in order to hang on to a salary. The German took his place.

I saw him the night before he left for France, and again we sat up talking. I did my best to reassure him by telling him how good he had been, but he was afraid he had bought his success. He told me—what I hadn't known—that he himself had put money into the club and that he hadn't been taking pay. "They hated my guts," he said. "They tried to make me feel like a scab." I pointed out that the applause of the audience was an objective proof of his abilities. "I used to pass out those crystals and jades," he said. "They used to keep me going to get them. But I got goddam sick of playing Santa Claus, so I quit handing out the presents, and just as soon as I quit, I flopped!"

I tried to tell him it had been late in the season, that no night clubs did well in June; but he immediately fell back on a doubt which I found it rather difficult to deal with. "What I do isn't art!" he insisted when I had wanted to convince him it was. "You know damn well it isn't! It's a fake—I just did it as a stunt." "It's not a fake—it's a trick," I said, "and it's just as good as a trick as a sonata by Mozart is good as a sonata." "Don't kid me, damn it," he answered. "There's always that silly little shell that you slip the balls in and out of, and that the audience thinks is a real ball, and there isn't any way to get rid of it. The whole thing is just a bloody fake!" "What do you want to do?" I asked, "—perform miracles? All art in that sense is a fake. Every work of art is a trick by which the artist manipulates appearances so as to put over the illusion that experience has some sort of harmony and order and to make us forget that it's impossible to pluck billiard-balls out of the air."

But nobody, I saw, could convince him—since he had been spurred by no need to make money—that what he had done had been really worth doing; and he was unable—what was more pathetic—even quite to believe that he had done it. The magician who had taught him, he asserted, had invented the billiard-ball routine. I saw that the conscience he had cheated in the days of the college rush had ended by becoming quite morbid.

IV

This was the last real conversation that I ever had with Wilbur.

The next time I saw him was much later, at a party that he was giving at his house to raise money for Loyalist Spain. In his immense uptown apartment, done in

brand-new Colonial style and full of delicate and tricky
French clocks, which Wilbur was now collecting, we
paid fifty cents apiece for cocktails. Wilbur performed
with his billiard-balls, and a popular Jewish comedian,
whom Wilbur had known in his night-club days, did a
monologue and a song. A Left singing group of young
men and girls put on a sort of cantata in which Don
Quixote and Carmen ended up by giving the Communist salute. After this, there was a money-raising speech
by Wilbur's latest wife, a wiry and fierce little woman,
indestructible and inexpugnable as a caraway seed caught
in the teeth, who had for years been an assiduous promoter of those Communist organizations that disguise
themselves as liberal groups. (Adele, whom he had just
divorced and whom he now considered hopelessly
bourgeois, was going around the world with a devoted
woman friend.) Wilbur himself was beaming: he would
slip about from one person to another, putting his arm
around their shoulders, exchanging confidential in-
formation, grinning and nodding his head. I saw that I
was surrounded by a brotherhood from which I was
completely barred, and I was reminded by their too
high-keyed cheerfulness of an evening I had once spent
with the Buchmanites, that well-bred evangelical movement of which the "house parties" where sinners confessed had been one of the pastimes of the twenties.

Wilbur saw me and came over to speak to me. "A
big success—what?" he said. "We must have taken in
two hundred dollars." "I hope it really goes to the
Loyalists," I answered, "and not just to Communist
papers and committees." I was a little bit sore at Wilbur,
because I had been invited to the party without being
told its purpose and had been asked to pay for my drinks.
He tried to explain to me that the *Daily Worker* was
"red hot," "a live wire"—the only paper that told the

truth about what was going on in the world. "It won't tell you the truth about Spain," I said. "It won't tell you that your Russian commissars are keeping supplies from non-Stalinist republicans and shooting people who criticize the Stalinists, no matter how Loyalist they are." "They only shoot renegades," he said. "Listen, old chap: I'm disappointed in you. I thought you were a progressive. I'm surprised to hear you sobbing about those rats! There's only one line-up today, and that's between progressivism and fascism. You've got to be on one side of the fence or the other, and I'd be sorry to see you helping Franco. But I suppose the old *rentier* psychology is something it's awfully hard to throw off. That little place in Hecate County!"

I had wanted to ask him, at first, how he had reconciled his old ideal of government by the élite with his championship of Spanish republicanism; but, as I watched him among his new friends, I perfectly understood what had happened. The Communism of the later thirties, as instilled by his persistent wife, did not of course present itself to Wilbur as a democratic movement at all, but as a kind of exclusive club which was soon to dominate the world; and it had provided him at the moment he needed it with a role that both flattered his vanity and appeased his moral discontent; an occupation that was guaranteed always to remain entirely unreal and never to let him in for any final responsibility. And did it not also provide a revenge against a world in which he had found no place? With all this, he was encouraged by his coaches to go on living, for the glory of Communism, exactly as he had done before. He could craftily enjoy the consciousness that, in giving elaborate dinners and taking expensive trips, he was merely misleading people and in reality serving a cause—a cause which was sure to triumph. As I saw him there chuckling and weaving, I thought, remembering college, that he *did* look, and more than ever, like a decoy.

But the greatest achievement of this phase of his life was getting on WPA. He was allowed to make a brief appearance in one of the Theater Project shows as a comic embodiment of capitalism who produced a lot of things out of a hat but finally broke down in his act and was denounced as a ridiculous impostor by shrill-voiced young people who represented the workers. His wife had had him smuggled in under the pretense that he was a destitute actor. When the Theater Project was abolished, Wilbur was out of a job, and he couldn't have been more bitterly indignant if he had been an expropriated sharecropper.

4.

The Princess with the Golden Hair

I HAD FOUND, in the course of the summer, that I was watching Imogen Loomis at parties. I had been seeing her and her husband for years, but I had always thought them rather boring—on the middle-class side of Hecate County. Then my regular girl of that period had had to go out to Pasadena, where she spent six months of the year with her children, and I had suddenly started gazing at Imogen. I wondered why I had never noticed how sensationally attractive she was.

I saw now that she was actually a beauty—a beauty of an unusual kind. My idea on the evening when I first really saw her was that she looked like a fairy-tale princess. She was wearing a white satin gown, and she had her hair done in a snood: not the kind of snood that later became fashionable—this was 1929—but a large bag of gilt net that caught it up so that it hung behind in a great soft round clot of gold. For Imogen did have golden hair. I had taken it for granted before, with my supercilious opinion of the Loomises, that the effect had been produced by "Golden Glint," a hair-wash then much advertized in the papers; but now I learned by inquiry and could see for myself that the gold was absolutely real: not merely pale yellow hair, but hair that had sheen, that shone. Besides this, her complexion was smooth and fair, and her eyes were of a deep-pigmented brown of a kind that is rare in blondes and gives them something of the challenge of brunettes. She was tall, and, when she had caught one's attention, one saw that her figure was beautiful, too, a little bit fuller perhaps than was fashionable at the end of the twenties. She appeared to me that evening, as I say, like some swan princess or Lovely Ilonka out of a Russian or Scandinavian story, who enchants one's imagination in childhood by way of those collections of fairy tales that were illustrated by H. J. Ford with wonderful Pre-Raphaelitized types of straight-nosed and clear-browed English beauty. Yet she dressed on other occasions in quite different clothes and reminded me of other heroines. Sometimes she wore *robes de style,* with tight bodices that brought out her breasts, and flaring richly-patterned skirts that gave her a *galante* eighteenth-century flavor; and sometimes she appeared with a loose-flowing gown and a sullen voluptuous mouth that were obviously derived from Rossetti. What these costumes had in common, however, was that they were all quite outside the fashion and all unashamedly romantic; and, going back over my previous impressions of her, I decided that my slowness in doing her justice had been due to this theatrical aspect. I was sufficiently conventional by instinct—I had to confess it to myself —to discount the beauty of a woman who shaded her eyelids and exploited her hair to play the role of the Blessèd Damozel. But now that she had emerged from her background, all the other ladies suddenly faded.

She had done nothing to attract my attention to her. I had thought her in the past rather shy, and I had long ago established with her a casual and cordial relation which I now found it rather hard to break through. But, meeting her one day at Helen Hubbard's, where the atmosphere was always hearty, I addressed myself to her with the obvious intent of getting to know her better, and found her unexpectedly responsive. I had begun by thinking her commonplace, and then, when I had had my revelation, had for a moment stood a little in awe of her; but she seemed to me now more intelligent than I had supposed her to be at first, and more human than I had imagined her afterwards. She rose to my compliments and questions, I thought, like one of the rare rainbow trout in our little Hecate County river: you would bring up nothing for hours but the infantile and flapping sunfish—pretty in their green and yellow, but spiny, with no meat; then you were jolted by a heavy pull, became steadily intent on playing it, and were amazed at reeling up triumphantly from those shallow muddy pools of April so large and iridescent a creature. I felt now on Imogen's part the waking of an unexpected interest. It was as if she herself had not thought that I should ever make an effort to know her.

I went the next Saturday night to an enormous, indiscriminate party, solely in the hope of seeing her. I found her this time in a velvet gown, sumptuous and wine-purple, with a white ruff that stood up so high and stiff that it made her look quite sixteenth-century. She was wearing gold-embroidered sandals of the high-heeled kind then in vogue that left the instep attractively unprotected; and she had parted her hair in the middle and plaited it in two gorgeous braids that were wound around her head like a diadem. She was sitting in a carved high-backed chair. "You look like a panel," I said. "Your highball is a regular scepter!" But I was soon at that point where I ceased to be conscious of any hint of fancy-dress in her appearance: I was absorbed into the world she brought with her. I pored, standing over her chair, on her lovely and large brown eyes—the kind that people used to call "liquid." They met me with quickness and vigor—though for some reason it still seemed inevitable that I should only be able to talk to her in banalities. She put out a cigarette, and I looked down on the coils of her hair encircling her maiden part, and on the stem of her long round neck as it bent away from the ruff—how swanlike I had not before noticed, since her way of carrying her head, with its broad jaw and its jutting chin, prevented it from having its full value; and I was moved by a quality about them that I could characterize only as "womanly" —womanly somehow in a way that seemed unlikely because it was no longer in fashion, and which yet could still inspire respect, even perhaps adoration. I smelled her perfume—too rich, too sweet? No: why should she not be fragrant? How the lovers of the Renaissance must have made themselves drunk with perfume!

"I want to tell you something," I said: she looked up. "But I don't think I can tell you here. Let's go into a room that's less crowded." "I don't like to move," she said, "once I've gotten settled somewhere. Can't you tell me here?" "There's too much noise to talk in this room —and I really have to make a speech." She looked at me again: "Let me finish this drink." I tried being amusing about the guests. She had been watching our host and Helen Hubbard: he was flashing his fine white teeth in his leathery and swarthy face that seemed now rather worn and battered, and Helen was giving him her wide boyish grin and her frank and fun-loving laugh that could be heard across the crashing uproar. "Helen Hubbard," Imogen said, "is getting to be a real Amazon, isn't she?" We had so many strapping girls out there that I had not particularly noticed it, but, in the light of my present comprehension of what it meant for a woman to be womanly, I saw that she was becoming mannish. "She'll never get married now," Imogen went on with conviction. "All she cares about is playing tennis." So completely had Imogen's world been seeming to me to exclude the common one that it startled me for a moment to hear her make the same kind of comment that another woman might make. But she soon turned romantic again: she remarked that our tall dark host, whom nobody knew very well, reminded her of Jean Lafitte. "Yes," I answered, "this extraordinary house does look as if it had been built with pirate treasure." We went on in this harmless vein, which seemed stimulating and almost brilliant, as her eyes, under their noble brows, warmed with a humor that I had not suspected, and I saw, as she lifted her head, that her nose, which showed straight enough from other angles, was slightly turned up in a way that broke the line of her Nordic beauty but gave her face an unexpected piquancy.

"And now you must redeem your pledge," I said finally, when her highball was down to its dregs. "Did I pledge something?" "I sound like an Arthurian romance—it's something about the way you've got your hair. You promised to let me make you a speech. Let's go into the other room." "You bid me come?" she said, dropping her eyelids and accepting the mediaeval role on a tone that was quite distinct from the kidding repartee of the era—almost as if I had met her in some fantasy which she had already enjoyed indulging. She got up from the chair with a dignity that seemed to me rather rigid. I thought that she was playing the queen with perhaps a little too much self-consciousness, and I reflected that she would be more graceful if she would allow herself to move more freely.

I took her through the deafening living room and

across the big dining room beyond, where the refreshments had been handsomely laid out but to which no one had yet come to eat them. There was a library that opened out of this, and we invaded its shadow and solitude, and sat down on a red-leather couch that was lighted by a heavy-shaded floor-lamp. "What I want to tell you is this," I began, smiling sincerely with my eyes. "I've been thinking about you some time and I've finally come to the conclusion that you are just about the most beautiful woman I've ever seen in my life." "Oh!" she replied; and went on in a little-girl womanly voice which I had never heard her use before and which seemed to me at first incongruous with the vision I had been having of her: "I've always heard that you were a great talker." "No," I insisted, "I mean it. I'm absolutely fascinated by you. I stare at you all the time." She smiled, looking straight before her, with a pleasure that, again to my amazement, seemed entirely naïve and childlike. "Let me see you," I said. She turned toward me. I gazed at her with seriousness, bemusement, and she met my eyes, lowering her lids, after a moment, in a gesture half alluring, half ironic. I kissed her on her back-curling lips, and she held her face firm; but at the end of the third kiss, she turned her head away. "You know, you have a kind of beauty," I went on, taking her hand, with its long, round and smooth fingers, "that's really completely mythical: you're like Mélisande or Isolde or somebody like that in a legend." She looked away and had her lips half-open and in her eyes that look of gratification. "It was funny"—she still spoke in the little-girl voice, which seemed to indicate a kind of submission—"your saying I reminded you of Arthurian romances. Ralph used to say I reminded him of the stories about King Arthur and the Round Table that he used to read when he was a boy." "With pictures by

Howard Pyle!" I knew what he meant exactly—but it
annoyed me to have it brought home to me that her
husband had discovered her first, that she had been
dressing this rôle for him. "But *you're* a great deal
more romantic than any illustration by Howard Pyle.
You're the original thing! Before I saw you, I couldn't
conceive that such people had ever existed; but I suppose there may really have been a Guinevere and that
she may have looked rather like you. But you have the
human quality, too,"—I couldn't seem to avoid these
phrases. "Guinevere was too sedate." "Guinevere wasn't
always sedate: she had her moments of weakness, you
know." "No: of course she wasn't, was she?"—I smiled.
"I don't know why I forgot about that."

"I must go back to the other room," she said, taking
her hand away and opening the lid of her compact.
"We've only been here about three minutes!" I remon-
strated. "Let me look at you three minutes more. Tell
me something that is none of my business: have you had
very many men in love with you?" "Only one: Ralph."
"I don't believe that." "Other people have talked, but
they didn't really mean it." She shrugged, and the shrug
had its coquetry, yet I felt at the same time that she was
humble. "You know, it's very queer about you,"—I had
suddenly the answer to my puzzle. "You're a beauty
who doesn't behave like a beauty." "How do beauties
behave?" "They expect to be admired and courted, and
you don't really seem to expect it. When a woman who
knows she's a beauty comes into a party like this, she
assumes she's the center of attention and usually makes
herself so—whereas you come in unobtrusively and go
and sit somewhere against a wall. Then beauties get
egotistic and inconsiderate of other people's feelings,
because they know that there will always be men who
will keep on falling in love with them, no matter how

badly they behave—but *your* beauty hasn't made you mean, you don't seem even to have any idea of the effect you can produce on people." "I can be mean, too," she said, bringing deliberately a Borgia-like cat-look into eyes that might almost have been dog-like if they hadn't been superbly human—as if some deep competitive instinct had been awakened by my remark. "But really you *aren't* mean," I said, "and you don't seem to know how wonderful you are." "I'm not wonderful,"—she put back the compact, and she seemed to shake off my flattery and become grown-up again. "You just imagine I am." "Well, all I can tell you is that I can't look at anybody else." "You've seen me around before, and I never could notice that it prevented you from looking at other people. There was a time when Roberta Evans was the only person around here you could look at— wasn't she?" she demanded bluntly. And she fixed me with humorous archness from under eyebrows plucked like moths' antennae. "That was because you always acted like a woman who didn't expect to be looked at, who didn't really want to be looked at." She abruptly got up from the couch: "I must go back," she declared. She had glanced away, listening with parted lips, and I felt she had not liked what I was saying. There were people in the dining room now; we could hear the jabber of voices. I followed her straight figure, and wondered whether I had sounded patronizing.

"When shall I see you again?" I asked. "I don't know,"—then after a moment: "You must come to our house," she said. She greeted a woman friend and at once began to talk with animation about their entries of dahlias at the Flower Show. "Shall I bring you something to eat?" "Please do." The friendliness was back in her eyes, and the kisses had given me confidence. I moved among the long white-draped tables, and my eyes

skimmed along over the silver knives and forks laid
out in even rows, the big gleaming silver coffee urn, pip-
ing hot above an intense blue flame and surrounded
by an elegant brood of little gold-rimmed coffee cups,
the polished white plates with their wide gold bands,
on each of which was placed a white napkin, the pink
ham and the ivory turkey which a butler was beautifully
slicing, the little sandwiches with cucumber filling and
the tender asparagus fingers daintily wrapped in bread,
the Edam cheese in glossy red balls as full of meat as the
yolks of great eggs, the delicious-looking chocolate
cake laminated in very fine layers with a light creamy
paste between. And I felt at that moment that Imogen,
like the sandwiches and coffee and cake, was lying spread
out before me: a rich repast to be had for the taking.

I was just about to ask them to dinner, after a week
had elapsed since the party, when Imogen wrote me a
note—I guessed that she was too shy to call me—and
invited me to dinner with them.

Their house was a mock-Elizabethan affair, half-
timbered and built of red brick, with clustering triple
chimneys, and diamond-paned leaded casements. It was
shut off from the road by a neat brick wall, and I entered through wrought-iron gates, knobbed on either
side with stone balls, and walked up a perfectly smooth
flagged path, among a variety of shrubs and small trees
—yews and cedars, azalea and laurel—that crowded the
rather narrow front lawn. These in some cases had been
planted so close to the house, itself muffled in ramblers
and ivy, that they must make it, I thought, rather dark.
I knocked with an antique bronze knocker in the shape
of an upside-down gnome at a door set in an ogival
doorway and embellished with curly iron branches that
radiated in from the hinges.

The interior, though I told myself I ought to have foreseen it, a little depressed me at first, as indeed the whole household did. In the living room, the walls were rough-finished in white and the ceiling was ribbed with big stained beams, and there was a marble Elizabethan fireplace, elaborate with baronial carving and rather too grand for the room, which they had brought over from England. Some Elizabethan chairs, however, dark, high-backed and spiral-legged, had evidently been relegated to the background in favor of more practicable furniture. On the walls were German colored reproductions of Giorgiones and Botticellis, and an Italian Annunciation: saints' gowns of pink and gold, golden haloes, in a paneled and columned gilt frame; and I noted in the bookcase, at a rapid glance, such items as Chatfield-Taylor's *Molière,* a complete limited set of George Moore, *Aucassin and Nicolette,* J. A. Symonds' *Life of Michaelangelo* and his history of the Renaissance, Vasari's *Lives of the Painters* in English, and a section of detective stories. The room was lighted only by candles in hydra-branched candelabra, and seemed swarming with Siamese cats.

Imogen received me in a gown, extravagantly mediaeval, which went even a little further than anything I had seen her wear before and which I felt was directly connected with what I had said to her about King Arthur. It was a dullish autumnal green, and had a train and a high neck, as well as a novel kind of tight long sleeves that fitted over the hands like mittens but left the fingers free. She wore also the snood of gold net which I had already so much admired and on which I had complimented her; and I felt that she was playing up to my interest in her mythical-heroic role and had perhaps a little overdone it. As she rose and came forward to meet me, I noted again the rigidity which I took for affectation of grandeur; and the chair to which she returned, an hourglass of curved arms and clawed legs, reminded me of the chairs from which Hamlet, in old-fashioned Shakespearean productions, invariably delivered his soliloquy. But then she was so staggeringly beautiful!—I was soon under her spell again.

Ralph himself did everything that required effort: he made cocktails and handed *hors d'oeuvres*. He was a quiet and amiable fellow, not short but not very tall, not homely but not quite good-looking. It was easy to forget his appearance on account of his small obscure eyes, of which it was hard to be sure of the color and which rather deprived his face of focus. His most salient feature, not salient enough, was his nose, longish, straight and pointed. His dark hair was smoothly brushed; his gray suit was perfectly pressed. There was no trace in anything he wore or said of Imogen's romantic imagination. He was one of those men in business in a moderate but very sound way who seem to live with the sole purpose of maintaining a margin of luxury that is always a little conspicuous and which implies for them a position on some upper level.

There were also Helen Hubbard, invited for me, and Ed and Kate Schwenk, a commercial artist and his wife, who were special friends of the Loomises but whom I knew only slightly.

It was queer and a little uncomfortable to have cocktails by candlelight. I sat down on one of the Siamese cats. Ralph handed me a curious cocktail in a kind of aluminium goblet; it was pinkish and he said it was an experiment—a "noble experiment," he added—with applejack, grenadine, lime juice and just a dash of Pernod. I asked Helen about the tennis tournament. We ate olives wrapped and skewered in bacon, caviar with grated egg, and tidbits of hot crabmeat and melted cheese on little round pieces of toast. Ed Schwenk went on telling a story in his harsh and high-strung voice from somewhere in the Middle West: "Well, I sent for the headwaiter, and I said to him: 'Listen here, Herr Kellner: if this is calf's liver, I'm Christopher Columbus. And what's more, these new peas—as you call them on the menu—have been frozen for at least a year—and what's more, those blueberry muffins were baked about a week ago, and they ought to be on display in that antique store across the street as genuine Victorian paperweights!'—There isn't *one single decent roadhouse,* where you can get a good dinner and a decent drink, in the whole of Hecate County!"

There was a good deal of talk about food. My feeling —so strong at first that it chilled my social responses— was that Imogen's milieu was unworthy of her; but, as the evening went on, I was forced to perceive how vital she was to her household and how much she enjoyed her rôle. We had dinner by the light of more candles at a long refectory table. The meal, of which I remember the courses better than the conversation, had obviously been planned with enthusiasm: there were copious shrimp cocktails in Russian dressing; consommé enriched with sherry; Mexican *enchiladas*—they had spent the spring before in Mexico and were going through a Mexican period—with filling so fiercely peppered that it struck us in the middle of the dinner, when we were expecting the customary meat course, with a terrific intensification of the motif of the shrimps and *hors d'oeuvres,* brought moisture about our eyes, and quite stopped the conversation; then half avocado pears brimming with peppery French dressing; and a compote of cut-up peaches, raspberries and smooth white almonds —the whole washed down, as they say, with bootleg red Chianti in blue and green glass Mexican bottles.

These bottles were effigies of the Virgin, and they pro-voked a good deal of amusement of a violently sophisti-cated kind.

We had coffee and brandy in the living room. It was cold enough already for a fire, and the fireplace and the dinner and the candles were now lulling me and mak-ing me feel comfortable. I sank into it all, and I sat bemused by Imogen's claret-warmed beauty. When she was flushed, it brought out her high cheek-bones; and her eyes in the candlelight seemed enchantingly both darker and brighter. She lay stretched out on a large French chaise longue, a real eighteenth-century piece, more ample than the modern kind and covered in char-treuse green, with a high carved cradle-like back. We talked about the pictures and the *objets d'art;* and the altarpiece by Fra Lippo Lippi at once led to Browning's poem. One of the Siamese cats kept jumping up on my shoulder, and when I would set it down in my lap, it would dig its claws through my trousers. But I was basking; my prejudice was dulled; and I even found Ralph sympathetic.

Ralph Loomis was an advertizing agent of rather a special kind. His job was to travel about and place in provincial newspapers the advertizing of New York hotels and various brands of ginger ale and lipstick. This involved him in amusing adventures, and he was telling us of a visit of the spring before to Oklahoma City. He had been taken for lunch to the local men's club, where he had heard a great deal of talk about a sport called "pulling the badger." Everybody seemed to be betting. He was invited to be present the next night "at a bout or a match or whatever it was." The place was the club auditorium, which was festive with flags and refresh-ments. The records for the last fifteen years had been posted up on the wall, and the members were studying them attentively. There was a pack of blooded hounds with a keeper, which they also examined with interest. Ralph was told that, as the guest of honor, he had been chosen to pull the badger that night. A little speech of introduction was made, which was greeted with hearty applause. Then a box like a kennel, with a small cage behind in which were seen lettuce leaves, was brought in and set down on the floor. The entrance was closed by a shutter which could be lifted by pulling a string that ran through a hook in the ceiling. They handed Ralph the end of a rope the other end of which was inside the kennel, and earnestly and carefully coached him. The rope was only eight feet long, and he was told not to go too close, but just to give it a hard straight jerk and quickly jump away. The spectators withdrew to the back and sides so as to leave him alone in the center of the room. The trainer had the dogs in leash and seemed about to unclip their collars; the man who was to lift the trap stood ready at a safe distance; a tense and expectant silence descended upon the room. The signal was a pistol shot. Ralph saw the door fly up; he steadily pulled the rope taut and felt a weight of resistance at the other end. Then he gave it a hard straight yank. A white object came hurtling out, splashing some liquid as he leapt aside. It was an old-fashioned chamber-pot.

The climax brought a crash of laughter, almost as if we ourselves had been witnessing the hoax in the clubhouse. Helen Hubbard roared and made everybody else roar. Imogen had a shriek which was a little off-key and self-conscious, as if her acquaintance with me had been so far on such a high level that she feared I might be disillusioned by the coarseness of her husband's story. I didn't much like the shriek, and yet it was reassuring to know that she had also this earthy side, as I felt she would probably have called it. And one could not dislike Ralph, as I had fully expected to do. He had told

his ridiculous story with a quiet and candid drollery; and
there was something appealing about him. One felt that
he was a little ashamed of his work: the business had
been his father's. And it *was* funny to think of Ralph
in his always correct city clothes springing away from
the perilous pot—though its contents, he made haste to
explain to us, had been nothing but plain water. I had,
besides, already discovered that his work took him away
a good deal, and noted that he would be gone the next
week.

Ed Schwenk, who was highly competitive, was now
stimulated to tell at great length about fraternity initia-
tions in some Middle Western college he had been to.
I laughed heartily at this, too; and I talked at some
length to his wife—who was wearing an embroidered
Cuban shawl, but kept lit, behind a rimless pince-nez,
a beaming and motherly eye—about living in the country in winter and the problems presented by children.
She had three sons: one almost out of Yale, one in
his sophomore year, and one just about to enter. She
was perfectly clear in her mind about the eventual
careers of the younger boys, but she was worried as to
whether the oldest one was going to be an artist or an
engineer.

Imogen talked about Italy. She and Ralph had visited
the hill towns; she told me about some old trip that
they had made through the mountains in a carriage when
the party just ahead of theirs had been held up and
robbed by bandits; and the great Sienese festival, the
Palio delle Contrade, which was just exactly, she said,
like going back into the Middle Ages, and about which
she became rather tedious. I felt that if she and I had
made this trip together, it would have all been entirely
different: vivid with passionate love and colored by imagination on something higher than the guidebook level.

We should afterwards have slipped away for a long and voluptuous holiday in some amusing little place by the sea where nobody ever came. The last time I had been in Italy, I had only done galleries and churches, and done them all alone. "Do you like to swim?" I asked. She had turned her head away to take part in another conversation, and did not now turn quite all the way back, but looked at me askance with her bright steady eyes. "We don't go to the beach very much," she said. "Ralph gets cramps when he swims—and I," she went on, after a second's pause, "don't care much for the water." It was true that I could not remember ever to have seen them at the local beach club; but I had an uncomfortable feeling that she had been able to look into my mind, and had seen me there doting on her body, golden and Giorgionesque, as she lolled on the sand and looked out at the sea on the beach below our little pink villa. Some sally of Ed Schwenk's caught her ear, and she went back to the general conversation, laughing loudly at Ed Schwenk's imitation of somebody's bad golf.

Yet I felt in her farewell no chill. She shook hands with me, still reclining, with a conscious touch of Madame Récamier; and I felt in the smile that she gave me some frank kind of acquiescence and gratitude.

I waited before calling on Imogen till two days after Ralph had left.

I did not phone but simply went round, and I found her outside on the lawn pruning a great crimson rambler. "It's the wrong time of year," she explained, "but it's keeping out all the light." She was operating intently and brutally, but with a certain ineptitude, lopping off enormous branches. She looked very charming and stately in a wide flappy garden-hat that gave her somewhat the air—she seemed always in costume—of a titled

English lady keeping her hand in on a large estate. I tried to help her in her struggle with the rambler, reaching up and pulling down the higher shoots. The thing had been allowed to grow wild with a rankness that was almost repellent. The stems were nearly as thick as tree-branches and had great thorns like the teeth of a circular saw: the blossomless sprays, when you tried to disentangle them, seemed actually to reach out and fasten on to you and grapple you into the bush in order to prevent you from clipping them. When we had finished, I picked up a sheaf from the ground. "Don't do that," she said. "They'll bite you. Let me put them in the basket. I've got gloves on." But there was much too much for the basket, and I loaded my arms with the biggest ones that still seemed purposely to hook me and stick me with their diabolic barbs. We dumped them on a rubbish heap at the back of the house.

Returning, we stopped to look at the garden. The air was dense and the day bright. In September the grass was still gold in the sun, and things still had that velveted look that was characteristic of our climate. It was as if the blues and magentas and oranges and gamboges and reds had been given fresh coats of color, and the petals of the zinnias and dahlias had almost the tissues of flesh. There was a profusion of many kinds of flowers which had originally been planted in a formal design but had now become rather confused and were brimming into one another's beds; and there were pallid and long-necked pansies and cornflowers sprawling on the ground that, as she said, she ought to have had cut back: "It's so hard for me to kneel," she explained. The flower-beds turned suddenly at the farther end into an ornamental vegetable garden, with gourds and yellow crookneck squashes that had been trained to grow on the wall, though some of them had dropped to the ground, and pumpkins that had been pedestaled on top of it "the way they have them in Italy." She had even more or less succeeded in training tomato vines to string prettily on little low trellises their globes of yellow and red.

As we slowly strolled back to the house, I dreamed pleasantly of a villa in Candeli, which I had visited years before. It would be fun—and so natural, so simple—to alight in such a villa and live there: with the fine-looking Sienese maidservant who could neither read nor write, the heavy-beamed cool-tiled studio, which could be equally used as a study, the yellow-stemmed coffee cups for breakfast with their scrollery of the Renaissance, the wide round-arched Tuscan doorways and the windows full of flowers and leaves and light, with the sheer drop below to the Arno, green and opaque as a pigment on a panel. Over everything, as far as one could see, the copious appeasing sun, and inside the appeasing of desire on the broad low Italian bed that seemed meant for nothing else.

This Old World mood on my part was picked up, as we crossed the lawn, by the sight of a small staircase with an iron rail that ran up the side of the house. "Where does that go?" I asked. "It just goes to the second floor." "It looks quite romantic," I said, "as if it led to an historic chamber." She walked toward it, and I found myself following her up. "I feel as if we were going to see the Glamis Horror," I remarked as we climbed the steps. "I'm afraid we haven't got any ghosts," she replied, after a moment's silence. I imagined she had stopped to think and did not know what the Glamis Horror was. It was supposed to be a monster, not a ghost, but I did not correct her, and we said nothing more till we had got to the top of the steps, and she had opened a little Gothic door, which was dark-stained and iron-hinged.

The door gave directly on a bedroom: cool and white-walled, with drawn shades. It smelled of woodwork and linen, and was dominated and rather crowded by a great Elizabethan bed with spiraling bulging bedposts, and a great flat-topped wardrobe that matched it. The somber magnificence of these was relieved by a few bright ornaments: a pair of pompous Chinese roosters, a clay garland of Mexican fruit, and a doorstop in the effigy of a marching grenadier. "We brought it from England," she explained about the bed. "We don't sleep in it any more. It took up so much space in the room. So now we give it to guests." She shot up some of the shades. I studied, propped on a table, a framed Elizabethan ballad: *The Story of David and Berseba*. It was a broadside with crude little woodcuts of men dressed in swords and cloaks and women in feathers and ruffs:

> *Her beauty was more excellent*
> *   and brighter than the morning Sunne,*
> *By which the King, incontinent,*
> *   was to her favour quickly wonne.*

> *She stood within a pleasant Bower,*
> *   all naked, for to wash her there;*
> *Her body, like a Lilly Flower,*
> *   was covered with her golden haire.*

> *The King was wounded with her love,*
> *   and what she was he did enquire;*
> *He could not his affection move,*
> *   he had to her such great desire.*

> *"She is Uriah's Wife," quoth they . . .*

"You know," I said, "every time I see you, you remind me of a different period—and sometimes you remind me of several periods all merging like a multiple exposure. It's as if you were all the beautiful women who had ever gotten lodged in men's minds!" I took her hands. "Let me look at your eyes!" I said. She held her head aside, masked by the heavy brim. "Please!": she lifted her face, and it seemed a little stubborn and scared, as if she thought that I wanted to scrutinize her in some curious or critical way. But I told her how wonderful she was and kissed her in solemn admiration, and stared again at her eyes, which now seemed both tender and bold.

I made her sit down on the bed, which had nothing but a sheet on the mattress. "I never thought I'd know you," I said, taking both her hands together. "You seemed like a romantic vision—the kind of thing one can't get over to from reality." "I never thought I'd know you either,"—it was the yielding little-girl voice. "You still don't seem," I pursued, "to belong to the real world I live in—you don't belong with ordinary people." "You're not like other people either." "We have something very deep in common." "I don't know: we hardly know each other." "We neither of us live in Hecate County: we're strangers among all these suburbanites. I'm really only interested in things that don't exist for them: history and art and all that; and you somehow belong to the world of those things"— was I being a little maudlin?—"as no other woman has done that I've ever known!" "I don't know where I belong," she said. She sat looking away, as she so often did, her big hat partly hiding her face. I tried to take it off, but she held it on with one hand, and said, "No: don't!" "I want to see your wonderful hair. You know, you have the most wonderful hair that I've ever seen in the world. It's like something that a princess lets down from a tower." "Let *me* take it off." She carefully removed the hat and with her smooth hands smoothed down her braids. I kissed them with a kind of ardor that partook both of reverence and of passion; but though I was summoning the pictures in the legends, I did not seem to be realizing the excitement that I had thought I should feel about her: her hair in this half-shaded light of the room looked simply extremely blond. I was putting my arms around her and was on the point of kissing her mouth when she pulled herself away from my embrace. "Don't do that!" she said. "Why mustn't I?" "Because I don't want you to." She had shifted her seat on the bed. "I don't like to be held," she said gently. I leaned over to her and kissed her without touching her with my hands. The kisses were quite real, and she returned them. She was certainly a real woman: she had that odor of a woman perspiring in a clean but light summer dress that took me back to the summers of my childhood when outdoor romps with little girls in the shrubbery had taken an amorous turn; yet her edict that I must not embrace her made me feel, as I went on kissing her, that she was somehow a sacred object from which I was still debarred.

But perhaps it would be like the hat: in a moment I should try again. In the meantime, I went on talking: "Who are you?" I asked. "Where do you come from?" "I'm a myth," she replied, with her coquetry. "But what part of the world do you come from? Or are you a universal myth?" "I was born in Minnesota,"—I could see it was a reluctant confession—"but I've lived in the East since I was fourteen." "Have you got any Irish blood?" "My father was born in Ireland—in County Galway. My mother's people came from Sweden." "Then you *are* a universal myth: you're Brunhilde and Iseult in one. I think you're really more like Iseult, though. But Iseult's eyes were blue, of course. Yours are much more exciting! Close them—let me see how they look." They were amazing: she had great rounded lids, with lashes that were darker than her hair—very noble and yet provocative. I kissed one and then the other: they were a little oily with sweat. Then I kissed her again on the mouth, and she seemed to respond with eagerness, pressing her lips against mine. I put my arm around her shoulder and my hand against her cheek; but immediately she shrank away. "Please don't do that," she said; then adorably soft and lisping: "Just kiss me." I put both hands on her ears and the coils of her hair; then I put them on her cheeks, which were flushed and hot. The logic of the situation impelled me to force her backwards, dropping one hand to her waist and trying not to bear on her shoulders. But she righted herself and slipped away. "Don't do that, please," she repeated, appealingly and yet with authority. In an ordinary affair of the kind, I should have pressed her with, "I want you so much! I can't think of anything else!" or something of the sort; but with her I did feel that it was vulgar to attempt to go to bed with her thus out of hand on a sheet in a closed-up guest-room; and I tried to play a worthier role. "I'm sorry," I said, "but I adore you so. I don't know what to do about you!" "There's nothing to do." She had been leaning back, propping herself with her hands, her lids half veiling her eyes; but now she stood up with decision: "I must go downstairs," she said, and straightened her hair in the mirror. Over her shoulder I watched in the glass the reflection of her anxious brown eyes, which seemed to me shining with love and aching with the strain of the moment; and her mouth that I had kissed half-open.

I kissed her again before we left, and she quickly

turned her lips away afterwards. I followed her out into the hall and downstairs into the wainscoted and tapestried smell that, like everything about the Loomises, was several degrees too rich. I noted little carved heraldic lions poised upright on the newel posts. "Wonderful little lions," I commented. "That's Ralph's coat of arms," she said. They had had it looked up, she told me, by the College of Heralds in London, and then had had the lions made by a wonderful old German woodcarver in Brooklyn.

"Would you like a cocktail?" she asked. We made a manhattan in the kitchen, which was quite non-Elizabethan and equipped with the latest developments in electric refrigerators and electric stoves. It was the maid's day out. We brought the cocktail things into the living room and set them down on a little low table. This table was made of tiles that had Goya's *Caprichos* on them; and we talked about Goya and his queer imagination and his affair with the Duchess of Alba. I had pointed out the Duchess in one of the pictures and spoken of the part she played in them. "Oh, yes," Imogen picked it up promptly. "The Duchess of Alba was his mistress, you know, and when she was banished by the Queen to her country estate, Goya went right along with her, and the Queen had to pardon the Duchess to get Goya to come back to Madrid." I had noticed that she did not like to be told things but was always impatient to tell. "I suppose she was really quite remarkable," I went on with a quickening enthusiasm. "She must have had a certain amount of brains as well as being extremely beautiful." "She posed for the Maja portraits, you know." "I've always thought it rather amusing that the one that's described as *vestida* should have been thought to be less improper than the one that's described as *desnuda*." "Yes: he painted it because her husband had heard that she was posing nude. The Queen was very jealous of her and burned down the Alba palace. They were wonderful people, weren't they? —the Spaniards. She used to send Goya dinners on magnificent silver plates, and according to Spanish custom the dishes couldn't be returned—they were a present that went with the dinner." "Yes, you have to have wastefulness, I suppose," I said, "to get the really greatest kinds of art." "Yes, I know,"—she seemed a little chagrined—"I can't be wasteful, though." "Why can't you?" She did not answer my question. "If I'd been the Duchess of Alba," she added, "I'd have had Goya come to stay with me in the country, and I wouldn't have cared about anything!" I did not quite grasp the point she was making, but she said this with a force and a boldness that made me believe in her greatness of spirit. "It's the Irish in you,"—I hastened on. "It's just as Yeats said: *Only the wasteful virtues earn the sun.* The Irish produce great writers because they're temperamentally prodigals—they're willing to squander their lives on the gratuitous work that great art demands; whereas the Scotch, on the contrary, are only really good at economics and moral philosophy: two departments in which the object is to minimize waste— whether of money or stress and strain—through accurate calculation. The Scotch are a fake in the arts because they always have to pretend that they're producing something more than they've paid for." "You talk so brilliantly," she said. "You're really a brilliant man, aren't you? I've never known a brilliant man." I can't say I wasn't flattered by this, but it rather stopped my flow of ideas. And in a moment she looked at her wrist-watch and announced, "I'll have to go and get dressed. Edna Forbes is coming at half past six to take me out to dinner."

We kissed good-by in the hall. I was ardent and loyal: she was loyal, too, but did not linger. I asked when I should see her again. "Are you going to the Fergusons' Saturday?" I was. "Well, I'll see you there."

I saw her at the Fergusons' and took her aside and paid her such court as was possible; but she didn't want to see me Sunday: Ralph was coming back that night. Then I had to go away for two deferred summer visits; then Ralph had his vacation in September, and he and Imogen took a motor trip to Canada; then they went to New York in October, and I found myself alone in the country, wondering what had happened to extinguish an affair of such promise.

I succeeded in having lunch with her, however, one day when I went to town. I took her to a good little speakeasy, smart, expensive and dark, where her face, under a felt cloche hat, in the light of the pink-shaded lamp, glowed tantalizingly out of the shadow like a glamorous movie close-up, detached from its trunk and untouchable. We talked about the people in the country. I told her how much I missed her; but at two-thirty she had an engagement. Ralph was away again now, but it turned out that she had made an engagement for every dinner and lunch during his absence.

I took her where she was going in a taxi, and in the taxi kissed her much. "We mustn't see each other," she said. "Why mustn't we?" "Because I'm married." "You've been married for sixteen years, and Ralph has had you all that time. Don't you think I deserve something, too?—I love you,"—I was sober and earnest— "I'm in love with you: don't you know that? Please don't refuse to see me." "I'll see you sometimes," she said, "but you mustn't be in love with me." "Why not?" "You don't really know me at all." "I want to, though." "You wouldn't like me." "I'd like you more,—I'd appreciate you more, than anyone else has ever done." "Would you?" She was pleased again and looked away out the window. "You'll see," I said, with quiet certainty.

We were pulling in at the Ritz, where she was going to have her hair done. "Don't kiss me here," she said, and quickly got out of the cab.

II

It may be that there is nothing more demoralizing than a small but adequate income.

I had been a pretty good student at college and had stayed on to get a Ph.D.; but I inherited some money from a sister of my mother's and decided to drop my thesis. I had specialized in economics. My father was an expert accountant who had first worked for the bigger insurance companies and then had made himself a position as what came to be called a "management engineer" —that is, a mathematician who figures out budgets and methods for grasping corporations; and I had been slated for something of the sort. But I loathed the idea of Detroit, in which my family now had to live, and I was interested in economic theory rather than in studying the sales and costs of the General Tires Corporation; so I had made up my mind to teach. I had, however, been affected by the radical wind that had blown at the end of the war (in which I had been too young to take part), and had come to be repelled by the indifference of my father and the employers' world that he served to the human needs of labor. I had called myself a socialist at college, and had found myself more and more at odds with the college Economics Department, where the professors were mainly apologists for the bankers on the board of trustees or people of the dry-goods and grocery type who had a sympathetic interest in business without the competence to be businessmen. I had, also, with no talent of my own, a very great enthusiasm for art; and what I really wanted most to work on and what the categories of college had no place for was an historical study of painting in relation to its social-economic roots. I decided to take advantage of my income to go into the subject for myself.

But the pressures of 1919 gave way to the spending of the twenties. I went to Europe to see the museums and stayed there for nearly three years. Life, of course, for an American was easy abroad; but then when I came back to New York, I found prices that made it hard to live in comfort. I had relatives in Hecate County, and I was able to rent from friends of theirs a most remarkable little place in the woods, situated on a charming little river, for considerably less than it was worth. I got to like the long quick drives between houses and the long drinks screened in by foliage—though I often told people they bored me—and my work, since I had settled in the country, was becoming rather desultory and languid. That summer I had hardly written anything, but had only read at histories of art and dense books on social background.

And now suddenly I found myself dissatisfied. The effect on me of the revelation of Imogen had been to make me feel rather worthless. I was carping and sulking in my tent, I was shirking the dust and heat (such phrases came inevitably to mind); I was missing something very important: the real dignity and glory of life. After all, despite his limited intelligence, Ralph Loomis had in some sense earned Imogen: had he not given her an Elizabethan country house, the certainty of winters in New York, and all those travels in Europe and America? And what did I have to offer her aside from my superior taste and my "brilliant" conversation? I knew that I must do something, be something. Jo Gates, my regular girl, who was at present in California, had never made me feel like this. First of all, I must finish my book. But for that I needed libraries, museums, the society of intelligent people. And I needed to be nearer Imogen.

I was not actually very near her in town when I finally found an apartment. She was staying in the East Fifties at the Vanderveer Hotel, and I landed just below Fourteenth Street. The rents in Greenwich Village in those days had gone up to join the uptown rents, and anything really good was away beyond my resources. But I took for sixty-five a month, which was more than I paid in the country, a single large room and a bath on the top floor of a house in West Twelfth Street between Sixth and Seventh Avenues. I moved in some of my furniture and pictures, and it was really not terribly bad—though I hated the daybed that was also a couch. At least it was an old red brick house with a white door and a little brasswork, which the landlord kept painted and polished; not one of those awful places with fire-escapes on the fronts and gummy yellow walls in the stairwell.

Between the first days of November, when I came to live in town, and the end of the Christmas holidays, I had a life in which I was at least fully occupied. I read purposefully; took notes, looked at pictures, and lay on my back on the confounded couch having maddening daydreams about Imogen, or walked the floor late at night, under the stimulus of a couple of drinks, trying to work out a strategy to win her. I was invited to the parties she gave and I cultivated her flavorless friends with the object of getting asked to their parties. I occasionally met Imogen for a drink or took her to an exhibition; and there were moments of silence and sighs, and moments when she told me she couldn't believe that she could ever so seriously matter to a man-about-town like me. It seemed to me by Christmas that I was lapsing to the level of an insipid little comedy that she amused herself by playing in public; I was a kind of *cavaliere servente* out of someone's eighteenth-century memoirs, in a perfectly wholesome America in which such things could not be real. Then she told me without warning or compunction at the grand finale of her season, a New Year's party that she and Ralph were giving in a friend's apartment, that she was going the next week to St. Augustine with her constant friend Edna Forbes. Ralph would be away in the West on his big early trip of the year. "Oh, why not stay in town?" I pled. "What am I going to do without you?" "You can write me," she said, smiling.

And when she went, I was faced by a blank. I did not have enough money to follow her, and I had just had a letter from Jo that she was not coming back from the Coast. She had declined to take alimony from her husband, and now she had lost half her investments in the catastrophic stock market crash. She had a home in California with an uncle whose pampered favorite she was, and she could not afford to come East. Our relation, though jolly and enjoyable, had ceased to be particularly exciting—like the even California sunshine that so rapidly wears out its romance; but I had always had the comfortable assurance that she would be back with me the first of the year: I had not had to be desperate about Imogen. But now Jo and Imogen both had suddenly left me flat—as flat as the pavements of winter in the season that follows the holidays. In the country I had always been braced by the conviction that I was digging in, and I had had the satisfaction of feeling that I was burning through the dull season, that the brain of a man was alive while the beasts were asleep and the earth was dead. But in town the damp thickens the smoke, the traffic seems marking time, and people spit in the subway stations. The only things that were fresh in the streets were the headlines—new words—on the newsstands, and most of these announced dismal events.

I took to walking in the evenings on Fourteenth Street, which had a certain animation and variety. I got to like the big-hipped cat-faced women of the photographs shown as lures out in front of the Fourteenth Street burlesque show; the announcements of moving-picture palaces bejeweled with paste-bright lights; the little music shops that sold big brass-band instruments and Slavic and Balkan records and had radios that blared into the street; the Field's restaurant window with the white-aproned girl, blue-livid under a mercury tube, making pancakes on a hot metal slab; the young women on the pavements, some of them pretty, Italian or Jewish or whatever, stopping to look in at the displays in the windows of the dress and shoe shops. It seemed to me that American manufacturing was making possible for all classes of the people an almost uniform standard of smartness. I remembered having been surprised when Jo, who always looked so well, had told me about buying cheap dresses at this very department store on the corner which was always proclaiming sales; but now I saw that these working-class girls were able to buy, at very low prices, well-designed turbans and sandals which to me were absolutely indistinguishable from the ones worn by ladies uptown. What a shocking injustice it was that they would now not be able to buy them, that the garment workers and shoe workers who made these things should be picketing these very streets in the de-

mand for a minimum to live on! I had always seen the
fallacies of capitalism, and now—moved perhaps at
once by self-pity and by self-disgust—I had a vision of
the economic system as a pitiful and disgusting fiasco.

In the restlessness of my after-dinner boredom, I began looking in on the dance-halls. The first one I visited
was desolating and soon drove me out again. Sparse
couples—uninterested hostesses and elderly stolid men
—were shuffling or revolving to monotonous music under lighting that was glamorless and garish. I wondered
whether they were all like that or whether there mightn't
be gayer places: was this the type of the popular recre-
ation that a city like New York had to offer? I decided
to give purpose to my outings by making a little socio-
logical survey; and I started at what I took to be the
top: a much-publicized dance-hall in the theater district,
which occupied a whole floor of a corner building. It
was open on two sides to the town, and seemed quite
wholesome, lively and bright. There were young men
who brought their girls there to dance as well as lonely
ones who danced with the hostesses. These hostesses
were all quite presentable, and most of them had good
quiet manners. They were forbidden to make dates on
the premises, and a very firm effort was exerted to keep
the place up to a decent standard.

The next evening I returned to Fourteenth Street and
tried a place called the Tango Casino that had always
impressed me, from the pavement, as the jazziest and
the toughest of these downtown resorts. It was situated
on the second floor, and displayed, besides a strung-
out electric sign, a crude picture, painted by hand, of
a man and a woman dancing; from its windows, when
they were open, there splashed down the jangling
unflagging music of a headlong and demoniac dance-
band. I climbed the dirty marble steps, steep and grim

as a staircase of Hell, and bought a long strip of tickets at the brisk little window at the top. Inside I found a dark and cramped box, which, in comparison with the other two places, had a certain vulgar mystery and richness, a concentrated atmosphere of violence. There was a small dance-floor, crowded with couples and hedged with waiting men, which was constantly being blacked out and suffused with purple or blue while the energetic Negro band played such tunes as *Three O'Clock in the Morning, Valencia* and *My Blue Heaven*. I soon found myself adhering to a chunky little wench, who had heavy mascara on her lashes and who told me I was a very good dancer. She proceeded, with even more importunity than the girls usually showed in these places, to remind me, by an enthusiastic reference to the size of her last partner's tip, that a "present" was always expected. She pressed the lower part of her body and her thick round knee against me, and she tended to make me keep her in corners, stuck tight to her and slowly turning, which was what she evidently thought I wanted. It was hard to get away from a partner till your tickets were all used up, but I finally gave her a dollar and left her. I then retreated to a blue-carpeted lounge which had bulgingly upholstered blue chairs and heavily pink-shaded lamps, and ordered one of the flat ginger ales that they were selling as set-ups for drinks. I looked the girls over there and liked none of them, and finally returned to the floor with the purpose of using up my last tickets.

This time I held out against the hostesses, who came after me like the pigeons at St. Patrick's. There was a market here, I had found: men lined up for the best-looking girls. I watched a pretty little one that I liked, and I waited through half a dozen dances till her partner at last left her.

She was slim and rather pale and had reddish hair and was wearing a blue dress. I was struck by her complete unconcern. Instead of coming to meet me with alacrity the moment she saw me advancing, she stood without catching my eye; when I spoke to her, she said simply, "You want this one?"; and did not even smile. I noticed that she was not made up, did not seem to have put on even lipstick, where the other girls heavily depended on their artificial mouths and lashes in the peachy artificial light; and when I talked to her, she paid out no patter but answered my questions briefly, in a toneless but not unfriendly voice. Nor did she glue her knee against me: we danced with a conventional interval. I asked her what her name was, and she said Anna. Her last name—when I asked for it—was Lenihan. It did not sound fancy enough to be one of their made-up names.

I invited her to come out for a drink when her duties as a hostess were over; and she replied, after a moment, yes, she might: she had just been about to ask me how to get to an address in the East Thirties—she was going to a party there. I was surprised that she shouldn't have known, but she told me that she lived in Brooklyn and had hardly been anywhere in Manhattan except the Tango Casino. She had to see a girl about something after the Casino closed at twelve, so that she would not be able to meet me till half-past or it might be later; and they didn't allow you to meet men on the street right outside the dance-hall, so I should have to wait for her a block away at the corner of Union Square and Fifteenth. There was something a little odd about it: I wondered why a girl so indifferent should take the trouble to make my acquaintance before going on to something else. It hardly seemed to me possible that she wanted me to direct her to where she was going.

I waited till one o'clock, in the abruptly cold February night, gazing south toward the gray open space where Fourteenth Street and Fourth Avenue merge at the corner of Union Square, so treacherous with traffic in the daytime, so abandoned and barren at night. I was just about to start walking home, rather exasperated and disgusted with myself, when she quietly and quickly came up, her face, between her hat and her fur, looking childlike and a little bit monkeyish. She had been hurrying but was quite undemonstrative in her apologies about making me wait. I took her to my rooms in a taxi, and she sat in the big armchair and had two cigarettes and one drink. "I'm all excited," she said—she was serious and almost white. "I'm going to a party that's being given at the Grover, and I've never been in a hotel before." "You must think I'm drunk," she said when I asked her whether she really never had. I believed her, though: she did not seem to care about making an impression on me. She did not smile and I saw that she was shy, though when she spoke, she was natural and quite direct in her husky little city voice. And yes, she was definitely pretty as those girls in the dance-halls went: her face was small and round, with gentle modeling and bluish-gray eyes that looked like little fine-sepaled flowers; and her mouth had a pink surface of lips which, entirely unobtrusive though it was, seemed expressionless and all of a piece as if it had just been kissed or was unconsciously inviting kisses. I went over and sat on the arm of her chair and put my arm around her, but she evaded my lips when I bent down to her face, and said simply and promptly: "Oh, no!" She soon crushed out her cigarette and declared that she had to leave. I tried to keep her, but she coolly got up and put on her fur-collared coat. I tried to kiss her again and managed just to graze her lips as we were saying good-by at the door. I sent her off to her address in a taxi, which was evidently a luxury for her: she protested about the expense.

She promised to call me up but didn't, and I looked in on the dance-hall again. I found her, and we danced perfunctorily, and she told me she would come the next night. I was doubtful as to whether to expect her: I didn't know whether what seemed her lack of interest were a reason for assuming that she would forget it or a reason for supposing she would come since she need not have troubled to promise. Yet I found that the chance of her coming had the effect of stirring up my energies to grapple with my aesthetic problems. I had just been rereading Clive Bell, whose doctrine of "significant form" as opposed to illustrational value had become so much a part of my thinking that I had never got my quarrel with it clear. But I saw now how impossible it was for me to accept his Platonic idealism which made art represent a reality independent of the vicissitudes of life; and I could never work out the relation between his theory of the history of art and my social-economic one. For Clive Bell, the school of painting that began with Cézanne was the herald of a great rebirth; to me, it seemed already to reflect the human decadence and the mechanical tyranny of a dying social system. Though I admired many abstract paintings, I tended to find in them the savage self-loathing, the helpless splintering, the self-immolation, of urban man in the modern world. And I was telling myself tonight that, if I were myself an artist, I should want to leave explicit in any painting of Anna some evidence of her tarnished prettiness.

She did turn up—as before, very late. That evening I made her sit on the daybed and presently she lay in my arms and I discovered that she was wearing bloomers. "Oh, doan do that!" she said. "What do you want me to do?" "Just love me." I thought of how Imogen had said, "Just kiss me," and I felt for a moment a flicker of fear lest this and the impenetrable bloomers might portend another frustration; but what Anna meant by being loved was something that went a good deal further than anything that had been possible with Imogen. She closed her eyes and became very hot and seemed to lose herself. She evidently *did* want a lover. But I never got beyond her bloomers, and at last she sat up flushed and looked away. "Gimme a cigarette," she said.

She promised to call me up at six in the afternoon on a day when I knew I should be home to answer. She failed to do so, to my irritation, but did call me two mornings later. "I'll explain every*thing!*" she said, as if she were really concerned about not having kept her word. She had told me that she lived with her mother, who was a fur worker at a place in Manhattan, and she had to stay home and keep house; and when she appeared that evening, she insisted upon making it clear to me that she had had to go out to telephone, because she did not want the family to hear her (she told them, when she came to see me, that she had stayed out with her girl-friend Doris) ; and that she had had to be attending to the kitchen at the time when she was supposed to call me because her mother had not come back yet; and that then the next day had been Sunday and everybody had been around and she hadn't had a chance to go out. I could see that she was in earnest and I was glad to believe her, though I felt that there was something left out.

This time her bloomers came off. She lay perfectly quiet, with her eyes shut, in her little stockinged feet. I did not try to make her go to bed, but only embraced her body through her old and rather wretched black dress, which, however, did not stifle my appetite with its stale smell of having been perspired in night after night at the dance-hall. Nor did I mind the cheap odor of powder, nor her breath, which was flavored with garlic. Her mouth was tonight so responsive—it seemed to spread, become fleshy and wet—that I forgot about everything else. But it was very soon over. She remained there beside me with her eyes closed a long time. Then, "Gimme a cigarette," she said, still with her eyelids dropped. She told me that she wore the bloomers to protect herself against the boys at the "dancing school," who sometimes took her out after it closed: "When they touch your bare skin, they go wild," she said.—"And then here I am in it with *you!*" She was rather grave about it; but later I made her smile when I told her she was pretty with her color so high: it brought out the red in her hair. She had a little shy grin that gave her dimples. "I'm homely—don't kid me," she said, looking away again. She wouldn't take money when I offered her some as I was dropping her at the Fourteenth Street subway; but said merely, "All right: good night," and slipped quickly out of the cab before I could kiss her good-by.

She came to see me quite often after that, though the intervals were sometimes long and our appointments rather uncertain. I noted all her visits in a diary which I had made a point of keeping that winter, in an effort to intensify for myself my perceptions of the things about me and my consciousness of experience, which I had felt rather dimming in the country; and I can best present my glimpses of this period—which seemed to me unreal at the time and which later I could hardly remember, so completely disconnected were they from everything else I was doing—through the entries I made at the time. I find them queerly sandwiched in between notes on exhibitions and reading, and sardonic observations on my social life.

February 20

Her soft little face with its white tender skin and its shadows in the softened lighting, as she was sitting half upright on the daybed—her round and attractive legs stretching out from beneath the short skirt. Her pale blue dress, as she wore it, had a certain smartness of draping. She said she was "skinny now"—she used to be "nice and plump"—they didn't like her any more at the Tango Casino, because she'd gotten so thin.

She had to get up early the next morning to collect the tenants' rent so that she could take her mother the money before her sister got a chance to collect it and keep some of it for herself.

She lives with her mother and her stepfather. They rent a little house in Brooklyn and sublet most of the rooms. They have an awful time when people don't pay because it's so hard to get a dispossess notice. They make her do all the cooking—and at night she goes to work at the Tango Casino. She also has to sleep in the basement, and she's scared of that damn furnace they have —when the pressure goes way up, she's afraid it's going to blow up the house, and once she had to rush out and get a neighbor to fix it.

Her mother is a Ukrainian, she says, and comes from some town near Lemberg; but her stepfather (with scorn) is a Russian. "His name is Alexis, but they call him Fatty. He's a big fat awful-lookin guy. We were measurin ourselves one day—we have a lotta fun when I'm not sore at-um—and he's as big aroun the thigh as

I am aroun the waist—twenny-four.—And my mother supports-um, she gives-um money. When I think of my mother livin with-um! When I go past the door of her room and see her cuddlin up to-um in bed, I could just go in and smack her! Hones'ly, it's an awful thing to say, but I'd rather have my mother dead than livin with a guy like that!"

Passionate for so frail and quiet a girl—blind kisses, nothing but those meeting mouths.

February 26

Tonight she arrived rather tense and strange: discouraged my kisses and smoked cigarettes. "I want to tell you something," she said presently. She did not look at me. "I didn't want to tell you before." "What is it?" "I doan like to tell you." She had evidently braced herself for a difficult and humiliating confession, and I was sure she was about to reveal to me that she was a parttime prostitute. But when I pressed her to go on, she said solemnly and as if it might end everything between us: "I'm married." Rather relieved, I laughed, and asked her whom she was married to. "His name is Daniel Lenihan." "What does he do?" "He's a bum. He told me he was an auto salesman, but what he does is steal cars.—I don't live with-um any more." "Where does he live?" "Doan ask me! He lives all over—lives with his friends. He comes to get my money at the dancing school every night—that's why I can't see you till so late. I'm afraid he'll find out I see you—I thought he was following me tonight—that's why I'm so nervous. He'd kill me." "He wouldn't really, would he?" "He'd do anything—he's crazy—he used to beat me up." "He couldn't get in here." "He'd wait till I came out." I went over to the window and looked down: a few dark figures strolled past—Greenwich Villagers on their way to delicatessen stores or coming home from the movies. Could anybody be lurking in a doorway? My first instinctive assurance that no such person as Anna described, even if he really existed, could possibly impinge on my rooms, where I was knotting my web on the history of art and where the telephone threaded me in with the web of my social relationships—this feeling gave way to a fear lest I might have been motoring in the jungle and have wandered too far from the car. "There's nobody outside," I said. "I'll go out with you to the subway when you leave." "I wouldun let you go out with me. If he saw you, he'd know I'd been up to something." "Is he jealous of you still when you don't live with him?" "He'd be sore if he thought I had a boy-friend." I tried to make her feel that my solid position would be somehow a safeguard against Dan.

"I've got a child, too," she went on: she was evidently very much ashamed. I asked her what it was: "A girl—four years old. The reason I can't go out in the daytime is that I have to stay with Cecile." We talked about the little girl. "You don't mind?" she said. "No: of course not." "I do, though." "Why?" "Because it isn't right." I tried to tell her that she didn't need to feel she had sinned since he had treated her, she said, so badly. "He brought a woman home with-um once,"—she tried to strengthen her case—"and went to bed with her right in the next room.—I wanted to get even with-um—that's why I went with you." I told her that I'd hoped she liked me, too. "I do like you," she explained, "but not the way I cared for Dan." "Weren't you ever unfaithful to him before?" "I was always so crazy about-um that I didn't want to do it with anybody else. When Dan was away, there was one boy that would throw me because he looked so much like Dan, and I'd dance with-um and I'd think about-um, and I thought if he ever kissed me, I'd just pass away—and then finally he took me out in-uz car and kissed me, and I didun like it at all: I was just disguss'ed and made-um take me home."

"But if you don't live with your husband any more, you ought to have somebody else." "You know it isn't right," she said. I urged upon her the obvious arguments. "I had a dream about you," she said at last, looking away and with a little smile. "What was it?" "What do you think? I dreamt we were doin it on the sofa at home and my sister came in and said: 'I guess you needed it pretty bad!'—I wanted a lovin so much one night last summer that I wasn't able to sleep. I used to let boys take me home and love it up in the hall, but I never did it with any of them." I kissed her and begged her to take off her dress; but she continued to sit there, intent and mute, staring into the darkness of her faithlessness to Dan. It was as if she had not broken her vows till she had let me know she was married: up to then she had been able to tell herself that I wasn't aware of her sin and that she was doing it just to spite Dan; but now she had to face the recognition that she was definitely betraying her duty.—Finally she said, "All right: you go into the bathroom so you won't see me."

Afterwards, when we were lying on the bed with my arms around her cheap slip—for, in spite of her having made me go away, she had taken off nothing but her dress—she returned to the subject of Dan. He had beaten her up constantly, she said. The day she came out of the hospital—she'd been all tore up having Cecile and they used to bring the young doctors to look at her, and Dan had been there one day when they put up a screen in front of her and made him stay outside— so as soon as he got her home from the hospital, he accused her of flirting with the doctors, and hit her and

knocked her down. She told me this as if simply in
wonder, and even laughed a little at the fantastic behavior of Dan. "He's crazy, I'm tellin yuh," she said.
"He'd take a cat, y'know, and put it up on a wall and
tie a string aroun its neck—and then of course it would
jump and it would hang itself and he'd stand there and
laugh. And he'd get up on the roof and try to jump
and catch hold of the branch of this tree. He couldn't
make it, but he'd go right back up and jump again and
fall down and hurt himself again. And in the winter-
time he'd roll off the roof into the snow. Oh, he's
cuckoo, I'm tellin yuh!"

She gave me this account of herself and Dan in such
a matter-of-fact way that it did not occur to me till
later that it followed a banal melodramatic scheme. It
was like the old "apache" dances, where the man threw
the girl around, or some sob-song of Mistinguett's.

March 3

She had borrowed a dress from Doris, her pal at the
Tango Casino.—"You wouldn't think it cost eighty dollars, would you? That's transparent velvet—the latest
thing." Black velvet skirt and a blouse—brass-patterned
and deep-stained with rose—that matches her bronze-
red hair.—She rips open a package of cigarettes with a
single slash of her thumbnail, splitting it down the
middle.

"I like it—I could be made love to forever." Dan, her
husband, she says, used to just roll on and off, but he
was different with other women. I asked her whether
she had never thought how short a time it lasted at best,
and she answered, Uh-huh, she had. But just as she will
never take a drink if I am looking in her direction, as a
dog will not eat when watched, so she does not like me

to look at her body. Dan had never seen her naked, and had never kissed her except on the mouth; but I finally persuaded her last night to let me take down her slip. She was cute: when I had liberated one little breast and was about to proceed to the other, she said with coquetry: "Only one!"

She is very responsive, though—immediately catches rhythms, is sensitive to any stimulation. She has fine, really beautiful hands. I wanted to kiss them, but she took them away: they were all rough, she said, from doing the housework. It is true that the right hand shows use: the fingers are thicker, less tapering and more strongly developed than those of the left, which are smooth, longish, well-shaped and white. The wrist is also more slender and rounds slowly into the thickness of the forearm. Her left hand is always cleaner. She tells me that she once played the violin.

She had got into the habit, in sleeping with Dan— as a gesture of affection and respect—of holding his penis in her hand. She said she couldn't go to sleep unless she did. She would curl up to fit my back and do this, but in the long run I found it uncomfortable.

March 11

I have put together a kind of biography out of several conversations with her:

She was born "down in the slums—in Essex Street, I guess"—twenty-two years ago. Her father had been "an architect," she thought, but I assumed this was an exaggeration. He had died of t.b., soon after he and her mother had come to the States, and had been buried in Potter's Field. Neither Anna nor her sister could remember him, and they had never seen a photograph of him; all their mother had ever told them was that their father had been very fond of them and had worried about them when he was dying.

Her grandfather in Austria had kept some kind of store and had had one of the finest houses in town, but he had somehow lost all his money. He had thought her mother was homely when his other daughters were so good-looking, and used to spit at her and drive her away from the table; and she had only married Anna's father in order to escape from her father. She hadn't wanted to have any children and had done everything she could to get rid of them, and Anna thought that that was the reason why her sister had turned out to be so terrible. I asked what was the matter with her sister. "She isn't quite bright or something—you'd never look at me again if you could see her. I think it's because my mother used to beat her—she used to hit her on the head something awful."

Her mother had put Anna and her sister, when Anna was two years old, in a charity home up the Hudson. They had stayed there for two years, and it wasn't so nice, you know. The sisters used to spank them every night; and they would line them up every morning to see whether they'd wet their beds, and if they had, they'd put the wet sheets over their heads and make them stand there until they'd dried. In order to get to where they kept the pots you had to walk to the end of a long hallway, and Anna would be afraid to go down there at night and would fall asleep and not go, but her sister would get her up and make her go, so that she wouldn't be punished in the morning. Her mother would come to see them, and Anna would be so upset when it was time for her mother to go that they told her not to come so much. They beat Anna across the knuckles because she didn't put her penny in the collection box for a statue of the Blessed Virgin, and her

mother saw the welts when she came, but she still didn't
take the little girls away. Finally they discovered at the
home that her mother was married again, and they
wouldn't let them stay there any longer.

When her mother first brought her to New York,
she'd never seen the high buildings before, and she was
afraid that they were going to fall on her and insisted
on walking in the middle of the road. She didn't remember this, but her mother had told her about it. Her
mother had married the furrier she worked for, but later
they had gotten divorced. Anna, after her years at the
charity home, had had the impression that her stepfather was nice; but her mother had told her later that
he never had liked the children and had accused her of
spending too much money on them. He had torn up
some photographs that her mother had taken of Anna,
standing with her violin and wearing a white lace dress.

She went to school for the next eight years. But her
stepfather and her mother or her mother and her sister
would have a terrible quarrel every night, and she would
go to sleep crying and praying, and would be thinking
about it so much the next morning in school that she
couldn't keep her mind on her work. Yet she evidently
had the instinct to learn: she writes a very well-formed
hand, never seems to misspell a word, and even knows
how to use commas—though her grammar is the same
as when she talks. The little notes she has occasionally
written me make a curious contrast with the letters that
I have been getting from Imogen in St. Augustine.
Imogen's writing is large and loose, and her spelling is
partly phonetic; her only punctuation is dashes. Anna
is impatient of her mother's bad English when the latter
will say "sinking a sonk" or talk about the clock's "tick-
ling." Anna is so much ashamed of her queer-sounding
Ukrainian name, which the kids used to laugh at in

school, that she will not tell it even to me, and as a child she took her stepfather's name, which he had partly Americanized. She had been proud of marrying Dan because he was an American husband; and among Ukrainians and Russians she got a kick out of being known as Lenihanova.

At home they'd always said that she was dumb and that she was the kind of girl who'd never get married. She tried to oil the sewing machine one day and used mucilage instead of oil and gotten it all stuck up—"You ought to have heard my mother!"; and she didn't want to drink her milk but would save it for the cats in the backyard. Once when she'd been a kid and her mother had put out poison for cockroaches, she had felt so sorry for the roaches that she'd catch them before they got to the poison and put them out in a box on the fire-escape: "Stupid things like that!—everybody used to laugh at me." She had gone to sing once in a Ukrainian choir that one of her aunts was in, but people had poked fun at her and it had made her too shy for her ever to try it again. The only good times she remembers to have had during these years when she was going to school were when her mother bought bicycles for her sister and her, and they used to ride them around. She has mentioned this more than once.

When she was twelve, she quit school and worked at home, and at fourteen she got a job wrapping up packages for the American Biscuit Company—she liked it because she was crazy for work. She used to bring home her pay every week—"I was such a good little girl!" she commented with irony for her innocence—and her mother would allow her fifty cents; till one day she heard her mother ask Fatty whether she could give Anna the money to buy a new pair of shoes. Fatty wasn't

doing any work himself, and that was the first quarrel
with anybody that Anna had ever had. Her mother had
taken up with Fatty before she had been divorced, and
the truth was they had never been married. Anna was
terribly ashamed of it. Her mother had been ostracized
by the family. The furrier that her mother worked for
now came from the same town as her mother, and he
and her aunt and the rest of them had had their Ukrainian clubs and their evenings when they played cards
together, but her mother had had no part in this life:
she would work all day sewing in linings, then she
would go to the movies, then she would come home and
cry. Anna sometimes shows signs of being worried lest
she, too, in her relations with me, may be proving she
is doomed to dishonor.

Anna's attitude toward her mother is a mixture of
love and repulsion. It is as if she had never got over
the frustration of the affection of her childhood. She
says that she has come to the conclusion that poor
people can't love their mothers the way she imagines
other girls do, because their mothers aren't able to look
after them and just knock them around; yet her life at
the present time seems to gravitate about her mother and
she has evidently never ceased to resent the presence of
Fatty. She and the old lady must, besides, be quite
antagonistic types. She says that her mother at fifty is so
strong that she'll live to be a hundred, whereas Anna
has never been strong. Anna used to have fainting-fits
as a girl and her mother would just let her lie there;
and she almost died when she was having Cecile, but she
was sure that if she'd been with her mother alone, her
mother wouldn't have gotten a doctor or done anything.
When she'd first been sick after Dan had knocked her
up (which had happened before they were married),

her mother had thought right away that Fatty had been sleeping with her—"He used to try to, but I wouldn't lettum"—and had called her a "hoor" in Ukrainian—"and that sounds awful in Ukrainian, y'know!"

As I put these details together, they sound like a tale of woe. Yet Anna has never a complaining tone, and if I comfort or sympathize with her, it seems to make her ashamed. "Oh, I'm not so bad off—I'm happy now," she said to me this afternoon. I asked her why she was happy. "Because I'm sure I don't love my husband no more." I said I'd thought she'd known that some time. "No: just in the last coupla months—I never was sure before."

I was later unable to resist asking whether she ever thought nowadays about me in between the times we saw one another. "Yes," she answered: "always."

March 17

Dan has gone home to Syracuse, where his family live, and Anna is feeling freer. He had grown terribly thin, she says. He couldn't have had any place to stay and probably didn't get much to eat. He knew all the people that kept speakeasies and he would go in and bum drinks. He was always drunk, and he was all diseased—she didn't know what was wrong with him. The last time he had come to the house he had told her he wanted her to hustle for-um, can you beat it?—and Fatty had thrown-um out of the house. The next night he had come to the Tango Casino without letting her know he was there, and had watched from the window till he had seen her come out, and then had dropped a paperbag full of water that had gone off right behind her, with a bang like a gangster's pineapple. After that, he had disappeared, but she had soon got a letter from him from Syracuse asking her to send him money. She says, as it were, hopefully, that she doesn't think he'll last long.

March 24

She turned up one night last week in the dress she borrows from Doris, full of excitement over a party she was going to with some of the dance-hall girls. There was a charming Rumanian doctor who had been coming to the Tango Casino lately, and he had invited them to his house on the south side of Stuyvesant Square. I had never seen Anna so cocky or so intent on enjoying herself; and I resented it as we always resent women when we find them exhilarated at the prospect of going somewhere to which we have not been asked. She treated me rather cavalierly, stayed only a very short time, and refused to let me kiss her much for fear of spoiling her make-up and hair. I saw her off with an accent of coldness and was annoyed even more after she left at the thought that I had come to depend on a girl from the Tango Casino who was so easily beglamored by a Rumanian doctor—probably a cheap abortionist.

The next time I saw her, however, she was perfectly natural again: affectionate and gentle and modest. I asked whether it had been fun at the doctor's. "Uh-*uh!*" she replied in the negative. "He was terrible. I couldn't go through with it." And I could never get her to tell me what had happened.

March 26

Her hair falling back from her forehead, reddish—she still wears it bobbed—straining back, with the pillow under her buttocks—her head hanging over the edge

of the couch—deep husky city voice: "Sweetheart!—
Oh, don't!—Oh, yes!"

She gets a sensation, she says, like a thrill that goes
all through her—sometimes it makes her toes curl: "I
want to scratch and bite—I don't know where I am or
anything." The doctor in the hospital had said that she
must be very passionate because the opening of her
womb was so small. Her cousin Sophie didn't care about
it, but she did it every night because her husband liked
it, y'know—he's a truck driver and he does it every night.
"That's why when Dan was in jail he thought I
couldun be faithful to-um—because I was so passionate.
I didun tell you before, but he was in jail for stealing a
car. When he got out, we must have done it for
twenty-four hours—he haddun had any for a year and
a half. The bed creaked so loud we had to put the
mattress on the floor. My mother was in the next room
and I didun want her to hear."

She is now so responsive to my kissing her breasts
that I can make her have a climax in that way.

March 30

It turns out that her husband's family are fairly well-
to-do. His father is a building contractor. They are
churchgoing Irish Catholics. To Anna they represent a
stratum so far above her own that she has always approached them with awe—though they sound from her
accounts of them, if anything, more awful than her
own people.

Dan had taken her to stay with them for a year just
after he and she had been married. He had written
them in advance that she was a great Russian violinist,
also a singer and dancer; and when she had arrived in
Syracuse, they had received her with tremendous en-

thusiasm: somebody had picked her best roses for her, and they wanted her to give a performance. She was so much embarrassed that she couldn't talk, and she got away to her room. Then her birthday came around, and it was another dreadful ordeal: they insisted on giving her presents in spite of her begging them not to. She had never learned how to thank people, make a fuss about things the way they did: "Oh, Aunt Alice, how beautiful!—how sweet you are to give me that!"—her people never said those things. When she saw that they were going to give a party for her, she went out of the house into a blizzard and stood behind a tree till she was so cold that she had to come in.

And presently they began to despise her. It dated from the moment they discovered that she didn't know how to play bridge. She caught them making fun of her one day, and after that she was afraid to say anything at all. They found, when they took her to mass, that she didn't know when to kneel and do things (she was used to the Greek Orthodox service); and when she got pregnant in Syracuse (the first time she had had an abortion), she couldn't stand the incense in the church and had to be taken out. Her father-in-law told her she was a heathen, and that her family weren't fit to keep pigs. They decided she would have to be confirmed: she and Dan had had a civil marriage, and they wanted them to be married in church. They sent her to a priest to learn her catechism. She didn't like him, and was struck by the fact that he would make appeals at mass for money for the church and the poor, and then go off in a Pierce-Arrow in the summer—she wondered that the congregation didn't seem to notice this but always treated him with perfect respect.

Then Dan, who was crazy about circuses, went away and followed one for weeks and left her alone with the family. Her father-in-law and her brother-in-law high-hatted her now when they were sober and made love to her when they were drinking. Her father-in-law used to accuse her of having gotten Dan started drinking, because he didn't want to admit that Dan was no good.

And yet when she had come back to her people, it had taken her a long time to get used to them, because they seemed to talk so loud and be so common that they made her uncomfortable now. Until she had gone to stay with the Lenihans, she had never learned to say "please" or "thank you." Her aunt and her cousin said what an ugly baby she had. Dan came back soon after she did, but he had already been around a week before he let her know, and she found that he had been spying on her to see whether she were being unfaithful to him. At the same time it was soon after this that she realized he didn't really care for her: one night when he had taken her to a speakeasy he had introduced her as just a girl and had told the people there he wasn't married to her but just was living with her. He hadn't cared for Cecile either. He'd go away and leave her with anybody—Anna would give somebody money to buy food for Cecile while she was out, and Dan would get it and spend it on himself, and Cecile wouldn't eat till Anna got back. And he would scare the little girl to death: he had knocked Anna down once in the street when she was holding Cecile in her arms.

She showed me a photograph of Dan: a black little Irishman with squinting eyes. I don't think I had ever quite believed in him.

April 3

——ing in the afternoon, with the shades down and all her clothes on—different from anything else—rank

satisfactory smell like the salt marine tides we come out
of—appetite, on these hurried occasions, increased by
dress, stockings and shoes, which would be dampening
and quite out of key at a regular meeting at night.

April 7

Anna has left the Tango Casino and got a job as a
waitress in Field's restaurant. When Dan had made her
work in the dance-hall, she had been all excited about it,
she had thought it was something like being an actress;
but she had gotten disgusted with it. Dance-halls of
that grade, I have learned, are vulgarly known as "rub
houses"; and Anna, now that she has left, has explained
to me that most of the clientele, whom she always refers
to as "greaseballs," come there to get an orgasm by
pressing against their partners. One of the girls, she told
me with a little embarrassed laugh, had come into the
ladies' room in a mess: she had it all over her dress.
"They're pigs!" Anna said.

But she puts in a pretty heavy week at Field's, has to
be on her feet all the time. They pay her a dollar a day,
which with tips comes to twenty a week. Some of the experienced girls make as much as fifty dollars. She has
never been a waitress before, and she was nervous when
she started in because she knew that she'd be so embarrassed the first time she was given an order! In spite of
all the miseries that have made her so humble, she has a
perfect little independence and does not like the idea
of running back and forth to bring unknown people
food—and I find that I do not like to have her do it.

She leaves Cecile in the morning at a nursery, and
comes back to get her at six. Her mother has left Fatty
and taken a room of her own, because he has started a
speakeasy on their premises; but Anna and Cecile are

still there, spending the nights in the basement. Fatty has girls and everything. "They pull down the blinds at ten o'clock and I don't know what they do." I asked what the girls were like. "They're terrible—what I mean, terrible!" One of them explained to her that she got three dollars a man and six dollars an hour. "She thought I was so foolish to work, yuh know, when I could do the way she did and make my fifteen dollars in a couple of hours every night." She laughed: it only seems to her comic. But it is no place for her and Cecile. Last night they had a big fuss: a man gave one of the girls a five and tried to get back two dollars change, and the girl kicked up a rumpus, and Fatty threw her out.

April 10

Things seem to be getting worse with Anna. She is always worried and tired. Her eyes protrude and her skin is dry and her face looks a little hardened. The girls in Fatty's joint have caused a great scandal in the neighborhood by giving all the men the clap. This morning when Anna was going to work, a woman stopped her in the street and made her a terrible scene under the impression that she was one of the whores. Her mother had told her to move out.

But I found, under her dullish and shabby clothes, the slim and white beauty of her body (she is now willing to have me see her nude) ; and her thirst for love revived as she held her mouth under mine for the pleasure of kiss after kiss or lovingly detained my tongue. The comfortable yet magic feeling of the fusion of intimate moistures when you lie still for a few moments together —human sub-super-human: her darling dark velvety eyes as instinctive in these moments as an animal's, as naked and unthinking as her body.

April 13

A crisis at Fatty's speakeasy. He is in wrong with the local gangsters: "He'd throw them out when they got drunk and noisy—he's strong, yuh know, and he han'les 'em rough." So one night about ten, when Anna and Cecile were asleep, three men came to the door and stuck up the boy who opened it. Fatty heard them say, "Stick 'em up!" and opened the window and called for the police, and then lay down flat on the floor. The room was dark, and when the men came in, they must have thought the big rubber plant was Fatty, because they shot at it three times. The bullets went through the glass and in through the open windows of the woman across the street and could have killed her, and the police told them that they would have to get out of that neighborhood. Cecile had been so scared that for days she had always cried when Anna had had to leave her.

April 18

Anna has just had a telegram from Dan in Syracuse telling her to come on at once: he has a "blood-clot on the brain" and is dying. She has called up to let me know that she is leaving right away tonight.

There are certain kinds of common disasters which, proverbial though they may have become, do not seem to have any actuality as sinister possibilities for ourselves. Railroad accidents and fore-closed mortgages are examples of what I mean. When they happen, we are reluctant to recognize them; and when we have been forced to, we are shocked and indignant. Gonorrhea is one of these. It was with horror that I found out what was wrong with me just as Imogen was coming back.

Ralph had gone to meet her in the South on his way back from his Western trip, so she had stayed away another month. If she had only come back sooner, I thought, I might have been made ashamed of Anna, of my sordid love affair. How wretched the whole thing now seemed!—and I brooded on Anna in bitter doubt. Had she been working in Fatty's joint? Had she been going with other men all the time? There were those parties she had been taken to by Doris, and I had always had doubts of Doris. True, as my doctor told me, she might have caught it long ago from Dan, and have had it and never been aware of it. I had absolutely no evidence that she had ever been unfaithful or that she had knowingly deceived me about her condition. But the snap in my sympathies occurred which sometimes takes place in one's relations with persons of an inferior class —though right up to the moment of the rupture one may have thought oneself on close terms of fellowship —when something has made special demands on one's tolerance, one's trust or one's patience. The instinctive suspicion of people who talk differently and live differently from us, the fear of the poor and the humbly employed, about whom we so often feel guilt—suspended though this doubt and this fear may have been by conscious or unconscious effort—spring suddenly to reassert themselves as we decide that such people are beneath us, just as they are supposed to be, in morals and human dignity as well as in manners and dress. It is so that the liberal, the sympathizer with labor, in the case of some conspicuous strike, will readily conclude, from the moment when a riot takes place on the picket line, that the provocation came from the strikers. I thought about Anna as she had lately looked, of the sour smell of poverty in her clothes, of a way she had of pinching my chin. I looked with disgust on the couch where we had had so much pleasure that winter, and glanced away when I came into the room.

It was almost May now. As I walked out one day along Twelfth Street past a row of brown and balconied houses, I beheld an unhoped-for mirage: a pile of red, blue and yellow flowers on a pushcart that moved toward Fifth Avenue. I say a mirage because the vision was blurred in the bright April morning light and seemed some flowering of the light itself, as this rose and filled the sky from the east and poured down into the streets its firm radiance. I walked behind these simple and de-lightful, these pretty insubstantial colors, as they passed across the Avenue eastward; and the gray of New York today had suddenly become luminous and soft where it had lately been monotonous and chilling, its massiveness gave satisfaction instead of being felt as oppressive. How graciously, after all, old Washington Arch closed the vista and opened a portal beyond! The whole quarter was soaked in a sun that was rich, for all its clarity, with whiteness; and it was as if Greenwich Village had ceased overnight to exist as a separate section, as the particular shell of houses and shops where one had lived, where one had hidden oneself, in the city: it had been flooded by the tide of light as a cave is flooded by water, till the gullies between the great buildings, which in winter had looked narrow and grim, appeared now—with pigeons fluttering on the roofs and odd garments flying from the clotheslines—as much exposed to the freedom of wind and light as if they had been the virgin hills of the island. The immense and dead modern city was gone with the gloom of winter. All that had been cleanly wiped out. I still had my taint, it was true, carried over from the dirt and the dullness; but that, too, would presently be purged away; and in the meantime Imogen was coming. She had written me a four-page letter. From under the sullen mute that my illness had imposed on my spirits, a swift quiver of excitement revived.

III

She greeted me with the Magnolia Gardens of Charleston as they had visited them at just their most glorious, with Williamsburg reconstructed by the Rockefellers, with the sliding panels and suspended beds which Jefferson had installed at Monticello, with her trancelike existence in St. Augustine, so easy, so sun-drenched, so cheap. She seemed to have spent most of her time taking sun-baths with Edna Forbes at some remote part of the shore where no bathers, she said, ever came. I had the feeling that she wanted to make me envious, and that at the same time she was trying to persuade herself that she had enjoyed all this more than she had—that she had come to be conscious in my presence of the deadly second-rateness of her life.

They stayed on in New York into May before going out to their house in the country, and I dined with her alone one night when Ralph had to take to the theater some newspaper editors from the West. I counted it a definite victory that for the first time in her life, she said, she had begged off from entertaining the "visiting firemen," as she and Ralph always called them. I knew from having seen her with such people that she rather enjoyed dazzling and charming them with her queenliness, her graciousness and her clothes; but she now let me understand by touches distinctly scornful that she thought the whole thing rather crass. I expressed for the first time my opinion that the people she saw were

dull. I meant it to apply to her personal friends as well
as to Ralph's business acquaintances; but she answered
that Ralph himself was bored by them, it was hard for
him to pretend to be one of them, that what he really
liked was reading and seeing the world, and that he was
a marvelous traveling companion. "Isn't he rather conventional?" I wickedly asked. She denied it, insisting
that he was wonderful at mixing with all kinds of
people: he had sat around in cabins in Kentucky drinking white mule with the mountaineers. I pressed my advantage: "But in general," I said, "you just go to all the
best hotels; you look up all the points of interest; and
then you buy a few appropriate objects and you take
them back and have them around in Hecate County." I
felt that I had reached her pride, and I went on to
counter her travelogue by regaling her with such favorite incidents of mine as the night at the Ritz in Paris
when Simon Delacy and Charlie Vezin had seized upon
one of the *garçons,* declaring that they had always
wanted to find out what was inside a waiter; the time at
the bull ring in Madrid when we had all taken a turn
with the bull, and Willie Gifford, who had not
jumped aside in time, had grasped the animal literally
by the horns, quickly leapt up on his head and ridden
around the ring sitting astride his neck, to the delirious
applause of the audience; and my romantic adventure in
New Orleans with the masked lady at the Mardi Gras
who had turned out to be a beautiful quadroon—at least
that had always been my conviction. I also told her that
she knew nothing about the underworld, and she answered that she couldn't imagine that I knew anything
about it either. "I *have* had some firsthand experience of
gangster life; believe it or not," I said.

After dinner, I picked up a victoria at the Plaza and
took her for a drive to the Park. It was mid-May, a

warm afternoon had brought a first gummy touch of summer; but the evening had cleared like cool water: it was neither too hot nor too cold; and my enchantment with Imogen of the summer before came to meet me like a rapturous dream that one knows one has somehow deserved.

"I like this rich horsy smell," I said, as we started out. "It reminds me of old livery stables the way they used to smell in my childhood." "Yes: I like the smell of horses," she answered—and added after a moment: "My father had a lot of horses." She had never told me much about her father: he and her mother had separated, she said, and she had come to New York with her mother when she was still in her early teens. I had felt that there was something painful and had never asked her further about it, but now I ventured to probe it a little: "Was that in Minnesota?" I asked. "Yes," she said, and, after another brief pause, went on: "My father had a big place out there." We passed a young hatless girl, walking her horse back from a ride. I had often ridden alone in Hecate County, and I saw Imogen in breeches beside me. "I used to ride but I don't any more," she said. I felt now, as I had felt with her on occasions before, that I had run into some kind of obstacle, as to which it was hard to tell whether it represented a secret or a simple reluctance.

But the drinks we had had and the privacy and ease of lying back, all tucked in, in the victoria released this time a burst of frankness. "I don't like my father," she said. "Is he alive still?" "Yes. He still lives in Minnesota, but I haven't seen him since I was seventeen. He treated my mother terribly—and he treated me terribly, too." "You must have a good deal of his Irish, though." "Yes: I have plenty of Irish.—He was a very handsome man. He'd been a great athlete in Ireland—he was a

famous football player. He was a war hero, too—he was
in the Sudan, and he got all kinds of decorations." "I
thought you must come of heroic stock—that explains
a good deal about you." "He was no good after he
came back from the war, though. He'd been spoiled by
all the applause he'd had—and he didn't know how to
be anything but a champion, and he wasn't able to settle
down to lead any ordinary life. He came to America
expecting to do great things as he'd always done before
—and he married my mother, who was a beauty—but he
didn't have any experience of business or any of the
things people do in American cities, and so he ended
up in the country with a farm—because he came from
the country. But he hadn't liked farming at home, and
he could never put his heart into it when he tried to be
a farmer. He never could make it go, and then he got to
drinking and—did horrible things to my mother. My
mother was a patrician, you see. Her father was a
Kommerseråd in Sweden, but he lost all his money, and
she came over to America and worked as a governess.
She didn't like the other Swedes in Minnesota, because
they were lower-class. She only had a few Swedish
friends—and the evenings when they came to see us, my
mother and they used to carry out all the aristocratic
Swedish drinking customs. You can't drink unless you
ask somebody to drink with you, and the hostess invites
everybody to drink in turn—and the gentlemen, when
they lower their glasses, are supposed to hold them for
a moment just opposite the third button of their uni-
forms or where the third button would be, and they
look solemnly at the man that they're drinking with
before they put them down on the table. But my father
used to spoil it by getting drunk beforehand and drinking freely whenever he felt like it." She seemed humorous about it, and I laughed. "It wasn't funny, though:

I used to cry because I knew how my mother felt, and I thought that it was so disreputable for Daddy not to drink in the Swedish way." "What happened to your father afterwards?" "He's still out there. I don't know what he's doing. I haven't seen him since just after I married. I don't want to talk about him: he was bad—he was bad to my mother and me. Mother left him and came to New York and supported herself and me by giving piano lessons."

She changed the subject: "That looks like a mountain range, doesn't it?" As the sun beyond the Hudson burned red, the wall of flat-surfaced buildings toward the south was losing its prosaic whites and yellows and taking on a grayness of shadow that made them seem almost majestic. Along the paths, dark pressed asphalt though they were, the spring greenery, still light and faint, touched the Park with a pleasant vagueness. I had a feeling of voyage and adventure as we looked up toward the varying skyline and I heard about the drinking customs of Sweden. It was a pity that there was no place in New York where one could get out of sight of those buildings; and we talked about Europe, half transported ourselves to the Wienerwald and the Bois de Boulogne, for there were lovers under trees and on benches as there are in every park in the world. I made love to Imogen with tenderness and grace: I wrapped up her legs more tightly as the air grew chilly and dim, and I took off her hat and kissed her while the decrepit but top-hatted driver walked his horse in the rock-walled cut. It was rather a wide-brimmed hat that she had worn tilted over one eye; and now, when I bent toward her face, she would turn her head in toward my shoulder, and when I had kissed her, would turn it away—so that she took on for me a new personality: she was tonight that old type of American girl, laughing-eyed,

healthy and frank, that had stood for the ideal in my
boyhood. It was curious how quickly the exotic impression produced by her account of her parents had been
transformed into something associated with ice-cream
sodas and sailor hats. The memories she had been telling me of her girlhood had stirred me to try to imagine
what she must have been like at that time, and it was as
if she had taken my cues to play up to a rôle I projected.

If only we had known each other earlier," I said as
we came out from the cut, after some moments of abor-
tive silence and with our hands still clasped under the
carriage robe. "You know you're the only woman that
I've ever really wanted to marry!" She sighed: "It might
have been nice." "You *know* it would have been wonderful, don't you?" She looked up at me from under
her shaded lids that were languorous from my kisses, and
gave me an inebriating love-bemused and longing-
solemn look; then she dropped her eyes again: "Sometimes I think it would have been—yes." "I'm still just
as much obsessed by you," I said. Her answer was a
quiet avowal such as I had never won from her before:
"I'm glad you're going to be in the country this summer. My life *is* rather dull in some ways. I thought about
you a lot in Florida. I wished we had been together
there." I squeezed her hand and held it more firmly, and
her strong fingers pressed mine hard, as if witnessing
some steadfast pledge that had not really been ex-
changed.

We lay back with our feet on the opposite seat and
gazed up at the buildings to the west which were lifting
above us now. "That looks like Notre-Dame, doesn't
it?"—she nodded toward a double-towered apartment
house. "I wish it were," I replied—"and I wish this
were a boat on the Seine. To tell the truth, it *is* something like a gondola." "It would be fun to be with you

in Venice!" she said. "You'd tell me all about the pictures,"—and she left her lips half-open. I felt that she
had quite succumbed, that I had only to put out my
hand; and I was filled with that happiness of the dream
that came to me because it was deserved. "Shall we live
in a big pink *palazzo?*" I said. "They're not very expensive, you know," she answered. "I'd like really to study
Venice seriously,"—I must curb myself, I thought, and
keep things straight. "I'd like to go into its commercial
history and find out how Venetian painting grew up
and declined with Venetian trade." "You'd read me
Byron and Browning," she said, with an appeal to my
dearness that I couldn't resist. Yes: of course we should
read Byron and Browning.

And this fantasy of our having met earlier and married and lived together slipped its tendrils into both our
minds and overgrew them like an unpruned creeper. We
talked about it together so often, we imagined it with
so much emotion and endowed it with such vivid detail,
that, for me and, I believe, for her, it seemed almost to
substitute itself for our real routine life of the summer.

I had been able to sublet my apartment, and I rented
again my old house with its half-romantic isolation. My
disease, though it did not become dangerous, was a
peculiarly tenacious case. My regimen made it impossible
for me to drink, to make love or to eat rich food—so
that there was nothing for me to do but to work at my
book with what the French call *un zèle acharné*.

Nothing to do except this and to dream about a destiny with Imogen. And I found myself lifted to a pure
exaltation of proud and devoted passion—a passion such
as I had not imagined even in adolescence. It was always
as a wife that I saw her now: I did not want any longer
to seduce her. I felt shame for the cold-blooded con-

cupiscence with which I had started my siege and could imagine no other relation but an open and wholehearted union.

The new situation, of course, involved a fundamental paradox. Though she was always right there within reach, though she often talked the language of love, I could not—both because of my malady and because of my moral position—really have her by putting out my hand, as I had felt I could do in the Park. I idealized her now as a wife; but she was actually the wife of Ralph Loomis; and if she had been unfaithful to Ralph, she would no longer have been the ideal wife. I was forced to admire her for qualities which stood between her and me, and kept me without hope in proportion as I worthily appreciated her virtues. Since the actual evidence of these qualities was the beautiful job she was doing for Ralph, I was obliged to approve of Ralph's household, and even to approve of Ralph—for did not Ralph and I have in common that we were both the adorers of Imogen and that we both adored her in her role of wife? I found that I was no longer attempting to drive a wedge between them. His part was to be the husband, mine to be merely the friend; but otherwise we seemed almost identical in our deference and submission to Imogen, in our contentment as we basked in the beatitude she shed.

Many evenings of talking, while they drank and I didn't, I spent with the Loomises that summer—I could usually outrange them about Europe, though Ralph had seen more of the United States; many games of croquet I played with them—I got to be a dead shot and could beat them; many picnics we had by the river—Ralph was better than I with the beefsteaks, but I used to supply vintage wines; many visiting friends of the summer did we invite one another to help entertain, and I scored with the brilliance and distinction of mine. I even became friendly with Edna Forbes—whom I had always hitherto found plain fare—because she adored Imogen, too. She was a tall, rather well-dressed girl, who never seemed quite to have ignited. She was ten or twelve years out of college, but she had carried along through her thirties all the mannerisms and habits of a college girl. She was always on good terms with men, with whom she never felt a moment's self-consciousness, because they never really interested her as men, nor did she interest them as a woman; but for Imogen she showed the enthusiasm of a permanent collegiate "crush." She was a pleasant-faced blue-eyed blonde; but if she was pretty, it was only to Imogen's profit: to be Imogen's good-looking, well-tailored companion, who would always do her perfect credit but never eclipse or compete with her; who would always, in fact, set her off. Edna laughed a lot good-naturedly when you talked to her, and—if I had been doing any drinking when we met—I had often found it easy to forget her and to think about something else, while she was anwering the questions I asked. But now I did not have this resource, and, after a phase of mild exasperation when I listened to the things she said, I began to probe her, stimulate her, work up conversations with her, and I had finally reached the point of telling Imogen that I thought she was awfully bright and that her comments on people were penetrating. These bright comments, I realized, were just the kind of thing that Edna and Imogen talked: they gossiped about the people they knew like college girls discussing their classmates.

Edna claimed certain days of Imogen's, and I had rather resented this at first; but I presently came to feel that Edna's claims did not conflict with mine, so I ceased to be jealous of her. Edna was not jealous of me because it seemed to her obviously right that people should admire Imogen. She accepted me as a personage at Imogen's court, and she never feared any evil, because she knew that my relations with the sovereign were as innocent as her own. One could hardly imagine even that Imogen's relations with her husband could involve, to Edna's mind, any intimacy superior to her own. She felt assured of an inside track in being able to talk over with her mistress Ralph and me both, and to hear her say things about us that she would not have said to ourselves or to either about the other. I, on my side, was braced by knowledge that Imogen dreamed much of a life she would prefer to be living with me if she had met me before she met Ralph, and I believed, though I may not have been right, that Edna did not figure in this fantasy. As for Ralph, he was, after all, married to her and knew that he could rely on her loyalty. So everyone had grounds for satisfaction.

Imogen, who had brought this about, kept the whole situation in balance, and she succeeded in creating the double illusion of being married to me in our common dream at the same time that she faithfully presided over Ralph Loomis's bed and board. I allowed her to assume —what else could I do?—that I had given up drinking to finish my book, and that I had given up trying to be her lover out of a fine consideration for her and Ralph; and there were moments, since my consciousness shrank from the truth, when I almost believed this myself: at least it was true that my illness, by imposing upon me a strict discipline, had cleared the path for my aspirations. And for me the fresh visions of boyhood that are later blurred by sensual experience and cracked in imperfect relationships, those visions that I supposed I had discredited and long ago left behind, had at last become identified with a being who, though still beyond my

grasp, did possess an objective reality. The first little girl
that one handles in the attic or under the dock may half
destroy the hair-ribbons of feminine pomp that one has
stared at from the back-seats of school; and the "pet-
ting" that prevailed at the end of the war among the
young people of my generation had tended to prevent
us from idealizing and marrying as soon as we were
out of college—as the chaster generation before us had
done—our first favorites among our well-brought-up
prom partners. But by the time you had had a good
share of the liberated love-making of the twenties,
which had gradually lost part of its interest by becoming a mere indoor sport; when you had lived through
one of its great heartstring-twisting, nerve-consuming,
miserable-making passions that had compelled you to
dash about planlessly from one country in Europe to another, that had sometimes won you passages of pre-
carious romance in the hotels and bars of strange cities
which seemed sets for the scenes of a ballet, and had
sometimes subjected you to torments which had driven
you to disreputable drinking with people you could not
tolerate sober—when you had finally waked up one
afternoon with bruises of which you could not remember the cause, with a drink-swollen double hotel bill and
a depleted book of traveler's checks, you had come to
feel a treacherous cheapness in the lively beloved object
who had just hurtled off to Vienna with a second-rate
newspaperman and you had begun to remember a world
in which the women made the basis of the family, gave
their value to the proprieties and conventions, and let
the men do most of the drinking. And now, finally, I
had known through Imogen the possibility of the perfect
partner, of the two indivisible people who spend their
whole lives as one, admiring and understanding and
caring for one another, longing for one another in ab-

sence with an ache that is also exultant in its sureness
of eventual reunion, and coming together in the brimming fulfillment of tenderness, of fondness, of passion,
of the unique need for one another—I had known, in
fact, the possibility of all that had once been meant by
"love."

For my time the word "love" had meant heartbreak,
the love that faded out or that one had to lose. To look
for "happiness" through love seemed naïve. But now I
even found myself seeing Imogen as the splendid embodiment of a type that I had not supposed I cared for
but for which an undeveloped desire must always have
been buried in the subsoil of my mind: the type of the
American beauty. This ideal, which had figured in my
childhood, in the pictures in magazines, as challenging
and piquant but chaste, had bloomed later into something more sensual, with arched eyebrows and kiss-
provoking lips, with deep eyes which, though still eyes
of good-fellowship, could be imagined as eyes of passion, and when I returned to my solitary house, so
obviously the house of a bachelor, my somber Cézannes
and Grecos, my papers and books on the couch, I returned to a projection of Imogen, in that tan jersey
that swelled with her breasts and those brown shoes
that laced over her ankles—a current style of clothes for
the country which in reality she never quite wore, and
with those marvelous hypnotic brown eyes that would
have glowed for me always at home as they had glowed
for me an hour that afternoon at somebody's cocktail
party. On my trips to see the doctor in New York, it
was Imogen in a smart city costume that I saw myself
meeting for dinner and telling my adventures with
paintings while she listened with a sympathy and interest which, in reality, her impulse to talk of her own
doings had always—because, as I told myself, our lives

had never actually merged—prevented her from quite showing. I was hardly even embarrassed when I found myself becoming infatuated with a flaming cigarette advertizement on the back-cover of a magazine: a lovely girl, photographed from life, with teasing and sincere brown eyes, posing against the background of a golden tobacco leaf and dressed in a clarion red that seemed a blast of blood-shaking emotion. I would leave the magazine on a table, so that my glance could leap casually to it whenever I came into the room.

This phantasm of the beauty of Imogen became thus a kind of denizen of my consciousness who dwelt there and who was yet not a part of me, with whom any contact was always unreal, like an illusion I had once seen in a night club, where one looked into a glass tank of water, and there seemed to be a pretty naked girl sitting on the bottom of the tank and diminished to the tininess of a naiad, who from time to time lifted her eyes and pretended to be smiling at the spectators, though one knew that she was somewhere else, that what one saw was but a reflection in a mirror and that she did not really see you as she smiled. But my bright refracted vision of Imogen would not even keep its physical outlines as a practicable human woman: the being of my imagination would identify itself, for example, with the big round crystals of a necklace that Imogen had one day worn, and her very personality—her shining eyes and the whiteness of her skin contributed to this—would seem to have become something crystalline, something ornamental, perfect and clear, incapable of being possessed; or a red peasant blouse that brought out her gold coils with an embroidery of gold-scrolling leaves, incarnadined my reveries all day with a deep stain of coloration that, irrelevant, formless and female, would smear my more coherent thoughts, yet, when I tried to recompose her image, melt away and slip from my mind.

This presence that was always with me and always assuming new forms was bound up with a real kind of poetry she had that was not merely her bodily beauty and that she rarely quite expressed in speech, but that seemed to be hanging about her without one's ever being able to put one's hand on it, or to come up from some deep source inside her that one was unable to tap at will. Imogen could sometimes perceive things or stimulate me to perceive things in a way that made me feel she had a magic, and this magic was all the more enchanting as well as all the more uncanny for the fact that rocket-clusters of color would sometimes take their flight from conversations that had otherwise been flatly banal; so that I came to disregard the banality and only to be conscious of the poetry, which haunted me now like a spirit, a spirit that spoke for me, too, a spirit of our combined sensibility. I would wake, after a nap in the late afternoon, just as the sunlight was fading to darkness, amid the waving of the leafage, abundant but vague, that shaded my house so darkly, hearing the sounds of a far locomotive and the cars humming by on the road beyond—and half fancy I could turn toward her on the bed here, where she, too, had lain down in the heat, and have her share with me all that world of the countryside, so voluptuous, so dulled and content, the eve of July and deep summer; or I would follow on horseback little blind-alley roads that twined among our inlets from the sea, where the thin grassy tongues of land ran out into the still reedy water, where a white summer cottage with a small smooth lawn was all but islanded in the smooth shallow blue, and where, dimmed by the distance, a gas tank loomed drum-shaped and shone with an aluminum luster that we agreed made it seem quite precious—I would stand and sniff-in the rank marsh and watch the water-birds that flew flappingly and dangled their legs, and I would see ourselves living in that cottage, where we had just bought the children a croquet set and were playing an hilarious game trying not to drive the balls into the water; or, when one of our bright Sundays had been spoiled by a gray remote rainstorm that threatened all day so that we had to give up our picnic, and it had grown at last too dark to read, and I had taken up the awnings and lain down for a nap as I heard the rain suddenly falling, I would rouse to an evening so lucid that we seemed, as she said, to be placed in the hollow of a great green-and-yellow melon—I opened the window, and we stood by it and felt on our sweaty cheeks the delicious fresh ice-cold air, and afterwards we went into the garden, where the rosebushes held drops of rain and the spare towering locust trees were stirring their fronds in a little wind, and we breathed the rich August air that had a smell, as we said, like chestnuts, and looked up at the white full moon, so perfect, so cool and so new, and at the smoke-gray clouds in the west that moved against a darker ash-gray—all those delicate things that I could not paint, that would be hidden in my unexpressed consciousness and lost with the drift of experience, if it were not, if it would not be for Imogen; or I would amble on my horse in September through the sideroads between big estates, the high hedges and wattled fences and low walls and well-valeted trees, traversing the carpet-like shade and the deep golden strips of the autumn sun, and remember the summers we had spent, consuming them all to the full, wasting neither sun nor rain, night nor day, monotony nor entertainment, beyond the long voyages, in foreign lands.

These summers when we went to Europe had on

Imogen a special hold: the actual summer in Hecate County, which I could sometimes imagine she was spending with me, she was spending, after all, with Ralph. She would see us in India, in Switzerland, on the Great Barrier Reef in Australia—anywhere she had just happened to hear of; and there were times when I could tempt her to dare to pretend that, instead of being properly married, we had finally run away together and that people mustn't know who we were.

But at last there came a summer that we spent—drinking dreadful martinis at a roadhouse—in a castle in the south of Ireland. I suddenly found myself cloyed with this idyl of gay Irish hunting and rosy-cheeked old Irish servants, and I insisted that the things she was having us do were far too expensive for us, that my income was very much smaller than Ralph's, and that my work involved arduous researches and years of modest living, even hardship. She took the new cue at once and shifted with equal enthusiasm to a little old house on Cape Cod, where I should write by the light of an oil lamp and she would organize my notes and type my manuscript, while the wind roared and pounded outside: "I'd work my hands to the bone for you!" she said, and this profession was no less sincere than any other of the things she had projected, but it struck for me a bad note of bathos: I saw myself getting muzzy over Prohibition cocktails, which had been served in depressing teacups, amid the hunting prints of the Hecate County roadhouse—these had suggested the south of Ireland dream-fugue—talking idiotic might-have-beens with the wife of an advertizing man, a woman I had been working on a year without making the slightest headway.

"Look, Imogen," I said abruptly,—"a debauch of the imagination is just as bad as any other kind of debauch —in fact, it's a good deal worse because the experience you get out of it isn't real. If you and I are going to run away together, we ought to do it and stop spinning these fairy tales!" I was all the more exasperated, of course, because actually I should not, at the moment, have been able to do anything about Imogen even if she had allowed me to carry her off.

"You know that we can't run away," she said, speaking softly but firmly and dropping her eyes.

"Then let's not talk all this rubbish," I answered. "I want you, but I want you not in a castle in Ireland that we might have gone to live in if things had been different—and that I loathe the idea of, anyway. I want you right here and now!" But I caught myself up and defined "here and now" in a way that would leave me a margin: "I want you this autumn—when we get to town!"

"I've told you," she retorted, "that if you feel like that, you'd better not see me any more." This was the move that she always made and that was supposed to block my progress.

"I'm sorry to be so irritable,"—I struck a candid and earnest note. "But the whole thing's been wearing me down!"

"It's been hard on me, too," she said, subsiding into her little-girl voice. "I'm very unhappy sometimes."

"Well, there's only one way to cure that," I declared, paying the check with decision. "I'll see you in town in the autumn!—Is that a pact?" I demanded.

"I don't promise," she said. But she blushed, and I felt I had a chance to dislodge her.

I was almost afraid at this point that Imogen had been putting a spell on me. I had not been able to get rid of my disease, and the doctor seemed puzzled and worried. Could it be possible that some queer acquies-

cence in the role she was attempting to impose on me
had been a factor in preventing my recovery? I demanded more drastic treatment; and the doctor, after a
brief and frank lecture on the risks of using silver
nitrate, cured me with it overnight. The balance of
forces was broken; again I could entertain real hopes.

The Loomises by this time—it was late in September
—had gone to town for the winter. They were living
in the Fifties in a West Side hotel—a place that was
just rococo enough and gay enough to please people
from Scarsdale and Larchmont. Ralph Loomis had great
quantities of "due bills" from the companies whose
advertizing he placed, and he and Imogen were able to
spend months using them up in the various hotels. They
apologized for this one, when I called on them, by
laughing about it a good deal. It seemed that one of its
advertized attractions was a breakfast in a cardboard
container that was poked in at you every morning
through a kind of slot in the door. They said it was a
wretched little breakfast and made you feel that you
had been put in prison.

I found with them on this occasion a small elderly
brown-faced man, an old friend of theirs, they said,
who was staying at the same hotel. The first thing I
learned about him was that the sight of the put-up breakfast had disgusted him so that morning that he had
hurled it down the hall after the waiter. Imogen was
delighted at this, and rather overdid telling about it;
and, as the conversation went on, I gathered that the
visitor was rich, and that he had originally come from
Columbus but lived on a ranch in Montana. I immediately became aware that he hugely admired Imogen
and that he had with her some special relationship.

She had been ill—one of a series of illnesses which
obliged her to go to bed for days, though she would

never tell me what was the matter; and the visitor had brought her a bottle of Moët & Chandon champagne, which we drank sitting around the bedroom. She was flushed with the champagne and attention, and she looked very lovely in a pink negligée and with mules of red and gold. Her big eyelids drooped and lifted too beautifully, and when she laughed, she would throw out from under them great beams of gratification toward the visitor from the West. It was *he* who was the hero of the afternoon, and I resented him with special rancor. It turned out that he had known her for years and that he always came to see them in New York. Imogen and Edna Forbes had once spent a summer on his ranch at a time when her health had been bad, and it had done Imogen a lot of good. He was urging her to come again: "Blackie still talks about you. He always asks me if I've seen you when I come to New York." Imogen explained to me that Blackie was the rancher's head man, a great card—a "splendid character" and a "real old-fashioned cowboy." They repeated witty things he had said, the rancher chuckling, Imogen roaring.

"I'n' she wonderful! I'n' she marvelous!" said the visitor, turning to me with the utmost geniality, when Ralph, who had had a phone call, had gone out into the other room. "She's a regular goshdarned Helen of Troy—and who wouldn't like to steal her?" "I can't be stolen, though," said Imogen. "Let me steal you both and take you back to Montana for a month!" "Ralph can't get away," said Imogen. I was relieved that she couldn't go, but the whole thing was making me uncomfortable. Not only because it wasn't possible for me to compete with the ranch and the champagne in their power to exhilarate Imogen, but also because, since his interest in her was evidently the same as mine, it was discouraging for me to see him so firmly and promptly curbed: it brought home to me my own situation. I was already aware that I had not been the first to discover the wonder of Imogen. There had been another friend of theirs, an architect, who, Imogen told me, had "claimed" to be in love with her and who had designed their house in the country and painted a dreadful mural that covered all one end of the dining room and included a portrait of Imogen riding a white horse. Later he had developed t.b. and gone to live in Santa Fe; and I had always taken it for granted that he must have been absurdly unworthy of her. But now suddenly I seemed to see that the dude rancher and the architect and I were all in the same boat. Should I, too, grow middle-aged hopelessly admiring Imogen, taking her out when her husband was busy—as it appeared that her friend from the West might perhaps have the privilege of doing if she were well enough before he left—and being told that she could not be stolen? Was it simply that the more you admired her, the more her eyes would beam?

Ralph presently returned from the telephone, and we talked about the Chicago gangsters. Ralph and the visitor both had done a good deal of business in Chicago and had had some experience with them. Ralph, it seemed, had even known Jack Dilling, a Chicago newspaper reporter, who had more or less worked with the gangsters and who had just been murdered that fall. "He didn't like me," said Ralph, "because I was handling Ottawa Club ginger ale, and he had an interest in a local company that made both ginger ale and beer. It was all part of the underworld tie-up. At first he tried to bribe me to double-cross my account—he offered me a rake-off from the beer racket. And then—when I brushed him off—he tried to intimidate me."

"Tell them how you went to dinner!"—Imogen's

eyes were now beaming for Ralph. "What kind of fellow was he?" I asked. "He was tall and thin and pasty
—and he had sort of colorless eyes that were weak but
rather uneasy-looking. He always wore a big fur-lined
coat that the gangsters had undoubtedly given him."
"Tell them about the muskrats!" Imogen eagerly urged
him. "Well, the way he tried to threaten me was amusing. He asked me to dinner and I went—this was before
he had let me see that he was acting as an agent for
the beer racket. He lived in an apartment that was what
you might expect of a fairly well-paid reporter, but
there were a few magnificent items that gave the gangster touch: a big gilt Louis XIV victrola, for example.
Dilling lay on the couch, with his coat off and his collar
open, and ordered his wife to do things. She was a
pretty little blonde who would have been perfectly all
right as the wife of a newspaperman, and was finding it,
I thought, a certain amount of a strain to live up to the
role of gunman's moll. But she was trying to do her
best by putting on as much make-up as a rhumba dancer
at Colosimo's. She just sat around and said nothing—I
tried to get her to talk, but she wouldn't: Jack evidently
had her stunned."—I remembered how Anna had told
me that, when she had first gone to work at the Tango
Casino, Dan had made her "plaster her face all up" with
two red spots in the middle of her cheeks. I reassured
myself by remembering that I, too—as I had said to
Imogen—knew something of the sinister race who in
that period so fascinated the public. "Tell them about
the dog!" said Imogen. "Well, he had a horrible little
Boston bull, one of these dogs with pink eyes that
bounces around, and he told me with obvious pride that
it had been on trial a couple of times for biting people.
They were people that, so far as he could see, he said, it
had a perfect right to bite."—"He wanted the dog to

be a gangster, too!" said Imogen.—"Well, he began by
going on about what wonderful fellows the Italian gangsters were—'They're just like you and me,' he said.
'And they're the most generous and hospitable people!'
He told me how he'd had Christmas dinner at the home
of Rudy the Rat or somebody, who had just slaughtered
three of his rivals in a garage, and how lovable the old
grandmother was, and how proud Rudy was of his children, and how the oldest boy played Verdi on the piano,
and what a good-looking brunette his wife was. He said
that Rudy had shot at her the week before, 'but she knew
how to take it,' he said. 'She's crazy about him.' " We
laughed. "He was just like a kid," Ralph went on,
"that's been reading dime novels or pirate stories and
wants to play he's a big hold-up man or a pirate."—
Could my interest in Anna, I wondered, have had an
element of the same sort of thing?—the contemptible
vicarious excitement of feeling oneself in touch with the
underworld and hearing about it at first-hand. "Well,
when he saw that that didn't go over with me—he'd
already made his little suggestion about giving me a cut
on the beer-needling profits—he resorted to terroristic
methods. He told me what had happened to the people
who had refused to play ball with the bootleggers. One
had been found thrown out of a car, one had had the
top of his head blown off, and so forth. 'He never knows
when it's going to strike or where it's going to strike,'
he said. 'If the boys had you down as a son-of-a-bitch,
you might be sitting here drinking cocktails and you
might never get out of this house alive.' Then his wife
came in from the kitchen—she'd been getting the dinner
herself—and asked Jack how to cook the muskrats. He
asked me in rather a menacing manner whether I'd ever
eaten muskrat. He said that a trapper in Canada, who
helped smuggle liquor over the line, had sent them

down to Mike the Punk or somebody, and that Mike
had wanted him to have some and had sent him a whole
barrel of them. 'He's the most generous guy in the
world!' he said. He took me out to the kitchen to see
them. He evidently hoped I'd be horrified by them—
and they did look pretty disgusting: they were packed
in a barrel full of ice, and they looked like the corpses
of skinned cats with the heads and tails and paws cut
off. Well, all Jack knew about it was that you boiled
them, so his wife put them into a big pot of water, and
we waited about an hour. We started on a bottle of
Canadian whisky, which had been sent as a present with
the muskrats—I think mixing the drinks was a part of
his attempt to get me down and make me more malle-
able. He kept on talking about gangster murders.
Finally, we attacked the muskrats. I think the truth was
that they'd cooked them so long because they really
didn't want to eat them—it turned out in the course of
the dinner that Jack had never had them before. But
even so they weren't cooked enough and were still
rather raw in spots. Mrs. Dilling wanted to put them
back, but I accepted the challenge offered, and I insisted on flying at mine and devouring it down to the
bone."—We asked what it had tasted like: "Fishy—
fishy and rank—and it was covered with a thick layer
of fat, which made it extremely messy; but I washed it
down with the dago wine—and then I demanded another muskrat. I'd noticed that Jack had lost interest
when he discovered that his own was bloody—he'd sent
it back to be boiled some more; so I tore at my second
muskrat in a way that was absolutely ogreish. I abandoned the knife and fork, and picked it up with my
fingers and gnawed it the way the muskrat himself
would have eaten a fish—getting the fat all over my
hands and face. In the meantime, I talked scornfully

but humorously about how filthy politics were in Chicago. Jack only picked at his muskrat, and finally he pulled off a leg that was a little raw at the joint and that he attempted to eat like a drumstick—and at this point he quietly disappeared and didn't come back for some time, while Mrs. Dilling and I had a very pleasant conversation about our favorite movie stars. Presently Jack reappeared, looking green around the gills. He said that the Scotch had been doctored—that some son-of-a-bitch had put alcohol in it.—So that was the late Jack Dilling, who thought it was a lot of fun when his pals used to line people up in a garage and fill them full of holes with a machine gun. I don't think anybody needs to shed any tears over him."

His story had all been told in a drawling and easy manner that seemed only casually caustic—the manner that was fashionable for the college men of the vintage of just after the war; but the effect on me was the opposite of that of his story about the badger hoax. I had already a sense of guilt—which was not any the less uncomfortable because I could never be sure whether I felt guilty at having tried to seduce Imogen or at not having succeeded in seducing her—and I had felt, as the story continued, that it somehow applied to me. I asked myself whether Imogen had not told him about my boasting of knowing the underworld; and I had even had the fancy that his description of Dilling had been meant as a crack at me. I, too, was tall and thin, and I had grown rather pale in my forest from the relative lack of exercise imposed by the demands of my cure; I, too, had been stained by that foulness.

But now I was free to retrieve myself—to be clean and sincere again, to assume the full moral stature to which I had never risen. It was unthinkable to go on living in that lazy and half-baked way. If I were not going to break with Imogen, I must make her divorce Ralph and marry me.

But two things I had first to accomplish: I must establish the ascendancy over Imogen which would be possible only after I had slept with her, and I must manage a bigger income. I decided to take action at once, and I persuaded an old friend of mine from college, a curator at the Metropolitan Museum, to give me a job in the painting department. I did not get any very great pay, but it was enough to make all the difference for me as between uptown New York and Twelfth Street. I took an apartment on Madison Avenue in the respectable lower East Seventies, within easy reach of the places where Imogen stayed during the winter. It was larger than my rooms downtown—it had a living room, a bedroom and a kitchen; and I bought for it a chair and a couch of that simplified "functional" kind which was at that time coming into vogue—very comfortable, with light-green cushions and low wide arms that drinks could be set on; a new cocktail shaker, nickel and glass, that did not leak when you shook it, like my old one; a formidable nickel-cased syphon that charged its own soda water; and new aprons for my colored maid, whom I had induced to come with me to the city. It was a walk-up on the second floor, just above a conservative florist's; and my new residence and work in that section of town—the comparative whiteness of the streets and the straightness and space of their vistas, the restaurants, so often empty, that had names like Tally-Ho and Cloverbrook, the trim ladies walking dachshunds and Scotties, the big green Fifth Avenue buses, the marbles of the Metropolitan and its hollow resounding halls, the slow careful handling of pictures and the silent consultation of scholarly works, the unassertive sober air with which one walked past the guards—all this seemed to lift me to a different plane from the one I had lived on in Twelfth Street. I also sold an article on Renoir to one of those smart fashion magazines that run photographs of modern paintings and of art treasures brought to this country, and I bought a black derby and a new dark coat.

I directed my efforts now, without showing any special ardor, to getting Imogen to come to lunch with me. I wanted to show her my new apartment. And I finally succeeded in this. She arrived twenty minutes late, and, avoiding the trap of the couch, entrenched herself in the modern armchair. But she drank two of my streamlined cocktails. She had just been to the Renoir show and determinedly talked about it. She was excited, and, under pressure of the excitement, she had one of her moments of eloquence. "They just melt on your eyes," she said. "They're what the French call *fondants*. They're all typical Frenchwomen just meant for sex—they marry and become mothers and just melt up in family life!" "You don't think that's the thing for a woman to do?" "A woman can be so much more. She shouldn't dissolve her personality in other people." "It's only by dissolving herself," I smilingly but sententiously replied, "that a woman can find her identity."

I was afraid that my perfect little lunch was almost entirely lost on her. She did not finish the avocado salad, which I had had because I thought she liked them, and she hardly touched the cream cheese and Bar-le-Duc. But I could see that she was dressing a new role for me: she had discarded her old romantic costuming and now appeared as a woman of the world. Her face was smooth and fresh from a "facial," and her cheekbones seemed thrown into relief so that she looked like Marlene Dietrich. "I've had my hair done a new way," she explained when I spoke of this. I made her take off her hat, and was enchanted by her new coiffure, a beaten and gleaming gold: she had at last had her hair cut short just at the moment when the fashion had changed and most women were letting theirs grow, and it was marcelled in exquisite ribbings with little clusters of curls about the ears. I told her my admiration. "I look different, don't I?" she said. "I look like something out of *Vogue*." "Yes," I said, "it's a new personality—a new kind of beautiful woman." But it was always a personality that did not want itself to be dissolved, and I had vowed to myself to invade it. I took her face in my hands to kiss her. "Oh, you'll muss my hair!" she protested. I kissed her carefully, respectfully bending; then sat seriously, holding her hand.

I told her how natural it seemed to me to have her sitting there in my place; how often I had seen her on the couch, whose color I had chosen as a setting for her; how hungrily, coming home from the museum, I had wanted to find her there and to talk about the day over a cocktail. "Yes: you'd tell me about the pictures," she replied in the way that annoyed me. "Edna Forbes was just saying how fascinating it would be to live with a man like you: it would be like having Bernard Berenson and a young man-about-town at the same time." "Now, listen, my dear,"—I moved—"we *mustn't* go on like this. It's immoral to want to be lovers and to go on wanting to be and not being. We're getting to be like that Browning poem about the Statue and the Bust" "Yes, I know," she said—she was troubled and looked away. I followed up by quoting:

> *"The sin I impute to each frustrate ghost*
> *Is the unlit lamp and the ungirt loin."*

"I know," she said more decisively. "I've thought about it, my dear, but I can't." "Just because you're married?"

"No—" "You know I want you to marry me—I want you to get a divorce." "Don't say that—you don't know anything about me!" "What is it I don't know?—tell me." "Oh, I can't!" "Why shouldn't you? I shan't mind, whatever it is." "Oh, no: I can't tell you!" "What is it? You know that I love you so that I'd understand anything about you. Now tell me what it is!" "I can't." "You must—it isn't fair of you not to." "Well, I'm not a well person, you know." "Aren't you really?" "I've told you I had trouble with my back—but you've never known how serious it was." "What's the matter?" I hoped now to find out and intently I applied my question. "I've got serious spinal trouble—I've got tuberculosis of the spine. It's what they call Pott's disease—isn't that an awful name? I've had it ever since I was twelve." "But you seem to get around all right—you just have to lie up occasionally, don't you?" "I have to wear a brace,"—it was the final simple painful confession. I put my arm around her and kissed her cheek. She had never let me do this before, and now I knew that it had been the brace: she had dreaded to have me feel it. "Why, my dear,"—I held her close—"you ought to have told me before! But why should you have thought it would change things?" I felt terribly sorry for her, and tender in a quite new way. The defiance I had thought I found in her, the alert and unyielding defenses, had been simply the shame of the brace—a cage, a humiliation, in which she had always to live. "I couldn't bear to have a lover," she answered. "You wouldn't want to do something that would hurt me.— And you wouldn't really want me now, anyway." "Don't say anything so silly, my dear." I smiled to get the tone back to gallantry.

"I fell off a horse when I was a little girl—one of my father's horses. I had to wear an awful jacket for almost two years—a thing with a rod up the back of my neck and a kind of a clamp on the back of my head like they used to have in old-fashioned photographers' studios.— My father wanted me to ride again right after I'd fallen off—that's why I can never forgive him!" "Well, that's what you're supposed to do with children—he probably didn't know how badly you were hurt." "I couldn't walk, I couldn't even sit up, and he wanted me to get right back on the horse!" Her voice became appealing as she revived her childish sense of injury. "He really kept a riding stable—I didn't tell you that. When he didn't make a go of his farm, he began hiring out the horses that he'd gotten for the family to ride. I couldn't bear his hiring out my horse that had originally been bought for me. I couldn't always have it when I wanted it—and then when I did ride it, I began to feel when people saw me as if I were just a stablekeeper's daughter—that I was only able to have a horse because my father kept horses for hire. He could never understand how I felt." "Wasn't he sympathetic when you were ill?" "He kept wanting me to try to get up and do without the brace. He didn't want to believe it was really bad because he didn't want to think he was to blame." "But was he to blame for your falling off in the first place?" "In a way he was to blame. My horse had been so much in demand that I'd gotten out of practice riding her and she'd gotten so she didn't mind me. The first time I went out with her one spring, I was galloping through the woods and she took a sudden turn down a path that led home and threw me off so that I hit a stone.—And he wanted me to ride again the next day!"

"But you don't wear your brace all the time?" "No: not all the time. I leave it off sometimes to go out in the evenings—though I have all my dresses made with high necks because sometimes I can't do without it—

and sometimes I can leave it off for quite a long time. But I always have to put it on again—my back has been worse lately—that's why I've had to be in bed." "You're still the most beautiful woman I've ever seen or imagined—it may have made you more beautiful in some way—I suppose there's a kind of light that's generated in people from pain." "I couldn't go to school—my mother taught me at home. I was bright and I ought to have gone and gotten to know other children. That's why I've always been so shy—I never went to school after I had my fall." "But you've made up for all that now: you know how to handle people—and you've done a great deal more reading than many women have who've been to college—and I don't see"—I ended, smiling—"why it should interfere at all with your 'love life.'" "I can't have children," she said. "You can have love, though, just the same." "Oh, I couldn't, I couldn't! It would make me so unhappy—and it would upset everything!" "It might make you happier, on the other hand." "Oh, I couldn't!—You wouldn't want to hurt me, would you? You wouldn't want to humiliate me?" "Why should it humiliate you?" "It would ruin my whole life and tear me all to pieces! You wouldn't want to do that, would you?—And then I wouldn't like you any more—I'd never be able to forgive you!"

I didn't want to press her at that moment. "I must go now," she soon announced. I tried to arrange for another lunch, but she was filled up for days ahead. "I don't want to see you for a while. It would make me uncomfortable to see you now that you know about me. You and Ralph and Edna Forbes are the only ones who know." She put her purse under her arm and left.

She left me in a state of emotion at once erotic and dolorous. Though my relations with Imogen were clarified and my intimacy with her in a sense advanced, I had to accept a check.

It was Saturday—I had asked her then because my Saturday afternoon was free, and I had not made any engagements; and now I had nothing to look forward to but an empty and futile day. I poured a highball of the genuine Scotch that I had specially laid in for the occasion but which Imogen had not touched, and I sat for an hour or more musing on Imogen and her story. The brace explained everything, of course: it had kept her from believing in her beauty; it had prevented her from giving herself. It was the brace that I should have to surmount; but did I really want to break Imogen down? I should have to work out a new attitude.

I had told the maid not to come back, so presently I left the apartment and, thinking I should dine alone, rather purposelessly started downtown. I wanted, I told myself, to brood quietly on my love for Imogen, to find out how, if at all, it had been altered by the afternoon's revelation. But, once I had crossed Fifth Avenue and was wandering among the West Fifties, it was as if I were relieved of a strain, a posture which had been cramping my spirit: I forgot about Imogen completely, as I had not been able to do in months. Here, as the night blacked and chilled the city, with the speeded-up pace of the season, I could feel the hot pulse of the appetite inside the hard shell of New York: it reached me from the electric signs that blinked rapidly through rhythmic dramas, in which chewing-gum brownies in green and pink bulbs pricked the night with their arrow-pointed caps; from the livid blue or white lighted names on night clubs that were blinded like harems; from the sight of young dancers in their street-clothes, with straight backs and well-developed ankles, whom their make-up did not make meretricious. I thought

about Anna. She had come back from Syracuse and written me during the summer. Dan, it turned out, had not
died, and she had left him in Syracuse. I had answered,
not mentioning my illness, but telling her I hoped to see
her when I should get back to New York in the fall.
And now suddenly I felt I must look her up. I went
into a coin-booth in a drugstore, and its dinginess and
stale cigarette-smoke took me back to my nights of
Fourteenth Street: as I dialed, my throb of excitement
was followed by a recoil of distaste. The thick accents
of Anna's mother spoke incredibly out of the black
transmitter and told me that Anna was now working at
a restaurant only a few blocks away on Fifth Avenue.

I walked around there, came in flushed from the cold,
self-consciously sat down at a table, seized a wine-list
and ordered a drink. Then for the first time I took in
the restaurant, which was not what I should have expected. The Field Company had lately been attempting to meet the popular demand for "Ritz," and had
substituted for their usual homely lunchrooms a kind of
Babylonian court, with glossy black-onyx walls and a
gilded cascading fountain, of which the thin even sheet
of water, trickily lit from below, looked itself a kind of
tinselly gilding. It seemed a queer place to be seeking
Anna, but I stared about and presently found her. She
was waiting at the counter for an order, and showed the
same cool detachment toward her tray that she had
shown toward her partners at the dance-hall. She masked
perfectly her surprise at seeing me when I sent her a
message by my waitress, and pretended no recognition
as she came over to me, unsmiling but blushing. She
appeared to me, after my dazzlement with Imogen,
rather dry-skinned and pale-eyed and plain under the
relentless glare of the lighting and in her yellow white-
aproned uniform which was the same in all the Fields'

restaurants and which reminded me of the sliced hard-
boiled eggs that invariably appeared in their salads. But
she smiled when she came up to my table, and I was
reminded how sweet her eyes were. In a few curt and
low-spoken words, with an eye on the movements of the
hostess, she reproached me for not having called her and
agreed to come to see me the next Thursday, which, she
said, was her afternoon off; and, as she departed to attend to a customer, gave me a roguish and sidelong grin.

She turned up looking very attractive—I had feared I
should find her sordid. She was wearing a short blue
dress and a new cloche hat for autumn, with the white
stockings and the blunt-toed black shoes that were part
of her waitress's costume; and her long-waisted slender
body seemed to me surprisingly smart, with the dress
caught up in front, as the fashion was at that time, and
scooped in under her narrow little buttocks. She had had
her hair waved for the occasion, and it smelt very clean
of tar soap. Her skin was quite fresh and pink, and the
color of her dress brought out in her eyes a pretty forget-
me-not look that made it extremely difficult for me to
suspect her of having deceived me. I found that I was
telling her what had happened to me in a more or less
objective way and in the stern but friendly tones of a
father who has heard about his young son's getting
drunk. She was obviously troubled and depressed. She
said that Dan *had* had something the matter with him,
but she didn't know whether it was that. She had discovered in Syracuse that he had some kind of a great big
sore—he had wanted her to sleep with him, but she
wouldn't. "Was that what was the matter with him?" I
asked; but her answer only further revealed to me the
incurious ignorance of the poor in regard to the diseases
among which they live and which they simply take for

granted as infestive plagues a little more mysterious than
cockroaches or rats: "They didun want to tell me what
was wrong with-um—they tol' me it was a blood-clot,
but I don't know what it was. He wasn't hardly conscious
when I got there, but then he came to and went out and
got drunk and came back and knocked me down and
kicked me between the legs and made a big cut and was
trampling on my face. His father came in and he tried
to beat up his father, and they had to call in the police.
—What I think is he'd just been fakin to get me to
come on there with-um." I reflected how far all this was
from the world that the Loomises lived in: they would
never have been able to believe it; I could hardly make
it real to myself. I could imagine the attitude of Ralph
to anyone who treated his wife like that, or even to
anyone who said he knew someone who did. Dan had
also come and grabbed her pocketbook just when she
was getting on the train to leave. He had told her he
would meet her in Utica and run her the rest of the
way to New York, so for her only to buy a ticket to
Utica. She had gone to the hotel he had told her and
had stayed there for two dollars a night; but he had
only sent a man with the pocketbook with most of the
money gone.

Her father-in-law's whole family, she said, had been
in very bad shape when she was there. The sister had
married a man who had afterwards turned out to be
married, and she had had some children by him and she
had finally come back home and treated the children
terrible. She took dope, and she'd scream and yell and
curse—she'd always say, "I want Anna!" "I'd stay with
her and keep her quiet, see. She'd threaten to kill the
children. My mother-in-law couldun do nothing with
her—she's crazy. And my father-in-law's sort of crazy—

and Dan's brother is just disgusted. Dan likes his sister, and he doan like to see her like that—I think that was what got him started drinking."

I took a vicarious pleasure in feeling how different my apartment must seem from the Lenihans' moral squalor. She was evidently amazed and thrilled. She watched me work the siphon with interest and slipped a Cole Porter record on the phonograph. She lay in my arms on the green modern couch on which I had pictured Imogen, and eventually we went to bed in my sober and white-walled little bedroom, with its two Renoirs and some new blue and green crêpe ties that I had hung on a corner of the mirror. The bed had been made up with clean sheets. It was the first time we had had a real bed, and it gave the whole affair a new dignity. I was careful to take no risks. She still seemed to me terribly appealing, and once, when I came back into the room, I found her curled up on the bed and was pleased by her eyes, very cunning and round—at once agate like marbles and soft like burrs—looking at me over her hips. When the rest of her face was hidden, they had, also, an unexpected depth.

Anna's visit relieved my tension. When I walked out of the house the next morning, I met a world that was well thought of, and deserved to be, a world that was sound and clear, and to which I was glad to belong. I worked at the Metropolitan; I also did serious writing; I had a mistress who came to see me. As for Imogen, she was slightly trashy; and, besides, it would be selfish and brutal determinedly to mount my guns against a woman, so romantic and so sensitive, who had always been partly crippled. What a formidable undertaking it would be to get her through such an emotional crisis! And, once I had set out to prevail over her, I should certainly have to see it through. I should have to detach her from Ralph and adjust her to the new situation. And, after all, wasn't it too mean to Ralph? He had been bearing all the emotional costs of her case, and did he not have the right to keep her? When I saw her for a drink two days later, I was gentle and affectionately friendly, and quietly forbore to press her.

But Anna disappeared into her darkness again. One day when I was waiting for her, she called me up and said Dan was back. She was going to take Cecile and go to stay with her sister in Manhattan, where he wouldn't be able to find her (her mother was back again with Fatty: they had moved to a different section, and Anna had been living with them).

I felt that her anxiety and the imminence of Dan had for the moment estranged her from me completely. She did not call me up for a week, so I finally stopped in at the restaurant. She hadn't been to work for two days —nor had her mother heard anything about her since she had gone to stay with her sister. Dan *had* found her again, it turned out; and when she finally reappeared, she was disfigured by a cut on her lip, an eye in the purple-and-green stage, and great bruises on her hips and thighs. She had had to stop working at Field's and was ashamed to go out on the street. Dan had waited for her outside her sister's and pushed her back into the hallway and beaten her up. He had accused her of being unfaithful, and she had been scared he'd find out about me. Then he had made her get into a car and driven her to a drugstore where they knew her, and made her persuade them to cash a check which she had just seen him forge in his father's name. Then he had taken her to a speakeasy and announced that she was going to live with him and that they were going to find a place right away. They had started to go somewhere in the car, but Dan's driving was now so screwy that a cop had pulled him in and taken them right to court. There Dan had made an impression by producing a Burns Agency badge, which he had kept from a brief period of detective work, and he had almost induced them to let him go when Anna couldn't stand it and gave him away: she told them that the badge was a fake and that he had just passed a bogus check. The cops had called up the Burns Agency and looked up Dan's record at headquarters and sent him straight to the Tombs. "I didn't want-um to get away," she said. "He's so clever—he can talk-umself out of anything! When they caught him and Fatty in a stolen car, he made them think that Fatty had stolen it, so that Fatty got five years and he only got one. And I didn't want to live with-um no more—I was afraid he'd kill me or do something to Cecile."

At first she had been ashamed to go home with her face. Her family had used to make fun of her for the way her husband beat her up, and her aunt that lived in Brooklyn and whose opinion she highly valued had, she said, remarked with approval on the fact that she hadn't had no bumps or bruises since she had taken up with me; but when at last she had gone back to her mother's and told them what had happened, they had had nothing but congratulations. They had said she had done right in betraying Dan, and Fatty was particularly pleased; but now she was tormented by conscience— she hoped he wouldn't get a long sentence. It seemed terrible to send somebody to jail when you'd loved them once so much. "You've never been so happy with me as you were with Dan, have you?" I asked. "I was never happy with Dan—I used to cry when he made love to me." "But you didn't always do that, did you?" "Not at first." Then she added: "You've made me feel different about Dan—you're the only person who's ever been nice to me."

I tried to reassure her by telling her that Dan must be really insane and that he was better off in jail. "I wish I didn't have to go back," she said—she had not got to my place till eleven. "I'm so tired—my eyes sting so. But I have to be there in the morning to get Cecile's breakfast and take her to school." I asked her whether she didn't want to sleep, but she put her arms around me, and we went to bed together; and that night I felt a satisfaction of possessing her perfectly, completely—my arms around her slim little figure, my tongue in her soft little mouth, and her slender legs twined over mine.

She slept, and I told her I would wake her at two. I took her to the subway in the damp winter morning, and when I found myself back, warm and dry, in the bed that still smelt faintly of arrowroot, it made me uncomfortable to think of her, sitting alone on a bench in the station through the hour-long wait between night trains and of her long dreary trip to Brooklyn, half overpowered by sleep. It was, after all, no light undertaking for her to come over to see me at night—especially when she was working at Field's and, after spending the whole day on her feet, was first obliged to go back to Brooklyn to give the little girl her supper and put her to bed. I must make her accept some money to buy Cecile and herself some new shoes.

Dan was sent to jail for two years; and though Anna had moments of remorse, she was obviously much relieved. She cast off now a good deal of the constraint that she had always felt in coming to see me; and I, on my side, accepted her more freely for the fact that she was detached from Dan.

I found it a continual agreeable surprise to realize that

she was not "common" and that the quality of her intelligence was good. She had in a sense never even been Americanized—that is, she had never been vulgarized as many children of immigrants were, who, in adapting themselves to our cities, had acquired bad manners and a blatancy that, for some reason, seemed much more offensive than any mere peasant crudeness of their parents. She had a Brooklyn pronunciation of English—an accent worn down on the lips of the crowd as the long Brooklyn pavements had been by their feet; but she had somehow, in simplicity and humility, escaped this New World barbarization. I recognized her temperament as Russian—or, more specifically, I suppose, Ukrainian: for she had little of the Russian volatility, and the cadences that were sad in her voice expressed a deadening of resignation rather than the Russian complaint. She was naturally cheerful, well-balanced, amiable, considerate and sensual, as the Slavs of southern Europe are: and there had survived through so much that was degraded and harsh, so much that, it seemed to me, was nightmarish in her life, a clear little power of perception and a cool little faculty of judgment, a realistic sense of the way things were that had never become embittered, a sensitiveness of feeling that had never been dulled and a humor that had never been coarsened. And I found all this very refreshing after my summer with Imogen's fantasies: there had begun to take place in my sympathies a shift that was gradual but rapid.

This change of direction was involved with—it may even have been influenced by—the recent set of my political feeling. In my walks on Fourteenth Street the winter before, I had taken to buying the radical papers —especially the Communist press; and I had now become addicted to reading them, and had been spurred to study Marx and Lenin more seriously than I had ever done before. The truth was, I now came to realize, that, in the days when I had considered myself a socialist, I had tended to think of Marxist revolution as a kind of thing that happened in Europe, that one read about in papers and books, and that one might passionately take sides and dispute about, as one could about Robespierre or Cromwell, but that never seemed an element in one's own real world or a conceivable possibility for America. But now I was becoming convinced that our well-to-do American groups did constitute a *bourgeoisie,* and that our American factory workers and farm-hands, our poor farmers and fruit-pickers and lumberjacks, were in process of being reduced to the position of a dispossessed *proletariat,* in the senses in which these words had been used by the great socialists in Europe and Russia.

I had spent Christmas with my parents in Detroit, and I had seen the deflated city spread out on the bleak flat land, with its banks collapsed, its factories stopped, and its blocks of stores and houses vacant. The great climax of my father's career had been his feat of devising for General Tires a marvelous coördination between the different departments of the business, producing, distributing and executive, by which conflicts were to be carefully worked out through a system of interdepartmental committees, so as to save needless effort and cost. Everything was taken care of in this system except the interests of the public and the worker, who had never been considered at all. But when I tried to make my father see this, it only became hopelessly apparent that he regarded the depression as an act of God like an earthquake, a drouth or a flood. He was a kind and good-natured man—there was always something boyish about him—and it troubled him that General Tires should have had to lay off its old hands: he contributed

with unusual generosity to funds for unemployment relief; but it sometimes made me childishly desperate to
be blocked, in my arguments with him, by his refusal
to see the logical reasons which would always prevent
the system from working and his total inability to imagine a world in which free enterprise did not prevail.
I suppose I always held it against him, too, that he
was culturally inferior to my mother and me. He was
proud of my mother's music, and, though I know he had
at first been disappointed with me, he had never tried
particularly hard to dissuade me from studying art;
but he had no understanding of either beyond rattling
off a waltz on the piano and decorating his office with
Remington prints of hunters, sunsets and moose. My
mother got restless in Detroit; the people in Grosse
Pointe bored her, and she had come to live mainly in
anticipation of her visits to her sisters in the East. She
confirmed me in my aversion to the city by laughing at
the respectful alacrity with which the members of the
oldest French families accepted "Mr. Ford's" invitations
to his antiquarian barn-dances and other entertainments;
and I finally became rude one day at a dinner where
people had been saying, apropos of the unemployed, that
the time had arrived when the Americans would have
to learn to use their leisure, and when somebody had
told with enthusiasm of having been present at the
Fords' Christmas party, where a hunchbacked and jolly
Ford worker, dressed up as Santa Claus, had handed
around the gifts. I felt that Karl Marx and Anna had
given me the right to be bitter.

I always felt guilty at the moment when I took the
train back from Detroit, on account of leaving my
mother alone there. I would torment myself for an hour
asking whether I shouldn't have lived there or at least
have made myself in New York the kind of home of

which she would have approved and to which I could have asked her for visits. I had been having these pangs of compunction since the days when I had first gone to prep school, and they had always had the effect of making me swear to myself that I would dedicate myself more earnestly to whatever was my ambition at the moment. Today, as I looked out on the Canadian farms, I had a clear and fierce revelation. I had been trying to show in my book how the painting of the nineteenth century had been influenced by the Industrial Revolution; and now I saw that the union of Imogen and Ralph was a striking dramatic symbol of the queer combination, under capitalism, of a disgraceful economic reality and a dissembling romantic screen. Ralph made the money in advertizing—that is, in hiring himself out to glorify whatever the industrialists were hoping to manufacture with profit; and Imogen spent the money on domestic settings and panoramas of travel abroad that made it possible for her always to fancy, and for Ralph part of the time to pretend, that their situation was other than it was. But the world of Anna was the real world, the base on which everything rested: she was the worker who gave all that he could give and who got for it as little as he could live on. I listened to her reports of Field's restaurant with the same kindling indignation with which I had been reading in *Das Kapital* the hideous industrial chapters. When she had first started in as a waitress, she hadn't been able to afford a girdle and had got in wrong for wearing rolled stockings, and they had put her at the very back tables, where you could only make a couple of dollars. Sometimes she had to stay on her feet all the time through the rainy days when no customers were coming in, and it made her bleed alarmingly when she was having her monthlies—she had never, she said, been right since

Cecile was born. She had hoped she might get made a hostess at the first place where she had a job because the hostess had been nice and liked her and pinched her arm and called her "you dear little thing"; but then this hostess had been transferred, and the new hostess had been terrible to them, and you couldn't throw up your job and get a job at some other Field's, because, if you just quit, you found yourself on a sort of black list and they wouldn't let you work anyplace else. And then her mother had suffered as a fur worker from flying bits of fur in her eyes and she had contracted an eczema of the hands which had made her fingers so sore that she had finally had to stay home and try to get them cured.

Anna did not herself play up, or even consciously lend herself, to my view of her as a victim of the economic system; and it may be that, on the one hand, I was feeling the need to justify on higher grounds the strong taste that I was beginning to have for her; and that since Imogen, on the other hand, was so difficult, I wished to believe that, as a bourgeois "escapist," she was not really worth having. Certainly my affair with Anna was saving me trouble and time: I had now only my evenings to write in, and, assured of seeing Anna at least once a week, I did not feel any longer, as I had done, the restless and irksome desire to contrive skimpy rendezvous with Imogen or to go dining and drinking out. In any case, I took a sharp pleasure, which was at the same time aesthetic and sensual, in the contrast between my meetings with Anna and all the other events of my life. I remember one cold winter Sunday when she had come in the afternoon, a day of blank uptown façades and decorous uptown perspectives, when I had gone to the deserted museum to look something up in a book, and, returning, I had felt it so incongruous to watch her take off her stiff pink slip and to have her

in her prosaic brassière: the warm and adhesive body
and the mossy damp underparts—the mystery, the organic animal, the prime human oven of heat and juice
—between the cold afternoon sheets in the gray-lit
Sunday room; and one evening when I had come home
from a party at which I made Imogen smile by my
tender and charming gallantries and kissed her hand
at parting, and then made love to Anna for the second
time, by a sudden revival of appetite after she had put
on her clothes to go, by way of her white thighs and buttocks, laid bare between black dress and gray stockings
—she was so slim that it was almost as easy to take her
from behind as face to face—while she kicked up one
foot in its blunt-toed black shoe as a gesture of playful
resistance or simply of wanton freedom.

In all this period of my meetings with Anna we had
only one unpleasant moment. One night when I was expecting her she called me up and asked me to come and
get her—something she had never done before—at a
restaurant on West Forty-ninth Street. It was a curious
and ignoble neighborhood—a kind of backstairs for the
entertainment district: there were cheap little restaurants
and bars, women's-wear shops with much lingerie,
Chinese restaurants with large signs that said "Dancing," and hotels at a dollar fifty a night. I identified
the little speakeasy with misgivings: it had the air of a
garage; and found Anna with a girl friend named Irene,
who was also a waitress at Field's and for whom I felt
an instant dislike. I thought Anna behaved rather un-
naturally: she would not let me take her away, but kept
insisting on my buying more drinks. These drinks were
the worst I had ever had, even under Prohibition: the
gin was stinging and raw. I felt that I had touched a
new stratum, which Irene represented, too. She did not
impress me as a tart, but she was common and covertly

malignant in some sort of special way. I felt, also, that she and Anna had some sort of special understanding, that she was putting Anna up to something. When I finally got them into a taxi, I offered to drop Irene at her subway, but she said she wanted to go to a restaurant where a wonderful man was working whom she described as her "big moment." Anna was all for my taking them there; and, to my surprise, when I firmly declined, became vehement in a way quite alien to anything I had known of her before: "You wouldn't do that for me!" she said. "All right! I'll never forget this!"

When I had finally put off Irene at her subway, I asked Anna what was the matter. She ceased to be aggressive, with her friend gone, but was sulky and wouldn't say much. I expressed a low opinion of Irene, and she answered that Irene was her best friend now, and that I didn't care about her anyway. "You must be getting tired of me," she said, "because you're beginning to pick on me." Later on, when I had her at home, I demanded of her several times whether she cared about me still. "I don't like the way you ask that," she said. "All right, if you don't believe me . . . I could say I did anyway, couldun I?" The cheap drinks and the Limburger cheese she had had, had given her a bad breath, and she complained of being sick at her stomach. Our love-making was perfunctory: we scarcely kissed and she turned her head away.

Our relationship was chilled for a week; then suddenly I knew one evening, from the way she was laughing with me, that I had all her confidence again. She said that the girls at Field's had all warned her that Irene was queer, but she had always refused to believe them: "I didun have no girl-friend, see, and I thought Irene was such a wonnerful girl-friend. She was always so nice to me, yuh know, and used to take me out and buy me drinks." But one night Irene had induced her to spend the night in her apartment in Manhattan. After Anna had gone to bed on a couch, Irene had rather embarrassed her by walking around the room with her clothes off; but Anna had dropped off to sleep, and then, the first thing that she knew, Irene had come over and was "down here." Anna had pushed her away, and wouldn't go with her any more. Irene had told Anna that night that her husband was a fag, and Anna thought maybe she hadn't always been that way but had gotten that way because he was that way. "I think she wants a boy-friend," she said. "You heard her rave about that guy in the restaurant."

Not long after this reconciliation, I went to a night club with the Loomises. Ralph's agency had lately extended its scope and now placed advertizing with radio stations as well as with provincial newspapers; and Imogen had appeared after Christmas with a beautiful baby-leopard coat, which brought up for me boyhood memories of a novel by Elinor Glyn, and a Welsh terrier called a Corgi, fox-faced and coffee-colored, which was completely under her domination and snapped savagely at everyone else. They were also doing the town at a rate that I had never known them to do it before, and that evening I had been weak enough to allow myself to be carried along on their spree, telling myself, however, that I was going to pay part of the check. But Anna's wages from Field's had lately been seriously diminished by her sending money to Dan so that he could buy himself food and cigarettes in prison, and I in turn had been giving her money, so that the scale of prices in the Coronet imposed on me a certain strain.

Edna Forbes was also of the party, and at one point

in the evening Imogen and she went away to the ladies' room and stayed about fifty minutes. During their absence, Ralph Loomis and I had a long conversation about radio. The fact that he was peddling the commercial "plugs" that made the radio programs so offensive contributed to my picture of the Loomises as symbols of capitalist culture; but Ralph rather deflected my antagonism by himself deploring the commercialization of radio before I had had a chance to mention it. "We ought to do as the British do," he said, "and have the whole thing directed by the government. Still, I suppose it isn't any worse than reading a story in a magazine and running up against a Campbell's soup ad. They do broadcast a lot of good music." And he described to me his ideal program, which would include the organ chorals of César Franck, a poetry-reading by Carl Sandburg, an analysis of current news by somebody from *Time* magazine, and a monologue by Robert Benchley, whom he had met and liked to call "Bob." I pointed out urbanely that the kind of thing he wanted would be impossible to achieve under capitalism, and he admitted that this might be true. The longer the two ladies remained away, the more I found myself warming toward him: he seemed so much less the exploiter than the victim. And since Ralph's current splurge of spending had not been in the least ostentatious, and since I could see that the badness of the radio had given him a feeling of guilt, I thought I might as well let him pay the check.

I had been wondering about the absence of the ladies, and Ralph finally showed concern. He must always, I supposed, have to worry about something going wrong about Imogen's back. "They're just talking about us," I reassured him: our solidarity now seemed complete. "They're telling each other everything they've done since they saw each other last." But they returned a few moments later—Edna in diamond earrings and a white satin evening gown that lent her a certain elegance and almost made her attractive; Imogen in black, with a cowl-like garment that covered her shoulders and back but left her lovely white arms bare and gave dignity to a beauty that seemed to me tonight—reminding me of Greta Garbo's—at the same time perverse and detached.

Ralph invited Edna to dance; but I simply ordered Imogen a highball. "You and Edna ought to dance together," I said kiddingly but rather crudely. "Do you think we're Lesbians?" she answered, with a coloring of cuteness in her voice and turning upon me her gorgeous eyes that exasperated me by seeming familiar when I knew they were far away. "No: I don't think you're Lesbians, but there's always a leak in your relations with men." "What do you mean by that?"—she smiled so determinedly that I knew I had touched her. "I mean that you talk everything over with Edna." "No, I don't." "You do: you tell her everything that happens to you. I've got to feel that everything between you and me is enacted in the presence of Edna." "There's nothing between you and me!" "Sometimes I feel," I went on, "that all the admiration I give you is just turned into a kind of device for you to get admiration from Edna." "I don't follow you," she said rather sternly. "You know,"— I tried to keep it amusing—"there are times when it all seems like something in a story in a woman's magazine—one of those stories in which the heroine is a married woman who manages to eat her cake and have it, too. She goes alone on a trip to the West Indies, and on the boat she meets a wonderful man who is glamorous, passionate and handsome. He takes her up on the top deck and kisses her while the moonlight is silvering the ocean. The reader holds his breath for several

columns because he thinks she is going to fall and just
throw over her husband and her family, but then, in the
nick of time, it turns out that the guy is a swindler
who has been fleecing the passengers at cards, and she
suddenly gets a cable from her husband in which he
tells her that he is meeting her in Havana. It has suddenly been revealed to him in her absence that he had
come to neglect her lately, and he is terribly in love
with her again, and so they have a second honeymoon in
Cuba. Everything has been perfectly painless, nobody
has suffered at all—but the woman who wrote the
story has communicated to the woman who reads it
some daydream she likes to indulge. The other woman
has been having that daydream, too—*she* would like
to run off with a man of the world—and now she can
imagine it more vividly and yet afterwards be left
feeling virtuous. And that's what you do with Edna, and
you do it at my expense." "What's wrong with that picture," said Imogen, "is in the first place that my husband doesn't neglect me, and in the second place that I
don't want to elope with anybody." "And in the third
place that I'm not a cardsharp—but if you really knew
about my life, I'm afraid you'd be just as much horrified."

I knew I was behaving badly. I did not see her again
for a month.

In the meantime, just as I, at that time, had felt the
impulse to confess about Anna to Imogen, so Anna had
come to shrink from visiting her husband in prison for
fear she should talk about me. She did not go to see him
or write him for nearly three weeks, she said, and then
she got a letter from him that made her cry. He accused
her of making whoopee while he was locked up, and

of being unfaithful to him. "But what Christlike creature," the letter went on, "am I not to forgive you? I
know that I am a phony crook and a liar and that I
haven't been fair and just to you, but I still love you like
I always did. Pay no attention to what other people say
about me use your own judgment. I am only in here
two years and that is only twenty-one months more and
I expect to live with you fifty years if you will have me.
I am going to be in the Washington's Birthday show
and the director thinks I am hot. I am going to sing a
song for you in the show bring Cecile over to see it."

But when she had gone to see him, she came back
more frightened than ever. "He looked terrible. He just
stared at me at first, and didun say anything, like he
was sore—then I talked to-um and told-um I still
loved-um and everything, and after a while he calmed
down. He thinks that everybody's through with-um. He's
a bad egg, I know it—he's just about as bad as they
come. I'm afraid of-um—I'm afraid he'll cut me up—
he said he wouldun kill me, because he doesn't want to
burn in the chair, but that he'd do something terrible
to me." She had used to wake up in Syracuse and find
him glaring at her with crazy eyes. He was so jealous—
he hadn't wanted her to dress well, had tried to make
her wear old clothes of his mother's.

And then Cecile had just heard for the first time about
where her father was. The kids had found out at her
school. They had asked her why her father wasn't home,
and then shouted: "Because he's in prison! That's why
he isn't home!" "That's a fine thing for her to hear!"
said Anna. "I still didun tell her the truth."

Then suddenly Dan died. She had known that there
was something the matter with him, because she had
used to see him in the morning with pus all over his
lips; they had had X-rays taken of his nose; and now

they said at the jail that what he had had was a tumor of the brain. They had operated on him on the Island, and he had died right away. They had notified her that his body had been sent to the morgue, and she and his father had gone to claim him. She hadn't wanted to have Cecile have to go to the morgue, but they were taking the body to Syracuse and she thought that she ought to see him. It turned out that she was tickled to death, because she had known her father so little and had always been looking forward to having him back.

Anna went on to Syracuse, and Dan's family gave him a Catholic funeral, with all kinds of expensive features paid for out of Dan's insurance—including a special coffin that was supposed to keep the body for a hundred years. Her father-in-law had tried to give Anna what was left of the life insurance; but Anna had refused to accept it because the last time she had been in Syracuse he had told her that it was she and her people who had ruined Dan's life. When she came back after her absence of five days, she found that she was out of a job. The manager wouldn't have her back. He didn't like her because he was a wop and once, when he had asked her, "Can you understand English?" she had come back at him with, "Yes: can you speak it?" And now she had been trying a week and she hadn't been able to find a job, and she wished she had taken the insurance. "Big-hearted me!" she said scornfully.

Dan haunted her still for a time. She slept, she told me, way over on the side of the bed, even when Cecile wasn't with her, for fear he might still be there. She had destroyed the X-ray photographs, and so hadn't been able to send them when he was going to be operated on, and she was afraid that he might have died for that reason. And then she hadn't gone to see him when he had written her the last time begging her to come. One night she read a ghost story in the paper—she thought it must be true because she'd read it in the paper, and she couldn't go to sleep all night for imagining he was outside the window. The way he'd looked at the morgue!—they'd just had him there lying on the floor, they hadn't even put him in the icebox with the others.

But the shadow eventually faded; and she seemed to me, almost as I watched her—like a crocus set free from dead leaves which have been keeping it stunted and bent—to straighten up and take on her own color. She was more self-assured, more mature, and she seemed to me, even, taller.

She came more often now to spend the night, which she had rarely been willing to do before. There was an interval when she was out of a job and when I gave her enough money to live on; and at this time she was freer and more mine and we were having more fun together than had been possible at any time before. She arrived fairly early one evening, when she had not waited for dinner at home, and I went out to buy her some beer and some delicatessen sandwiches. While I was doing this, she took a hot bath, and when I got back I found her combing her hair and looking very pretty and clean in a pair of my white pajamas that had several buttons missing. I was beginning to cease to feel, as I had the winter before, that she was a wisp of irrelevant romance that I had brought home from a Fourteenth Street dance-hall, a beast or bird picked up in the fields that could never be a household pet; and tonight she was there before me as the creature I had actually caught: a pretty little Slavic girl, with a round face, a flattish nose, nice soft hair that was parted in the middle and that tonight seemed rather blond than red, and clear, for-

eign, light-green eyes that slanted up a trifle at the
corners and that looked as if they had been washed like
the rest of her. And she smelt sweet of powder and soap
—I had bought her some first-rate cosmetics.

She curled up against the wall on the couch, and I sat
opposite in the modern armchair, and she ate sandwiches and we both drank beer. I talked about the Russian Revolution: "I know," she would say, and I could
see that she did know it as a serious fact on the horizon
of her mind. She had heard it discussed by her Ukrainian relations—some, shopkeepers, some, garment workers; but she had no political views; and when I tried to
make her understand that a working-class government
in Russia might have repercussions over here, that business slumps with the hardships that they inflicted on
people like her family could only be prevented by a
socialist revolution put over by people like them, I felt
that I was merely embarrassing her by consigning her
to the category of a "working class." To tell her that
the fur workers like her mother, the garment workers like her cousins, and the waitresses at Field's like
herself were expected to dislodge their employers and
the big figures she read about in the papers and to make
themselves the rulers of society—must seem to her, I
could see by her silence, to be thrusting on herself and
her people a rôle for which she knew they were not
fitted and for which I must know they were not—so that
I soon began to feel silly and insincere; and my Marxist
way of talking seemed at the same time to imply that
Anna and her family were at present such "under-
privileged" beings as to have been practically outlawed
from humanity, when the fact was that she and I, in
our manners with one another and in the freedom with
which we had both bound ourselves, as it were, by emotional contract, were meeting on equal terms—so that to

force into the situation the conception of the Marxist proletariat was to be guilty of, not merely bad taste, but of violence against everything that was good between us. I found myself embarrassed, too—and dropped the subject and gave her more beer.

Soon I was laughing with her over her cat, which had just been having kittens. They had taken in this cat from the street. "My mother likes cats," she said, "and Fatty, he likes cats, too—so she always has plenty to eat. She was going to have kittens, so we gave her a box. But she had to have somebody aroun—she wouldun let me leave the room, so I had to stay in the kitchen all the time. Finally, I had to go out, and when I started to go out the door, she ran over and bit me in the leg and dropped a kitten. So then she had her kittens. It's funny how they eat the afterbirth. The kittens wann-ed to nurse just as soon as they were born. They all began to yell like hell.—Cecile just loves them to death, but I'm afraid the old cat will scratch her." Cats played quite a part in their lives. She had told me that when she was little, she had used to save milk for stray cats; and once she had been upset about finding a little kitten in the street that had been all chewed up by a dog, and the children had been torturing it and throwing water on it; she had gone to a policeman and he had told her that the S.P.C.A. was closed after five, and he had laughed at her and said it would die; so she had gone to a drug-store and they had laughed at her but sent a boy out to kill it with chloroform. As I watched her, lying back on the cushions, I saw that she looked rather like a kitten herself.

She said that she had been all tired out with the cats and her sister's children, whom she had invited over to Brooklyn to celebrate Cecile's birthday. She had been comfortably relaxed by her bath, and the beer had made her sleepy, and she did not feel much like making love. She carefully cold-creamed her face, and we went to bed in perfect tranquillity. For me, too, it was a kind of relief to share thus in her relaxation, to have her gentle young body beside me all night in my own bed. I had said good night in the dark to the cunning shadowed hollows of her eyes and kissed her twice on her little mouth, and she had turned from me away toward the wall. As I lay with my arms around her and sometimes pressed against her, she would say, "Well, let's go to sleep!" but responded with a soft little pressure; and finally I turned her around.

The next morning at eight o'clock I came out and found a capable young woman in a well-cut and -hung green dress ironing her apron in the living room. She had got a new job at Krafft's and that day was going to work again.

The whole evening and night were to leave on me through everything I did the next day an impression of sweetness and dearness, of affection and satisfaction.

And in the interval of five days before I saw her again, I found my hunger for her becoming obsessive. I noted that I was getting into a phase where I constantly imagined I saw her in people I passed on the street who might hardly have anything in common with her; and, as I walked through the rooms of the museum, in certain of the Italian madonnas, and in the grave little New England bride of the American Hawthorne's *Trousseau,* who did not really look much like her either but who had something unpretending and childlike that I had come to associate with Anna. But when she came to me next, she was ill: she had been menstruating, and her work at the restaurant had as usual made it worse. She had not wanted to confess this at first, but at last she lay down on the couch and mentioned that she felt faint. She had dark places under her eyes, she was pale, and her hair looked dull. She complained that she could not eat the food at Krafft's, because she had to see it all the time and she knew how lousy it was, but that, when she had come home after work, she had not had the energy to go out and get vegetables and milk and fruit, so that she hadn't had anything to eat but pork, which was what Fatty always got. Her mother used sage tea to dye her hair, and then she would eat out of the saucer she'd made it in, and this disgusted Anna and took her appetite away. And she had also had a fight with them which had upset her.

She was not used to having people take care of her. She was always surprised when I brought her things, if only a drink of water or a light—which she said Dan had never done; and she had never let me send her to a doctor. But I got her to go to bed and drink part of a glass of sherry. I sat beside her and held her left hand and noticed again how finely it was shaped. The desire with which I had awaited her had been subtilized and diffused into tenderness. I said to myself suddenly, "I must love her." I told her I would sleep on the couch, and let her have the bed to herself and had to quiet her "Oh, don't's!" and "Oh, no-o's!" "Say something sweet to me," I begged her as I kissed her goodnight on the pillow. She said, "Darling,"—and then added: "I can't say it,"—and, touching her breast: "It's all here."

She called me in the morning the next day I was to see her and told me she was sick in bed. I made her promise to get a doctor, and she wrote me a note that she was better (she never would phone me when her people were there, because she tried to keep up a pretense that she spent her nights out at a girl-friend's). But when I called up her house two days later, her mother told me that Anna was still in bed, and the old lady spoke English so badly that it was impossible for me even to be sure that she understood the questions I asked—so I felt I must go over to Brooklyn and find out what the situation was.

I had never seen her house or her family, and the journey brought a certain suspense. When I went down into the black dugout of the subway and took the train that banged and hurtled through the straight narrow tube, it was as if I were engaging myself in some logical course of procedure which would force me to a harsh recognition I had hitherto kept at a distance. We shot out of the tunnel at Brooklyn Bridge, and I looked down, through the rows of dark girders that wove back and forth like a mechanical loom, on the city shown in dark silhouette above a livid and leaden water that seemed to shine at one edge white-hot, and on those streets of the East Side, where Anna had been born, with their dingy roofs packed tight for miles, shouting here at the escaping train, from the walls and the tops of their buildings, their last cries to come and buy fine values—in raincoats, in furs, in candy, in laxatives, in five-cent cigars; and I was caught for a moment by a vision of that immensity of anonymous life, which, though I knew it only through Anna, had thus come for me alive at one point like the screen in the blotted theater that is peopled by the animated shadows of persons not really present, whom one never may see in the flesh—though in this case I knew that they existed and had the heat and the accents of life, and that the dramas they acted were real; and I was moved by a kind of awe. Then we went down into the blackness again, and finally emerged from the tunnel in a raw landscape of tracks and garages, gas tanks, one-story factories and bleak little cheap brick houses in which the factory workers evidently lived. This was Anna's own country, I said to myself; I might as well accept it at once.

But I was surprised when I got out at the stop which was the closest to Anna's address. I walked along under low-columned cloisters, pale brown and a little more gracious than anything connected with the subway on the Manhattan side of the bridge; and emerged from the subway steps into the sunlight of a whole new world, which seemed to me inexplicably attractive. It was Twelfth Street just off King's Highway, not far from Coney Island and Brighton Beach; and there was space and ocean air and light, and what seemed to me—it was what most astonished me—an atmosphere of freedom and leisure quite unknown on the other side. The great thing here was that there were so few high buildings—the tallest were apartment houses than ran only to seven or eight stories, and there were not very many of these; and for the rest, one found little brick shops —delicatessen stores, beauty parlors, drugstores, billiard rooms, kosher butchers and newsstands with Italian and Jewish papers—that had been relatively newly built and that looked absolutely toylike. These cropped up in patches at intervals among streets that were exceptionally wide and that seemed to go on forever, yet, more or less of a sameness though they were, had somehow escaped from the abstract monotony characteristic of American cities. They were planted with rows of young maples, now beginning to be green with April; and the houses —double affairs though they were—placed each at a good distance from its neighbors, seemed quite independent dwellings, not unpleasantly paired, rather than cramping partitioned units, and though they were all fairly small, had been planned with, I thought, a pleasant

eye to the amenities—for each had its own little backyard and garage and its little privet hedge on the street,
its latticed shades in the windows, its arched doorway
with a diadem of bricks that rayed out around the top,
and its little flight of steps in front with an ornamental
patterned stone bowl in which nasturtiums or geraniums
grew. These avenues and houses were further redeemed
from their tendency toward uniformity by the children
with whom they were populated and who, even in this
period of poverty, seemed remarkably healthy and clean.
There were babies being wheeled in baby-carriages that
had what seemed to be a great luxury of springs and
young girls with mature round breasts that bulged out
under the surfaces of their sweaters; and there were also
their ample mothers leaning out of the ground-floor
front windows, and occasionally a black-browed Sicilian
in suburban American clothes tinkering with his car, or
an old Jew walking solemnly and stiffly, a derby hat on
the front of his head, pulled down over his somber eyes.

I found Anna in one of these houses—to my surprise,
one of the neatest and cutest. I remembered—though I
had previously forgotten—that they had only moved
into it the fall before and that she had talked about it
enthusiastically—"Oh, do I love that house! I sit right
over the radiators!"—as if it had been the only one of
her homes in which she had had enough heat in winter; and had hoped they could rent rooms to boarders
so that they wouldn't have to give it up. But I hadn't
divined its attractions.

I felt better as I rang the bell, but when her mother
had answered the door and I had followed her down
to the basement, I saw that they were certainly poor
and I grasped what it meant to be poor. They had only
three rooms to themselves, and they had to cook or
sleep in them all. They were submerged in that close

smell of poverty—of boiled clothes, unaired bedding and smoke and grease—which seems a permanent half-suffocated state just this side of complete extinction; and Anna was lying on a formless bed, a mattress propped on wooden legs so that it was only just off the floor, amid gray and tumbled sheets. Her first feeling was one of horror and almost of indignation that I should come there and know how they lived. When she saw me, she began to cry; and when I sat down beside her and took her hands, I could feel how tense she was. "Oh, why did you come?" she cried. "I didn't want you to come!" She was awfully pale—so much so she frightened me: she must have lost a great deal of blood. The doctor had been to see her; but she wouldn't tell me what he had said till her mother had left the room. There was something the matter with her ovaries, and he had told her she ought to have an operation; but she didn't want to have an operation because her Aunt Sophie had had one and had never been well since. It was hard to make her talk about this, and I suppose that my own mind, by a reflex, collaborated in shutting the problem out. She had been doing the crossword puzzles in a tabloid and I was afraid the pocket Webster she was using was inadequate for this purpose. The feeling that pressed forward in my mind was that I ought to get her a bigger dictionary.

Anna's mother was round-faced and squat, and her nostrils were rather snoutish. I could see why the slender Anna always talked as if her mother were the botch of the family; yet she had strong and bright round green eyes that were queerly but undeniably handsome. She did seem of cruder stuff than Anna, and Anna did not want her to talk to me. "Go away! This doesn't concern you!" she shouted with a fierceness and rudeness that I had never seen her show before. I thought that the old lady

was fond of Anna in spite of Anna's jealousy of Fatty,
but that, tougher and coarser than her daughter, she had
been so much knocked about by life and so much crushed
by immovable burdens that she could not afford to care
much about anything that happened to her children or
herself. As for Fatty, who had loomingly presented himself, I had always tended to take it for granted that
Anna's descriptions of him were distorted or exagger-
ated; but they turned out to have been entirely truth-
ful. He was enormous: both tall and obese; and he
resembled in an incredible degree—even to the sharply-
peaked circumflex eyebrows, though he lacked the ferocious glare—that hectoring and menacing giant of the
old Charlie Chaplin comedies from whom Charlie always had to escape. I had not quite believed Anna either
when she had told me once how sebaceous he was—
"If you pick up a glass, it's dirty!" she had told me—"if
you pick up a plate, it's dirty! The doorknobs are all
greasy from his hands!" But now I found that this was
perfectly accurate: I discovered after I had shaken
hands with him that he had left a deposit on my fingers that resembled a layer of lard.

He was affable and extremely respectful—though it
was true that he could hardly speak English; and, in
submission to Anna's objurgations, he almost at once
withdrew. Anna's mother came back after a time and
said something in Ukrainian to Anna. "She wants to
give you tea," said Anna, seized again by distress and
disgust. "The way she has tea, she drinks it in glasses!
And she talks about a doughnut, but it's not a real
doughnut—it's just an Austrian doughnut!" I accepted
and consumed the refreshments—explaining that I liked
the glass and did not mind the holeless doughnut—and
when her mother had left the room, Anna put her arms

around me and pulled me down to kiss her. But, "Oh, what did you ever come over for?" she said.

The next morning I had quite a hot argument with Charlie Dumaine at the museum, the friend who had got me my job. I had discovered that he still regarded Whistler as one of the summits of modern painting just as he had at college, and that he could not understand my insistence that the museum should buy Braques and Picassos. I declared that Whistler's famous passage about the Thames clothed with poetry by the evening mist and the chimneys becoming campanili, was one of the most pathetic, if not one of the most ignoble admissions ever made by a modern artist, because it showed that he was absolutely incapable of dealing with his environment as it actually was. Better to break things all up, etc.

I did not eat at the museum, as I usually did, but walked over to Lexington Avenue and had lunch at a cafeteria alone. On my way, all the pressure of my disquietude about Anna and of my discontent with my work was suddenly relieved and my spirits leapt up, as I caught sight of a bold readjustment, a course that might seem quite impossible to others, that would upset my personal life, yet one that I was perfectly free to pursue. This course was to throw up my job; sublet my too-expensive apartment; and go to live near Anna in Brooklyn! I would rent one of those nice little houses and Anna would come to see me, or live with me perhaps and keep house; and so, hidden away from my friends and immersed in the life of the people, I should achieve my insurmountable book. I should not even go out for weekends to Hecate County, as I had thought of arranging to do: the memory of it sickened me now. I should take Anna and her little girl for holidays to

Brighton Beach and Coney Island, to Far Rockaway and
Sheepshead Bay—names which now blew in from a
summer sea, with bright bathing-suits and girls playing ball, a natural and simple and delightful world of
people who worked and had little to spend but who
came for their fun to the beaches. There they were, just
a few miles away, just beyond the dark bulk of the city,
and I had hardly even seen them!—And there I should
break with that bourgeois past in which I was still embedded; so I should drive myself out to that inexpen-
sive level of living—free from social obligations, from
waste—where the real analytic and creative thought as
well as the building and the production were accomplished.

Anna was up by the end of the week, and when she
came to see me again, I at once put my plan before her.
She was silent and seemed rather glum, and I was afraid
that she did not like it. But it took me a little time to
penetrate to her point of view and find that she was
filled with dismay at the prospect of the scandal I
should cause her. She had always been painfully
ashamed of the fact that her mother was not married to
Fatty—her aunts almost never came to see them, and
when they did, Fatty couldn't be there. Anna had always told her family that she didn't do anything with
me (though I could hardly imagine they believed her),
and she didn't want Cecile to know anything about me
because she had never forgiven her own mother. I did
my best to convince her that it wasn't at all wrong for
people to live together, and that she shouldn't blame her
mother either; but she said that it wasn't right and that,
whenever she came home from seeing me, she wasn't
able to go to sleep till she had prayed to God for for-
giveness. And it would just make them laugh at her and
pick on her to have me around the corner.

So my idyl of seashore and toylike streets faded out between the walls of my apartment. I had somehow missed it again.

IV

But the incident increased my respect for her and compelled me, I found, to take her more seriously. We were now on a very firm basis. I had come to rely on her in certain ways. I felt that she really knew me, as Imogen had never done. For Imogen I had simply been a character in an imaginary romance she had lived, the man with whom she had dreamed of eloping ever since she had married Ralph; but for Anna I was an actual person whose behavior and personality she was able to observe and gauge as she did those of other people. She would chide me in her straight little way when I had done too much drinking during one of her visits, and she always knew at once and was anxious when my nerves were under a strain. And at the same time I found that I could talk to her about matters that I had at first never mentioned: the dissonances between members of my family, the competition for power at the museum, the fantastic behavior of my friends. Wherever it was a question of relationships, she seemed perfectly to understand; and I could see from her remarks and inquiries that her notions about my affairs were fairly accurate ones. When I showed her pictures of paintings, she went directly to the figures as people, commenting on their physical characteristics and probable personalities. She saw rabbis in Greco, waiters in Grosz, greaseballs and gangsters and fairies in the groups of the Italian Renaissance. The nobler gentlemen and ladies of the portraits she would gaze at with silent attention; and she made me a little jealous by her interest in one of Velasquez's soldiers when I found that she had looked him up one evening after I had gone to get her a drink. What had been most unexpected to me and one of the things that brought us closest together was that we shared a sense of the comic. She appreciated the things that amused me as few women of my acquaintance did, and she would ask me for further stories about an idiotic girl I knew who had first divorced her husband and bought an island near Nantucket because, as she said, she had always wanted an island; then had had the former husband visit her and had married him again in the village church with many rapturous telegrams to friends; but had soon after run off with the driver of a gigantic transportation truck—because she had always wanted to ride in a truck—and had finally "found her destiny" in New York as organizer of a Communist hunger march. She also liked me to mimic my boss at the museum, who had queer habits of hiding from people, and his elderly woman secretary, who was afflicted with a compulsive mania for setting things at right angles on other people's desks when they happened to be out of the office. She always noticed very clearly herself what people did and how they talked. And I on my side was never bored by her stories about her family and their neighbors, which were told quietly and were never repetitious. Her life in the new house that she loved so had become quite real to me now: I saw it all through her humorous and lucid eyes. She had even a gaiety about it that was carefree by comparison with her muted tone in the days when I had first known her on Twelfth Street—though the shyness and the shadow returned when she talked about the things that were squalid.

There were, for example, her mother's Polish boarders. I had never before been given the full sense of how

much the Russians scorned the Poles. Anna's attitude
toward these two crippled workers—within the limits of
her gentle disposition—had the arrogance of a conviction of superior race. One of them had worked in a
furniture factory and gotten the ends of his fingers cut
off and was collecting sixteen dollars a week while he
was hoping for a settlement of two thousand; the other
had broken a bone in his foot by dropping something on
it, and was also collecting compensation. I expressed a
ready sympathy for the Poles as the victims of industrial
accidents; but Anna told me that she was practically
certain that they had both done these things on purpose in order to get the compensation. And then they
were so vulgar! They always brought everything back
to women. If one of the Pollaks got into the car with
Fatty, and Fatty said, "This car is cold—I'll have to
give her gas," the Pollak would say, "Just like a
woman!"; if he said it was a cheap car and didn't run
good, the Pollak would say, "Just like a woman!" I remarked that I had known a few Polish women and
found them extremely attractive, with their tingling ef-
fervescence and their slanting eyes. "They're not attractive," said Anna. "Why not?" I asked. "Cuz they're
Pollaks!" She did condescend, however, to go to a
Polish picnic, to which one of the boarders had invited
her. She had had a good time, she said, because she
usually felt with other people that she wasn't as good as
they were—"like with Dan's family, yuh know—but
with Poles I feel I'm better than they are. Great big
women—you ought to see them! Their dancing's just
the polka and hopping around. I sprained my ankle and
it's sore today. And the men don't do nothing but boast
—they don't do nothing but talk about how many
women they've had and how much money they've
made."

And then there was the Ukrainian who had taken her out. He'd been a crook for the last sixteen years, and he claimed that he couldn't be caught. He had driven her to Coney Island and told her about his racket and tried to persuade her to work with him. She was to promise to marry an old Swede that he'd picked out in Bay Ridge and get him to put all his money in the bank for her—then she would disappear. He told her he'd been working with widows for years. He had had a good-looking fellow who worked with him, a regular Valentino, who was absolutely irresistible to widows; but the guy had gone into the bootlegging business, and now he had to have something new. He had told her that he wanted to marry her, but it had occurred to her that she was a widow herself. He had tried to take her upstairs in a restaurant, and she had made him drive her home, and on the way she had told him that she didn't like his car, which was a lousy old Buick with a cockeyed fender. But then he had turned up next time with a brand-new Chrysler—"I was kind of flattered," she said, with a little smile of confession. "If he could buy a new car just to please me!" "How do you know he bought it?" I asked.

The whole story made me angry and uneasy. She was a free prey for men again, and I felt that I ought to protect her; yet I supposed I had no right to prevent her from going out with other men if she chose. "We ought to live together," I said earnestly. "This is all wrong, the way we're doing!" "I wouldn't want to live with you," she answered. "I'd just be sitting at home every night worrying about you when you were out." "But you'd go out with me," I declared. I had thought lately how quiet her manners were and how pretty she could be made to look. "And what would I talk about?" she said. "My family and the Polish boarders?"—I had been telling her how much this entertained me. "I wouldn't want to meet your friends—I wouldn't know what to do. I had such a terrible time with Dan's family that I wouldn't ever want to do anything like that again!" I suggested that she might find my friends nicer than the people in Syracuse.

But then Imogen was upon me again like some creature of enchantment in a folk tale that appears to the hero three times.

It was the middle of June, and they had gone to the country; but she called me up one Saturday morning. She was in town, and I arranged to have lunch with her, putting off till an afternoon train a weekend I was to spend at Port Washington. At once the old excitement flickered. I walked over to Central Park and all the way down Fifth Avenue. The sky was a pale blue, and the Plaza reminded me of gaieties that I had known there when I was just out of college and the hotel itself still new. "I'll miss you this summer," she said. "The people *are* dull out there." "What do you do?" "We do just the same things." I felt that she did find her life empty, and that I had become at last an old friend, one of her so few real intimates to whom she could talk. "I've been learning to do flower arrangements, though. You know, the Japanese make an art of it, and I've been reading a book about it. You can arrange a single flower so that it looks just like a Japanese print. Dotty Scope and Edna and I have gone in for it in a serious way. We're going to get them to have a contest of flower arrangements at the flower show this year!" Her intensity increased as she talked: it was so that she spent all her passion, and I suddenly perceived with a pang how unspeakably tragic her life had been, how it had all, like her back, grown crooked. Was she not perhaps the perfect example—such as one rarely met outside fiction—of the "great soul in a small destiny," and had I not, perhaps, let her down?

We went for a drive in the Park in memory of the spring before, and she looked very pretty in a pink summer dress, and everything was soaked, through our drinks, with an other-worldly softness and color. "What are you going to do with your weekends?" she asked with a shade of slyness. "Take trips to Coney Island—Staten Island—Rockaway Beach." "Who are you taking to Coney Island?" "Nobody: I'm going alone." "All alone?"—she was thinking a minute. "Have you ever been to Rockaway?" "No." "You'll never go there but once. . . . You won't go alone, though. You've got a girl." "What makes you think so?" "I know you have." "Who do you think she is?" "She's somebody you don't want people to meet—so how would I know who she is?" "You're absolutely wrong about that"—I brushed it off with self-conscious lightness. I was jolted by her guessing so much, and shocked by the fear that she was right in her idea that I was ashamed of Anna.

She took occasion to tell me that Ralph had gone to Old Lyme to spend Sunday with his mother; and I felt that I could perhaps have induced her to stay over in town for dinner. "You know," she said, "you're the only person that I've ever lied about to Ralph." It was as if she wanted to make me feel that in some sense she had given herself. But I had promised my friends on Long Island. I said that I would go out to Hecate County for a weekend or two that summer.

When Anna came to see me in the middle of the week, I noticed a change at once. She was wearing a new red dress, and I felt in her a new self-assurance. She sat down in the big low-built chair and crossed her

slim well-shaped thighs and began to smoke with a poise
that I had never quite seen her assume. Even her hair appeared more abundant—she had just had a new kind of
hair-do.

She told me at once what had happened. She had
been having for some weeks an embittered feud with
one of the Polish boarders. It seemed that he had been
in the war, and they thought he was crazy on account
of it, because he couldn't talk about anything else. They
couldn't understand what he said, because he talked
some queer kind of Polish that was different from the
Polish they were used to. They got bored with him and
didn't want to talk to him, and then he got mean with
them and used to kick Anna's cats, and one day he had
made a beanshooter and shot one of the backyard robins
that Anna had put up a box for. Anna had bawled him
out, and Fatty had tried to bawl *her* out, because he
said she ought to be nice to the boarders—and then
Fatty had called her a "hoor" and she had called him a
bastard and a pimp, and he had said that she ought to
pay rent, because he was supporting her all the time.
"Can you beat that?—when I do all the work!" she
laughed, as she always did, without any trace of irony
or harshness. "I told him that *he* was being supported,
not me—my mother and I supported him—and he went
out sore and stayed out all night. And in the morning
they called up from the police station and said he was
being held for disorderly conduct. I was so tickled I did
a dance and everything." They had let him out later,
but had kept his car. Anna had never spoken to him
since. But the great thing was that her mother was so
disgusted with Fatty that she had picked out a new
apartment and was going to take Anna to live with her.
Fatty had got the idea that he'd start up another speakeasy, and he hadn't given her mother any lovin since

July Fourth last, and he talked about how he had a girl that he paid a dollar fifty and how she played with him and did everything, and Anna thought the moment had come when her mother would leave him for good. And she had the Poles down so now that they didun even dare to look at her. The whole thing had made her feel so good that she wanted to giggle all the time. "Give me a cigarette," she said.

But later on she fell asleep beside me. She was still rather thin and needed rest. Then just as I was dropping off myself, she suddenly came to life and sat up over me and shook me with her straight little arms. "I'm strong, huh?" she said. "I can fight! How'd yuh like to see me fight about you?" She had just had a dream, she said, that the girl-friend I had told her about had come in there, and that she, Anna, had been fighting with her. "One night I went to a restaurant with Dan and there was a girl there that sat down at the table with us—and she was picking up her dress and making up to Dan— and I flew at her and we had a fight. She got me down on the floor and was tearing my ear and I bit her in the thumb, and we heard afterwards that she got an infected thumb and had to go to the hospital with it. I was all het up—I was just like a puppy after it's had its first fight. I learned to fight Dan, too. At first when he used to beat me up I'd just crouch down in a corner and wait till it was all over—but then later, when I saw it coming, I'd crash a chair over his head. When I really got good and mad, Dan couldun stop me nor nobody!"

I shut my eyes and was beginning to drowse before she had finished her cigarette; but she suddenly slapped me on the stomach, which happened to be lying bare. I reacted with a nervous shudder. "Can't take it, huh?" challenged Anna, with humorous but unusual tough-

ness. "I used to do that to Dan, and it would make-um
so sore he'd forget he wann-ed it!"

"Ralph," said Imogen, "has gone in for the topiary
art. Don't you know what that is? It's clipping box and
privet bushes into all kinds of little shapes." She showed
me two cockeyed bells and a fairly successful lady in an
Elizabethan skirt. "They have special gardeners to do it
on the big English estates. Ralph was getting to be quite
good at it, but he's had to be away so many weekends
that they're beginning to look all fuzzy, and I'm afraid
they'll just turn back to bushes if he doesn't get a chance
to trim them. I can't do it, because I can't bend down."
I inquired about Ralph's mother. "She's not really sick,"
she declared. "She just works up all these complaints so
that she can get Ralph to come and stay there. He's only
spent one weekend at home in a month." The sky had
suddenly clouded, and large drops of rain were stain-
ing our clothes. As we turned to go into the house, I
glanced aside at the queer little staircase.

She made gin fizzes in enormous high glasses, and we
drank them lying back on the couch, and gazed out
through the leaded windows at the darkened yet fresh
green leaves against the background of the gray-silver
sky, and heard the rain coming down in a splash as if
the sky were momentarily shaken. I remembered that
feeling of a house in the country on a long rainy summer day that had been pleasant in afternoons of childhood, when we had had to stay in and had played
charades: the comfortable damp within doors, the wet
by no means threatening outside; the wind stirring a low
sound of surf in the trees and blowing rain about the
trees and the gardens—a mere flurry of shade and wet
that was easily, amusingly, endured, since one knew that
the sun-dazzled summer world would soon open about

one again. Tomorrow or even today the glare would be back on the tennis courts, on pale sands and striped beach-umbrellas, on the shiny upholstery of topless cars; but I had really, as I was now telling Imogen, enjoyed just as much, if not more, those begloomed afternoons indoors when we had made up our riotous dramas and when, as I did not tell her, I had once kissed a pretty cousin with whom I had gone into the next room to whisper about a word to act out. Imogen leaned back on the couch and beamed at me from beneath her big eyelids with brown eyes that were themselves almost childlike.

The rain was soon past, and it was clear again. "Come over to my old place with me," I blithely proposed. "I've got to get some summer clothes that I left there." We were comfortable friends now. We set out among hedges and trees dripping rain beneath a brightening sky. "You know," I said, "these drops of rain remind me of the memories of you that I've been having all this spring. They've been hanging in sort of little gouts of glamor on all kinds of commonplace things, down here and in town both—some of them have rainbows in them—I try to shake them off, but new ones are always forming." "You shouldn't do that," she said sweetly. "They were hung there to make you happy." "Were they?"— I gave her a look, affectionately, seriously, lightly. I was silent, a warm feeling of confidence coming to life in me again for a moment; but I wondered what it was possible for me to count on. Yet, after all, weren't Imogen's back and the brace taken for granted between us now? We ought not to feel self-conscious about them. She pointed out to me a yellow warbler with a sinuous canary neck flickering in and out among some shrubbery. And farther on, when we had turned into the

driveway that led to my old place in the woods, I saw a
beautiful purple finch with that rosy metallic orange
that they have about the head and neck; and I thought
that it would be nice to show Anna the quick vivid birds
of the country, so much finer than the robins and the
sparrows that she fed in her backyard—yet not luxuries
that one had to have money to breed, but free and self-
sufficing beings that had evolved their own colors and
voices and would come to live in anybody's trees—since
they were, of course, their own trees. And the squirrels
of which Imogen had said that they were bouncing along
on the grass like slowed-up tennis balls—they did not
need those well-rolled lawns: they would have come to
take food from Anna's hand, no matter in what house
she had lived, just as the vagabond cats did in Brooklyn.

The house was musty and dark, and it imposed a kind
of heaviness and sadness, as to which it was impossible
to tell whether it were due to a desolate memory of the
sterile idle life I had lived there or, on the contrary, to
a feeling of compunction that the cushions and the green
wicker furniture should be languishing through a Hecate
County summer with nobody to enjoy what they had
to give. I opened some of the windows in the living
room and went to rummage among put-away blankets in
closets that were suffocating with moth balls. Imogen
explored the whole house and criticized the way I had
arranged things: the room I had taken for a study
would have made a much better guests' bedroom; I
ought to have hung a big picture over the fireplace.
When I had found what I wanted, we sat down on the
couch, and I persuaded her with an ease that surprised
me—since we had lately been rather formal—to take
off her hat and the raincoat and lie down with me on

one of the beds. "I'm afraid your aunt will come!" she said. "It doesn't belong to my aunt. It belongs to some friends of hers—they aren't even here this summer."

It was queer, and so unlike what love ought to be—though we had cultivated long spells of kissing that involved running my tongue over her eyelids and that were the sole consummation of our meetings. The room, with its bare mattress, its slipless pillows and its pulled-down yellow shades, smelled close and provided no setting: I half knew that the thing was impossible. When I had been putting my arm around her, I had felt for the first time her brace—"Oh, don't!" she had said, shrinking—and I had had a swift chilling vision of a harness of steel and straps; but I was moving toward the round solid thighs, not at all, I thought, the thighs of an invalid, which showed through her short country skirt. She checked my hand and took away her mouth before the end of another kiss: "We mustn't do this, dear. We must go!" Her big eyelids, however, were drooping; and her body, for once, had relaxed with the abandon of being in bed; but—perversely—she evidently felt that she had to do violence to this. "Let me go," she said gently but resolutely. She sat up, and we swung about; but I put my arm around her and kept her on the edge of the bed. "Do you know what you are?" I said suddenly. "You're what they'd call on Fourteenth Street a 'teaser.'" "No, I'm not," she protested, after a second's pause: like a child who has been told she has freckles; and she went on, interrupting my reply: "So you got yourself a girl on Fourteenth Street and became a crusader for the working class! So that's what your Marxism is made of!" "Why shouldn't it be made of that?—as well as of other things," I demanded. "There are some very fine things on Fourteenth Street— that can't be seen from further uptown." "I know all about proletarians," she said,—"much more than you ever thought of knowing. You don't know about the working class at all. My father was a Galway peasant, and I'm half a peasant, too. You're not earthy enough to understand peasants. You'd never get along in Ireland! That's why you didn't want us to live there." "My dear," I answered, "if you're an Irish peasant, you're the kind that's really a queen." "That's true," she said. "My father's family were kings of Ireland in the early days. They were broken and turned into outlaws by the English occupation."

"Look, my dear," I said, taking her hands. "Come to me sometime in the city, won't you? You were made for love, and I love you. An Irish queen like you," I went on with a tender smile, "ought not to be afraid of love!" "I'm not afraid," she said. "You mustn't worry about other things"—I was going on to reassure her, but "All right," she cut in. "I'll come to you two weeks from now—if Ralph goes to see his mother." "You really will?" I took my cue, hardly believing, insistent and ardent. "I'll come Saturday afternoon—about three. Don't have the maid there." "Of course not," I said— I could hardly catch up, she was going so fast. "Call me Friday morning at eleven." She got into her raincoat and put on her hat, looking at herself in the mirror.

When we were out and walking along the drive, I could see that she was very tense. She talked determinedly of other things with overgaiety and overanimation. It was tremendous to have brought her to that pitch, yet I was somehow disconcerted a little.

I saw Anna toward the end of that week, and she had relapsed from her high point of hopefulness. Her mother, after all, was not moving. The eczema—"athlete's foot"—had got so bad on Mrs. Litvak's hands that she couldn't go to work any more, and she and Fatty quarreled every morning about whether he should start a speakeasy or not, and it upset Anna so that she wasn't able to eat any breakfast. Her mother would wrap her hands up in rags and then would leave the old dirty rags all around the house, and Anna couldn't stand it. She was even afraid to let Cecile eat the things that her mother had cooked on account of the discharge from her hands, and this hurt the old lady's feelings, and made the situation worse.

She worried all the time about Cecile—it had got worse as Cecile grew older. The little girl had had something wrong with her vagina, and Anna had found a tin whistle in it, and it had turned out that a little boy-friend had put it there. She was afraid she was bad like Dan. The little girl was bright, so bright that she'd been able to skip a grade at school; but she wouldn't mind her mother. Anna would do her best to explain to her why she mustn't run in the streets, and when she'd finished, Cecile would say, "Can I have some ice-cream, Mama?" When she stopped her from reading in bed, Cecile would just lie there and look at her with wicked black eyes like Dan's. She wanted to bring her up right, but she didn't know how to teach her. The only thing she knew to do was to make her kneel on beans the way the nuns had done with Anna and her sister, but Cecile had soon found a way to shove them back under her knees. Anna said that she had got so, at last, that she beat Cecile all the time—that was the only thing that had any effect on her; and Fatty tried to take Cecile's part, and then there would be a fight.

I had seen Cecile several times, and my impression of her was not a bad one. She had dark hair cut in a bang, a flat little nose like Anna's, and big dark eyes that were both piercing and self-contained. It was true that she

was a little on the tough side: she talked a language of
the Brooklyn streets that made Anna's seem soft and
well-bred. When I had taken them to the circus in
March, Cecile had gazed in utter silence; and when I
had offered to buy her some pop, she had growled something I could not make out, which turned out to be, "I
want some, but Ma'll holler." When I had urged them
on one occasion to spend the night in my apartment and
her mother had asked her how she would like it, she had
hoarsely retorted: "Like fun!" She always seemed to be
glaring at me; but for Anna she had a smile of the eyes
that was loving and confiding and childlike in such an
unexpected way that it gave me a kind of pang. "She
adores you," I said. "She's a nice little girl. She isn't ab-
normally bad—you're too much afraid about her. I
thought she was very cute and good. She's pretty, and
she's very smart. You mustn't worry about the tin whistle
and things like that—all children do those things." Anna
rapidly became so gay that I was puzzled for a moment
to account for it, but soon realized that it was due to
relief over my telling her that Cecile was not depraved.

It did get on my nerves rather, though, to hear her
go on about her sister. This sister, she had at one time
confessed to me, had in her girlhood been for a while
on the streets and used to go with chauffeurs and sailors,
and take them up to her room. She was deaf in one
ear, Anna said, because her mother had hit her when
she was young, and Anna thought she was half-witted,
too. She was married to a taxi-driver in Manhattan, and
had three children who were always sick, with measles,
scarlatina or running ears. She was now going to
have another, and there was nobody but Anna to be
with her. Her husband had had her fall downstairs, with
the idea of bringing on a miscarriage, and thus both
getting rid of the baby and making grounds to sue the

landlord for ten thousand dollars on account of the bad
condition of the stairs; but the miscarriage had not
come off, and when they had tried to pretend she was
seriously hurt, all they had gained was to get put out
of the house. They would have no place to go after the
first. Her sister had thought it would be a fine idea to
leave her husband altogether, because in that case she
would be able to qualify to get her children accepted in
a home. "Imagine," said Anna, "having children to put
them in a home!" Anna at one time had had the idea of
taking an apartment with them and thus escaping from
her mother and Fatty. "But it's just as bad," she said.
"It's worse. I can't bear to see them so poor, and I give
them all my money. That's what I did when I lived with
them before." And I even got rather disgusted with the
affair of the Polish boarder when I learned that he was
doing his business and wrapping it up in paper and
putting it on the floor in the bathroom so that Anna
would find it when she cleaned. I had a reaction of instinctive impatience against the badness of both her al-
ternatives: I did not want to hear any more about either
of them.

We made a date for her next day off; but in the
meantime I was troubled by the feeling that I ought
really to prepare myself for Imogen, that I should pass,
before the final epiphany, a period of vigil and fast in
order to make myself worthy of her. Should I not have
to go back into the dream? Was it not there, after all,
that I should meet her? So I called up Anna and told
her that a friend was coming to stay with me, and I
would let her know when he left. At the same time I
sent her some money to buy clothes for Cecile and herself.

Yet, as Saturday afternoon was brought closer by

Time's rolling camera and the meeting came forward to engulf me like some angle of a room in a film, some corner in regard to which the spectator has been keyed to the tightest suspense by the knowledge of the presence there of some sinister person or weapon, so I found that some queer apprehension like dread was dulling my vibrations of excitement, and that I was tending to shut out the whole prospect and to apply my attention prosaically to my routine at the museum or to trivial contacts. Was it the fear of not proving myself equal to the rapturous exaltation of spirit which the occasion demanded of me but to which I had never yet risen? Was it a dislike of being unfaithful to Anna? Was it constraint at the thought of the brace: of the practical problems it presented and the danger of doing something to wound Imogen? Or was it perhaps a queer kind of horror that sometimes touched me in connection with Imogen?—something that I could not account for, that I could not even tie up objectively with any of her traits or acts.

At the same time I was still in suspense as to whether she would keep her promise; I wondered how I should feel if she failed me—I was afraid I should be utterly sunk; and I looked forward with relief to a decision when Friday morning I picked up the phone. I found Imogen at first so abrupt that I thought she was shying again; but when I put it to her: "Well, how is it for Saturday?", she replied: "A little after three," and I knew that she would really come.

The next morning I woke very early, and I found myself possessed for some minutes by a vivid perverse evocation which I had been trying to refrain from indulging. I saw Imogen lying naked in her brace; but the brace did not discourage desire; on the contrary, it stimulated me oddly. It was a harness which showed silver on her white lovely skin, which pressed tight on her feminine softness, which would fetter her, would hold her half-helpless, while I intimately invaded and enjoyed her and compelled her to shudder in submission under the hard non-conductive metal.

Then I thrust the vision away as impracticable, morbid, misleading, and got up and took a brisk cold shower before I sat down to my breakfast. It was now the second week in July, and the town was baking and glaring in the somniferous New York heat. In ten minutes I was sweating again, dressed only though I was in pyjamas. I told my maid, over the coffee, that she was not to come back, and I was rather annoyed that, after waiting so long, I could not have had better conditions.

I killed time without exertion and did not go out—alternately reading and dreaming. I half wished at moments, as I lolled on the couch and breathed its close smell of cloth in hot weather, that I did not have to make so much effort as this rendezvous was bound to involve; yet I was nervous and did not wait till two before I set the apartment to rights, took another, a hot-and-cold, shower, got dressed and put out glasses and ice.

She came on time at twenty minutes past three, and I felt that she had kept to her purpose. "To go through with it" was the phrase that occurred to me as we labored through some flat conversation about people and things in the country. It was as if she were looking at pictures of new fashions and people in Florida before having a bad tooth out. I had a moment of being so much embarrassed about the whole procedure of sex that I could sustain myself only by approaching it as an inevitable surgical operation. But when I finally took her in my arms, I was roused by the warmth of her body even in the sweltering day. "How perfectly beautiful you look!" I cried. "Do you like my dress?" she asked, letting her head rest against me. I did: it was a sheer black chiffon, through which the pattern of her slip showed darker and her arms, so white and so round, looked prettier than if they had been bare. I had never seen it before and it occurred to me that she might have bought it because I had told her in May about a boyhood infatuation of mine with a picture called *The Last Day of Summer* that had hung in the Metropolitan: a slender brunette in a black chiffon dress who was sitting at a café table, with, before her, a slim-stemmed manhattan, in which the cherry showed red. "It looks just like that picture I was telling you about that I used to have such a crush on." "Yes; I thought it did," she said shyly, but gratified.

She did not, however, lend herself readily to my ardent and expert induction. She had thought the thing out for herself. When I tried to have her lie on the couch, she insisted on finishing her cigarette; and when I tried it the second time, she said decisively: "Let me go into the other room." But she remained on the couch a moment, brooding with her great round brown eyes, as Anna had done on the evening when she had first been unfaithful to Dan. "Don't frighten me, will you?" she begged, at once pleading and giving me orders.

She picked up a small overnight suitcase. "You let me go in here," she said, and disappeared into the bedroom. When I heard her close the bathroom door, I slipped in and snatched my bathrobe and got into it and hovered in the other room. I waited a long time till I feared I had waited too long; then I softly called out "Hello!" and she answered from the bedroom, "Hello." I went in and found her under the covers in a dressing gown of dull rose-red. I put my arms around her and kissed her, and then told her how pretty the dressing gown was. "I just got it—it's new," she said. I found to my surprise that she was nude underneath, and I did not at that moment remember that there had ever been a question of a brace. I wondered at her breast. It was perfect; round and white, with a small pink nipple; and it inspired me almost with awe, like an object of luxury and ornament, after Anna's meager little breasts that seemed scarcely more than cute spots for kisses. "I'm afraid they're not pretty," she said. "Oh, yes, they are: they're marvelous—incredibly so!" "That one was spoiled when it was held in too tight at the time I was having a baby. The other one is better." "But you didn't have a baby?" "No: the doctor thought I oughtn't to have one." "They're both perfectly lovely!"—I kissed them. It seemed to be true that she doubted her beauty; but this somehow made it harder to praise it. I was actually embarrassed and baffled by a body which surpassed in its symmetry anything I had ever expected. I suppose that, though I had not imagined it, I had been fearing some deformity or at least defect; but, even if I had not, I should hardly have been prepared for a woman who—alone in my experience—did really resemble a Venus. She seemed perfectly developed and proportioned, with no blight from her spinal disease: she was quite straight and had the right kind of roundness. I found that I was expressing admiration of her points as if she were some kind of museum piece, and that she seemed to enjoy being posed in the setting of the fresh rose sheath, as if some frank and unashamed self-complacency coexisted with her morbid self-doubt. "I have too much flesh on my stomach," she said; and, "I know you don't approve of stained toenails—but I like them": she had colored them red. But what struck and astonished me most was that not only were her thighs perfect columns but that all that lay between them was impressively beautiful, too, with an ideal aesthetic value that I had never found there before. The mount was of a classical femininity: round and smooth and plump; the fleece, if not quite golden, was blond and curly and soft; and the portals were a deep tender rose, like the petals of some fleshly flower. And they were doing their feminine work of making things easy for the entrant with a honeysweet sleek profusion that showed I had quite misjudged her in suspecting as I had sometimes done that she was really unresponsive to caresses. She became, in fact, so smooth and open that after a moment I could hardly feel her. Her little bud was so deeply embedded that it was hardly involved in the play, and she made me arrest my movement while she did something special and gentle that did not, however, press on this point, rubbing herself somehow against me—and then consummated, with a self-excited tremor that appeared to me curiously mild for a woman of her positive energy. I went on and had a certain disappointment, for, with the brimming of female fluid, I felt even less sensation; but—gently enough—I came, too.

Lying beside her, I thought with wonder how well-modeled and -cushioned she seemed after Anna's hard protruding little thigh-bones. I had got so accustomed to Anna that I hardly knew now what to do with such a luxurious woman. And it was horribly hot: our lovemaking had left us dripping and sticky. Imogen, completely prepared, had brought a douche in her bag, and a bottle of something precautionary—though of course I was taking the proper precautions. I mused with a certain detachment, while Imogen was away in the bathroom, that in my principal love scenes with her there had always been something not right: the big sheeted bed brought from England; the raw mattress in my shut-up retreat; today the unpleasant weather.

When she returned, I embraced her with gallantry. "I didn't frighten you, did I?" I asked. "No: you didn't frighten me," she answered in her intimate little-girl voice that could hardly pronounce its *r's*. I told her how astoundingly she justified the impression I had had of her beauty: "You have the loveliest body I've ever seen!" "Really? The very prettiest?" "Your back is beautiful, too,"—I had seen it when she got up from the bed. "Did you think I was deformed?" "No, of course not; but you talked about yourself in such a gloomy way. —Let me see it." I made her turn over. It *was* unbelievably beautiful: from the shoulders she curved in to a vaselike waist and her torso was just balanced by buttocks that were rather hard and tight, but had two sculptural indentations, great dimples above the hips. I was applying kisses to these when, "Please don't do that!" she said, wincing. "My back is very sensitive there." Contrite, I turned her around. "It's a pity it's so hot," I said, "just the first time we've ever been together." "Yes, it's hot.—You're not happy with me?" "Of course I am. I've never seen a woman like you!"

"I must go soon," she said before long. "Why? I thought you were free for today." "I promised to meet Edna for cocktails." I had at this a moment of sinking, a cold and indignant suspicion that she was going to tell her friend about the whole affair. "Did you have to make an engagement with Edna? Why couldn't you have had dinner with me?" "You're selfish," she said, with an exasperating touch of the pouting little girl. "You want me all the time. But you can't have me all the time—and it's best for us not to see too much of each other—you've had me this afternoon—you promised me you wouldn't make demands on me. It was hard for me to do this, you know, and now I've got to go and collect myself and get back to my life again." "Call up Edna and tell her you can't come and we'll go down to the Moneta on Mulberry Street—nobody we know would be there in summer. Or I'll bring you in dinner from Longchamps's." "I can't—I mustn't!"—and she added: "It's not good for me to go without my brace." This blocked me: I couldn't suggest that she might go and put it on and I would meet her. "I forget about your back," I said, smiling. "You're such a marvelous physical specimen." "Sometimes when I overstrain it, I have to spend weeks lying down." "I'm so sorry, my dear: please forgive me!" "I took it off for you." "Your back doesn't hurt you now, does it?" "No: it's all right for awhile." "You don't have to go right away?" "Not right away, but soon. What time is it?" It was only half-past four. "I must go at five," she declared.

I detached my mind from the clock, and returned to contemplation of her body. "You want me?" she anticipated me by asking. She lay quite still, as she had done before; then, as before, she made me remain still while she began that little movement of her own which brought her, after prolonged muted minutes, her almost secret consummation. I now made her close her superb round legs, and looked down on her great brown eyes that always seemed so female and open, though she soon turned away from my gaze, and on her yellow disheveled hair—she had let it down when I asked her—which she had now had cut to shoulder-length. I pored on her and tried consciously to realize how lucky and how happy I was to be possessed at last of the love I had longed for; but the delight of the climax when it came—even with her there in my arms—did not somehow connect with my vision.

"I must go right away, dear," she said, when she

came back the second time from the bathroom, sitting
down on the edge of the bed and immediately getting
up again. I lay there as if she had left me behind and
watched her with a sudden dissociation. I was struck by
the preoccupation—so different from the perfunctory
or mechanical method more usual with hurried women
—with which she had proceeded to dress; by the intentness with which, at each stage, she looked at herself in
the mirror. It was true that at every step she did manage to look amazingly attractive, and I found that this
began to annoy me, as, even after our hour of love-making, and contrary to the general rule, she became to me
more sexually desirable in proportion as she put on her
clothes. "I have beautiful clothes," she said, as if she
were talking to herself; and I could see that they were
all newly bought. There was a slip which had large
flowers in green and blue, and I thought with impatience that, by wearing it, she had spoiled the effect
of the black chiffon dress with which she had aimed to
please me by recalling *The Last Day of Summer*. It had
been the trim smartness of the girl that had attracted
me so much in the picture, a smartness which had meant
for me in boyhood all that was worldly and gay in New
York, and Imogen had so fatally missed it with those
large flowers that showed through from her slip.
But her legs in sheer gun-metal stockings had taken on,
now she was dressing, the lusciousness, the sensual appeal of ideal legs in silk-stocking advertizements, and
this seemed to me extremely unfair.

She packed her bag in her efficient way, put on her
hat, and was ready to be off. I saw that it was futile to
detain her, and she insisted on going alone. But we sat
down for a moment on the couch. "This has all been
so wonderful," I said. "So wonderful it doesn't seem
real!" Her answer surprised me and threw me out. She

said, in a curious way, not affectionate but rather detached: "This must be a great moment of triumph for you!"

Well, it must be, I thought when she had left me—I had been after her for nearly two years. But I rather resented her saying so; and, in any case, the desire had at last been fulfilled, and now that I did not have it, I found, after a moment, that I missed it. I had lived with that desire so long, had depended upon it so much: it had always been shining within me, it had always been promising some day to redeem my more commonplace experience, and now suddenly it had been extinguished. I poured myself a good-sized drink and sat down in a kind of daze.

Then the telephone pulled me up. It was Anna. She wanted to come to me—she was just leaving Krafft's. I knew that I had treated her badly, that I had told her I should call her and hadn't; and from *her* calling me in this way, I got the impression that she was anxious and suspicious—perhaps in some kind of trouble. I did not want to tell her not to come and hurt her feelings or fail to help her. It was natural for me to say, when she asked me, that my imaginary friend was gone and that there was nobody there in the apartment.

While waiting for her, I finished the highball, and I was stupefied rather than embarrassed when she arrived, looking very slim in a little blue suit and new shoes that she had bought with the money I sent her. She had something of that quality, I thought, that I had liked in the old New York picture. She grinned at my highballs and hebetude and my general air of disarray—I had taken off my necktie in the heat—which she supposed me to have achieved by myself. She chided me laughingly and gently: "How many nights have you been drunk?" she asked. I knew that she was glad to be with me again, and I could not help confessing to myself that I was glad to have her back. But I was worried by the realization that I should certainly have to offer to make love to her: if I failed to, after our long separation, she would be sure to suspect the truth. I laughed with her for half an hour, telling her of the visit of a friend which had actually taken place years before; then I kissed her in the way we were used to, and was rather surprised but relieved to discover that the familiar stimulus produced the familiar results. I had made up the bed in the bedroom and closed the bedroom door; but I forestalled a move on her part to go in there by pretending an imperious hunger, and, with a readiness that rather surprised me, made love to her on the living-room couch.

I asked her afterwards how things were at home. "Cecile's been a good girl lately. When I got home after the last time I saw you, I told her that you thought she was a nice little girl and that I wouldn't beat her any more if she was good and did what I told her. I'm not so much worried about her.—She looks good in her new clothes, too—I want to bring her over for you to see her."

So something I had said had carried into their miserable life in Brooklyn. I was on edge and unquiet with the faint queer nerves that come with excess of satiety, and I was haunted by an apprehension lest the successful duplicity I was practicing might fail me after Anna had gone and leave me quaking with moral horror. But the fact that Cecile and Anna had responded in this way to my touch made me feel a gratification and self-confidence such as I had not, that afternoon, ever enjoyed during my rendezvous with Imogen.

The weather got worse than ever. When I came back

at five from the museum, I would pull off sopped shirts
that had lost their form and drink gin-fizzes that only
made me more soggy, seeming soon to ooze out through
my pores and to merge with the humidity of the atmosphere. I lived like a sponge under water.

I was expecting another flight from me on Imogen's
part, and when I phoned her on Monday morning, she
told me curtly to call her Friday. Anna had said, in leaving me, "Saturday night, huh?," and I had let the arrangement go, thinking that I should never see Imogen.
But Imogen, when I called her again, did say that she
would see me on Saturday, and I had to tell Anna not
to come.

She arrived a little tight about four, after a lunch
with a woman friend, a divorced former neighbor of
hers. I had already had a couple of gin-fizzes, and I
made her a drink at once. Ralph had gone again to stay
with his mother. "She's not really as sick as all that,"
said Imogen, with positive assurance. "She hasn't really
had a stroke—it's just a little embolism. Her sister died
last fall, so Ralph feels that he ought to be with her,
but she always has a maid who takes care of her."—"I
don't go to see her much myself," she explained in answer to my question. "She and I don't like each other.
She thinks that I'm an upstart—and I think she's a
spoiled, vain old woman. She expects to be treated with
homage as if she were a dowager empress. And she's a
professional dealer in lavender and old lace. She gave
me a set of Chippendale chairs and an oval mirror and
some other things just after we were married—at least
we thought she'd given them to us. But later she asked
for some of them back, because she said they didn't
go with the new house.—And it wasn't as if she'd inherited them—she'd bought them herself at auctions
and things. It wasn't as if they were real family pieces."

She seemed to me less remote and romantic than at any of our meetings before. But desirable—with brute brown eyes and with the marvelous breasts and body of which I had now had the revelation. Yet when she turned her head for a moment to put out a cigarette, I caught in her three-quarters face, with drooped lids, piquant nose and half-opened lips, a glimpse of that tormenting beauty which I knew that I had still not possessed. Was it somehow beyond me? above me? It did not matter that she seemed to me today even a little coarse. I sat beside her and kissed her and put my hand over her breast and said, "There's gold in them thar hills!"—adding at once, for fear that *I* was getting coarse: "I always think of you somehow as golden." This pleased her. We were both rather drunk. "I'll have to take off my brace," she said. "Don't come in till I tell you."

I felt nothing of emotion and little sensation. This time I did not let her anticipate me: when she said, "Wait a minute, dear," I did not stop but tried to find out what she wanted, and I had my own climax first. I had been going on for so long and had applied such variety and delicacy that it seemed to me incredible I should have had no effect. But again she did it all for herself, and the throb to which she finally attained seemed fainter than the time before. We had both been rather dulled by the drinks; I had a feeling of languid bafflement: it was as if my love had all been liquefied into the moistures of our bodies and the weather without my ever having been able to enjoy it. "We'd have to see a great deal of each other," I said, "in order to be perfect together." "No: we're not perfect, are we?" she answered, after a brief pause; she brooded another moment. "You frightened me. You promised not to frighten me." "I'm sorry: I didn't mean to." "You kept begging me to go to bed with you, and now you don't like me!" I protested "It's just that *you're* so perfect that it makes me feel that I'm not perfect." "No: I'm not what you want—I knew it! You're used to a different kind of woman. I ought never to have given in to you at all!" "I can tell you with absolute sincerity," I said, "that you're the most beautiful woman I've ever known and that I've cared more about you, I've loved you more, than I ever have any other woman!" "Have you really?" —she was pleased again. "Of course I have: you know it." "I've never really believed it." I caressed her; for a few minutes we did not talk. Then, "You don't know how serious this is for me," she said. "I've never done anything like this before—and I feel all the time that people are going to know when they see me—Laura Bright said I looked so vivid—I'm afraid of looking too well. And I'm afraid that something awful will happen—that Ralph will be killed in an accident. It means so much more in my life than it possibly can in yours!" I had the feeling that she was arguing a case, trying to redress a balance against me. Or was it really that I shrank from acknowledging the seriousness of what I had done?

I went in and tried to make more drinks, but the gin had given out, and I called up the bootlegger for more. When I came back, I found her sitting on the bed in her slip. "Will you help me with these straps?" she asked. It was the brace. I saw it first from behind, and it was different from what I had imagined. It was a harness of leather thongs, steel uprights and rubber pads that hardly suggested a hospital but rather something that was used for sport and could be bought at Abercombie and Fitch. "I didn't want you to see it," she said, "but I can't buckle it up myself—I can only get it off." I reached down in some perplexity for the strap-ends.

"Wait: I'll take this off," she said. She pulled the slip over her head. I was somewhat abashed by what I saw. There was a collar around her neck, and two straps that came down over her shoulders and held up a small band of steel which stretched across her chest and two pads which went under her arms, rather like a *décolleté*, below which her lovely bare white breasts emerged in a perverse and provocative way. When she sat down on the bed, however, she clasped the slip against them. "Make it tighter," she said. "Another hole. I haven't been wearing it tight enough, and my back's been getting weak again. I used to wear it so tight that it made me sore, but I've been letting it get too loose. . . . Is that the tightest it will go?" I shrank from making it sink into her flesh; but, "No: put it in the last hole," she insisted. "I have to have it to hold me up—otherwise I'd flop right over. I know that it's perfectly ghastly—I'm sorry you have to see it!" She was flushed, and her cheekbones stood out when I had finished and turned her around. "You look quite exciting in it," I said, taking hold of her bare upper arms and making her face me as we sat on the bed. "I'm so sorry," she said. "Kiss me." I pushed down the arm that was holding the slip, and she gave me a heated kiss, the most passionate she had ever offered, as I pressed against her bare breasts; and for a moment I had the idea of making love to her just as she was and proving my indifference to the brace. But I was afraid that it would be impracticable or unchivalrous. The thing really scared me a little. And I simply went on kissing her and praising her in a way that may have seemed to her deliberate and made her suspect pity. "You'd better get dressed," she said. "Your bootlegger will be here in a minute!"

I put my clothes on in the living room, and she had just come in dressed when the bell rang and I pushed

the buzzer. Imogen stopped apprehensively. "It's just
the man with the liquor," I said. It was only one short
flight up. I opened the door with alacrity: "Come in,"
I said in a daze. "Hello, Skinny!" cried a loud and
cheerful voice. It was my old nickname from college;
we were invaded by a pair of little piercing eyes, an
impudent and sharklike grin, a long pointed aggressive
nose, which I recognized with deadened shock as belonging to a friend named Art Niles. He was a very
up-and-coming young lawyer, a partner in a smart firm,
who fancied himself as a man-about-town. He had with
him a little brunette, rather pretty but not quite first-
rate, whom he introduced as Mrs. Newbold. I presented the visitors to Imogen, but did not dare either
to mention her name or to invent a fictitious one. "The
name is Loomis," said Imogen, smiling and shaking
hands with a *savoir-faire* that I was glad to have her
show, though she did seem rather middle-class. "I'm
glad to see you, Art," I said—my aim was to be cordial
at first, then pretend we had to get away somewhere.
"You *ought* to be glad to see me!" he declared, giving
us a blast of his bumptiousness—he was obviously already well lit. "I ought to be one of the most *welcome*
guests that's ever come into your door! I've got a bottle
of *brandy* here such as you haven't seen in a *blue
moon!*"—it was the ironic emphasis of our college days
that carried off commonplace phrases. "Oh, goody! A
self-charging siphon! If there's anything I love, it's a
self-charging siphon!" "Here: you'd better let me work
it," I said. "It's likely to shoot all over. The charge
can explode, too." "It can't be too highly charged for
me! I'm so damn *highly charged* myself right now that
the only *danger* is that I may *blow out* the siphon." He
filled the glasses with short high-pressured spurts. He
had a collegiate buoyancy and brashness that always

made things seem amusing and what we used to call "fast." Imogen commented *en connoisseur* on the rarity and excellence of the brandy: I did not like to see her overdoing it with her hearty and ready responses. I could see that Art thought her attractive but he made me uncomfortable by treating her a little as if he classed her with his own companion, who turned out to run an antique store. He did not hesitate to tell dirty stories, and Imogen laughed at them too loudly. When it was a question of going out to dinner, I tried to say that she had to catch a train and had only time for a bite; but, to my surprise, she allowed herself to be swept away Niles's tumultuous insistence and we found ourselves, after a plunge in a taxi, in a place called the Parisian Divan.

This was a restaurant with a plush-curtained front window, in which Art loved to make himself a figure, ostentatiously selecting wines and giving special directions to the waiter. His firm was still making money, and he was still "having fun" just as he had done when he had first got out of college: it annoyed me that he should show himself so indifferent to everything that had been happening in the world. And I was puzzled by the behavior of Imogen, which seemed to me almost brazen. Was it simply the result of bravado, of an attempt to convince Art and his companion that she had nothing to feel uncomfortable about?; or was it that Art's kind of thing was the kind of thing she really liked?—I remembered the man with the ranch. Wasn't she being a little perverse? After dinner, I mentioned again that she wanted to get back to the country, but we went on to a place of amusement that Art Niles considered tops. This was a beer garden where you sat at tables and watched a childish old melodrama, called *The Drunkard*, performed for comic effect. Every line that was pounded and yelled got an exploding response of laughter; and it was as if the stupid howling we did, almost like organized cheering, were a defense against the badness of the times and the horrible summer heat. But in Art's case, exhibitionistic impulses had been heightened at the same time as his humorous sense, so that he was constantly going off with a bray during the in-between passages of the dialogue at which the audience as a whole did not laugh; and he carried the ladies with him: Elsie Newbold laughed merrily and metallically, but Imogen absolutely roared. I kept up my laughter with the needled beer, into which the waiters were sweating and which seemed to me as sickening and false as the assumed sophistication of the audience who were bellowing in savage derision at something not less crude than themselves.

They and we took separate taxis outside. "I'm not going out to the country," she said. "I'm staying in Laura Bright's apartment. She's out of town for the weekend." "Come to my place a minute." "All right, for just a minute." "What have you told Ralph you were doing?" "I've told him that if *he* went away every weekend, I was going away weekends, too." I gave her a long taxi kiss.

The gin I had had sent in was still unopened there. I had never known Imogen to drink so much. "I don't know why I've come up here," she said, as I handed her a gin-fizz. The charge in the siphon had given out, and I had had to make the drinks with plain water. "Well, how did you like Art?" I asked. "I liked him all right. He's very gay." "Art Niles doesn't know there's a depression on—he thinks he's still making whoopee in the twenties." "And what do you think you're doing?" she retorted with a slight change of tone. "I think," I replied, after a moment's thought, "that

I'm becoming extremely demoralized from being in love with you." "You don't love me really: you hate me!" she said. "It's the same thing, isn't it?" I answered. "No: it isn't the same thing. Ralph loves me." "Does he love you every minute?" "Yes." "I'd love you every minute, too, if I had you all the time like Ralph." "But you can't have me all the time, so we'd better not see each other." "You're jealous of Ralph and his mother—that's the reason you're doing all this. I don't think you care a damn about me." "I don't think you ought to complain. I've come to you—I've compromised myself." "No, you haven't." "Those people have seen me here." "I'm sorry about the people—it was stupid of me to let them in." "If it got back to Ralph, he'd kill me!" "He wouldn't kill anybody, would he?" "When he feels that somebody has double-crossed him, he's very hurt and very resentful." I remembered the story of the muskrats. "He trusts me—his whole life is based on me. If he should ever find out about this, he'd go all to pieces—he might shoot us both!" "But Ralph won't know. Why should he?" "Those people might tell somebody else that they saw me in your apartment." "I'll see that they don't." "But if you speak to them, then they'll know I've been having an affair with you! Suppose I should meet them somewhere!—How can you complain about yourself and say that I'm ruining your life when you've made me do all this?" She began to cry: I sat down beside her. "I didn't say that —I"—"Yes, you did—you said I was demoralizing you!" "Don't! don't! I love you so that I'm jealous of you—I can't bear the idea that I don't have you"— "You say that you love me"—her big childlike eyes were running enormous tears, as she sat on the couch leaning forward and with her legs stretched out and her ankles crossed like a little girl sitting in a swing—"and then you say horrible things to me! Nobody has ever said such horrible things to me!" "I'm sorry. Don't you want a drink? I didn't mean to say anything horrible to you." "I can't drink it without soda!" she said. "Now that you've had me,"—she laughed—"you don't care whether I have any soda in my drinks!" "I'll go out and get some right away." "And leave me here alone?" "Maybe I can call the bootlegger." She went on laughing: "You make love to me—you make me come to your apartment—when you're in love with another woman!" "No, I'm not." "Yes, you are"—she kept laughing—"you told me!" "No, I didn't." "Yes: you admitted it. She's some tart—and you want to treat *me* like a tart—you introduce me to your friends and take me around as if I were some *demi-mondaine!*" "No, I don't." "Yes, you do!" I thought her mirth was sounding rather overwrought. "Do you know that I went without my brace for days?" . . . "Did you?" "Because I didn't want you to see the marks . . . and now my back is strained. . . . And I took it off again today. Sometimes I have to go to bed for weeks!" Her laughter was getting out of hand. "I'm so sorry. You mustn't think I don't appreciate it. If I should never be able to see you again, I'd always be grateful to you—I'd always know how fortunate I'd been—because I'd seen how beautiful you were!" But this only brought a renewal of laughter: "You just want to hurt and insult me! . . . You make me do what I don't want to do—and then you scold me—and try to hurt me!" "I didn't mean to hurt you." "Yes, you did"—she could only sob it out between gusts. "It hurts me to make love when my back is sore. I can't sleep with Ralph sometimes for weeks!" "Do you like to have him strap on your brace?"—I had said it before I could think, and I hardly knew why I had said it. She let loose at me a gale of laughter that was nothing but howls and gasps. I had never seen hysterics before, and I was shaken but rather disgusted. It occurred to me that the people on the floor above might think I was strangling a woman. When she spoke again, mouthing great sobs, I could hardly understand what she was saying: "You *do!*—you like to torture me!— You're just like my father! you'd like to beat me!—I never cared about my father after he beat me!" . . . She was off again, and everything I said to her only proved to excite a new paroxysm—a blast that, escaped from pressure, was at the same time attack and appeal, and that raged to make everything dreadful.

But she soon began to rein herself in, stopped laughing, sobbed thickly in spasms and finally sat staring and pale, with a kind of fright in her eyes that looked a little too intense to be acted. She got up and restored her make-up, gazing aghast into the little round mirror and dabbing her tear-ravaged face. "I must go home," she said.

When I came back, I was confronted by the mess of the day: the soapy drops of the rainbow of Imogen. There were the drinks in which the ice had melted, the siphon that no longer functioned, the ash trays overflowing and filthy; the wet towels on the floor in the bathroom, the rumpled bed which had never been opened but on which I found bobby pins, the modern couch which I had bought with such confidence but which now seemed defaced and defiled. A little breeze was coming in through the window; but now it would soon be morning and the sun would be stewing us again. I had derived a certain satisfaction, in the heat of the afternoon, from hitting on a sponge under water as an image for myself in the humidity; and now I figured Imogen and me also under water, but in the guise of those sea anemones which, in moments of desperation, exgurgitate their own stomachs. To formulate even a phrase, in my general submergence and wreckage, seemed to give me a spar of sense to snatch at.

She of course declined breakfast with me when I called her up the next morning, but told me to call her in the country. I was lonely and extremely depressed when Anna rang me up the following evening. Our engagement had been for Thursday, but she wanted to use her day off to take the little girl to Coney Island, and she asked if she could come on Tuesday.

I was unable to get Imogen in the country when I had called her the two following mornings; and, after sourly brooding about her, I thought I had at last put her out of my head when Anna arrived late Tuesday night. I had had quite a lot to drink, and she remained for me rather remote. In a blurred way I heard her tell me, through the all-obliterating heat, that Cecile had "hannun assident" (I noticed now the debasement of her consonants)—she had fallen and cut her lip; and that Anna had finally persuaded her sister to come over and have the baby with them in Brooklyn, but that her husband had drawn up a paper which he wanted Anna to sign in the presence of a notary public and in which she was supposed to agree to pay for both the rent and the food in the event of his being out of work, and even to put up two months' rent for them to live in some other apartment, if they turned out not to be satisfied—from which Anna concluded that her brother-in-law had every intention of stopping work as soon as they should have moved in at her mother's. She felt so foggy, she said, that when she had been coming over on the subway, she had thought she was going crazy: she couldn't remember which station to get off at. It was partly arguing with her sister and her husband;

partly the injection she had had at the clinic; partly that she had gotten all blistered up from a four-dollar permanent she had had; partly that she hadn't had much sleep, since she had gotten up very early in order to do all those things before work. And then when she had gone home to give Cecile her dinner and was starting right out again to come back over to Manhattan to see me, she had tried to pick herself up with a drink of Fatty's awful gin that he got at thirty-five cents a quart, and it made her feel worse instead of better. When I tried to caress her breast, she turned away and said: "That don't feel good."

I explained that this was due to the heat, that I did not feel very well either, and invited her to try some whisky. The drink did revive her: she became quite lively and wanted to play the victrola. There was a number called *Mean to Me* which I particularly abominated —it was the other side of something amusing—but which Anna always wanted to hear. One of the stanzas ended as follows:

> *You treat me coldly*
> *Each day in the year!*
> *You always scold me*
> *Whenever somebody is near!*
> *Dear, it must be—great fun to be*
> *Mean to me—*
> *You shouldn't, for can't you see*
> *What you—mean—to—me?*

I knew that she would soon put it on and I waited with nerves wincing. "Oh, don't play that awful thing!" I broke out. "Just once," she said with a kitten look. "I don't think I can stand it," I said sharply.—"You know the reason you like it: it makes you sentimental about

Dan!" "That's the way I used to feel about-um," she confessed at once. "Of course it is, and what you really want is somebody to beat you up the way he did!" "Like hell I do!"—she laughed. "You want somebody to step on you and knock you around!—that's the reason you don't really care a damn about me!" "What's biting you?" she asked with a grin, but looking at me in amazement: "What's happened to your motorcycle cop?"—I felt myself slipping in some awful way— "Have you seen him again lately?" She had told me about this cop, who was on duty near where she lived and who had been nice to her and Cecile and had helped them get through the traffic. After that, he had recognized her when he saw her again, and he had even given her a note to a hostess at Krafft's, who had given her her present job. I had found myself a little jealous that Anna should have been helped by another man, and I had always had a suspicion that there was something left out of the story, since it was difficult to imagine that the cop, without getting some special encouragement, had gone out of his way for a girl whom he had merely helped across the street. She had told me with a little giggle that he was good-looking and she kinda liked him. "I haven't seen him since I told you," she said—"since he gave me the card for Krafft's."

But to me it had all become plain—what an idiot I had been not to see it! She had for weeks now been two-timing me with the cop, who was no doubt a dashing guy on his cycle and who would appeal to her much more strongly than I did; she was going with him to Coney Island—that was why she would not see me on Thursday—and she had got her new permanent for him. She was tonight just standing me off with the shortest possible visit when she was too much used up to be anything but doleful. She did not even hesitate now to show her indifference toward me—had she not refused to let me touch her breast? Yes: she only kept coming to see me on account of the money I gave her. "Goo' Lord! I'm the best girl living!" she protested as I began to accuse her. "Only you—that's all!—I wanted to take Cecile to Coney Island, because I've left her alone so much lately. If I'd been with her, she wouldun have had that fall." I insisted that the motorcycle cop was going to take them to Coney Island on his cycle; and I remorselessly continued to question her till I finally saw her grow sullen in her quiet and resigned way: "All right," she said, "if that's the way you feel about me, you don't want to see me no more. . . . Where would I have time for another guy? . . . All right: I'm going!" She did not go; but as I hacked at my cruel indictment: "I'm going, d'yuh hear me?" And she went.

I made myself another drink with a proud and determined hand. Now at last I was done with Anna! I was glad—I confessed to myself—to be sure that she had never really cared about me. How absurdly I had romanticized her, overrated her! Hadn't she probably always had other men? After all, my case of gonorrhea had never been fully explained. My affair with her had set up a strain that had been warping my whole life!—And now I must conquer Imogen—that was what Imogen wanted: to be conquered. She had never found her master, and she needed a master: it was obvious in all our relationship. She wanted me to dominate, to direct her; to get her away from Ralph; to teach her what it meant to make love; to liberate the passion that was blocked in her and that spent itself in petty and futile ways. That was what they all wanted—it was what Anna wanted, too. I couldn't be for Anna a motorcycle cop; but I could be for Imogen a consort such as Ralph had never been.—It would require my deepest sincerity and my steadiest strength of purpose. It must be now the prime object of my life that would take precedence over everything else—yes: even if, so late in the day, I had to resort to my father and go to work for General Tires, in order to finance her divorce. After all, I was a trained economist and should always be able to turn it to account, and a certain amount of experience in industry would be valuable for my writing: it would give me a firsthand insight into capitalism. I would, I swore, the very next morning, call up Art Niles at his office and ask him about divorce procedure: divorces had been one of his specialties. And how I wished I could tell Imogen tonight! At any rate, I should get her in the morning! I stood staring at a vision of her maddening breasts bursting out from under her harness.

But when I called her, I again could not get her—it was strange that no one answered at her house. I rang up Edna Forbes and learned that Imogen had gone away on a visit to friends in Vermont: she hadn't been very well and she needed a rest, and August in Hecate County was so frantic that she was not going to come back till after the season was over. Ralph was to join her later. Edna's smug and friendly tone enraged me: I was sure that she knew all about everything and was handling the situation with quiet tact. When I got back that afternoon, I expended an hour and a half trying to put through a connection with Imogen. There was a farmhouse a quarter of a mile away, and I had them send somebody to get her; and at last I heard Imogen's voice as indistinct as a disembodied spirit that can hardly get through from the other world and as guarded and non-committal as a political prisoner of the Fascists who is allowed to see a newspaper interviewer. I passed on to her both these similes as pleasantries, but they were not very amusedly received, and I got the impression that Imogen was not sure they were not somehow offensive. I could make no real contact with her—she answered my questions briefly; to apologies and professions she would simply reply: "Yes: all right." She didn't want me to come up there: no place for me to stay; she wasn't well, had come away for a rest. "I'm writing you," I said. "All right." I hung up, feeling angry yet guilty.

I had beside me another drink—I was multiplying my drinks before dinner—as I called up Art Niles's apartment. He was out, so I called Elsie Newbold. I had several times spent the evening with Art and Elsie and Elsie's partner. Now I learned that Art and Elsie were out. I invited the partner to dinner; and, although she had already eaten, she came out with me and drank while I ate. I brought her back to my apartment and made love to her. She was a stocky blond girl from Nebraska with a certain cornfed sex appeal. She had a wide and genial mouth and a way of pronouncing her r's that made you think she was biting with her strong even teeth through something nutritious and thick; she made Nebraska seem rank and attractive. She painted, and we talked about painting, and I became quite exalted over Breughel, and almost imagined that she and I were figures in one of his pictures: a lusty boor and his wench having a good bout behind a haycock. I can only remember admiring her enormously thick white thighs and pasturing on her ample breasts that flattened out when she lay on her back. I had the illusion for a moment that I was free of both Imogen and Anna, and that I was starting on a new and more wholesome life; but when I came back to my apartment alone, I found it rather creepy again from the women who were no longer in it but who had somehow left, on the couch

and the chair, the scenes that had taken place there—
and I put myself to sleep with a highball.

The next day was Thursday, and I woke up with the
consciousness that it was the day I always counted on
Anna, but that I should not be able to see her. I should
have to see Martha instead. But Martha I hardly yet
knew, and it was impossible for me to talk to her about
painting without first getting absolutely tight. I saw
now very clearly that Martha was not a figure in a picture by Breughel, but a serious and honest little girl, to
whom I had given some reason to believe that I was
beginning a serious affair with her. I called her up and
asked her to dinner. Then I got through my day at the
museum with an effort of coördination. I did not write
my letter to Imogen; all that, I found today, was a distant dream, a dream I did not want to return to. But it
came to me disquietingly and with daylight clearness,
before the afternoon was over, that Anna had not really
been unfaithful to me, that I had worked the whole
thing up myself. I went straight from a shower to the
girls' apartment, but we all had dinner together instead
of my taking Martha out. I was under the impression
that I was drinking less because between our martinis
and our highballs we drank nothing but beer during
dinner.

The next morning I had moments which disturbed
me by skirting an insane kind of panic. There was a
Gainsborough in my office that had been set on the floor,
and I knew that I did not want to pass too near it because I had felt an irrational impulse to put my foot
through the feathers. It was plain to me as I walked
along the galleries that the guards were all going mad:
I would find them in the Far Eastern Wing, where
visitors seldom came, muttering to themselves; and I
could see that it must be a strain for them to spend

hours alone on their feet in the presence of those spider-like deities and those dizzying oriental patterns, or even of a roomful of paintings, pictures of people in extravagant costumes, carousing and loving and hunting, which were totally irrelevant to themselves. It would be funny if someday one of them should—what?—snatch up a bronze statuette and brain that little woman in the duster who was silently making a copy of Bastien LePage's Jeanne d'Arc—and then himself give the alarm—would they suspect him?—would his finger-prints be found on the statue? I rallied myself at lunch-eon, which I ate by myself—though the caramel custard at the end affected me a little like the Gainsborough. I should not have to work tomorrow, but could I even get through the day? Why not beg off on the ground that I was ill? Not very good policy, as my father used to say—they would know it was only a hangover. But to hell with it! From the lunchroom I phoned Charlie Dumaine, whom I had lately been snubbing about Whistler. "You look absolutely gray!" he said. Nettled and ignoble, I went home. There was no letter in the box, of course; but my maid had left a note which I impatiently made out as, "Miss Stout say she want you to call her." Miss Stout was Martha. I flopped on the bed with a feeling that I had literally been flattened, like the characters in the *Katzenjammer Kids* comic strip when steam-rollers spread them out into pancakes. It was a question, I presently decided, of whether Imo-gen could or could not have children. If she could not, I should hardly be justified in taking her away from her husband. She had sometimes, at our recent meetings, slipping back into her earlier fantasy, discussed the question of our having children as if it were a real possibility. She had perhaps not wanted to risk it for Ralph's sake, but would she be willing to do so for mine?—and should I allow her to endanger her life? My mother would be glad, I knew, to have me carry on the family—my sister would never marry. It would be something I could do for my mother to make it up to her for deserting her in Michigan. I wrenched myself away from the bed and made an effort to take on human dimensions. I brushed my hair, buttoned my vest, tightened the knot of my tie; then I walked across town to the Park and took a bus to the Public Library.

It was cooler outside; I felt steadier. I was not afraid I'd slip on the steps as I climbed the immense marble staircase; and I waited in relative calmness for my number to come up on the board. I have forgotten now what I found out about the influence of Pott's disease on childbirth, because I soon became interested in something else which drove this problem out of my mind. In the catalogue I had noticed a monograph, published in New York in the eighties, on *The Hysterical Element in Orthopaedic Surgery,* and I had had the curiosity to send for it along with a large recent work on the general subject of orthopaedic surgery. I was so struck by what I read in the first of these—a pioneer study, apparently —that I looked the matter up in the second, and sat poring with a dreamlike feeling that I myself was imagining the book. What I learned was that a large number of cases which had the aspect of spinal disease and even of congenital deformity had been found to be neurotic shams. It was sometimes very difficult, said the modern authority, to tell the real cases of spine trouble from the false; but the latter could usually be checked by the following characteristics: the "neuromimetic" patient complained of extreme local sensitiveness (just as Imogen had done when I touched her back), whereas the real diseased spine was not painful; the spine in the counterfeit case could not always pretend not to be flexible (as Imogen's obviously was), whereas the genu-inely tubercular spine tended to become helplessly rigid; the "expression of apprehension" characteristic of Pott's disease did not appear in the imitated cases; and, finally, the symptoms of the real disease were more or less un-changing and permanent whereas the feigned symptoms were varied and capricious. The false cases usually had their origins in accidents such as falls just as the real ones were supposed to do, and there were instances in which local doctors without special lights in this field had gone on being deceived for years. I remembered that Imogen had spoken of an elderly family physician who had attended her all her life.

Every symptom thus listed by the specialist dropped into a pocket I knew like the billiard balls shot by an expert. I was disquieted and even appalled. I looked up at the great gold coffered ceiling that made the shelter and the canopy for thought, for cool study and the prob-ings of reason, and I strove to readjust myself to a totally new conception of Imogen. Did she know that she was living a fraud or had she always thought her malady real? In either case, it was unutterably gruesome. I looked down at the book again: "They wear their pads and straps," it said, "so tight as to produce excoriations, insisting that they do not give them comfort otherwise."

It was queer to be delivered of Imogen. At first it made me empty and giddy. As I went out, I had a worry-ing vision of pitching down the mountainous staircase. But I righted myself outside. In the dear New York streets of summer, I found myself sustained and stiffened by a mood that grew constantly stronger as my nervous constraint relaxed. It was a feeling of satisfaction—philistine and disloyal though this perhaps was—at the idea that Imogen was bogus, that the Ideal had been adolescent mooning, and that I was free to take my

pleasure where I found it—I noted and pardoned the
banal phrase.

Should I call up Martha; tall drinks? I was at liberty
to have all that now. Instead, I dropped in at Krafft's
and sat down at one of the tables served by Anna.

She pretended she did not see me, but I asked one of
the other girls to tell her that I wanted to speak to her.
She stood beside my table and said gruffly: "Well?" But
it did not take me very long to summon back her little
smile and to make her agree to come the next evening.
I called up Martha and told her I was ill—which was
in a sense true—and that I was going out of town for
the weekend.

Anna was dulled and subdued. "That's what you say,"
she answered when I tried to tell her how much I cared
about her. "You weren't so nice to me the last time,
you know." She resumed her sober complaints, but this
time I did not mind them. She said that it was impossible for her mother's hands to heal in the hot weather,
and that the family were now on city relief, and that,
aside from what Anna could contribute, they had only
four-fifty a week to live on. She did all her eating at
Krafft's, and—though Cecile had plenty to eat—they
were getting along at home on one or two meals a day.
"They were sore because I had my hair done—but after
I've been at my sister's, I get afraid that I'll get to be
like that, too, and I hadn't had my hair done for a year.
The gas was turned off last week because we owe the
gas company fifteen dollars and eight-nine cents, and
they thought I ought to have paid it." Her cousin, the
garment worker, who was also out of work, had broken
open the back of the meter to turn the current on, but
the company had found out and sent in the cops. Anna
said she couldn't stand it when anything like that hap-

pened: she had gone out in the backyard till the fuss
was over. They had had nothing hot to eat, and had
finally borrowed an electric burner. "What's going to
happen," she asked, "to all the people who haven't got
jobs? I'll always be able to get along, but what's going
to happen to *them?*"

She lay in my arms without interest; I had done all
too good a job in breaking up our love affair. Her arms
looked thin with their little blue veins.

"Last night"—she was brooding aloud—"I got up to
see if the door was shut, and it was standing wide open.
You know what we think, don't you? We think it
means that somebody is going to die." She had been
scared that it was Dan who had come back to haunt her
the way he had threatened to do. He had told her once
that if he should die, she'd have to die, too. She thought
she ought to say a prayer and burn a candle for him.
She felt that something was going to happen. They had
told her at the clinic again that she ought to have an
operation. "Why don't I hurry up and die, huh? Why
don't I commit suicide? I told my mother once after
Dan died that I was going to commit suicide, and she
went right out and tried to get my life insured." And she
returned to her obsessive idea that she had never been
normally strong because her mother had not wanted to
have her and had tried to get rid of her before she was
born. "She gave me that fur coat, though, after Dan
died. Mr. Rosen owes her a couple of hundred dollars,
and she made him give her a coat."

She was ill—she was seriously ill; and I had been
doing nothing, had been allowing her to get rapidly
worse—while I was worrying about Imogen and her
back! "Look here," I said, "I want you to go right
away to a doctor who's a friend of mine. I want to find
out what's the matter with you and have you get the

proper treatment. I'll make an appointment tomorrow, and I want you absolutely to go!" I had to wrestle with her shyness and her morbid fears, but one could count on her basic good sense. She went, and the doctor reported to me that Anna "inside" was "a mess": she had a cyst in one of her ovaries, and had been generally ravaged by something that looked like a gonorrheal infection. She ought to be operated on at once.

And from that moment I vowed to Anna the devotion of a kind of cult, as if I could retrieve my neglect of her. (Martha Stout was now away in Woodstock, where she was taking two weeks' vacation—she had behaved like a remarkably good sport.) I made Anna have the operation in the early days of September, when the weather was turning cool. She was frightened and depressed at first, but accepted it with her usual quietness. I went with her up to the hospital. She had taken Cecile the night before to a movie that had a revue, "because I might kick off or something." They had all cried at home when she left, and she had bawled her mother out; but she confessed to me she was dreading the moment when I should have to go and leave her there. This came sooner than we had been expecting, for the nurse quickly appeared in the waiting room and told me that they would put her to bed and begin getting her ready right away, so that I couldn't see her again. She had brought nothing to the hospital but a toothbrush and one or two other toilet articles, which she carried in the zipper-fastened pocket of her little sealskin muff that had been given her by her mother with the coat, being too much ashamed both of her nightgowns and of the old valise which was her only bag, so I went out and bought her slippers and a dressing gown, a pot of blue African violets and some Japanese narcissus bulbs, and sat down in a drugstore and wrote her a letter. I left them at the hospital to be given her when she came out of the anaesthetic. I went home and spent the evening alone.

They took her into the ward—I learned later—and put a screen around her, and shaved her from the breasts down; her skin was so tender that they scratched her. Then they rubbed her with ether and swathed her in a big bandage. She was frightened, but it made her feel important, and she found that she was rather enjoying not having to do housework and get meals. She had cleaned house and attended to everything the last day or two before she left home, and now it was distinctly pleasant to feel that other people were doing those things while she was just lying in bed and being waited on. She had manicured her hands for the occasion, and she had had her hair done again, though they had said to her jeeringly at home: "They won't be looking at your hair!" The nurse woke her up in the morning, and lifted her on to something on wheels, and took her up in the elevator and wheeled her into the operating room. The next thing she knew she was lying in bed, looking out through long windows that opened on nothing: she could see that she was way up in the air and imagined she had been taken to another world. The doctors and nurses were talking and fooling around with pans and bandages, and she thought that she hadn't had her operation and would have to go through it all again. Then she began to be sick at her stomach and conscious of insistent pain, and they were giving her morphine to dull it.

I was not allowed to see her till the following day, and I could not go up before evening. I had to wait till her mother had left her, since only one visitor was allowed at a time. From the moment when I saw Mrs. Litvak, I knew that the prospect was distressing. The pressure of a special anxiety had been added to her usual burden. "She's nervous," the old lady told me. "She didun wan' me to stay. But I t'ink she likes to complain." I found Anna lying stiffly with her head back—she hardly opened her eyes. When I asked her how she felt, she said only: "I've got awful pains." I told her that I had talked to the doctor and that he had said she was doing well. "He don't know!" Anna replied. "Aren't you beginning to feel a little better?" "Worse." Her voice was low and unreal; it scarcely made any contact with me. A spasm of pain began, and my holding her hand annoyed her. She pulled it away and frowned, wincing with her mouth. She had not been able to eat, had had nothing but a little water, and she looked so terribly frail that I felt life was running thin. They had taken out both tubes and both ovaries and had cut off the neck of the womb. She seemed dreadfully clean and pure, with a delicate ivory look, as she lay between the white bedclothes and under the electric light. "Are they bad?" I asked. "Terrible," she breathed, with the awful simplicity of suffering. Her face with its eyelids lowered and its common Slavic nose had a dignity that made me silent. I knew that she did not want me to touch her; I could only sit and see her writhe in a new convulsion of pain. She complained of the "gas" in her throat and put a finger to the back of her tongue. I asked her, when the pangs had passed, whether she had got my letter and liked the flowers. She nodded; she was away beyond me; she could not have read the letter. I felt that she was exercising restraint so as not to be irritable with me as she had evidently been with her mother. They came to give her a shot of morphine, so I left her. When I kissed her good-by, she murmured in a voice that I could hardly hear but as if she were speaking impersonally: "I am going to die tonight." "What? Oh, no, you're not," I replied. "I can't stand another night like the last!"

I went home on the subway sickened. It was as if all my faculties were jammed, and I were helpless to think, feel or imagine while Anna hung half out of life. I lay in my bed in the dark, and kept saying aloud, "Oh, darling!" If I could only have had her there with my arms around her! She had come to my apartment so many times, sensible and smiling and curt, mindful of her relationships and duties, smoking her cigarettes. In that room of mine, too, now a bachelor's cell, she had stiffened and stretched back and closed her eyes—but in the shudder of passion then, for the positive response of life, instead of from faintness and pain. I thought of her poor little body with its feminine apparatus never to be complete again.

I could not relax in sleep. Tonight for the first time in weeks I had not had the three or four highballs that usually kept me stupefied till morning: my visit had stopped me from drinking as it had stopped me from everything else. I could achieve nothing better than a half-sleep that reminded me of the fakir's spiked mat. Then, suddenly, with a shock, I had the impression that the telephone had been ringing. It was the hospital—I had given them my number—they had called me because Anna had died. I leapt up and dashed into the living room, snatched up the receiver and said, "Hello," but there was only an unbroken buzzing.

I went back to bed and was tortured by a fear that I had missed the call. Oughtn't I to ring up the hospital and find out whether or not they had called me? Yet now, becoming quite wide awake, I knew that there had been no call, that it had been merely my straining anxiety. And now very clearly, with a hideous insistence—in the sleepless sobriety of the drinker who has tried to go to sleep without drinks—there pressed upon me a question, a conviction: didn't I really want Anna to die? I cared about her, I had come to depend on her; and yet she was impossible for me: under everything I wanted her to die, because that would do away with my problem and make life more comfortable again. Tonight when I had thought I should lose her, should be relieved of responsibility for her, I had been under the impression that I loved her as I had never loved her before; but it was all sentimentality, hypocrisy. I regarded now with horror and disgust my broodings of a few hours back, my dwellings on her agony in the hospital, my contrast with our former enjoyments. All that —I accused myself now—had been the maudlin and maniacal tenderness that is the other side of unconfessed cruelty.

What was making me cruel?—frustration? The fact that I could not decide either to put through my book or make money?—that I could not succeed, through the book itself, in reconciling economics with aesthetics?— But at the bottom of this, all along, had been my two years' frustration over Imogen. She had beckoned me, bedeviled me, blocked me; and finally, even in yielding, she had involved me in a new kind of stalemate that resulted in hellish scenes, a relationship of mutual torment. And hadn't I, in consequence of this, got to the point where I wanted to hurt her?—hadn't she told me so that horrible night in July?—and hadn't I, complacently and quietly, been compensating for my failure to do so through the sufferings of poor little Anna?—deriving a satisfaction from her husband's bad treatment of her, from her anxieties over her mother and Cecile, from seeing her as the wretched butt of the brutality of the capitalist system?—from having her, by reason of her poverty, of her humility, of her gratitude toward me, at the same sort of insuperable disadvantage as that at which Imogen had for so long held me? And now was I not really gloating, under pretense of pity and fear, over, virtually, her disembowelment?

Then, just as I was subsiding again into a slumber of nightmare and nerves, the telephone did ring: the mechanical steely shriek cut me awake like a whip. I listened and heard it again. Yet it was almost a relief to be summoned to take hold of something screaming and real. It was a telegram and dazed me a little: I asked them to read it again. "Arriving town Sunday morning ten forty-five from Rutland taking afternoon train country. Imogen." I remembered that I had written her an affectionate letter, trying to put things on an amiable basis.

I smiled with self-satisfaction, drank a highball and went to bed.

On my next visit, Anna seemed better. In the late afternoon light, she had no longer that deathlike beauty: she looked more human, though the tint of her face was flat and her hair without sheen and stringy. The sun hurt her little gray eyes. She had slept only half the night; but her pains were not now so bad, and the doctor was tapering off with the morphine. She said she did not mind being touched, and faintly but distinctly from time to time she would return my hand's pressure; once, when my face was near hers, she moved her head to kiss me.

I saw her very clearly now in this bare and sober atmosphere of the hospital and against its neutral background. It was as if her personality here had been purged and thinned down like her body till it appeared in its simplest essence; and it was as if my morbid paroxysm of the night before had purged me, too, of

my false emotions, so that at last it was possible for me
to form a conception as I had not been able to do before
of what Anna was like in herself apart from her home
and from her relation to me. It was plain—and cor-
roborated my feeling at the same time that it somehow
surprised me—that the people in the hospital adored
her. When she had first come into the ward, the other
patients had taken her for a child and had not thought
it right to discuss with her their gynecological ailments;
but when the nurse had been shaving her for the surgery, she had made them all laugh by saying, "It took
me seven years to grow that crop!", and before long the
livelier women were making jokes about "my operation," and then had found out that Anna had more
awful things the matter with her than any of them.
Anna said that she and they had a lot of fun together,
but that they were all going out of there soon, and she
would be left all alone. "But there'll be others coming
in," I reassured her. "They couldn't be such a good
crowd!" she said. The nurses were nice, too. But some
things that she had heard had worried her: she had
been told about a room that was just across the hall
where they took people when they were dying; and one
woman who had been in the hospital a month and
showed no signs of getting well had come into their
ward and complained and cursed and made everybody
very uncomfortable.

Her mother arrived, and they were cunning together.
Mrs. Litvak, quite neckless and shaped like a cask, with
her glittering round green eyes, her round and platelike
face and her nose with its two round gaping nostrils,
looked rather like a mother pig sitting stolidly beside
one of her litter. But when Anna, with a new assurance
that she seemed to have derived from her hospitalization,
remarked to her that she (Mrs. Litvak) was behaving

better today because she hadn't done any crying, her eyes became immediately moist. She had brought Anna a picture of Cecile, whom they did not want to visit her yet. "Are you treating her all right?" asked Anna. "I beat her. I t'row her out de window," said her mother with unsmiling irony. Anna was afraid, she had told me, that they wouldn't give Cecile milk and eggs and other things they didn't have themselves; and she was afraid that the Polish boarder would play with her when he was drunk, as Cecile had once told her he had tried to. She now learned from her mother that Cecile had been going every day to the movies, and she was afraid she was up to some mischief because they didn't change the picture that often. "She sees de same picture twice." "You hadn't ought to let her do that," said Anna. "Who's doing the laundry?" "I do it myself." *"You* can't do it account of your hands! *You* oughtn't to do it! Get somebody to do it!" I saw that it was making her nervous to have both of us there, so I left.

When I came in the next evening, she was suffering. They had left off the morphine injections, and she was having to live through the pain. She had got them to move her on her side, and, when she heard me, she made no movement, but simply told me to come round the bed. Her eyelids dropped again over her eyes. She was afraid there were "complications": all the other women had been moving around at the end of five days, and she had been there four. They gave her enemas, which hurt her terrible: "When my time comes," she said, "I can't stand it!"; and she felt hostile toward the doctors and nurses. Cecile had been there that day, and when she had seen her mother's flowers, she had said: "Flowers are for happiness or they're for when people die—but these flowers are for happiness,"—an echo, I guessed, of what someone had told her, perhaps with malicious intent. Anna hadn't been able to remember it and had had to ask the woman in the neighboring bed what it was that Cecile had said. "If I die," Anna said in a low voice to me, "I'm afraid they'll send Cecile to a charity home—like they did my sister and me—I don't want that to happen to her." "You're not going to die," I said, "but I'd always see that Cecile was taken care of. I'd never let them send her to a home." "How could *you* take care of her?"—she had closed her eyes: I was afraid that her pains were beginning again. "I'd send her to a good school." "You couldn't afford to pay for her." "Oh, yes, I could," I declared. She reached for the bell, and I rang it. The nurse came in, and I went. When I kissed her good-by, she gave no response.

It was Sunday the next morning. I called up the hospital and asked about Anna, and they said she was doing well, but that was what they always said.

I met Imogen at the ten forty-five. She was for her rather tanned and wore a blue traveling dress. She was a little bit too businesslike, it seemed to me, and made an urgency of going straight downtown to Laura Bright's apartment: she wanted to take a bath, she said, and make herself look decent, and I did no more than suggest that my apartment was a good deal nearer. I thought that she might at least have let me wait for her in the living room at Laura Bright's; but she told me to come back at a quarter to one, and I was grateful at the same time for a stimulus that stiffened my loyalty to Anna.

The apartment was on West Thirteenth Street, and I killed time by walking over to Fourteenth. I bought a copy of the Communist paper and took it to read on a damp bench in Washington Square. I had not been getting it lately, and it seemed to me now rather false in tone. From my bench I gazed about at the phenomena of Sunday noon. It had been raining during the night and looked as if it might rain again; and there were people sitting alone, as if they had no place to go: a Negro girl with worn-down shoes and a grisly rush of teeth to the front, and a man lying asleep on a newspaper with one hand behind his head, bare arms showing hard and brown. A pretty young mother went past with a homely and dirty baby in a baby-carriage. Washington Square, I reflected, was a sort of intermediate belt between the foursquare uptown New York of big residences, offices, stores, and the downtown of old streets now degraded: the Italian swarms, the squalor of the docks; it was a landing that led to the basement. I got up and walked down through Macdougal Street, which had always kept its ugly name and which still suggested gangs of city hoodlums. I wondered where Essex Street was, where Anna had thought she must have been born. I would find out and go down there someday—I should hardly have time to now. I walked emptily over to Broadway and came back by Astor Place and Grace Church.

I found Imogen now quite refreshed. She had changed to a new dark-green suit that involved a kind of plaid silk blouse. I felt that she again wanted to shine for me: the green, yellow and red of the plaid set off her spectroscopic shimmer, and brought out the gleam of her hair under the green of a helmetlike close-fitting hat. I took her to the Lafayette, and we ate among the cream-colored paneling, the more or less Corinthian columns, the light hairpin-backed chairs and the ribbed windows that looked out at Ninth Street, on the platform at the end of the spacious room that had the air of a serious French restaurant but was never sufficiently cozy for intimacy. She followed my lead, I noticed, in order-

ing two eggs Benedict; and she told me about Rutland
marble. "They have so much marble up there," she explained with her factitious enthusiasm, "that they make
the sidewalks of marble—and the front steps of people's
houses. It's just like Roman days!" I asked her about
her illness, and she quickly passed over the subject by
saying she was all right now. I told her that I had been
living more soberly and introduced a certain note of
portentousness into the gravity and decorum that already
prevailed. Did I want her to feel that I was sadly concerned about the turn our relations had taken, that I
reproached myself for our evening in July?—or did I
want her to perceive that something else had cast its
shadow and alienated me from her? At that moment I
still hardly knew. "Why don't you come up to my
place?" I suggested with friendly politeness when I had
paid and tipped the waiter. "I can't: I've got to catch
the four-thirty." Ralph had come back two days before
in order to spend the weekend with his mother, but she
had to go out to the country to get things started running
at home.

We walked down into Washington Square, and I
spread out the *Daily Worker* on a bench that was still
rather wet. "Is that all right?" "Yes: I guess so," she
said. I found we were getting stalled: the cocktails of
lunch were wearing off. There were even more children
around, and it was difficult to feel any sort of privacy.
"You don't really want me, though!" she said suddenly,
as I was telling her how much I had missed her when I
had gone to the Russian Ballet with a party of stupid
people and had kept thinking how much I wanted her
there to drink in the color and the movement with
her half-open lips and her rapt eyes. "Oh, yes, I do,"
I answered, and paused to think what to say next;
but she went on: "I'm sorry I was so horrid that

night, but I was upset from meeting those people and everything." "I know you were. I was, too. I felt terribly about the whole thing. I'm sorry I put you in that rotten situation." "You like to hurt me, though!—you like to humiliate me!" "No, I don't." I went back in my mind to check up on my attitude in presence of the brace: surely I had been all right!

A little girl on roller-skates fell down and began to bawl. Everybody stared at her a moment; then I got up and went over to her, and Imogen followed. "Where's your sister?" I asked. There had been two of them when I sat in the park before. But the little girl went on howling: she had, as a matter of fact, hurt her knee rather badly. We wanted to take her to a drugstore to be bandaged, but she told us she had to stay there till her sister came back. I wrapped the cut at the drinking fountain and tied my handkerchief around it—whereupon, in a defiant spirit, she went back to her roller-skating. "That other girl," I said, "had no business to leave her alone like that." We were back on our bench again. "I used to be left alone all the time," answered Imogen, competing for pathos. "I didn't have any father, and my mother used to be out most of the day teaching other people's children." "You were older than that, weren't you?" "Oh, yes, but I didn't know what to do with myself. Mother thought that none of the children on the block where we lived were good enough for me to play with—and then I wasn't able to do anything very active. I used to make up long romances in which I was always the heroine and always terribly oppressed and persecuted. I was a princess who'd been locked up in the castle of a horrible ugly monster—something like Beauty and the Beast—and then, finally, all of a sudden, the monster would turn into a prince, who'd been in love with me all the time. And then all the locks would fly open and all the chains would fall away—they'd had me chained to the bed; and the trumpets blew and everybody bowed before us—and we were going to be married and be King and Queen. Later I worked it out with more historical background —I was Mary Queen of Scots; but I made up my own story about her: the executioner turned out to be my friend. He was a nobleman whose duchy had been stolen, and he beheaded a wax figure in my place, and took me away with him to live in France." "All that wasn't awfully good for you, was it?" "No: I suppose not," she acknowledged after a moment, rebuffed. "I know I'm awfully queer. I'm sorry I'm so queer—I don't want to be. It's like that fairy story I used to make up. I've always thought that someday there'd be somebody who would come and break open the locks."

I was silent. "But tell me about *yourself,*" she went on. "Something's been happening to you." My restraint became portentous again. "Well,"—I paused a moment before I came out with it—"you were right when you thought I had a girl-friend who belonged to the prole-tariat,"—I gave the word an ironic emphasis that depre-cated her invidious view. "I knew you did," she said, but this time she did not look up at me, and I felt that she was masking a shock. I told her the story of Anna, and, though I kept it sober and brief, I made it sound sufficiently romantic: my meeting her first in the dance-hall, when Imogen had been away; the menace of Dan and the gangsters; her agony and the operation and my worry for fear she wouldn't pull through. Imogen sat silent, impressed: for once she made no effort to assert herself, though I was expecting her at any moment to tell me that she had been just as ill. "You really love her," she said at last. "You never really loved me." "You know I did, but you wouldn't let me." "I let

you," she quietly reminded me. "Yes, my dear," I retorted; "but, as you always said, I couldn't really have
you." "And you've really had this Russian girl?" "Yes,
I suppose I have." "Why don't you marry her?" "I've
thought about it. She'd really make a wonderful wife,"
—and I went on about the good qualities of Anna.
"Goethe married his cook," said Imogen. "Yes, and
think of all the painters who married their models,"—I
was prepared to develop the theme—"women who
knew nothing about their painting and yet made them
happy as women. They didn't worry about their social
position because the life that an artist leads is outside all
the social positions. The artist makes his own position,
which is about the nearest thing you can get to being
above the classes. The great painters got their subjects
out of the people when they didn't have to paint portraits for a living. They exalted them as John the Bap-
tists and madonnas and Josephs and Christs—and what
have we got by our American artists? They've salvaged
a few New England fishermen and a few Greenwich
Village kids as homely or wistful types, but they've done
nothing to transfigure the ordinary people, to bring out
what's really in them.—Not, of course, that our material
is quite so good as the material they had in the Renaissance. Our people have been all pared down and
flattened out by the industrial system—and they've been
living among buildings without faces so long that
they've hardly got faces themselves. Yet when you think
of all the human dignity, all the courage and endurance
and loyalty, that are still unspoiled in a city like this"—
I gestured toward the East Side—"you want to do something to vindicate it!—especially now that they're not
even getting the food that this country can provide in
such quantities and are being turned out of their houses
—and very pleasant little houses a lot of them are. The

competitive process has produced incidentally a great many excellent things, but now it has made it impossible for people to get those things—and the ignorance and impotence and imperviousness of the Hoover administration are closing down on the country like a darkness. I will say for the Communists that they've got the guts to go on bawling in season and out of season that capitalism won't work and will have to go!"—"Are you a Communist?" Imogen asked. "No, I'm not: I wouldn't do as a Communist; but I can certainly see the necessity for a sounder society than the one we've got, and for some kind of better life than this life that we all live!" —"I'm sorry I couldn't be what you wanted," she said. "I know you're a brilliant man and that you want to have a career that's different. I wish I could go with you, but I can't. You wouldn't want me, besides." "I'd want you all right," I was answering; but she looked at her wrist-watch and cut me short: "I must go to get my train," she said.

I had noted with gratification that her hand was trembling with tension.

As soon as I had left Imogen at the station, I took a cab and went uptown to Anna. She had had, it seemed, her first good night's sleep. She could sit up and smoke cigarettes, and the creaminess of her face had a tinge of pink. The new blue dressing gown I had given her brought out the blue in her eyes, which were peculiarly lively and clear. She felt, as she said, "ambitious," and had been manicuring the nails of a patient who was too weak to do it herself. The head of the "social service" came in and said a few words to Anna and tickled the back of her neck with her forefinger, and Anna, as soon as she had left, repeated the gesture on herself, with a grin at me, half mocking, half pleased. And presently a patient in a bathrobe drifted in from another ward, and demanded with a friendly sharpness: "How do you get to be a pet?" I could see that she had on the floor a certain reputation; and she enjoyed being imperious and important. When her mother came in later on, Anna began at once to bring an indictment against Fatty in an authoritative tone that surprised me. She had learned from someone else in the family that he had locked Cecile out of the house and that somebody had found her crying. Then, as soon as she had expressed herself thus, she seemed to feel that she had gone too far: "I'll be nicer when I get out," she said. "I won't be so bad-tempered any more, because I won't be sick all the time." I could see now that, just as she was liked in the hospital, so she commanded from her family a special respect: in some way they depended on her as I myself had come to do. The kind of thing she gave them, I thought, was the kind of thing she'd given me when I had told her, on a previous visit, that in my worry I had taken to liquor: "Drinking won't help," she had said, too gentle to be sharp and too ill to joke, but with a kind of detached severity; and that evening I had gone to bed sober. Now my talk about Anna with Imogen had intensified my appreciation and made me feel that I must make a decision as to what I should do about her.

Her Aunt Sophie was visiting her that evening. Anna hadn't let her come before, because, she said, she was "too dramatic"; but I found her good-mannered and quiet. Like her sister, she was rather short and bun-shaped, but better-looking and better-dressed. Her brown eyes showed intelligence and a certain poise, and she spoke English quite correctly and with relatively little accent. Anna told me the next day that Aunt Sophie had tremendously cheered her up by assuring her that it wasn't true that Anna's mother, as she had always be-

lieved, had just let her father die and wouldn't do anything for him, and that she had been mean to Anna
and her sister. Aunt Sophie and I left together so that
Anna could be alone with her mother; and when we
looked back up, from outside, at the window where
Anna was sitting, she waved to us, animated and smiling, a slight little figure in blue, through the ebbing
September light.

I went downtown with Aunt Sophie in the subway,
and we talked about Shalyapin and *Boris Godunov,* and
she told me about Chaikovsky's *Mazeppa,* which the
Ukrainians regarded as their national opera. She thought
there would soon be a war in Europe unless America
did something to stop it. I saw from Aunt Sophie that
the family really belonged to a small bourgeoisie. It was
actually a case, not of Anna's emerging as something
mysteriously superior, but of her mother's having somehow fallen below the family standards. Poor Anna herself suffered so from the illusion of sharing her mother's
disgrace that she had never been able to bring herself
to do the things that, in Aunt Sophie's opinion, were
proper for a Ukrainian girl: to go to the dances at the
Ukrainian club and get herself a nice Ukrainian husband.
Aunt Sophie was correct and conventional in just about
the same fashion, and cultivated and interested in public
events to just about the same degree, as my own aunt
in Hecate County. It may still have had something to do
with my recent conversation with Imogen that Anna
and her aunt and her mother all seemed to me so sympathetic that evening. They had qualities, I was telling
myself, that Anglo-Saxons and such people lacked: a
human response to life, that was humorous, considerate,
quiet. I liked to think of what old Mrs. Litvak had said
about the Japanese narcissus: "They want to be left

alone,"—as if they had been beings one lived with and whose habits one had to know.

I knew that I had scored off Imogen, and when I was back in my apartment alone, I wondered whether I had hurt her feelings.

I went over to see Anna in Brooklyn the Saturday after she got out of the hospital. They had given her a little room to herself, at the back of the house on the second floor, which smelt of some kind of cheap varnish that they put on the doors and the woodwork. She was still very weak: she had tried to take a bath and had not been able to get out of the tub. She had got dressed and made up for my visit, but the little brown dress with her in it looked as if they could have passed through a ring like the fabulous oriental silks. She didn't want me to kiss her hands because she thought they had grown so thin; and when I put my hand over her breast, she said: "There's nothing there any more!" But the night she had first come home she had had a dream that was fine, and she knew she was going to be all right. "What was the dream about?" I asked. "What do you think? You and me. We were trying to make love on a bed that had a woman already in it, and there were people all around." "That was from being in that ward for so long,"—I gave her softly an amorous kiss and found that she flushed in response.

One day at the hospital, however, I had been rather surprised at being asked to wait. I had put it down to some treatment or necessity; but two days later the same thing had occurred, and, as I had sat watching the people come and go, I had noticed a little lean stooping man with small blue eyes and a pointed nose who left the building just as I was summoned. "Who has just been to see you?" I had asked. She had been obviously wor-

ried and depressed: "I didun want to tell you," she had
said, and then explained that it was a fellow named Stan
whom she had met at the Polish picnic. He had afterwards come to see her, and she had allowed him to take
her to the movies. He worked in a Norwegian drugstore over near Prospect Park. "He likes me," she had
confessed to my questions. "He *must* to come to see me
in the hospital. But I don't like-um—I won't lettum kiss
me. I didun want you to know about it!" I now asked
her a little disapprovingly whether Stan had been coming to see her at home. "Oh, yes!"—she mocked his
simple-minded persistency—"he's been here every day.
He says he wants me to marry-um.—Oh, don't worry!—
I don't like-um. My mother and Fatty think he's fine
because he comes and plays pinochle with them in the
evenings—but *I* couldn't like a Pole!"

At this moment her cousin Leo, the garment worker,
paid a call with his wife and their little girl. He had
olive skin, round black eyes and a long, perhaps Jewish
nose. His wife—a Czech—was pretty and nicely dressed,
with blue eyes and a knife-like profile. I found them sympathetic, and the child seemed nice: she was a good deal
quieter than Cecile and had gentle pale blue eyes. They
were all rather pale and thin. I had heard something
about Leo from Anna, and we talked about the garment
trades. He was a marker and cutter, and had once made
good money; but he had gotten a black eye with the
Amalgamated through belonging to one of their locals
that had been captured by a racketeer. He hadn't known
at the time what was going on, but now the union
wouldn't give him a job. He hadn't had any regular
work for almost two years now, and he wasn't able
even to pay his union dues, and that made the situation worse. Now he was working for the CWA for
thirteen dollars a week, which wasn't even enough to

buy food—they had a two-and-a-half-year-old baby as well as the little girl. I asked him what he was doing now and he confessed, with a shame just discernible in a moment of hesitation, that he had started in with a shovel. The boss had told him that he seemed intelligent, not like most of these guineas, and had promoted him to be a field clerk, but he had found that this didn't help, because he got just the same pay and only had worse headaches. Now he owed over a hundred dollars rent, and the landlord threatened to evict him. Leo said he knew the man meant it: he was a wop who'd been in plenty of shooting, and his wife had a bullet in her abdomen.

He picked up Anna's old violin, which she had got out and had been fooling with a little because she wasn't able to do any housework. She had spoken of this violin, which had been brought over by her father from Europe and which was the only relic of him she had. She had told me that it was supposed to be a fine one, and had talked once or twice about selling it; and now I was surprised to discover that it did bear Stradivari's label and was at least one of the good imitations. Leo played on it a little old polka and started the overture to *Poet and Peasant.* Then he stopped and said, "I can't remember it,"—and he and his family took their leave.

As they were on their way downstairs, Anna quickly called in her mother and whispered to her to tell them they could stay there in a little room they had that was vacant. Anna showed signs of crying. Leo always had bad news, she said. He had been to Aunt Sophie for a very small loan, and she had told him she couldn't give him anything—their business was too bad, she said. And then she and her husband and their daughter had taken a trip to Europe just to see the Ukraine again—

and the money they spent on Eliena! Leo's visit had upset her so much that she went on to upbraid me, too, in
a way she had never done before: "You and your
friends," she said, "go out and make whoopee"—I had
been trying to amuse her with a story about an evening
I had spent with Art Niles—"and my people can't even
pay their rent!" I tried to tell her that some of my
friends were painters who were badly off, too, and
had been living on the artists' dole; but I had been
startled by her outbreak of resentment over a contrast
which, though to me always dramatic, I had got into
the habit of assuming she took as a matter of course.
Yet for them the depression was always going on like
a flood that swept away their houses, set them adrift in a
heaving waste and might capsize or drown whole families—a flood that never finally subsided; and the atti-
tudes, I knew, that I assumed to myself and in my conversation with others meant nothing in that bare room
in Brooklyn where Anna and her garment-worker cousin
were so sober and anxious and pale.

I was struck, too, by her exacerbated awareness—
which never seemed to relax for a second—of the presence of Fatty in the house. All the time that she and I
were conversing, she seemed to be able to follow every
movement that this monster was making downstairs.
"He's speaking English, so he must still be talking
to Leo," she would note as if to herself; or, hearing
him in the kitchen, "He's nasty to my mother," she
would tell me. "He calls her 'old whore' and 'old
monkey,' and I can't stand to have him call her names
like that!" He would come in to see her, she said, and
sit down and just manage to squeeze into the armchair,
and then he would have to brace himself on the arms
in order to pull himself out. But she no longer laughed
about him. She had given him some money to buy

things, and he had come back with tangerines, which she hadn't told him to get, and only forty-one cents of change: "Was I furious? I jumped out of bed and started to run downstairs after him, but I strained myself so that I felt lousy and had to lie down again." He had taken away the mattress from the chair that opened up into a bed and that Cecile had been sleeping on, and she and her mother and Cecile had all had to sleep together, and then she had found the next morning that he had given it to the Polish boarder, who hadn't paid his rent. When she had slept in the same bed with her mother, she used to put her arms around her and hug her in her sleep, and her mother hadn't liked it and had taken to lying at the bottom of the bed. It seemed to me that these family relationships were actually poisoning Anna. Since she had come back home from the hospital, she had even taken to brooding on a project of getting Fatty deported from the United States. He was a Russian and he couldn't speak English, and he was no good over here anyway. At other times she was able to convince herself that the moment had arrived at last when it would be possible to get her mother to leave him. He had just had a summons for parking his car in some place where parking was forbidden, and she thought he couldn't pay his fine and would have to go to jail for a few days, and then she would get an apartment and make her mother move out. The lease was up the first of October, and there was no profit in the house any longer because none of the boarders was paying his rent. The one they liked best was a cook who had had a steady job when she came, but she had slipped at the place where she worked and injured herself internally, and now she couldn't work till she was well, and her son hadn't been able to get a job. She was trying to collect compensation, and Anna's Polish suitor, Stan, had

told her that he had a friend who was a very smart
Polish lawyer and that he would get him to do something about it. But, anyway, Anna's mother had to go
back and work at Rosen's next week—"and she can't
always support-um: he don't do nothin.—But she
loves-um, damn it!" she ended.

I left Anna, letdown and abashed. It was as if I had
somehow imagined that by sending her to the hospital
to be cared for, by getting her first-rate surgical attention, I could somehow change the shape of her life, establish it on a more comfortable level. But now I saw
that she was back, with no place of her own and conse-
quently no life of her own, in that same hopeless
situation, humiliating, taxing, tormenting, from which
I offered her no escape. That night I drank too much
again, and it became to me perfectly plain that I ought
to take a house in the suburbs and have Anna and her
little girl live with me (I didn't quite dare to bring
her out to Hecate County, where my house belonged to
friends of my aunt's). It would be foolish to return to
Martha. I had succeeded in not seeing her at all—
though I felt rather mean about it—since she had been
back in New York from her vacation; and Art Niles had
intervened for me by explaining to her that old "complications," as he said, which I "couldn't do anything
about" had "come back on me" and got me "in a jam."
She was not the kind of girl who would bother you;
and my evasion was made easier for me by Art's complacent assumption—of which, however, I did not
approve—that neither Martha nor Elsie Newbold was
a woman to be worried about, because they were self-
supporting and wanted, themselves, to be independent
and were, in any case, not the "type of girl" one married. But just as I had got to the point of achieving a
certain elation and had put Beethoven on the victrola,

the telephone rang and Art Niles's keyed-up voice insisted that I should come over to Elsie's: they were all there and had a bottle of applejack. I said no and felt sore at Art for behaving so irresponsibly; but, the moment after hanging up, I was stirred by a desire to go and at the same time depressed by the realization that I was back in my old mess again. I carelessly concocted another drink and had difficulty finding the next record. It was dreary and rather unhealthy drinking alone like that and playing the phonograph for oneself. Suddenly it was clearly revealed to me—as if liquor had opened a window—that Anna had never been honest. She had had that Pole all along without my ever having suspected his existence, and how did I know how many others besides. That time when she had got herself a permanent wave, though they all were so poor at home—if it hadn't been done for the cop, it might well have been done for the Pole. He must have given her the money for it. And I had been troubled by my own infidelity!

I took a taxi at once to Elsie's, and, with the illusion of a complete liberation, spent a bibulous evening with them. I did nothing to reëstablish my relations with Martha, but talked to her as if on the basis of a friendliness of long standing that was full of warmth and charm.

I was rescued by a *dea ex machina* in the shape of my old girl, Jo Gates. She had just received one of her dividends, which the company had been passing during the last two years, and she wrote me in haste and by air mail that she was "leaping on a train" for the East.

I met her four days later at the station, got her checked in at a Park Avenue hotel, and took her straight up to my apartment. I had at first had inhibitions about seeing her: I had some fear that all the things that had

happened might make some difference in my feeling
about her, mixed, I suppose, with an apprehension lest
something might have happened to her which would
make her feel differently about me. But from the moment that we were having our first drink together, it
seemed to me that I had never in my life been so glad
to see anyone again. She smelt of Chanel 5, she wore
gray mottled snakeskin shoes with enormous French
butterfly bows that gave a pertness to her long well-
shaped legs, and she had brought me a bottle of brandy.
She came to bed right away, as a matter of course, with
happy eyes wide-open in the daylight. She took rather
longer than I did, but she finally went off like an alarm-
clock, and afterwards talked gaily for three quarters of
an hour until we were ready again. She regaled me with
all the gossip of Pasadena, Santa Barbara, Los Angeles
and San Francisco. "Isn't it perfectly mad?" she would
say. She told me about the burning of the clubhouse
and how nobody knew whether it had been done by the
boy-friend of a certain lady to get rid of some incrimi-
nating letters that the steward was threatening to black-
mail her with, or by a certain suspicious husband who
thought he was smoking out his wife's love-nest; and
also how Percy Martin had finally decided to marry the
ex-Follies girl he'd been keeping, who said she'd had
fourteen abortions and was pretty as green paint; but
one Sunday when he'd brought around a friend to call,
and had notified the girl that he was coming, he'd found
her sitting naked on the john and reading the funny
paper, with the bathtub full of bottles of champagne: "I
think it was rather a good thing to do," said Jo, "Sunday
afternoon being what it is—but it *ruined* her chances of
marriage!"

My tension was relaxed: I talked volubly, too. "I
thought I'd find you all full of girls," she said. "No: not

exactly," I answered—and I gave her a rapid summary which rather misrepresented what had actually happened but which made me feel better as I worked it out. I tried to convey the impression that everything was over with Imogen and Anna both. She told me that in the two years since she had seen me she had only had three lovers, one of them just for a week before he went back to Canada and another just for an evening when she was awfully bored and tight, and that she had not liked any of them so well as me.

And she told me how Reggie da Luze had been showing a visitor the sights and had taken him to Montecito. The visitor had admired the places, but "They're all whited sepulchers," said Reggie. Just then they came to the archery butts. "What are those?" the visitor asked. "That's where the married men practice shooting, but this field is just for the sissies—the real he-men are up on the range practicing with forty-fives and buffalo guns." "And where do they shoot the clay gigolos?" the visitor asked. I laughed very hard at this. It was so different from Imogen's world, and it was the world, after all, that I belonged in.

When I went to see Anna again, I found her very much excited over the birth of her sister's baby. Her sister had come to stay with them, and the child had been born there the day before. Anna had been so much distressed when the baby was on its way that I was surprised to see her refreshed and delighted. It was a boy, and they had asked Anna to be godmother; she referred to it as "that wonderful baby." I was a little bit annoyed by her high spirits; and yet I was unreasonably impressed. This was something women couldn't be indifferent to, the leap of life renewing itself. It picked them up like a switched-on current of which they had

been made the conductors; and Anna was as helpless
now not to be happy over her sister's baby as an electric
bulb not to burn. She knew as well as I did what the
chances were that any offspring of her sister's would be
wonderful; but the same instinct that made her so
prompt to respond to the contacts of love stirred her
to exhilaration over a child brought out healthy and
lively. We could hear its little whining cry as it woke up
and groped for its supper. "I can't have any more now,"
she said, "so it makes me feel good to be a godmother."

I inquired about Stan, the Pole. He came in every
night, she told me. What did he talk to her about? "He
talks about-umself, like all Poles. He talks about all the
big shots he knows in Brooklyn—and how he's go'na
do this and that for us. He talks about the Norwegians
he works for—he says all Norwegians are crazy. They
can't be any crazier than Poles! He takes photographs
and he talks about that. He had one of his photographs
exhibited in some show. To hear-um talk, it was a big
sensation!" For a moment I had a kind of twinge when
I learned about his exhibiting photographs; but I had
decided what I ought to say. "Look, Anna," I began,
"please be honest with me. If you want to marry this
fellow, you mustn't let me stand in the way. Maybe you
ought to marry him. Do you think he really cares about
you?" She was silent, became suddenly grave. "I
wouldn't want to marry a Pole," she said. I was sitting
on the bed beside her and—whether in an effort to soften
the shock or from an impulse to reaffirm our old close-
ness against the pressure of Jo and the Pole—I put my
arm around her shoulder. She laid her head on my chest.
I could smell that her hair had been newly washed and
had that fragrance of arrowroot. "Did your girl-friend
come back?" she asked suddenly.—I had told her long
ago about Jo. "Yes, she has—but it isn't that. I thought

maybe you'd be happier if you were married." "It wouldn't help for me to get married," she answered. "I'm never really happy or anything.—So you're done with me," she said in a moment, taking her head away. "I'll always love you—you know that," I insisted, "but I thought maybe you wanted to get married." "I don't want to marry Stan," she said.

She closed her eyes when I kissed her good-by, as she always did when she was kissed. Her way of taking love was solemn as well as eager and sweet. But it was the middle of the afternoon; I was about to go away on my vacation; and I was glad to feel as I left the house that I did not love her so much.

I fell asleep among moonlit trees, in the first wintry chill of autumn, under blankets, familiar and clean, that felt comforting and smelt of moth balls. It seemed to me that Jo and I were living together now in a house, and that Anna was somehow with us. She was friendly and smiling and modest, though, in contrast with Jo's spick-and-spanness, she did look a little drab. But the whole occasion seemed to be genial, and the three of us went somewhere together. Then Anna was a kitten I was carrying—then something had happened to her: was it perhaps that she had been bitten by a dog?—when I had carried her a little farther, I saw that she was bleeding on my hand. Then I walked into a luxurious house that was ugly, heavy and crude, where I did not know the people. There was nobody at home, so I began to shave in a bathroom made of black and green marble. Then the people were around me and I was talking to them—everybody was having cocktails; but the kitten had been shrinking up. I kept reminding myself while I was talking that I ought to put hot water on it or something; but I delayed for such a long time that there was at last nothing left in my hand but a queer little oblong thing, like a cocoon with a round hole. I finally turned on the water and held it under the faucet—a very tiny stream of warm water played on it very gently; and it shrank after this all the more—I couldn't seem to do anything about it. At last there was nothing left but a little round thing like a cell that got dropped out of my hand on the floor. I knew, of course, that I ought to look for it, and I did look for it but I couldn't find it—so I gave it up and almost forgot it and went on talking to people.

I awoke to the smell of my house, none the less homelike for having been shut up—I liked the feeling that things had been well put away. What a relief to be there among trees, and alone, in that bright weather of autumn!—the sun on the rough white walls, the Navajo blanket with its red and green angles, the chest of drawers in which a family of field-mice had once built a nest among my manuscripts. I had brought my colored maid along, and it was pleasant to see the plates at breakfast— they always made the food look attractive with their curly Italian birds.

After breakfast I walked out for my mail. The woods were now an ocean of yellow where the billows were the tops of the trees. On some the leaves were shading from lemon to rose and on others they had already turned rusty. In spots they were dropping profusely, and from the moment they lay on the ground, all the life faded out of their color. Through a clearing, as I drew near the road, I could see, on the lawn of a neighbor, a tree playhouse they had built for their children—and I thought of Cecile in Brooklyn. I stopped near the gate for a second to watch a gorgeous gold-banded wasp feeding on a rotted apple that, among the large yellow leaves, lay crushed in a rut of the drive.

There was a letter from Anna in the post-box. I had told her to write me there, and she had done so with a promptness that put me on guard before I had opened the envelope. It began:

I have told Stan I would marry him. He don't want me ever to see you again, so I guess this is good-by. I am all right now. They told me at the clinic I can go to work soon. Don't call me but just write and type the address, because I have told Stan I wouldn't see you and somebody might tell him. This is good-by. Thanks for everything.

Love,
ANNA

I made my appearance that afternoon at a cocktail party the Loomises were giving. All the textures and shapes of people's well-kept-up places showed cold-washed and brilliant today in the strong October light and almost made looking at color and form an object in life by itself: the sides of a white garage gave planes of incontaminable candor; and a fire-hydrant, new-painted red but topped with canary-yellow, woke the eye like a gladiolus. Here again were the Elizabethan house with its dark angles sharply humping out of the shrubbery; the green privet hedge, grown higher; the flagged walk; the Gothic knocker. In the cavern of the close beamed interior, I met a clatter and a play of deep color: women's suits of autumnal green, sweaters of blue or tan, bronzed forearms and red seasoned faces. On the window seat were golden-brown cushions, newly in-stalled since I had been there last, across which the sun streaked old gold from the long Elizabethan panes. There was a blaze in the marble fireplace, and that first feeling of people in the country digging themselves in for the winter and brought together for entertainment and warmth. I congratulated Helen Hubbard on her winning a cup that year; I had a generous conversation with Edna—in the course of which we laughed a good deal—without my being conscious of a word we said; I inquired of Kate Schwenk whether her problematical oldest son had turned out to be an artist or an engineer, and learned that he was in Venezuela. Imogen looked handsome in maroon, and with a new way of doing her hair which bound it down very flat over her ears and caught it up tight behind in a bun. I thought she was cultivating a new personality. She was dressed for the first time since I had known her in conventional country clothes, very smart and expensive-looking, of the kind that I had imagined her wearing when she should finally be my wife, but which she had now, I thought, arrived at through an eager emulation of her new local crony Bess Filsinger. Bess Filsinger was very rich, and Imogen had shied away from her and called her a *"parvenue"* when the Filsingers had first come to Hecate County; but now she said that Bess was really "a good sort" and "fun," and it seemed to me that I had noticed with Edna that Imogen's old confidante was making an unusual effort, as if her tranquil authority were threatened and she were trying to keep in touch with Imogen by warming up an understanding with me. The only trouble about Imogen's costume was that she was wearing brown suède shoes with laced ankles on an occasion when she had given the impression that she expected more formal dress.

I asked her about some new statues that I had seen through the leaded windows, and she at once took me out on the lawn. The marble figures were the Four Seasons, which Ralph had brought back from New Orleans and which they had placed in the four corners of the garden. Ralph had also caught up on his topiary work—his mother was now much better; and he had even made a bird with a fan-shaped tail, though its neck was a little disappointing and looked as if it had been partially plucked. "He brought back some *cylindres,* too." "Where are they? I didn't notice them." "We put them upstairs in the guest room. Would you like to see them?" "Yes." She led me over to the little staircase that went up the side of the house. As we climbed, I remembered the day when we had mounted that staircase first and I had mentioned the Glamis Horror. Had it been there? Had it been Imogen's brace? Had it been partly my own weakness and morbidity? We entered the little door and stood before the black marble mantelpiece and looked at the tall crystal tubes with their vaselike flare at the top and their glazing of a flower-design. "Oh, they're hurricane glasses," I said. I had not been sure what *"cylindres"* meant. "Yes: they kept the candles from getting blown out.—Very useful things, don't you think? Sometimes you have to have transparent walls to keep a flame alive." I acknowledged it: "Yes, I know"; and I was clouded at once by a doubt. Had the nobility of Imogen, her body and spirit, always been just beyond me?—were they there now within my reach, if I could only rise to my role? Had I behaved like a vulgar rake? "We put them up here," she was going on, "because we thought that the Elizabethan bed was the only thing in the house that they went with—the only thing that was big enough for them. Those plantation houses down there, you know, are grand like nothing else in this country. You imagine that all the people who lived in them must have been six feet tall—the way people look in Velasquez's portraits." I had just a glimpse for a moment—and seemed to tremble on the verge of illusion—of our life in a plantation mansion: Imogen all in white with a crinoline and a double row of golden curls,

moving down a wide curving stairway amid the glitter
of immense candelabra. I lifted down one of the glasses
and examined the elegant tracing, holding it between
my palms and carefully putting it back. After all, dear
gay Jo, who did know how to dress, was coming out
there to stay with me that weekend. I talked expertly
about the specimens of Southern decoration in the American Wing at the Museum, and we casually passed out of
the room.

Downstairs Ralph was telling Ed Schwenk about his
adventures on the Mississippi, and Ed was laughing so
loudly that other people had gathered around. Ralph
had always wanted to travel down the Mississippi on a
steamboat from St. Louis to New Orleans, but it turned
out that there was no more regular traffic and that
even the excursion steamer had lately been discontinued.
With great difficulty he had run down a boat which
occasionally made the trip with cargo and would perhaps, he had been told, carry passengers. He had succeeded in persuading them to take him, but the trip had
proved uninteresting and interminable, and he had had
to play cards with the captain and mate. They did not
even want to play poker, but went in for a card game
called skid, which they said was an old-time river game.
In skid you had to bet on every turn of the cards, and
the captain and the mate always won from him and
were always running up their bets. Ralph knew that the
game was crooked and pretty soon he figured out how.
He had also begun to suspect them of purposely slowing
up the voyage in order to win more money from him.
Finally, at Cairo, he had gotten them drunk and compelled them to play poker with him and won some of
his money back. Then that night, when they were blotto
in their bunks, he had slipped ashore with his suitcase
and taken the train to New Orleans.

Ed Schwenk was haw-hawing his head off at Ralph's innocence and resentments and ruses. Imogen was listening with her lips apart and prompting him with details he had omitted. When he told about rowing himself ashore and explaining to the watchman on the dock and catching a milk train at four in the morning, her face lighted up with a smiling elation; I saw what my jealous egoism had prevented me from seeing before: that Imogen adored Ralph's stories, that they had all been created for her and that she herself had partly created them. Out of his halfhearted pursuit of a career that he disliked but that did not really seem to her so bad as it did either to me or to him, she helped him make an Odyssean epic that had its excitements, its humors, even its heroisms. Ralph could figure as a hero for Imogen precisely because he was always a victim, and there was nothing in his stories to disturb her with the fear of male domination. She could sympathize with Ralph's escapes because she shared his sense of maladjustment, of being always at a disadvantage; and she listened to his adventures like a child who is delighted by Jack and the Beanstalk because, like Jack, it finds itself among giants. She had helped him to achieve this epic, as he had helped her make a legend for herself out of Ireland and Siena and Mexico—all those settings in which she could reign, in which she could admire herself, because Ralph was always there to be dazzled.

All this was what they gave one another; but she and I, for all our romancing, could never have a world in common. It was Anna—I saw it with a sharp surge of feeling released by my second cocktail, as I looked out the window toward the garden where I had dreamed of a villa at Candeli—it was Anna who had made it possible for *me* to recreate the actuality; who had given me that life of the people which had before been but

prices and wages, legislation and technical progress, that
new Europe of the East Side and Brooklyn for which
there was provided no guidebook. She had given me this
vision—I had lived on it, not on Imogen's infantile fairy
tales; and she had given me something else—something
that could not be accounted for in terms merely of her
fine little humor, her clear little sense of things, her
gentleness, her appetite for love. It was somehow the
true sanction for life; but what was it and how had it
grown? Out of deep and sustained feeling? in a natural
purity of spirit? Such phrases did not really touch it. It
was something so strong and instinctive that it could
outlive the hurts and infections, the defilements, among
which we lived—so organic that it could not be an-
alyzed. She had transmitted a belief and a beauty
that could not be justified or explained. Nor could they
ever be paid for or sold.—And what had I been able to
give in return? What had I to compare with these? My
passion for painting, perhaps. But I had not been able
to give her that.

Yet it must have been that passion which had brought
me to her through the prison of the social compartments,
across the clutter of the economic mess, and that had
kept me with her, happy, so long; and, as Bess Filsinger
came over to me, protesting that I was snooting them by
myself in a corner, I was felled by a sudden glumness as
I knew, and found it bitter to know, that I was back now
in Hecate County and we should never make love again.

5.

The Milhollands and Their
Damned Soul

ONE APRIL in the early thirties I happened to visit on successive evenings two houses that presented a contrast and as to which it would never have entered my head that they had any close connection with one another.

The first of these was Warren Milholland's. I had known him when I was a student at college and he was a young English instructor. In those days the English department stopped short with the Victorian age and did not admit the importance of any American writers at all. You were given to understand that Hazlitt and Lamb were worth studying but never told to read Thoreau; you were allowed to believe that the opium consumed by De Quincey and Coleridge was the legitimate food of genius, whereas Poe, with his laudanum and brandy, had been a shabby and dubious character who would not have been elected to a college club or received at a faculty tea; and you heard Cowper referred to respectfully by professors who made fun of Walt Whitman. Warren Milholland arrived among us as the prophet of a new literary era. He talked to his classes about Masefield and Shaw, and he made them read *The Portrait of a Lady* and the poetry of William Vaughn Moody. I did not take any of his courses because I never could see the point of studying modern English literature in college if you had no difficulty in reading English, and I never thought he knew much about anything or showed very much real taste or intelligence; but it was pleasant to have him around, and I was always on very friendly terms with him. Later on, in the middle twenties, when he had given up teaching for journalism and started a fortnightly magazine called the *Booklover*, he had sent me books on art to review; but I did not get in touch with him again after I came back from my years in Europe, and it was now a long time since I had seen him. In the meantime, he had gone on to manage one of those "book clubs"—the biggest one: The Readers' Circle— that selects a new book for its members each month, and had more or less left the review in the hands of his younger brother Jim. I assumed that he had been reminded of me by some sections of my *Nineteenth Century Painting* which had been coming out in magazines, for he had asked me to a cocktail party.

As I walked into Gramercy Park on a fresh April afternoon and saw the neat little grilled-in preserve of grass and the clean old brasswork and bricks, I found it rather pleasant to remember the literary and artistic associations which also touched that part of town with charm: John Barrymore and Edward Sheldon, O. Henry and James Huneker, Luchow's and the Players' Club, William Chase's house in Stuyvesant Square. I would not have admitted at that time that I was much impressed by any of those names; but it flattered me to feel that I had now won some right to take my place in that milieu. After all, Chase had followed Whistler, that thin pennon of our art in the eighties; and Huneker had talked about Matisse and Cézanne over his beer in the back room at Luchow's. It was then with a certain pride that I climbed the steps of Warren's house to the little black ironwork porch and rang the old pale polished bell in the green frame of the handsome white doorway; and it was fun giving my hat to an aproned maid and plunging into the high-ceilinged room that extended through most of the bottom floor.

This room was so crowded with people that it was some time before I penetrated to the Milhollands and an even longer time before I discovered that the party had been given in honor of a woman writer whose latest novel had been taken by the Readers' Circle. She was a middle-aged South Carolinian, frumpish in a lacy old-fashioned way, and was exchanging with a pansy reviewer, who doted on her every frill, pungent plantation retorts for fastidiously-phrased compliments of the nineties. I found no place in this conversation and tried, also without satisfaction, an Irishman just arrived in New York whose picture of Irish letters was entirely composed of malign little anecdotes and who declared that it was definitely impossible for anyone to appreciate *Ulysses* who had not personally known the Dublin prostitutes described in the Night-town scene; and a smiling and smooth little Frenchman, who had recently been admitted to the Academy and who made me feel rather let-down as I realized the unexpected facility with which the elegance and the clear formulations that one had always admired in French literature could be turned to the confection of banalities for the American women's magazines.

The Milhollands themselves were all there. I finally found Mrs. Warren, rather bewildered and lost in the party. She was a physics professor's daughter, whom Warren had married young, and she had always remained a faculty wife, merely becoming more nervous and vaguer under the demands that were made on her by their life in New York. Now she asked me whether

I had had a cocktail, but she had obviously no feeling for cocktails, and did not make any real contact with the celebrities that she was trying to entertain. She had even less taste than Warren, I reflected as I glanced at the bookshelves that kept literature well down toward the floor and where the classics that Warren had taught at college were now mingled with the miscellaneous products of the days when he had been writing in the *Booklover* that Carl Van Vechten was the American Congreve, Joseph Hergesheimer the American Flaubert, and James Branch Cabell the American Anatole France. I remembered that the week before he had turned up in the *Booklover* again with an announcement that Nancy Timrod, the Southern novelist whom I had just met, was "a Jane Austen with a sense of beauty and a flair for salty folk speech."

Jim Milholland, a tall round-shouldered bald bachelor, with horn-rimmed spectacles and doglike jowls, stood holding one of their grapefruit-juice drinks and joking in a sallow way with the publisher of Miss Timrod's book, who looked like a rather badly dressed butler. Jim knew nothing about literature at all and did not even, I think, much like to read. He had several times cut my reviews as if it were something that could be done mechanically simply by clipping off the final paragraph or chopping every paragraph in half. I only nodded to him; but I was quite picked up by a talk with the kid-brother Milholland, on his spring vacation from Yale, where he had been carrying on the tradition of the professorial modernity of Warren by much more audacious methods. Spike, as he was always called, had started a new college magazine in opposition to the ancient *Lit*, and he was passionately enthusiastic in a challenging and unconstrained way that made me feel that I already belonged to a superseded generation. He flashed and crackled with a romantic kind of Marxism that he had caught from Malraux and Trotsky, and he regarded the writers of the literary movement that his brother had helped "sell" to the public as economically so ill-instructed that for the thirties they hardly counted. He was not, however, disagreeably arrogant or contemptuous in a cutting way as I am afraid I had been at that age; he wanted to persuade, to be liked, and he played on one an eager smiling charm enhanced by a crest of dark hair that had an effect both untidy and dashing, and a pair of black eyes whose expression was always perhaps a little more vivid than that of any of his other features. I put his blank places down to boyhood and thought him the most attractive of the Milhollands. He admitted with ready generosity that men like Sinclair Lewis and Dreiser had done something to point out the diseases with which *laissez-faire* economy had infected us; but he foresaw for the immediate future a literature of poems and manifestoes with which the factory hands, the farmers and the office workers would be bombarded by revolutionists from airplanes. If a capitalist war were declared again, he believed it could be stopped by these means, and he was even taking lessons in flying.

Later Warren came over and made me sit down on their old rather worn college sofa. "I want to talk to you about something," he said, in his genial and homely manner that reminded me of my father. Warren had a boyish accent and clear though rather beetled-over eyes that had always commanded my confidence; and he wore one of those unpretentious mustaches, characteristic of my father's era, that, shaved off squarely at the ends as they were, with no smart points or rakish flourishes, make one wonder why they should have been thought ornamental. I was surprised to see how stout he had grown. "Oh, what I wanted to talk to you about," he began, after a question or two as to how near I was done with my book and who was bringing it out: "George Paine is working on a survey that covers the modern period in painting. It's going to be about the most comprehensive thing that's been done on the subject in this country. It begins with Moanet and Mannet and comes right up through Rivera and Benton. George has tried to explain, so that the ordinary person can understand, what the modern painters are up to—and he's been pretty successful, I think——" "I've never been sure," I put in, "that George Paine knew what the painters were up to." "Well, the reader gets the pictures, themselves—fifty-two reproductions in color. We think they're just as good as anything that the Germans have done in that line." The "we" showed me that the book was to be distributed as a "selection" of the Readers' Circle and had probably been written to order for it. I must have been moved by some author's instinct of competition and self-preservation, for I answered: "I hope there are some eye-popping nudes for the benefit of the ordinary person." "Yes: we have some fine nudes," he said. "But, to tell the truth, it always seems to me that some of these modern paintings that pretend not to be pictures of anything are the most suggestive of all. You know what Gertrude Stein says: when art tries to be abstract, it merely becomes indecent." He laughed, and his look through his glasses—though it had once seemed as limpid and fresh as the waters of some James Whitcomb Riley brook of his native Indiana, in which he must have gone fishing in his boyhood— gave a glint of a certain shrewdness. The sound of his laugh itself, which at college had been rather nervous with the consciousness of the heresies he was uttering, had now a certain fullness, a deeper tone, which denoted self-satisfaction.—"Oh, I think George Paine knows his modern art!"—he went back to my doubts about it. "I thought you might like to review his book: he has the social angle you're interested in." "That's being over-done now," I demurred, "by people who are trying to use it to cover up their ignorance and lack of taste." "Well, that doesn't apply to George: he handles the social aspect in a perfectly sane and balanced way—he doesn't let his theories ride him. We wondered whether you mightn't like to do a piece about the book in the Christmas number of the *Booklover*—I thought it would be right up your alley."

But this book by George Paine was the first that I ever refused to review for the Milhollands. I realized that there would now be conditions imposed which I had not had to worry about in writing for the *Booklover* before, in the pre-Readers' Circle days: I should have to say the book was good and I should have to make it sound important.

The next evening I went out to dinner with an amusing little man in the publishing business whom I had known as a poet and drinker during his year and a half at college. I had run into him in New York from time to time, and now he had looked me up because he had heard I was writing a book and he wanted to sound me out for his publishers. This firm was called Haynes & Kendall, and my friend's name was Si Banks. He took me to a place in the East Fifties, a former speakeasy and now a muffled restaurant, where we had some rich food and a great many drinks—all, he explained to me, at the expense of the publisher; and then to a little evening party at Flagler Haynes's apartment.

This apartment was altogether remarkable as a specimen of the taste of the period, and I was impelled to make some notes on it in my journal. The living room was done in white, but it had been given a queer harlequin effect, at once abstract and tinselly, by woodwork painted red and black, looped gold window-curtains of some heavy-looking material, and several portraits of women and men, all by the same hand, in which an unsuccessful effort had been made to introduce an element of modern distortion into immovable academic formulas. There was an aluminum cocktail-shaker, a cylinder with a sudden bulge, like a life-preserver, in the middle, which was surrounded by mushroom-shaped goblets that had cylindrical feet but no bases. A double vase filled with red and pink carnations was constructed, also, of shiny nickel cylinders, one considerably bigger than the other; and a table-lamp produced the impression of a pile of immense round glass crackers, surmounted by a blue paper shade with a pattern of half-moons and stars. The furniture was all low-slung and functional, and gave you the feeling that the people were more or less lounging on the floor.

The host, when we came in, disengaged himself from the furniture, the company and the cocktails, in a way that made one feel that the occasion was not a party over which he was presiding but a species of mixed smoker in which he had become involved and at which he was unable to feel himself altogether self-assured or comfortable. He was a smallish lean man, rather haggard, with lank dark hair that kept falling over one temple, and a nose that was disconcerting by its inadequacy, like the nose of a mummy or skull. He wore brown tweeds and a buttoned-down shirt and had a gold Phi Beta Kappa key on his watch-chain; but one felt that his collegiate gentlemanliness, of a wholesome and Western sort, had been partially soiled or infected by some taint that it was difficult to name. One could not be sure that he drank too much, that he was dishonest, or that his wife was unfaithful; yet there was something slightly furtive about him, and something that always seemed out of key. He smoked a pipe, but he smoked it nervously, as pipe-smokers rarely do, and was always knocking the contents out of it and probing it with a wire cleaner, while he told you some publishing story that made him forget what he had intended to do with it: when he returned to it, he would start to fill it, then remember that he had not finished cleaning it and have to take the tobacco out.

I could not tell whether he were married or not to the woman who had done the paintings and whose name seemed to be Lydia Moffatt. She was a blonde, who must once have been quite luscious and who was by no means even now undesirable—smooth and round, with a pink complexion that sometimes looked like strawberries and cream, sometimes a little blowzy, and very pale fair hair that she demurely parted in the middle. There was something oddly dated about her, something of the small-town pretty girl of the early nineteen hundreds, who has emancipated herself in New York and who wants to appear in the know. She grinned broadly and laughed a good deal, tightly wrinkling up her eyes, and her mouth was painted ripely with mauve, as if in a frank appeal to be kissed. Though I had understood the place was Haynes's, Miss Moffatt spoke rather ostentatiously of "my view" and "my cocktail things," and was flirtatious to a degree that appeared extreme if she were actually married to him. She so overpraised an article of mine—with a combination of hard Western *r*'s and phrases like "utterly fascinating," which seemed to have been picked up in London from some rather out-of-date milieu—that I became quite disgusted at the thought of it, and it seemed to me that the style of the article itself had too much flavor of *fin-de-siècle* fine writing of the school of George Moore and Arthur Symons.

But I soon became aware that to hold the floor was the prerogative of Brian Sykes, a brilliant and "exciting" poet. I had always admired his poetry, which had meant a good deal to us in the twenties, when it had first been appearing in the *Dial*. It had come to us like a series of explosions that had smashed-in the conventional windows and had made a polytonal music of the crashing, tinkling, gleaming of the panes. I was surprised now to find that his voice had the pure whinnying timbre of Harvard. He was a Haynes & Kendall author, I realized, but he appeared rather disdainful of the company. He had lately made a trip to Europe and had written an exhilarating book which was having a certain success. His line had been the opposite of that of the exiles of an earlier period, who, beneficiaries of the rate of exchange, enjoying the smart bars and beaches, had jeered at the United States and talked about the art of living: Brian Sykes, who, residing in Minetta Lane and seeing nobody but his girl and his admirers, had managed to remain totally indifferent to unemployment and closing banks, now went abroad to rail at the insecurity and poverty, the anxiety and the political messiness, of Europe on the edge of a second war. He had not found the fine things he remembered: what he had really hoped to regain there, I think, were the gusto and the reckless high spirits of the years of his own youth. In any case, he had interlaced his travels with flashbacks to the French girls of his army days and a trip he had made with friends to the Pyrenees, and had happened for the first time to bring within reach of the ordinary reader the erotic and romantic interest which he had concealed from the public in his complicated poems. I now learned, in the course of the evening, that Flagler Haynes had financed this expedition. He was evidently proud of having done so and of having Brian Sykes on his list, but when someone called attention to the fact that Sykes's four-letter words had appeared in this travel book with only their initial letters, he showed signs of uneasiness—though I found it impossible to tell whether this was due to shame at having emasculated them thus or embarrassment at having printed them at all. There was a moment, after we had first come in, when Brian Sykes had held himself in abeyance till he had had a chance to size me up, test me out by my reaction to his sallies, amalgamate me with his previous audience, and reassume his domination of the room; but he was off again soon on his act, which our arrival had interrupted. "That was the party of the season!" he said, improvising in his high-pitched and headlong way. "The party to destroy parties! Si—who was our gracious host"—he bowed in Si Banks's direction—"kept telling people who asked for the john to go to the door on the landing—which was the room of an exceptionally unattractive young lady—whom Si desired to annoy"—"She'd been complaining to the landlady," Si chuckled, "about the noise we were making at night." "So a constant stream of well-liquored gentlemen were pouring into her room—opening their flies as they came. I apologized with my usual gallantry—I got the impression at first she was pretty—I saw her against the light and I thought it was a romantic adventure—but then she turned around and she wasn't pretty at all!— and she said to me very bitterly: 'It's happened too many times!' " "Why couldn't she lock the door?" one of the ladies asked. "The lock was broken," said Si. "You can never get anything fixed around there," he added with a curious complacency that I had seen him exhibit before in connection with the squalors of his Bohemian life, "because nobody is ever paid-up on the rent."—"But that was only one of the sensational incidents," Brian Sykes fizzed on. "Bee Marsh bit Harry Adler in the shoulder and Elsie was furious with her and said she was going to have Harry treated for rabies—she'd just been reading about Pasteur!" He was scoring his laughs now on every line.—"Bess has been getting ferocious lately," put in Si, with his choking chuckle. "She bit me one night in the shoe and left a whole row of toothmarks." "Speaking of biting," said Sykes: "I went to the Zoo this afternoon. The animals were all wild with spring. The bears were necking, and the racoons were ——ing, and the baboons were masturbating. One of them, who had no girl friend, was looking gloomily into the adjacent cage, where a passionate party was going on—he looked a little bit like Flagler, in moments of doubt and depression—when he's gazing into some other publisher's cage and sees him screwing a desirable author—he had an expression exactly like Flagler's when he's worrying for fear some novel of Floyd Guthrie's isn't going to do fifty thousand!" So he went on like one of those Fourth-of-July fireworks called Devil-Among-the-Tailors that sputters with sparks, emits colored stars, now single, now double, now in clusters, and finally pops off with a climax of whistling and whirling imps.

"Hey, drinks! On your feet, Flagler!" said Lydia Moffatt with vivacity. "Highball? Tom Collins?" she demanded of the guests, pointing at them with peremptory sprightliness. Flagler picked up the tray. "You don't know how to make Tom Collinses!" she said, putting one of the goblets on it and flashing her wrinkled-up grin that may once have been fascinating and still remained smug. *"I'll* have to make them. Men really turn out terrible drinks—the bartenders ought all to be women!—Come in and see my dining room," she bade me, seizing me with one blond arm and propelling me toward the door—I had expressed an interest in the living room. The dining room was rose and gray, and contained some irrelevant examples of not bad mahogany furniture. I admired an old-fashioned flower-piece. "Yes: it's cute, isn't it? All these Americana are Flagler's, and they've only just been installed.—We're living together, in case you didn't know.—They're a pain in the neck to me because they don't go with my modern things." The kitchen was also remarkable: it had a fancy yolk-yellow dish towel, an elaborate electric refrigerator that lit up like a window display at Cartier's, and pastoral eighteenth-century wallpaper with green bridges, cascades and groves. "Si tells me you're doing a book," said Haynes, as he got the ice out of the trays while Lydia was squeezing lemons. "Of course there's this book of George Paine's, which the Readers' Circle is taking, but it's only a popularization." "George Paine is a dope!" whipped in Lydia. "I've always thought there'd be a public for a really good book on modern art—I tried to get Roger Fry to do one." "What did he say?" "He wasn't interested." "Poor Flagler: he's always having brilliant ideas for great books that people won't write.—Now, my love, that's *not* the way to work that corkscrew. Let me show you: you don't pull on it at all, you just twist it around— like this." "I'm going to—I know." "No, you don't!" —she laughed with maternal indulgence. "You always try to yank it out." "I've been wanting to do a series," Haynes went on, relinquishing the bottle to Lydia, "of really bang-up guides to special subjects. To sell for about a dollar apiece but really comprehensive and authoritative: one on painting and one on music—a bird guide and a butterfly guide—volumes on stamp-collecting and numismatics."—"That's really what the whole thing is for"—she gave me an old-fashioned wink. "He's a coin collector himself and he wants to write a book about it!" "It would cost a lot to do it right," Flagler went on undistracted. "You'd have to have a lot of illustrations—but in the long run it would pay its way, because it would go on selling for years like the Home University Series"—— "Now, look out: they're pretty full!" said Lydia, setting the tall Tom Collins glasses on the tray, which was already crowded with highball apparatus. "I was going to make another trip," said Flagler. "There's room for them if you just go *piano piano.*—That's the boy—the-e-ere you are!—now, don't spill! don't spill! don't spill!"

"Do send me that manuscript, old man," said Haynes when I was finally going. "I'd be awfully glad to see it."

I was living in the East Fifties then, not far from Flagler Haynes's place, and Si Banks and I walked downtown together. On the way I became so much interested in what he was telling me about the publishing world that I asked him to come in for a drink.

He was tight, and, as was characteristic of him, he soon dropped any professional discretion that he might have been supposed to exercise as a representative of Haynes & Kendall. "Why, Flagler," he explained, "started in as a sort of protégé of the Milhollands. For a while he was on the staff of the *Booklover,* and then he got money from somewhere and set out to publish magazines himself—he bought a lot of old magazines that were already on their last legs and they all died on his hands—and then he went into the book-publishing business." "And is that going to die on him, too?"—I knew that Haynes & Kendall was a new and rather small house, and I was wondering whether it would be wise to give them my book if they wanted it. "Oh, no: I don't think so. We're doing pretty well. Brian's book has been more of a seller than anybody expected it to be—and we've got that wisecracking cookbook that's sold a hundred thousand. Flagler is trying to get Brian to write another travel book that will be taken by the Readers' Circle. You know, the Milhollands would never touch Brian before—they wouldn't publish his poems in the *Booklover* and they always gave him nasty reviews, and now they're trying to cash in on his success.—You know," he went on, "the Milhollands make Flagler take their risks and their losses for them: that's really become his function in life. They couldn't be seen in public saying anything good about Brian till he'd somehow been made respectable—and Flagler had to bring out two volumes of his poems— which didn't do anything from the publishing point of view—before he produced this more popular book. Flagler's really the Milhollands' *âme damnée*—you know that French expression?—somebody who does all the dirty work and takes all the raps for someone else, while the other person goes around with apparently clean hands and enjoys universal esteem—like the portrait of Dorian Gray."

We were sitting in my apartment now; he had a sparkling drink in his hand; and it was stimulating him to one of those flights of extravagant imagination which, with his schoolboy cheek and charm, sometimes made him a delightful companion. "It's the result of a c-compact with the D-Devil—that's wh-what the M-Milhollands have really d-done!—they've made a big deal with the Devil." He had a tendency to stutter, which got worse when he drank and which he exploited for comic point. "They've sold Flagler into b-bondage to the Devil to take the c-consequences of all their crimes while they g-go on g-getting away with everything. There's a normal proportion of failure that everybody has to let himself in for; but the Milhollands have evaded their share and put it all off on Flagler. Everything they touch prospers—look at the *Booklover* and the Readers' Circle and that awful little book that Warren got out on *How to Write and Speak English*— when he can't write a decent English sentence. But poor Flagler has to fail for himself and for the Milhollands, too. There could have been absolutely no reason in the world apart from a diabolic bargain why Flagler should have given up the *Booklover* when it was just beginning to make a big profit, and frantically begun borrowing money to buy up old decaying magazines. It was grisly. I was still getting out *Galimatias*—you remember my little magazine? It had started by being a monthly, but by that time it was coming out only about twice a year. But Flagler s-smelt"—he gave his half-chortle—"the odor of p-putrescent type, and he asked me to lunch with him and his partner. It was an interview that chilled my blood. The partner was a somber fellow— I've never seen or heard of him since—he seemed to keep his eyes closed all the time—as if he were dead himself. The first thing he said when we sat down was, 'I didn't get any sleep last night—I haven't any appetite for lunch.' I couldn't see that his loss of appetite followed from his not being able to sleep till, as the conversation went on, I r-realized that he must be a g-ghoul. He'd been p-prowling around at night and s-sucking the b-blood of some magazine—and that was why he couldn't eat. Presently Flagler leaned forward and said, with a horrible flicker in his eye: 'I've heard a rumor that *Galimatias* is just about to quit.' I shouldn't have wanted to sell him the name, even if I could have edited it myself, because it wouldn't have been the same thing—I wanted to keep it n-non-c-commercial. If it was going to pass out, I thought it ought to die as it had lived—as an organ of the *avant-garde*. I wanted to get out one more number. I had an idea"—he bubbled at the thought—"for a review of Theodore Merriman's poems—he'd just gotten the Pulitzer Prize. I'd discovered a wonderful passage in St. Augustine's *De Civitate Dei*—in which he's trying to prove that Adam and Eve, before they were expelled from the Garden of Eden, must have been able to beget children without the incentive of lust and gives various examples of cases in which people have controlled their organs and even compelled them to do certain things for which they were not intended—there are people, he points out, who can wiggle their ears and their scalps and bring up things that they've swallowed from their stomachs, and so on—and he says, also: *'Nonnulli ab imo sine paedore ullo ita numerosos pro arbitrio sonitus edunt, ut ex illa etiam parte cantare videantur.'* " He translated and went on: "I wanted to do an article on Merriman the month that he'd gotten the prize, when the Readers' Circle was whooping him up and sending out his new book —I was going to put the sentence at the head of the review and have the title, *Ut Cantare Videantur.*" I burst into surprised laughter: it was true that, since the Pulitzer Prize and the sponsoring of Merriman by the Readers' Circle, nobody had said in print how mediocre his poetry was, and one even heard him spoken of now as already a national classic.

"But what reason did Flagler Haynes give for buying up all those old magazines?" "He'd succeeded in convincing himself, by some very queer calculations, that if you could only get together under one management a lot of old periodicals that were losing money, you could somehow or other make a profit. What happened, of course, was simply that he lost more money on five magazines than he would have on just one. The partner was supposed to be a business man—he had been dabbling in magazines for years. But he had undoubtedly been sent by Old Gooseberry to mislead and encourage Flagler—and to provide him with more used-up magazines—what's that word?—exs-sanguinated."

"But what finally happens to the bargain? Does Old Gooseberry just prey on poor Haynes and let the Milhollands go scot-free?" "No: the debt has to be paid in the end. It's r-regulated by D-Divine Justice." "But how did they persuade Haynes to take the punishment for them in the meantime? What is *he* getting out of it —if he simply has to suffer for their sins and is damned to eternity, anyway?" "He gets a sort of special exemption from certain of the worst r-rigors. He can't be totally damned because he's got a lot of good deeds to his credit—things that the Milhollands were afraid to do or that it wasn't to their interest to do. He has to fail, but he escapes a bad conscience." "He *does* have a bad conscience, though," I said. "He's full of a conviction of guilt if I ever saw anybody who was." "That's really *their* guilt," explained Si. "He does have a feeling of guilt, but he doesn't know precisely why, and there isn't any real moral reason why he should have it to that degree—beyond the ordinary skulduggeries of the publishing business that most publishers get fat and complacent on. It seems to Flagler that his conviction of sin is due to all sorts of different causes: his risks with his partner's money, the contracts he gives his authors, and so on. But he feels just as guilty when he does something worth while which apparently turns out well—like publishing Brian's books. He thinks that he's feeling uncomfortable because Brian had always been a scandal before he published this travel book and he's afraid that the next book he writes may turn out to be scandalous again; but what he's really suffering from is the shame that the Milhollands ought to be feeling for having behaved so disgracefully about Brian. Eventually he'll slough off this vicarious guilt—when the day of reckoning comes—and he'll be compensated in some fairly substantial way.—But what he gets out of the arrangement in the meantime that probably induced him to accept it is his intimate relation with the Milhollands, which gives him a kind of support he needs. He knows he has a certain security in his career of continual failure, because it's the obverse side of the solid gold Milholland coin—he can be sure that he'll always have resources enough to keep on making disastrous mistakes—he can be sure of lasting as long as they do." "Yes," I contributed, "it *is* true, isn't it? that in a sense he's one of the Milhollands himself. There's something in his voice and his manner that reminds you of Warren and Jim: that folksy Western accent and his spectacles and those tweeds he always wears—a sort of surface of collegiate smartness combined with the genial appeal of the old-fashioned foursquare American. But in Flagler Haynes's case—I see what you mean—something rather queer and sinister has happened to it: it's somehow being eaten from within."

"And of course," Si went on delightedly, on a further inspiration, as he poured himself another drink with an intent but deliberate hand, "Flagler's left holding the bag for Warren's other deviations, too." I asked him what deviations. "His sexual career of crime." "What do you mean? I can't believe he's had one." "Lydia": he looked at me in his sly amused way. "You don't mean to tell me——!" I exclaimed. "She was

W-Warren's great passion." I found myself astonished and shocked. "Did Lucy know about it?" "I don't think so. Warren had a little apartment in which he pretended to work. He was leading a double life—like any pre-depression broker. I believe he had etchings in his place. He used to be wonderful when he was telling you about it. I was working on the *Booklover* then, and he'd occasionally take me out to a speakeasy and talk about himself at great length—he was trying to catch up with the romance of the twenties. He would say that he regarded his double ménage as a perfectly 'civilized arrangement.' Lucy was still his wife and very dear to him, and he still discharged his domestic obligations—but Lydia was able to give him something that Lucy never had—and he said that he believed it was possible to love more than one woman at once, that a man may have several sides that have to be satisfied by different women. He'd get just that tone of mealy-mouthed reasonableness that he used to assume in college when he was telling us about the good points of D. H. Lawrence and H. G. Wells." "But why did he give Lydia up?" "If you can ask that, you don't know Lydia. She bedeviled him in all kinds of ways—she got to feeling that her position was humiliating and she persecuted him to take her out, so that she could be seen with him in public as his official girl—and she did succeed in getting him to go with her to a few opening nights and things. But he was smart enough to know that it was time to call a halt. And Jim finally made an awful fuss when something came out in a gossip column—though of course that delighted Lydia. But the *Booklover* is principally read by schoolteachers and provincial librarians and all kinds of people like that. And then there was the Readers' Circle. Of course Warren's idea always was that the people outside New York liked to hear about the liberated life of the 'civilized' city sophisticates—but, as Jim pointed out, it was one thing for the editorial committee of the Readers' Circle to serve it up to them in appetizing books and another thing for them to illustrate it in public. That's always been the great problem of the arts in America: how to eat your cake and have it, too. As Howells said to Edith Wharton about *The House of Mirth* on the stage: what the American public wants is a tragedy with a happy ending.—In any case, Warren dropped Lydia. She raised absolute cain, because she thought she wanted Warren to divorce Lucy and marry her, but she was making such hysterical scenes that Warren got really scared and turned her over to Flagler. She had to settle for having one of her pictures included in George Paine's book on modern art. George was sore as hell and tried every possible device to get out of it; but he couldn't stand to run the chance of having his book not taken by the Circle, and he wouldn't risk a showdown with Warren. Warren had handed him a list of artists whose work would have to be represented: he said that it had been compiled by a committee of experts on painting. Lydia was one of the experts."

"Did they ever try to sound you out as a candidate for *âme damnée?*" "Well, Warren took me to Lydia's one evening and then said he had an appointment and left me alone with her there." "What happened?" "She told me that my face had something very sensitive and pure about it, that I looked like Charlie Chaplin and Edgar Allan Poe, and that she'd like to do a portrait of me." "And did you let her?" "No: I told her she was a damn lousy painter and that I didn't want to be painted by her."

When he had finished his fourth drink and was getting a little sloppy, I explained that I had to go to bed.

He had got me quite wildly hilarious about the Milhollands and Flagler Haynes, but I wasn't at all sure, when he left, that I wanted to give my book to the latter.

II

But Flagler Haynes that summer took a house in Hecate County that was not very far from mine, and since one couldn't help feeling sympathetic with him and respecting his aspirations, I eventually signed a contract with his firm.

Si Banks and Lydia Moffatt were constant guests at Flagler's, and I went over to see them quite often. There was nobody else out there that year who could talk about books and pictures. He had rented a pretty awful house, a kind of suburban Italian villa with a roof of corrugated green tiles, that had been built by a New York doctor at a place called Spackman Point. This meager and rather marshy lump of land, which bulged out into the brackish water, had at one time been the object of an effort at high-pressured real estate development, but, though the streets had all been laid out, few houses had ever been built, and there was something especially desolate about the sidewalks and the gravel roads, now becoming overgrown with grass. The doctor—for reasons that nobody knew—had spent only one summer in the house. It had been vacant for two or three seasons; and Flagler was the first tenant. Our theory was that the owner had furnished it with the equipment from his waiting room—for everything had that professional impassive, wholesale and ominous look. One found green-upholstered couches and chairs that were discolored but still very hard; tinted etchings of Notre-Dame and a couple of other churches; a fringed lamp in a Japanese jar; and a painting of a barefooted Turkish girl, coquettish and picturesque, with a pair of curl-tipped slippers beside her. From the porch you could gaze out over the water toward a gas tank on the opposite shore; and the nights, at once suburban and unhumanized, were made brutish, without the commuters who had not built their houses there, by the insistence of swamp-bred mosquitoes, monotonous whippoorwills, and moths that bumped, flapped and swooped.

There was also a tennis court, which had been tufted with weeds and seismically cracked but which Flagler had had cleaned up and rolled; and we played a great many doubles, which were rather discordant and queer, due, on the one hand, to Si Banks's unreliable form and his propensity to clown when he missed and, on the other, to the frantic anxiety which Flagler brought to the game—a seriousness quite out of proportion to the attitude of any of the rest of us. I came gradually to realize, after I had signed with him a contract for my book, that it was true that Haynes & Kendall—I had more or less discounted Si's fable—were not doing very well. Flagler had expected an enormous sale on a book called *An Outline of Sex,* and had printed many thousand copies; but it had turned out—as Si told me he had warned them—to be too late for either outlines or sex. "Can you imagine anything flatter, at this time of day?" said Si. "The Milhollands would have known, without a moment's hesitation, that the book was absolutely impossible." Si's attitude was detached in the extreme about everything connected with the business; he never—save for purposes of frank comedy or with the betrayal of a deprecatory twinkle—pretended to identify his own interests with those of Haynes & Kendall. "Flagler'd intended to follow it up with a book called *An Outline of Communism*—but by the time he'd have been able to get it out, the public would have been oversold on Communism just the same as they are on sex.—Have I told you the wise saying of Old Dr. Antichrist?: *Marxism is the opium of the intellectuals.*" I laughed, and Si snickered. Dr. Antichrist was a recent creation of his. "You ought to get out a book of those," I said. "I'd publish some in *Galimatias* if I could only raise the money for a new number. Here's another political maxim: *In times of disorder and stress, the fanatics play a prominent role; in times of peace, the critics. Both are shot after the revolution.* Here's another: *All Hollywood corrupts; and absolute Hollywood corrupts absolutely.*" "That's not quite so good," I suggested. "I'm c-counting on the most brilliant ones,"—he defended himself—"to carry off the ones that aren't so brilliant. In any collection of epigrams, the witty ones make the others sound witty. That's true of Oscar Wilde's plays—it's true of La Rochefoucauld, too."

Brian Sykes also came out once. They were finding it extremely difficult to get him off on the trip through the United States which was supposed to provide a Readers' Circle book. He had insisted upon writing a play in verse, which was taking him a terribly long time and which Flagler didn't dare not to publish because he was deathly afraid of losing Brian to some other publisher. And, on the weekend when Brian visited Spackman Point, he never gave Flagler a moment's respite from delirious flights of ridicule at the expense of the house and its arrangements, implying that if he had known about them, he would never have come out at all; and he worked up, the second evening, after a swim in the bilgy water, such a disgusting satiric picture of the fatuous travel journal which he declared Flagler wanted him to write that the poor fellow was never to summon the courage to speak to him about it again. He also broke the strings of a racket by slamming it down on a net-post in a temper and exhibited it as the last straw of evidence of the utter flimsy absurdity of Flagler's place—the plaster, indeed, had fallen in the living room—and, by metaphor, of his publishing business. He made passes at Lydia in a way that would have remained rather kiddish if Lydia had not welcomed them so openly. He was much better-looking than Flagler, with high cheekbones and slanting eyes that gave him a touch of the faun.

Lydia was out at Flagler's at least half the time and might almost have been the lady of the house. She would not assume, however, any real responsibility for running it. She would arrive, bustling and smiling, with brisk exclamations of "Glad to see Mamma?" and "Well, children, shall I make you a drink?", and plunge out into the kitchen with an air of taking the whole thing in hand and providing for the comforts of the helpless men; but then soon would emerge complaining that the Irish girl had been impertinent and that Flagler would have to give the orders himself. And so she would bring out new pictures to substitute for the colored etchings and command us to move the furniture about with a view to making the rooms more "livable"; then conceive some grievance against Flagler and neglect to buy in New York the napkins or glasses that were needed: "Well, this is your house, not mine— you've let me see that very plainly. . . . Before you went away last Monday, you overruled my orders to Molly. . . . Why, I'd told her to have tuna fish for lunch, and then you told her to have cold cuts—you know how I hate bologna and salami and all those things." She was one of those exasperating women who are extremely dependent on men yet spend the major part of their lives repudiating them or trying to take them down. Lydia had two methods of taking men down: babying them and harping on their faults. She would be constantly *aux petits soins* in a way that would drive you crazy—putting a footstool under Flagler's feet or a pillow behind his head; fetching him kleenex from the bathroom under the pretense that he had a summer cold, and, if he failed to use it, holding it to his nose; suddenly snatching his drink out of his hand in order to fix it in some special way that she insisted was the way he liked it—all this timed so as to make it impossible for him to put over some story he had started or even to carry on a consecutive conversation. On the other hand, she would seize upon Flagler's bad judgment, Si's toping or my difficulties in finishing my book, and rib us about them with her jolly grin that she unpleasantly combined with a choppy laugh. If anybody attempted to retaliate, she would immediately burst into tears, leave the room with a deadly unobtrusiveness or call a taxi to take her to the station. She would make Flagler terrible scenes about his using up all her time and involving her so much in his life that she was not able to do her own work, then weep like a little lone waif because he had not thought to pay her rent. In moments of contrition, she would tell him that she knew she had been behaving like a silly child, that the only thing she wanted in the world was to paint a few really good pictures, and that she had actually been angry with herself for having accomplished so little lately and had only been taking it out on him. But when she did consecrate herself to her work, she made everybody acutely aware of it and we all had to suffer from the strain—though, actually, she spent very little time alone—of her solitary and selfless effort. She would announce—she liked best to do it when she knew that, for some special reason, Flagler wanted her to come to the country—that she was going to "take the veil" and stay in New York for weeks; but, after two or three days of this, a call about five from Flagler would make her dash for the next train out of town. She would protest that she couldn't bear it to think of Flagler, poor lamb, going out on the cook's Thursday night out or trying to wrestle with dinner himself. By the time she got to the country, however, it would usually be so late that we would have to go out to dinner, anyway; but, afterwards, back in that ridiculous house, we would sometimes have a gay silly evening. When Lydia had had quite a lot to drink, she could be amiable, quite witty, and charming; and when I had had a lot to drink, I could feel her blond and firm fascination.

One Friday I had come over to play tennis and found Warren Milholland there. Si Banks had asked me to dinner when I had called them up that afternoon, but when I arrived at Spackman Point, I realized that Flagler had not known about this. He usually said, "Good work," when he learned that I had been invited; but today I felt a certain bleakness and drew the conclusion —though too late for me to leave—that he would have preferred no other guests that evening. Lydia, I found, was not there; and I assumed he had some business with Warren.

Dinner seemed rather constrained. Flagler could not pretend to be anything but seriously preoccupied about something, while Warren was ostentatiously genial, yet could not help having the air of an important man of affairs who has had to take an evening out to chat and joke at the house of a subordinate or of an old friend he has passed in the race, and, with Lydia gone, I had the feeling at times, when the conversation ran on the book business, that I was eating with some sort of committee. Warren did, however, talk at some length—and from the point of view of content rather than of market—about a book that he had been writing on early New England. "The witchcraft rumpus," he said, "was all just staged for political purposes. The Mathers and the reactionary clique were trying to block the movement for self-government that was going on then in the New England churches, and they worked up the witchcraft scare as a red herring to get their congregations excited and take their minds off the real issues." I caught Si Banks's humorous eye, which had nothing to do with history. I remembered that he had lately suggested that the *Booklover* ought to fit up a small room as a natural-history museum for Warren's zoölogical clichés, which included the man-eating shark that editors were free to attack, the dead horse that it was futile to flog, and the sacred cow that had to be respected. The red herring also belonged in this exhibit.—"They played on the people's superstition," Warren was going on, "and they intimidated the whole community till nobody dared to criticize the preacher for his opinions on church government or anything else, for fear they'd be accused of witchcraft. When a minister found attendance dropping off, he'd circulate a story—as one man did—that 'a great noise' had been heard one night 'all up and down the town, with rattling of chains and a horrid scent of brimstone'—and next Sunday a big crowd would show up in church,"—Warren was shrewd and droll. "That's going to be a swell book," said Flagler. He got up with a certain abruptness and took a bottle of liqueur from the sideboard. "Do you want to try this Benedictine? I'm afraid it isn't very good. It must have a faked label because it seems to be synthetic—like everything else. The liquor's been a goddam lot worse since Repeal even than it was before." "That's

another thing the Puritans wished on us," pursued Warren, not to be diverted, though I had thought Flagler
wanted to change the subject,—"the idea that drinking
is a sin. That would never have occurred to the godly
monks who put up the original Benedictine. But the
Puritans thought that the Devil was in the brandy or
rum bottle, too." "Maybe the Devil was in Cotton
Mather,"—I broke in on his humorous shrewdness, suddenly finding myself impatient and stimulated to self-
assertion—"when he got people to hanging one another
as witches. There was something awfully bad that was
always cropping up in those early New England com-
munities. Jonathan Edwards, too. He was guilty of
spiritual pride in an absolutely satanic way. His congregation at Northampton were perfectly right to turn him
out of his church: he'd got to a point of snobbery where
he wouldn't admit people to communion unless they
were able to satisfy him that they'd had a religious experience which was as pure and exalted as his own. He
himself finally had to confess that the Devil had somehow got a foothold in his big religious revival." "I
thought you were a radical," said Warren, "and didn't
take any stock in religion." "The Anti-Social is the
Evil," I said, getting out of it with a smile, and it *was*
rather odd, I reflected, that I should seem to be raising
this issue.

I was wondering what line I should take when an
upsetting interruption occurred. The weather had been
horribly muggy, and we had been eating in our shirt
sleeves and, all except Warren, with our neckties off
and collars unbuttoned; but a great sudden gust of
wind now burst in through the open windows and blew
the tablecloth up over our glasses and plates. We had
already had a growl and a rumble. Flagler got up to put
down the windows. And now we heard the frontdoor

bell ringing—a long ring that lanced the air like light-
ning. "It looks as if it's going to storm, as they say in
New England," said Warren, who had a summer place
in Massachusetts that was not too far away from New
York. "It's a gentleman to see you," said the maid.
Flagler looked up at her a moment in doubt, as if he
were going to ask the name; but then he turned to Warren and simply said: "We'd better go out." Still carrying on the conversation, Warren got up from the
table: "I want to talk to you some more," he said,
"about this question of sin and the anti-social. It interests me very much just now."

Si Banks and I sat on the porch, which was screened
in but did not exclude the mosquitoes. "I wonder who
that is," said Si. "Some prospective angel, I guess. Warren's trying to help Flagler raise money to get Haynes
& Kendall out of its hole." He asked the maid to bring
the whisky and ice, and we immediately had an after-
dinner highball. The thunder broke a little closer and
a sprinkle of raindrops fell. At the end of a pensive
silence, Si commenced to chuckle to himself in a delightedly childlike way that had something to do with
the prospect of unlimited access to liquor. I asked him
what it was that amused him, and he stuttered at
framing his thought: "You-you-you don't think it's
Old N-Nick, do you?" "I shouldn't be surprised," I
replied. "Warren was certainly sticking his neck out
just now.—Why is it so absolutely intolerable"—I
went on, after a moment's thought—"to hear him talk
about New England history?" "He comes from Indiana," said Si, who was himself a rather depressing
example of the decadence of the New England character. "They don't acknowledge the reality of Evil out
there, any more than they recognize good writing." "I

don't come from New England either," I answered, "but I can't stand his liberal smugness—it makes everything seem so easy. Writing history is perfectly simple —moral problems are perfectly painless—and life becomes completely uninteresting!—It's just like the Readers' Circle and the rest of the things he does. Why isn't the Readers' Circle all right? It's a good thing to distribute books—it's true that, outside of the East, there aren't enough bookstores in the country—and some of the books they send out aren't bad; and yet the whole thing is disgusting." "The trouble is," said Si, speaking straight in a way that had become rather rare with him, "that in literature, just as in anything else that's serious, nothing's really any good at all that isn't based on the recognition of the very best that's ever been possible. If you begin recommending the second-rate—let alone the third-rate and the fourth-rate, as the Readers' Circle sometimes does—you're not gradually educating people, as Warren claims he is, so that they'll be able to appreciate something better: you're simply letting down the standards and leaving people completely at sea. The most immoral and disgraceful and dangerous thing that anybody can do in the arts is knowingly to feed back to the public its own ignorance and cheap tastes. What the Readers' Circle has been doing is not a bit different in principle from what the Hollywood producers are doing when they say they have to make the kind of pictures that will appeal to millions of moviegoers." "But do you think Warren knows the difference between first-rate and second-rate stuff?" "Of course he does. Otherwise, he wouldn't be d-damned. In the days when he was teaching literature, he unquestionably didn't get everything that there was in Shakespeare or Milton, but he must still know perfectly well that they're in an en-

tirely different class from Theodore Merriman and
Steve Benét—who write just about the same kind of
poetry that the ordinary man would produce if he'd
gone in for writing poetry instead of for investment
banking or selling real estate." "Don't you think they
write the kind of poetry that Warren himself would
write? What makes you think he ever had any real
idea of why Shakespeare and Milton were worth reading?" "You never took his course," said Si. "He really
wasn't bad in those days. He used to wow us with *My
Last Duchess* and the finale of *Dr. Faustus*—only I always used to claim"—he giggled—"that he ought to
have made Mephistophelis say, 'Why, this is Yale, nor
am I out of it.' I think that the cult of success that they
all seem to get at Yale has had a good deal to do with
Warren's career. He wants to get tangible results that
he can show when he goes back to college." "But still,"
I said, "people have to make their livings,"—my second
instalment of Scotch and the satisfying realization that
I was well past the middle of my book had put me in a
charitable mood. "You can't condemn people too
harshly for the things they have to do to get money in
the set-up of capitalist society. After all, the academic
world wasn't any too hospitable to Warren. I'm sure that
our English Department let him go for bad reasons—for
the very things he was doing that they ought to have
done." But Si was implacably earnest: " 'He did it for
the wife and kiddies'—that's an excuse that doesn't go
in the arts. If a p-person is really serious, he has no
business to get himself tied up with other kinds of
responsibility. If he doesn't feel that what he's doing
is more important than raising a family or keeping up
a standard of living, he has no business trying to do it
at all." I remembered that Si himself had more or less

abandoned his family. He still gave his wife part of his salary and was always talking about it in explanation of the dismal little room in which he lived when he was not visiting Flagler, and he thus lent a certain flavor of virtue to his lodgings, his dress and his drinking; but the truth was that his wife had a job of her own and mainly supported their young son herself.

"This weather is funny," I said. "The wind has been blowing in, but it doesn't make things any cooler." "It's all like those b-blasts of hot air that come out of the funnels of st-steamers.—It's not going to rain either," he added. The pattering of drops had stopped. There was the sound of a car driving off, and we both became rather silent. "I don't think there's anything to worry about,"—we heard Warren's voice working on Flagler in its drawling and complacent way. They came out through the screen door and joined us on the porch. Warren poured himself a highball, as if it were a gesture learned late in life which one did not perform with ease but to which one addressed oneself; and I thought that he had lost since dinner some of his assurance of the big lawyer or executive; but, returning to the New England divines, he carried on with the meek bravado with which he had somehow at college gone counter to academic convention. "Why, Edwards is a man," he said, "that I think is very much overrated. Some of his writings like his famous sermon about *Sinners in the Hands of an Angry God* are sonorous and vigorous enough pieces of old-fashioned rhetorical prose." (Warren's ineptitude at literary characterization was goose-pimpling and almost infallible: *sonorous* and *vigorous,* I reflected, were not in the least the right words for Jonathan Edwards's wire-strung persuasion.) "The only trouble is they ain't true. I can't feel the force of an argument when the premises rest on beliefs that can't be accepted today by any scientifically educated man." "You don't believe that we're just hanging over the Pit, with the devils like hungry lions ready to fly at our throats?" "Well, it's hot enough to think so tonight." He pulled a timetable out of his pocket: "I've got to catch that eleven-twelve. How can I call up a taxi, Flag?" "I'll take you." I noticed that Flagler seemed, for him, rather *dégagé* after the nervousness he had shown at dinner. "Why, those terroristic sermons that they used to preach"—Warren went on with his explanation—"were just their way of getting people worked up and selling them religion when the market was low—like Buchman and Bill Sunday." "My theory," I perversely insisted, "is that the Devil was in Jonathan Edwards and had dictated the sermons themselves."

At this moment the telephone rang, and Flagler went in to answer. It was Lydia. From Flagler's replies, I could imagine the kind of thing she was saying: she was evidently complaining of the weather, declaring that it was impossible for her to work in New York and making a grievance of the fact that Flagler had suggested she might not want to come down because he was going to talk business with Warren. (Lydia, I am certain, would have liked nothing better than to have had two of her lovers together and to have tried to make them both uncomfortable by playing them off against one another.) There was an interruption, thus, of a moment, and a pause that became queerly prolonged. "I don't think that this liquor is quite first-rate," said Warren, putting down his glass. "There's no reason why it shouldn't be now; but I suppose that Flagler is right: you can't keep these bootlegger liquor dealers from trying to put over inferior goods—any

more than any other kind of merchant.—Why, the
Devil is a waning force. He really hasn't counted very
much since sometime in the eighteenth century. But Edwards was a shrewd enough Yankee to be able to exploit
his reputation. He took over the old hawk of Hell—
the old talk of Tell, I mean"—he laughed and shook
his head: "he took over the old hamfire and dalmation
—dear me, this bad whisker seems to me getting be all
misked up.—That reminds me of that description in
King Lear"—he tried to pull himself together with boyish frankness and a short laugh—"when you fellows
used to take my course, don't you remember?—that passage—I'm reminded of it by that word I coined—my version of"—he took it warily—*"hellfire and damnation—*
do you remember about the cliffs of Dover":

*"How tizzy diz to cass one's eyes below
Hangs one that gathers hamfire; dreadful trade!*

I can never remember what hamfire—*samphire*—is,
but I always think of it as something loathsome—a
loathsome discreditable trade!—Excuse me." He got up
suddenly and went inside. As Si said, he had been like
a fly that was beginning to feel the effects of having
been sprayed by one of those insect guns.

To my surprise, in the lull that followed, I heard
Flagler being amiably firm about not letting Lydia
come out, and finally hanging up in a way that treated
the question as closed without giving her any pretext
for taking offense. He came out and settled back in his
chair and put his feet up on the railing, and I felt in
him some new sense of freedom. When Warren, after
a quarter of an hour, did not come back from the
house, Flagler went in and found him lying on a bed. He
had been horribly sick, and, though he made a great

effort to be lucid, good-natured and candid, was evidently more or less drunk. He insisted, however, upon leaving and we got him on the last train to town.

Ten days later I was reading one of the liberal weeklies and came upon a long communication sent in by some professor of history. It asserted that the chapters of Warren's book which he had been publishing in various periodicals were out-and-out plagiarisms. Warren, the writer declared, had lifted the ideas, the research and, in some cases, the actual words from a doctor's thesis written years before by one of his (Warren's) own students. There were sentences printed in parallel columns that did appear to bear out these charges. The man who wrote the letter seemed animated by some specially bitter resentment, and there were several rows of dots which suggested that the editors had left the most scurrilous passages out.

I am afraid that I felt rather relieved. The next day Si came over to see me in a state of sardonic glee; he had read the communication, too. "You know what happened that night?" he twinkled. "It w-was the Old Man who was there. The contract they'd made with him was up, and Warren was due to take the rap." "You mean this scandal is the rap?" I asked. "Well, no—I don't believe it's exactly what Warren let himself in for by the contract. He would have had to bind himself over to w-work directly for the Old Man—probably without ruining himself at first, though, in the eyes of the general public. He would be much more useful to our friend if he kept his good reputation. But Warren, when his bargain expired, refused to deliver the goods. He'd become so successful and self-confident that he thought he could brush off the Old Man himself.— And now he's lost his reputation anyhow." "But nothing that Warren's ever done has been anything but a second-rate version of something by somebody else. Why should *this* make any difference to his public?" "All those schoolteachers and jerk-water college professors who swear by what they read in the *Booklover* and who have written theses themselves?—all those nice Middle Western ladies who have been doting on what the Readers' Circle has sent them? Did you know that the man who wrote the exposé is having it printed as a leaflet and sent around all over the country to the little local libraries and newspapers? He must be some former colleague of Warren's who's envious of him and hates his guts. The Old Man knows his business all right! You can't drop him like an indiscreet reviewer!"

III

But then the whole thing was smoothed out. The scandal was explained away. It turned out that the young man who had written the thesis—and who had died in Santa Fé of t.b.—had got all of his ideas from Warren himself in a seminar which Warren had conducted—though neither Si Banks nor I could remember that Warren at that time had ever shown the faintest interest in the literature of early New England. The *Booklover* published a statement, which had evidently been draughted by Jim from material supplied by Warren, and it was sent out to the subscribers of the Readers' Circle.

So that for Warren the affair had no bad consequences. The Readers' Circle continued to flourish, and other "book clubs" of the kind were started to sow and reap in the field it had opened. To have your book taken by one of them, Si told me, meant royalties and advertizing which would otherwise be impossible for anything but a best-seller. The selections of these organizations came eventually, in fact, to drive out most other books from the arena of public attention. They got preferential treatment from the *Booklover* and the literary supplements of the Sunday papers. The publishers and the book clubs, according to Si, had got to working pretty closely together, and most of the book departments in the newspapers and magazines simply chalked up the literary stock market as reported by manufacturers and distributors. There were men that did regular reviewing who were advisers to book clubs or publishers; and by the mid-thirties there was such perfect coördination that one could be quite sure, any given week, of finding the same new book featured in all of these papers. I remember one Sunday when a Readers' Circle biography of a famous American naturalist had just appeared, and the same picture of the fur-bearing marten was reproduced on both the front pages of the two Sunday literary supplements, just as, the week before, the same biographer had been given the place of honor in the *Booklover,* and a picture of the naturalist had appeared on the cover. The book was one of those fictionized absurdities by an inaccurate and sentimental woman who did not hesitate to tell you precisely what, in any situation, at any moment, was going on in the mind of her hero or even in the minds of the animals—till one did not know which was more embarrassing, the biographer's love affair with her subject or the great naturalist's love affairs with his fauna:

"She [the female possum] watched him with half-closed but unblinking green eyes. Who was this bearded intruder striding into the comfortable fastnesses where her family had dwelt for centuries, which had been sacred to untold generations of South Carolina possums since before those upstarts, the humans, had come with their heavy boots that crashed through the underbrush instead of slipping daintily through the twigs, with their harsh shrill voices that frightened the wood folk and caused them to shrink into their green retreats? But she did not shrink now, she stood her ground. Merely signaling to her babies with an invisible twitch, the quick unobtrusive warning of the patrician Southern mother, to lighten their hold on her tail, she tensed her muscles for instant flight, yet she did not drop from her branch. Clinging with a negligent grace and pretending an utter disinterest, she met the stranger's gaze. She could see from his deerskin jacket, from his moccasins and his leather leggings, that he was stoutly protected against claws and teeth; and she sensed in his prehensile fingers, strong as stout sycamore roots yet sensitive as the branches of young birch trees, in his curly and uncombed locks that had a wild tendril-like quality, a sympathy with the sylvan background that somehow made her feel at home in his presence, and a masculine self-assurance that was challenging and at the same time magnetic.

" 'Hello there, my gal—that's a fine brood of youngsters!' he had stopped and was smiling up at her.

"At the sound of his Yankee accent, Amanda Possum narrowed her eyelids by a scarcely perceptible hair's-breadth. It was too late now to play dead. Instinctively she knew with certainty that he would not be taken in by the trick—and the truth was that she rather despised this traditional swooning of the Southern belle. Was it that something fine-nostriled and straight-lipped about him had kept her from the customary subterfuge? Coolly aloof and patrician, she gave him back his glance.

"He reached in his pocket for his sketchbook, and a quizzical yet clear-eyed smile brought creases to the sun-bronzed face. Something was making Amanda's heart pound so loudly that she thought he must hear it."

At least this was Si Banks's version. He and Flagler were particularly bitter about the suffocating publicity for this book, which had not allowed, as they said, anything else to breathe that week. Haynes & Kendall had hoped to get some special attention for a book they were bringing out themselves—a long work on sociology and history by a late-nineteenth-century Pole, which a fanatical Polish disciple had induced Flagler to get him to translate on the ground that it was of greater importance than either Spengler or Marx. This translation, when it was finally delivered, had turned out to be in such very rocky English that Flagler had had to pay someone else to rewrite it, with the result of producing a text that the translator would not accept. The Pole made Flagler hysterical scenes and threatened to get an injunction against him to prevent him from publishing the book; and the problem of revising the translation was, thereupon, turned over to a Russian, who knew something about Polish and whose English was almost perfect. But the Russian had long spells of illness, during which he would write Flagler for more money, and, if he failed to get it, send his wife, who would wait in the reception room for hours and then so desolate Flagler with the cadences of her low-pitched Musorgskian voice that he would give her another check. Between her visits, the Pole would come in and complain that the Russian was impossible: he was a drunkard, he spent his time writing poetry of a hopelessly old-fashioned kind, and his grandfather had been an official in the Pole-persecuting government of Alexander III. When the work was at last published, it sank almost without a bubble. Most of the notices appeared in the Left Wing press, the readers of which could rarely buy it and where it mainly aroused hostile polemics. But poor

Flagler was now personally involved with the Russian and the Pole both, and had to go on helping them out for years.

He had also taken major losses on Brian Sykes's play, which he had advertized at much expense in the attempt to exploit the success of the travel book but of which he had hardly been able to dispose of four or five hundred copies; and on the novels of an excellent Englishman, who had never sold well in this country and was regarded by the trade as "rather special": his books, reissued by Flagler, were enthusiastically reviewed by his admirers but otherwise fell rather flat. Si Banks had further added to Flagler's difficulties by conceiving the idea at one time that he was capable of writing successful detective stories. He did two—bringing them out under a pseudonym, though he had never yet published a book under his own name; but his storytelling was quite amateurish, and the amusing satirical notions on which his plots were based were rather over the heads of the public who buy mysteries to read in bed.

In the meantime, Flagler Haynes, for reasons that it was difficult to guess, went on spending his summers at Spackman Point. "It's convenient to town," he would say, "and I feel as if I belong out here now." Three autumns after the summer I have just described, he even took the place for the winter. Haynes & Kendall was doing so badly that Flagler was seriously strapped. I happened to hear one day in town that they were actually going out of business and I wondered about the prospects of my book. I had that spring resigned my job at the museum in order to get it finished, and it now wanted only revision. I, too, was staying on in the country, so I went over to Flagler's that Saturday with the intention of bringing the matter up.

It was one of those spells in November when it turns gray and rains for days, as if the show of the year were all over and the lights turned off and the stage being washed—a long swabbing and sousing and mopping that makes the world of lawns and roads uninhabitable and even discourages us from looking out the windows. And the interior at Spackman Point was today almost equally dismal. The oil heating, like so many other features of the house, had turned out to be rather defective. A few of the heaters were boiling, but most of them were not working at all, and one of the pipes, Si told me with his elfin and unanxious smile, was leaking and flooding the cellar. I found him swaddled in sweaters and croaking with a bad cold, reclining on a brown leather couch in front of a fireplace of small dense brown bricks, in the room that Flagler used for a study. He had attempted to build a fire, but he was hopelessly inept at this, and the damp wood was merely smoking, while Si resorted to whisky to help him forget his miseries. When I came in, he prodded the logs and lighted a number of matches, but with no more than momentary results. The whole room had a peculiar cheerlessness, with its large lamp—a gold fluted column and a shade of cerise satin —on the table behind the couch; its jolly Scotchman tobacco jar, with a china tam-o'-shanter for cover; its glass-paned bookcases of the desolating kind that you buy separately in any quantity desired and pile up on top of one another; and its golfing and hunting pictures in the taste of the early nineteen hundreds.

"Lydia and Brian are upstairs," he said. "They've g-gone to bed to keep warm. Flagler's meeting Jim Milholland at the station."—Then, after a moment's silence, during which I could see that his mind was swimming in alcoholic bemusement: "Do you kn-know about the scandal?" I did not, but was immediately told. The story was absolutely fantastic and quite made me forget my own affair. One of the features of the *Booklover* for years had been a kind of "agony column" which had originally had some connection with various kinds of literary business. We had sometimes used to read it for amusement, and when I had looked at it in its earlier days, it had seemed to consist mainly of appeals from "gentlemen, cultured, traveled, fiftyish," desiring correspondence with ladies who "loved books and fireside chat," and "women of refinement, conversant with the arts, fond of theater, concert and opera," who wished "to banish ennui by interchange with mature well-bred men, free from philistinism and provinciality." But of late years, I was now told by Si, a new element had been seeping in, and the page was almost as full of advertizements by "gentlemen of robust constitution" in search of "non-prudish ladies responsive to the new dance rhythms," "Ganymedes who were at home in French and Italian and enjoyed European travel," "watchers by the Well of Loneliness" and "alumni of Dr. Birch's School," as one of those Paris journals that is openly devoted to pimping. And now a terrible thing had happened. The American Purity League, a vice-hunting organization, had recently got wind of this and were about to bring the *Booklover* into court for carrying indecent advertizements. "But Jim Milholland couldn't have known what was going on," I exclaimed on my first impulse. "He and that little managing editor and that old lady who went to Holyoke can hardly even be aware that such things exist." "It seems that Jim had been ordering pornographic literature," said Si with a delighted gleam, "from a man who advertized *'Curiosa.'* They found his name in the publisher's books when the Purity

League raided the place." I remembered, now I came to think of it, that Jim *had* called my attention one day to a volume called *Confessions of a Nun,* which had been lying on his desk. "Ever see this?" he had asked. . . . "They didn't care what they printed in those days"; and then had added, as if he were trying to make its presence there look respectable: "It was a phase of the anti-clerical movement before the French Revolution." It now occurred to me that *Confessions of a Nun* had perhaps been the only book in which I had ever heard him show a real interest.

"The most d-disastrous thing, though," went on Si, "is that the Purity League sent out a girl to answer the male ads and one of them turned out to be Jim. He met the agent in Central Park and they sat around and talked on a bench. He told her his name was George R. Brown. He made another date with her, and the second time he took her to the movies and rubbed against her knee; the third time he took her to a hideaway in the Fifties that it turned out he'd had for some time, and showed her pictures by Aubrey Beardsley"—"Stop!" I interrupted. "I don't want to hear any more. I suppose he went on to Rops. Poor old Jim!—I dare say that his life has been awfully lonely and dreary while Warren has been having himself a time." "The damaging part of this is that it gives the impression that Jim had been deliberately exploiting the whole thing—whereas he may not, as you say, even have known about it.—Unless,"— the look of impish humor revivified his pale puffed-up face—"unless he's entered into a c-contract with you-kn-know-who to misconduct himself in public." "What do you mean?"—I had forgotten Si's theory. "Why, Jim might have signed an agreement to do evil and make himself notorious so that Warren could keep a clean reputation. You know, that's exactly what's happened! That's the way that Warren succeeded in dodging the consequences of that plagiarism scandal. When the forces of darkness cracked down on him and he saw that he couldn't get out of his agreement, he sold Jim to the Old Black Creditor, too—it must have been a three years' contract, with Flagler still taking the losses and Jim, at the end of that time, paying the price for both himself and Warren—because Warren seems still to be all right: he's probably bought himself some extra years of grace by getting Jim to let himself be damned sooner." "But how would he ever have been able to talk Jim into it?" "He would have told him that the Readers' Circle was a national institution and a great deal more important than the *Booklover*—and he would also have told him that the personals would brighten up his bachelor life—and he would also have misled him by pretending that the Devil couldn't really get him: that there was no great risk of exposure, because the majority of the readers of the *Booklover* wouldn't notice what was going on and those who did would have no objection. Jim has always had faith in Warren—Warren is the success of the family and rescued Jim from Indiana, where he was a teller in the local bank—he never got to go to college, you know. He does everything that Warren tells him. But then, of course, the Devil has seen to it that a big exposé shall occur—of course, the Devil runs the Purity League." "Would it necessarily be fatal to the *Booklover?* Couldn't they just abolish the personals page and make some sort of explanation? The subscribers out in the sticks never know what's in the New York papers." "Well, I've been working on a scheme, as I've been lying here, to make everything seem all right to the subscribers. There's no reason why the whole scandal can't be perfectly well absorbed and assimilated. What Warren ought to do is to publish one of those deadly symposiums asking various literary men to make statements on the situation. Symposiums are reassuring: the point is that if you propound a question and print enough answers to it—it doesn't matter how absurd or contradictory they are—people somehow get the impression that the problem has been satisfactorily dealt with. I've just been composing some comments for the various poets to make. You could have people guess who they were—it could be a puzzle contest, too—and a symposium combined with a puzzle contest would be irresistible to *Booklover* readers.— See if you can guess this one—it's from a poem called *Milholland's Tangent: The more we knew of him, the less we knew.*" I guessed correctly.

"Here's another," he said:

"The embarrassing moment in the empty room."

"That's very good!" I laughed—"though I don't think he'd write those two *em's—embarrassing* and *empty* both.—What else?"

"Well, here are some lines by one of the younger men:

"The doors broken down, the methodical search of the files,

The waste-baskets captured, the commands against looting sent out"—

At this moment Flagler and Jim arrived. They had with them a middle-aged lady whom I had never seen before and whom I took for some reviewer for the *Booklover.* She was dressed frumpishly in an obsolete fashion, and there was something rather creepy about her. She had hair that showed reddish streaks of dyeing, a hat with a bird's wing on one side, a white chiffon blouse with a cameo at the neck and a high whalebone collar; and she had kept on an old lank fox boa that was somewhat the worse for the rain. She was pale and uncomfortably tense, but she had put on a blazing layer of rouge and she kept talking with unnatural vivacity and laughing in a way that was genteel but irrelevant to the mood of the company. "I hope that you agree with me about Byron," she said, while Flagler was working over the fire and getting more materials for drinks. "We were just discussing the subject on the train—a brilliant man, of course—at moments, a great poet—but the one thing that it's impossible to forgive him is what he did to poor little Claire Clairmont. One can concede a good deal to genius—I've never found it difficult, for example, to forgive De Quincey for taking opium—and Jean Cocteau, of course, takes opium, too: another brilliant man!—after all, De Quincey cured himself, didn't he? —and that's the great thing!"—she gave her sharp out-of-date social laugh—"all of us can't be cured, of course, but that's no matter. As I was saying to Mr. Milholland just now—I'm an old correspondent of Mr. Milholland's—we've been writing each other letters for months, but we never met before this afternoon, and I couldn't resist being so forward as to jump on the train with him and come down here—I hope you'll forgive my intrusion, but it isn't every day that one is lucky enough to have a talk with James Milholland—I knew it was he all the time, in spite of his wicked pseudonym—because [archly] I compared the letters I got from Mr. George R. Brown with a letter he'd written a year ago declining so courteously an article I'd sent him—wasn't that clever of me? When I romped right into the office today and confronted him with the evidence, he couldn't deny the soft impeachment"—she laughed as if it were all very delightful—"and so we've been having the most enthralling conversation.—But, to go back to Byron!"—she laughed again, in apology for her divagation—"we must grant the man of genius

his privilege of disregarding the social conventions—
but Claire Clairmont is another matter!—I *know*
Claire Clairmont—I have seen her and talked with her
just as plainly as I'm talking with you now—I've felt
her helpless and hopeless love for Byron—just as if she
were my own sister—and one thing I can tell you,"—
she smiled in a smug and dictatorial way—"she wasn't
the least bit in the world like Henry James's picture of
her—in *The Aspern Papers,* you know—*The Aspirin
Papers* I always want to call it,"—she gave a sharper
and less well-bred cackle—Jim Milholland responded
with a painful smile—"aspirin was about Henry's speed
—I don't often resort to slang, but sometimes it seems
the most picturesque way of expressing certain things—
not a drug to stimulate the faculties but a drug to cure
a headache and let one just go quietly to sleep—Henry
wouldn't take opium or coke, oh, no!—But what were
we saying about him?—Oh, about *The Aspern Papers*
—if you ask me, Henry James was the governess."
"You m-mean *The T-Turn of the Screw,* don't you?"
suggested Si. "I decidedly mean *The Aspern Papers,* because it's all just the same thing. There's always a governess in Henry James and Henry James is always the
governess—a prudish old man in women's clothes and
in love with the master of the house—and always one
of those beautiful English estates—you have a lovely
place here, by the way—it reminds me of Mrs. Jack
Gardner's—she knew Henry James, intimately of course
—he often used to come to the *palazzo* when he re-
visited the United States, and some say there was something between them, but *that* I don't believe—I don't
think he was capable of passion. She told me that he
said to her once: 'My dear Isabella,'—you know how
he talked: she described it as ceremonious and groping
—'My dear Isabella, in these so charmingly secular,

these more than mediaeval cloisters, one expects any moment to see Fra Angelico pop out with a delightful dinner pail.' But, after all, admirable writer though Henry James indubitably is, one doesn't want to find oneself deprived of all one's secondary sex characteristics!"—As I looked at her, I saw that she herself was desexed in the way that the insane sometimes are, so that her feminine features were shrunk to an unfeminine pinchedness and dryness. She was holding us, I realized now, by the spell that the lunatic is able to impose, sweeping one along with a furious force that has no natural origin or object. We had at first tried to reply to the things she said, but had ended by sitting silent. Jim Milholland was meek in a morris chair that was a part of the nineteen-hundred interior, with both his arms stretched out along its flat arms. I noted the cleanness of his cuffs and his long knotty rural fingers: presently he shifted his hands and held them above his vest, with the fingers interlocking and his elbows on the arms of the chair. His gaze behind his glasses was dull and his doglike jowls were drooping; his eyes and his wide mouth betrayed withdrawal and worry. I felt for the first time a certain mild sympathy for his cuffs with their simple gold cuff-links, his steel spectacles which gave to his face a suggestion of professional austerity, and his not badly selected plaid tie, worn with a soft shirt that buttoned down. Yes: he had risen above the bank-teller class.—"And that," the crazy woman was saying, "is the reason why I'm utterly convinced that William James *did* come back from the other world and dictate to Alfred North Whitehead—Alfred Whitehead had never written philosophy before, he'd just been a mathematician!"

Flagler dropped a log on the fire and ripped through the skein of her talk. "I'm sorry it's so cold," he said.

"It gets colder in the lower circles," said Si Banks aside to me; and his remark started a train of thought which presently led me to reflect that, if Jim Milholland's hour had sounded, Flagler must be due for a release—a conclusion which did not at first seem confirmed by the scene that I overheard when, in my need to escape the visitor, I had broken away from the company and was going upstairs to the toilet. Flagler, too, had gone upstairs for some purpose; and, though I caught only a snatch of the interchange as I was on my way through the hall, I realized that it belonged to the climax of a drama that had long been building. From the half-open door of a bedroom, I heard Lydia's clear quick voice ringing out in a humorous and impudent way that it seemed to me would provoke me to kill her: "We were just bundling, Flag—just talking about the harvest and the husking-bee.—Brian came in here to get bromo-seltzer." And Brian's yelping tenor: "Well, really, I must say, Flagler, that if you insist on living in an igloo, you oughtn't to be surprised if your guests double up!" It seemed odd, as I thought about it in the bathroom, that Flagler should answer quietly: "Come downstairs—there's somebody here I want you to meet."

And soon after I returned to the study, Lydia and Brian appeared—both of them flushed and rather subdued. Brian's habit, on seeing new people, had always been to shrink away and skulk on the fringe of the company, from which he would harass the conversation with heckling challenges and insulting asides, and presently engage in a counter-conversation with someone who was sitting near him—a performance of which the derisive hoots and the constantly increasing loudness would soon hamper the other talkers and eventually give Brian the center of the stage. But now Flagler put his hand on Brian's shoulder in the friendliest and easiest way and propelled him toward the lunatic booklover. "I want you to meet Mrs. So-and-So," he said, with, for him, rather unusual discourtesy, "who is unquestionably one of your fans.—This is Mr. Brian Sykes: a greater poet than Byron and a greater Don Juan than Henry James—to paraphrase Housman on a famous occasion— I'm sure you know the story." "A. E. Housman—there's an enigma!—a very strange man," she cried—"I presume you mean A.E. and not D.H.—There's something distinctly strange about that affair with Gerard Manley Hopkins!—those letters they wrote one another—they sound like two lovers—and then Housman not publishing Hopkins' poems—but of course there's something strange about all of us if the truth were only known!"—she laughed. Jim shifted the position of his hands again and pulled his legs in, as if somebody were taking a swing at him, and I was trying to collect myself to switch her away from this subject, when she suddenly turned on Si. "You stutter, I notice," she said, as he stared at her, doped and dumb. "Whenever I hear a stutter, I know there's a psychic defect. I don't mean to be invidious, of course—all great literature grows out of defects—like Somerset Maugham's club foot.—And that's where your 'sprung rhythm' comes in—didn't Hopkins have a stutter!—There's something that's frightening in all of us—if you ask me, the whole world is frightened—it's frightened of going insane—and what have we got but the great writers?—though even Thomas Mann nods"—"The Joseph series is one big snore," put in Brian, who was enjoying the visitor and who was always delighted at a pretext for belittling a distinguished contemporary.

"Well!" declared Flagler emphatically, knocking out his pipe on the mantel, "if the writers are the only thing that stands between us and the complete *Untergang*

des Abendlandes—and I'm not sure you're not right—
we might as well give up the whole game." He had just
made himself a drink and was standing in front of the
fireplace, rather round-shouldered, as he always was, and
with his usual somber look that contrasted with his neat
brown tweed clothes; but his voice, as he went on, had
a resilience and his tone a self-assurance that surprised
us and commanded our attention. "Personally, I'm absolutely sick of the whole damned literary racket—
when you come right down to it, what is it but huckster-
ing in a lot of greasy daydreams? You take fantasies
that people have made up because they can't travel as
much as they want to or haven't got anybody to sleep
with, and you get them set up by a printer and bound
between two board covers and you organize a business
to distribute them. You hire space for advertizing to tell
people that, if they'll part with three-fifty, they can be-
fuddle themselves with this fantasy. The fact that it's
spelled out on paper makes them almost think it's real.
And the same thing is true of the big reputations. What
was Byron but a fat neurotic man who suffered from a
deformed foot but had happened to inherit a title and
some money? He didn't really care much about women,
but he'd succeeded in exploiting his ideas of what his
emotions ought to be like till the women would actually
swoon if he so much as came into a room—our visitor here is still steamed up about him.—And Brian,
in a more local way, is in the same situation as Byron—
he sells the public little syncopated pipe-dreams about
himself in bed with beautiful girls. People have to solve
crossword puzzles in order to be able to get in on them
—and for some reason this makes the highbrows feel
all right about indulging themselves—and, for some
reason equally cockeyed, this literary pandering gives
Brian such a conviction of innate superiority that he

thinks he doesn't have to have any manners or even any ordinary decency." Brian had turned red and intent, but did not make any reply. "And so, I say, to hell with it!" Flagler went on. "The whole thing becomes repulsive. There's going to be a great stink raised now about the pimping personals in the *Booklover*—but actually these Swedish masseuses and things are about the most respectable wares that the *Booklover* has ever advertized. They at least give some tangible satisfaction instead of just teasing the imagination. So I'm done with imagination-titillaters! I might as well announce to you folks, in case you didn't already know it, that Haynes & Kendall is about to be liquidated. I'm going to sell the whole thing to Macmanus—and do you know what I'm going to do with the proceeds? I'm going to buy a dandy little sailboat because sailing's always been the only thing in the world that really made me perfectly happy. It keeps you away from books and it keeps you away from women. I'm going to be out sailing all summer, and in the winter I'm going to spend my time just sitting around the Yale club bar with red-faced old grads who like boats!"

"Bravo, Flagler!" said Brian Sykes, in his offensive way—"That's the greatest dramatic speech I've heard since I saw Walter Hampden play Shylock.—That picture of you as a rollicking old boat-lover is one of the most splendid things of its kind since Franz Hals did his carousing boors!" Flagler looked at his watch: "And now, Mrs. Whoozis," he said, paying no attention to Brian's jeers, "you have just time to catch the five twenty-five, which will get you into town for a latish dinner.—And you're taking that, too, aren't you, old chap?" he turned amiably but firmly to Brian. "You'd better get your things packed or you'll miss it."

Brian said, "I see," and left the room. Lydia burst

into tears and immediately phoned for a taxi. Si Banks sat solemn and stunned. Even Mrs. Whoozis seemed daunted. She offered me a benzedrine tablet and swallowed a couple herself.

At this moment the doorbell rang: it was the plumber to attend to the heating.

Jim Milholland stayed overnight, and Flagler drove him to the station the next evening. But poor Jim did not get on the train. He took a room at a local hotel and shot himself that night with a revolver that he had brought with him from New York. He had written a note to the management, expressing his regret at inconveniencing them, requesting them to notify Flagler, and enclosing the price of the room and a moderate tip for whoever should clean up. He had carefully packed his clothes, dressed himself in a suit of pajamas, spread out the Sunday paper on the bathroom floor—he had bought it in the lobby for the purpose—lain down on it exactly in the middle and put the revolver to his heart—which, though less certain than shooting in the head, he must have preferred as less messy for other people than spattering his brains about.

As Warren said, "Jim was a gentleman to the end." "I have lost," he wrote in the *Booklover*, "not merely a brother, but a colleague, with whom a close association of many years never ceased to be stimulating and helpful. He was one of the staunchest and rarest souls that it has ever been my privilege to know. *Ave atque vale, frater!*"

IV

Yet Lydia, as Si later told me, did a lot of explaining and made her peace with Flagler in a tearful telephone call. Flagler did not sell his business but went into bankruptcy and never bought his sailboat. Warren put him in as editor of the *Booklover,* which now dropped the personals department and got out several special numbers devoted to educational publications and symposiums on large general questions; but the paper did not prosper and was allowed by Warren to ebb away till there was little to be found in it save puzzles and reviews by the provincial schoolteachers who made up most of the surviving subscribers and whose interest was encouraged by this means. Warren, I remarked to Si, must have signed with the Black Man a very long-term contract—longer than poor Jim would appear to be worth, especially now that he'd been collected. "Oh, he's signed a new agreement," and Si. "He's given him some kind of lien on Spike. Haven't you noticed lately?"

It was true that Spike Milholland had changed very much since the days when I had first met him at Warren's—not yet out of college, very Left, and full of his idea of scattering poems from planes. After a year or two of unpaid work on a small non-Marxist radical monthly, he had, through Warren, got a job doing a book-column on one of the morning papers, and had achieved, toward the end of the thirties, when serious literary journalism was sinking extremely low, a considerable reputation and following. This had led to a radio engagement to broadcast ten-minute reviews of new books, and here he had scored a prodigious success. It was curious to see how easily the impudence with which at college he had challenged the English department by publishing, in his rebel paper, an article called *William Wordsworth: Renegade* and his gift for the kind of wit which the twenties had called "wisecracking," were now diverted from their original objective of "Revolution the American Way"—to quote the slogan

of his Left magazine—and spattered in a meaningless
commentary on the products of the publishing season,
which, keeping up, in its earlier phases, some of the
appearances of a "social slant," soon relaxed into almost
perfect harmony with the views of the publishing trade.
On the radio and in his column, he had now, to all in-
tents and purposes, subsided into the role of the salesman who tells you, in a men's-wear shop, that he can
show you some fine silk shirts or that, if you don't care
for anything in silk, he can give you something nice
in rayon: if you did not want a pretty good novel, he
could recommend a crisp new detective story; but his fast
tempo and his boyish manner, his indefatigably resourceful wit, won him a special kind of standing
as a promotion man and earned him a gigantic salary.
I met him one day, during the war, at a party that had
been given by the publisher of my book on nineteenth-
century painting, for a man who had written a novel
about the crew of a bombing plane, and I was struck
by the streamlined model, adapted to the needs of a
new era, which Spike had succeeded in developing out
of the standard Milholland personality. He had kept his
upstanding hair and the grin that carried off his in-
solence, but I could see that these were now being exploited as part of a deliberate performance. He had not,
however, lost entirely his capacity for passionate feeling:
he was excited about World War II to a degree that I
recognized from the previous one as only possible for a
civilian non-combatant. He was married and had two
children, so was exempted from military service, but he
took a vicarious interest in the bombing of German
cities that had almost become an obsession. He had done
a little flying in his college years, and he now haunted
aviators and airfields. Berlin had just been partly wiped
out when I saw him again at this party, and he told me

that he considered that the pilots of those planes had done more for literature than any "goddam novelist or poet" who had been writing during the last twenty years. He had complained, in his earlier phase, about what he called the "betrayal" of his generation by writers like Eliot and Pound whom he had at one time enthusiastically imitated; and it now seemed that this generation had also been treacherously "betrayed" by the Marxists whom he had admired later. His indignation at the thought of the fatuity of those who had believed in the "historic role" of labor in face of the menace of fascism now almost reached the pitch of hysteria.

In the meantime, the book clubs had been multiplying and becoming more and more shameless, and Spike had been cashing in on these, too. He was the principal name on a committee of selection for a scheme called the Treasure Seekers, which represented a bold variation on the original book-club idea. "How would you like," their advertizements demanded, "to have the foremost critics in America, with their expert knowledge, their mellow wisdom and their infectious and gargantuan gusto, come into your home and talk to you of the books they have loved and prized? How would you like to have them send you every month the literary finds they have made? These lovers of reading have spent their lives appraising and enjoying books, and they know that the books most worthwhile, the books that we keep and read again and again, are not always the much-publicized best-sellers, on which we sometimes find that we have wasted our time. They are books that may have passed unnoticed at the time of their publication, books that a big crime or a war that absorbed your attention at the moment when you were reading your morning paper may have prevented you from knowing about. Or they are books which may have been put in the shade by other books of a similar character which appeared at the same time, but which are deserving of a permanent place in every booklover's library. "Spike" Milholland and the experts who assist him have sailed all the seas of literature and they have delved in its remotest lands like the seekers after buried treasure. Their joy when they find a good book is like the thrill of the romantic adventurer when he spies the gleam of Spanish gold, and they want to share this joy of discovery, not merely with one another, but with every man and woman in America who knows and loves good reading." This disparagement of current best-sellers, this enthusiasm for neglected merit might have appeared rather surprising in a Milholland if one had not known that, as Si informed me, the jubilant discoveries of the Treasure Seekers were simply more or less recent books that had not sold when they first came out, so that the publishers found themselves with embarrassingly large stocks on their hands. Instead of remaindering them in the usual way, they had hit upon the brilliant expedient of unloading them through a special kind of book club. This in some cases led Spike, to be sure, into a certain inconsistency as a critic, since the books that he was now rescuing from oblivion, with an excitement he was wild to communicate, were sometimes, precisely, the books that, as a reviewer in his daily column, he had condemned or dismissed or ignored; but no one seemed to notice this.

At the same time, in a different quarter, far from vindicating the sounder values, he was involved in a project for gauging the coarseness of the coarser public appetite and providing it with a diet made to order for it. Spike was one of the advisers to a conspicuous firm who had achieved an immense success by scrapping completely the old-fashioned inhibitions which made publishers still want to appear gentlemanly or to enjoy the public prestige of being supposed to represent good taste, and by frankly setting out to sell books in a similar spirit and by similar methods to those of the circus promoter or the patent-medicine vendor of seventy-five years before. It was strange that it had taken this spirit so long to get into the publishing business; but, now that it was there, it was plunging ahead with an exuberance of exploitation so heady as to be irresistible even to Spike Milholland, who had somehow hitherto succeeded in regarding himself as a popularizer of things worth popularizing—"a barker for Parnassus," as he said. The new plan was to take a poll of what the public liked most to read in those sections of the country where book stores were scarcely known or missed, and to get the kind of thing manufactured that would appeal to this half-literate public. The products would be marketed through the mail-order catalogue of a colossal Middle Western department store, which was the only periodical that was known to reach large numbers of these people. They could thus order standard books at the same time they ordered standard furniture or farming tools or children's clothes. This was a great deal more profitable than the Treasure Seekers, which had not turned out tremendously well, and Spike got his cut for suggestions as to the kind of thing that could be supplied to these layers of the population to which the Readers' Circle was not able to penetrate. A certain slight tension of rivalry began to be felt between Warren and Spike.

Both of the two surviving Milhollands now showed in their personalities the peculiar effects of power. Warren's face had grown solemn and set, and he was like one of those steel-company officials who give you the impression of being owned and driven by an organism bigger than themselves which makes them feel their strength and importance, yet keeps them anxious and never leaves them free. Spike was like a man who had made good in the publicity department of a big motor company, as I had seen them with my father in Detroit: he was friendly, frank-spoken, full of jokes, and yet somehow slightly menacing and unpleasant, because he could not help giving the impression that he was a part of something oiled and metallic that was running at terrific speed and with which one could no more monkey than with the old-fashioned proverbial buzz-saw. One felt this more and more after the end of the war, when Spike had no longer any cause to grow fervent or furious about, at the same time that, with restrictions on paper removed, the book industry was pounding full blast.

This industry now played directly into the hands of the moving-picture producers, who had swallowed up the theater in the thirties and by the mid-forties were making great inroads not only into the field of fiction but even into those of biography and history. It had always been the habit of literature to fall back on stock characters and stock situations; but in the traditional fables of stories and plays there had usually been a certain consistency: a villain, a virtuous woman, a tragic romantic hero could be counted on to keep up their rôles in accordance with accepted conventions. But Hollywood had by this time discovered that the shadows that were printed on films did not need even this simple continuity. The choppy sequences flew by so fast, they faded from the screen so completely, that the audiences could be made content by merely being allowed to sit in a darkened and perhaps air-cooled house, watching backgrounds displace one another and human figures shift back and forth while the sound-track paid out a kind of dialogue which was similar to that of the balloons in the mouths of the characters in comic strips. No logic, no firmness of outline of even the most elementary sort, were required at this stage of the films, and these qualities were beginning to vanish also everywhere else in our writing—the Milhollands were dealing more and more with the simple commercial "processing" of words for the purpose of lulling this audience with blurry feelings and flimsy images, and their scruples about ballyhooing bad writing had pretty well been destroyed by the influence of the monotonous superlatives that were plastered on movie previews. It was queer, at this time, to see Spike, who must still have been sustaining himself with the belief that he was loyal to the best, confronted by the writers who had emerged from the services at the end of World War II and were trying to do serious work. He patronized them, rebuked them, passed them over. It troubled him when he knew they were good; for, whatever his real instinct told him, his whole energy, his whole equipment, were now unconvertibly adapted to interesting the public in something else.

What this was was very soon to be made manifest in way that was almost apocalyptic.

One day when I had come down to the Village, I ran into Si Banks on Eighth Street. I had undertaken to do for my publisher, who was following the current fashion of celebrating the national culture, a short history of American painting, and I was going to see some American primitives that were on show at the Whitney Museum. I had not seen Si for several years, and I was depressed to find him shabby and unshaven almost to the point of beggary. His hands quivered and his speech faltered, and there were sometimes long embarrassing intervals during which, unable to manage a word, he could only make smacking sounds. I thought he must have been drinking a lot. He first asked me for a cigarette, then, as we walked along the street together, tried to touch me for ten dollars to pay his rent. I had only two dollar bills, but felt guilty at not being able to help him. I was afraid that he did not believe me and when he asked me to stop in at the Cruller Shop, where he said he was meeting Flagler, I went with him to prove to myself and to him that my friendliness was not affected. Yet I dreaded this session in the Cruller Shop. What I shrank from, I think, was close contact with the underside of Milholland success.

The Cruller Shop was a flavorless place that combined being clean and well-managed with exploitation of the Greenwich Village tradition. There were mediocre paintings by known artists on the walls and framed poems by poets of the twenties, none of which had been, as was sometimes the case in the older Bohemian cafés, presented to the management as payment in kind but all of which had been specially procured for the purpose of creating glamor. Yet what was left in that part of town of the artistic and literary population still tended to go for drinks to the Cruller Shop, where it mingled with the ordinary apartment-dwellers and the visitors from out of town and was almost indistinguishable from them. I had one day had lunch there with an artist who had done admirable satirical drawings in the Communist magazine, and I might, I felt, almost have been lunching in one of those uptown hotels to which publishers and editors take you. We found Flagler there sitting at a table alone, and he, too, seemed in rather wretched shape. He looked more saturnine and dampened than ever: his wide mouth was drawn down at the corners, his spectacled green eyes were diminished to slits, and the nostrils of his inadequately salient nose seemed cavernous and dark like a death's-head's. He had always, through his publishing adventures, kept up in his dress, talk and manner a certain masculine raciness and snappiness that somewhat counterbalanced his funereal aspects; but I felt now for the first time, with a certain distress, that he had definitely passed into decline. The *Booklover* had been finally converted into a sort of biweekly publicity sheet distributed by the Readers' Circle, and Flagler had been removed from the editorship as too literary and not businesslike enough. For two years he had been making a living, rather ignobly and with no margin for luxury, as a publisher's reader and reviewer. I did not then, however, know this, and I asked Flagler what he was doing. "Nothing much. I've just finished a job of research—for Freddie Pratt's novel." "It's one of those long historical rigmaroles," he explained in reply to my question, "that takes typical American characters through every goddam war and national event from the Revolution on." "Is it going to be any good?" "It ought to be: it's got all the best battle-scenes that have ever been written in this country: Cooper, George W. Cable, Ambrose Bierce, Stephen Crane, Thomas Boyd." "How are the in-between periods handled?" "Lydia did most of that part—she's always had a gift for free fantasy, but she hasn't been able to write—and now all that she's had to do has been to spin herself some wonderful daydreams and to let Freddie put them into sentences— if you can call what he writes sentences." "Five generations of marvelous women," said Si, coming to life with his drink—"with every other generation a Cinderella. And they're like Lydia: they're always having a struggle between their careers and the men they love.—And there are *two* of everything—that's the great selling-point! There are two American families, not just one. It's like the old traveling Tom shows—don't you remember how they always used to advertize two Topsies and two Simon Legrees?" "But what's the point of the two families in the story?" "Why, one in the North and one in the South! There was Lydia Boudinot who went to France and became the American Rosa Bonheur and there was Lydia Gaylord who ran the plantation and kept the carpetbaggers at bay after her menfolks had been killed in the war.—And finally there was the Lydia Boudinot who lived with a Czechoslovak labor leader and later became a WAVE and married Lord Louis Mountbatten." "What did Pratt himself contribute besides the prose?" "Isn't that enough?" twinkled Si. "Nine hundred pages of typing that are less trouble to read than a road-sign!" "Fred did contribute something," said Flagler—"he contributed the great natural disasters—the drouths, the cyclones, the floods. He's a trained meteorologist, you know." "He used to do the w-weather reports," Si explained, "on one of the morning papers. —I tell you this book has got everything! They even called me in to inject a good shot of pornography." "Macmanus," Flagler continued, "is putting on the biggest promotion campaign that's ever been seen in this country. They're taking double-spreads in the papers and claiming an advance sale of three hundred thousand copies. Of course it's a complete fake—that many copies haven't even been printed. They sell them on paper to their own warehouses—they have branches in all the big cities. There's no actual demand for the book, but even if it gets bad reviews, it won't make a bit of difference: they'll put it over as a big best-seller, whether anybody wants to read it or not. That's what the publishing business has gotten to be.—Then a cheap edition in paper that will sell a couple of millions!" It was true, as I had been brought to recognize, in discussing my own new book with Macmanus, that the market for cheap paperbound reprints susceptible of being sold by the million was exerting a new kind of pressure on even the long-established publishers in their ordering and selection of books. I had found, for example, that, when I proposed to Macmanus a new life of Thomas Eakins, they had asked me to do, instead, a short survey of American painting that could be disposed of more easily in the drug stores, the cigar stores and the railroad stations.

At this moment in our conversation, with its slow drinks and its morose humor, we were jarringly invaded by Lydia, who sailed down on us like a svelte gray seabird that alights with short eager shrieks and a spasmodic flapping of wings. I had never seen her so well-dressed before nor playing with so much assurance the role of woman of the world. She had evidently just had a "facial": the cold-creamy smoothness of her complexion seemed hardly to be creased by her grin; and her hair, which had been done in scrolls, seemed to have taken on a deeper yellow, like fine-spun molasses taffy. "I can't stay a minute," she said, pulling off her paler gray gloves, which were also very new and smooth. "I promised to go to Spike's—he wants to sort of rehearse his speech—and he wants Freddie and me to be there.—An old-fashioned without the sugar—*without the sugar,* mind!—Well, how are all you children?"— she smiled upon us gleefully, with a self-conscious sweetness. "Me, I'm in a dither—I've just been to Brooks with Freddie helping him buy a suit. Did you know that Connie always bought his clothes for him all the years he was married to her? That's the reason he always looked that way. I saw to it that he got a good cheviot— something like one you used to have, Flag. He's going to be transformed: you'll see! But I can't do anything in time for tonight about his old 1920 evening clothes—

they go back to the days of stiff shirt-fronts!" I gradually became aware that the great cause of Lydia's excitement was an occasion which I had read of in the papers but to which I had hardly paid attention. That evening the first program was to be broadcast of the nation-wide television hookup, and Spike was to appear on this program and talk about the Frederick Pratt novel, which was to be distributed by the Readers' Circle and which had been saved for publication that day. "Would you mind very much, Flag," asked Lydia, "if I went with Freddie instead? His daughter was going to go with him, but she had to get back to school a day early—and he says he won't go alone and that there's nobody he'd be willing to ask—you know how shy he is: he's just like a great big kid on the verge of his first dance! I offered to take him and rally round him, poor lamb—I thought you wouldn't mind,"—she smiled in the gay good-natured way that meant she hoped she was giving him pain. "Go ahead," replied Flagler, impassive. "Oh, good news, by the way!" she went on, as if she had been saving this to make him feel better: "Spike has talked to Furstman-Fraser and they're going to come through with a couple of grand—one for me and one for you. He told them that if Freddie had had to go to work and do all the research himself, it would have taken him six months longer, and he says that that seemed to impress them. I told him that if it hadn't been for me, the book would never have been written at all, because *I* had given Freddie all the love interest." She smiled her smug ecstatic smile. "What about those b-bedroom scenes I w-warmed up?" demanded Si. "And, after all, I was the person who suggested the whole idea of having Nancy Gaylord be the mother of Walt Whitman's illegitimate child.—It's terrific," he said, turning to me. "He meets her at the Mardi Gras and lays her on a cotton bale—she realizes then for the first time that the Yankees aren't all as bad as she'd thought." *"I* put in *that* touch," said Lydia.—"Well, I'll try to get you something too.—And now, chickadees, I must fly—I told Freddie that I'd inspect him before he went out.— It's awfully good of you not to mind, old thing!"—as she got up, she squeezed Flagler's forearm. "He really needs somebody to hold his hand!" She smiled convulsively again and left.

"I've got a feeling," said Flagler, finishing the dregs of his drink, "that I'm going to skip the whole thing. It's bad enough to have to hear Spike put out his literary jive on the air without actually seeing him jitterbug around. Why don't you fellows take my tickets? There's a double bill on Greenwich Avenue with a monster and a mad doctor and I think I'll go round and catch it— that's the only type of art, I find nowadays, that's able to hold my interest." "All right," agreed Si, chuckling, as if our going would be a mischievous and priceless joke. I was curious enough to consent. Flagler paid for all our drinks. "Why not have another?" stuttered Si— "You don't have to go right away, do you?"—and immediately snapped his fingers for the waiter. I had an instinct to get away but some spell that he exerted held me, and he had already given the order before I had had a chance to say no. Flagler handed me the broadcast tickets, pulled an old soft hat down over his eyes, thrust his hands into his overcoat pockets, and, gazing straight ahead, seemed to drive his round spectacles out the door like the headlights of some obsolete motorcar.

"Have you been doing any writing?" I asked Si. "I've been doing some first lines of poems," he replied, with his quizzical glance. "Why just the first lines?" "Well, indexes of first lines of poems are sometimes absolutely amazing—they're better than the poems themselves. The other night I read the index of an anthology to some people and they thought it was a great modern poem—which they didn't quite understand but felt they ought to be impressed by.—Would you like to hear the ones I've composed?" He took out of the side-pocket of his coat a confused wad of soiled papers, which included the remnants of a small paper bag that had once contained peanuts. "I live on peanuts now," he said. "They're nutritious, they only cost a nickel and they completely take the edge off your appetite. In fact, if you get through two bags, they make the idea of eating abhorrent.—Let me read you these. They're not arranged yet in alphabetical order the way they'd have to be for an index—I'm going to do that later when I've got some more." He read, and I was punctually appreciative.

"The poponut-thrower's paramour is pounded to pulp and rind . . .

John is just a gimcrack to Maidy . . .

Beshrew me, wench, the monk is fair . . .

If you put it on the market list, the past will come to-morrow . . .

Stain it a gravy yellow, Ludlow . . .

Old pale wild roses that poison the dawn . . .

Provincetown, prison of poor little fish . . .

The rain on the roof says, 'Woof, woof!' . . .

There are wombats in your belfry, Cousin Beastly . . .

'Bang me a Missa Solemnis!' The bellringer's fingers were cold . . .

The little hard bugs are back again . . .

Say not of Amaryllis she is dull . . .

Give us a rouse, landlord!—the hunters have taken to hop! . . .

Dimvale Midvale, the omnipresent Puritan peri . . .

Fade low, fade slow, Papa has come a new cropper!" . . .

"Why don't you publish them?" I suggested. "Where?" he asked, pleased by my laughter. "If I only had *Galimatias!*—I read them to Spike the other night and they almost drove him crazy." "What did he say?" "He was absolutely indignant because he thought I had wasted his time. He'd taken for granted that it was a book I was writing that I wanted him to help me get published. He's got his schedule organized, you know, so that he's doing something definite every minute— and something that will bring in cash. He must make sixty or seventy thousand a year. He told me that that kind of thing had been all right in the frivolous twenties but that today it was the literary equivalent of vagrancy and disorderly conduct—he insinuated that it ought to be punishable by law. You know, the very mention of *Finnegans Wake* makes him foam at the mouth—the idea that Joyce took seventeen years to write it!—when, of course, he might so easily have been doing something to prevent Pearl Harbor from happening. You remember that, when *Finnegans Wake* came out, Spike just dismissed it with a crack. I insisted on reading him parts of it one evening, and he actually began to sputter and gasp. You know how ordinarily he's never at a loss—how he can always rap out the right thing!" "He used to be a poet," I said. "He must have known there was something in it." "He's pretty jittery nowadays, I think—he's under such high pressure all the time—and I suppose he's all on tenter-hooks just now about making his first appearance on television—afraid he won't be 'telegenic,' as they call it. If they don't come out right, they're finished—just the way it was with the talkies, when the actors who didn't have good voices found themselves thrown out of work overnight. He'd just be scrapped like an old-fashioned radio set—and now he must be lying awake nights, worrying for fear his physique won't be able to live up to his voice. He's had to take off weight and go for a work-out at the Yale Club every day, but I don't think he'll disappoint his fans. Think what a moment that's going to be when he first brushes a boyish hand through that shock of upstanding hair—why, a vibration will run through the wave-lengths that will make all the windows rattle!"

I paid for the drinks, but when the change came back, it was Si who picked it up. He did this with a roguish and impudent look that made it impossible to reclaim the money. The look said: "That's the way I am: there's nothing you can do about it!—it's like those crazy first lines of poems at which you've just been laughing so wildly." I had intended to take him to dinner at my club, in spite of his slightly hobo-ish appearance; but I now told him I had a dinner engagement and would meet him at the broadcasting studio. Yet I reflected with a shade of compunction, as I dined on clean linen alone, that the incorruptible line also incurred its price and brought its own kind of demoralization.

That evening we sat mute and immobilized, admonished not to make any sound, while Spike stood up against a gray screen under the blaze of a battery of banked Klieg lights that must have made a début in television almost as much of an ordeal as a questioning by the New York police, put on the spot, as he was, to prove himself viable in this medium, under pain of debarment from public appearance, by two monster-like cameras on trucks that glided backwards and forwards, converging on him with cyclopean lenses, and by a microphone suspended from a crane, like the antenna with its suspended bait of one of those gaping-mouthed angler fish. He was not performing for us, poor Spike: we felt no direct relation with him. The radio had already dissociated the owner of the voice from its hearer, and now television was making it possible for men to stand in one another's presence without any of the immediate give-and-take that had always guaranteed in the past some basis of responsibility between human animal and human animal. Actually Spike was before us grinning, sweeping his hand through his hair, timing his deadpan cracks and holding up a copy of the novel; but he was hardly aware of the New Yorkers there who had been invited to see him perform: he had been diminished and multiplied like the model for a colored advertizement, a clever little well-dressed homunculus that gestured and stepped about and wanted very much to please while real life-size people were sitting around in their living rooms and watching him or looking away, getting up to search for a match or to answer the telephone, or were saying to one another, "He don't look as young as I expected!"—and while his amplified mechanical voice that came out of the apparatus and not from the lips of the shadow filled the room with its dark hollow sound. In exploiting his personality, Spike Milholland had become quite depersonalized: he was a mere point of intersection by the great corporate lines of interest of the new television company, the several radio companies it had swallowed, a company that made powder for jelly desserts and that was sponsoring this first big program, the great merger of publishing companies that was speculating on the Frederick Pratt novel, and the national propaganda bureau that had continued, since the end of the war, to work on public opinion at home as well as abroad.

"In the winter of 1812," he began, in the accurate and crackling way that had always picked up his radio audiences, "the Russians drove out Napoleon, who had invaded their fatherland. Fifty-seven years later, Leo Tolstoy completed *War and Peace,* the epic of the liberation of Russia. It is now a hundred and sixty-seven years since the American Revolution, and up to the present it would have had to be said that the United States of America had as yet no national epic. I said 'up to the present,' just now; I should have said 'up to this morning.' Recently our national density has carried us into Europe—we have been called by our national destiny"— he snappily caught himself up—"to play an historic role in the Pacific and in Europe both; we have repelled, not one, but two enemies, more menacing than Napoleon ever was; and we have rated at last today—I say it in all seriousness and in absolute confidence—our own American *War and Police.*"

We could see that for one rocky moment he hesitated as to whether to correct himself, but he decided to sweep on, with an energy that made him a little overemphatic.

"The name of Frederick Morse Pratt may not perhaps be familiar to all of you. But I am here to tell you tonight that my prediction is that by this time next year the name of Frederick Trapp will be known"— He stopped, grinned and called out his boyish charm.— "My first appearance on television seems to be making me go up in my lines: I can't see you but you can see me, and I'm feeling almost as nervous as if you were all sitting right here in front of me.—Well, I was talking about Frederick Pratt. Who is he? He's an American writer who has learned the American way—a product of our American system, who has nourished himself on our bones and has our democracy in his—there I go again!"—he smiled briefly, but he could not conceal this time his anxiety and irritation—"what I want to say is that Fred Pratt is as American as hominy grits, as American as a soft-shell crab"—he paused for the fraction of a moment as if this had not been the comparison he intended; but forged on: "His parents were poor—he had to drop school when he was ten, and he soon found himself adrift—adrift in a world—our American world—that makes a man prove his mettle but that offers every man a chance. Fred Pratt worked as movie usher, mirage gemanic"—he pulled himself up again, but there seemed nothing for it but to plunge ahead: "He was a freight clerk and serda-joker." "Joyce is having his revenge," burbled Si in a voice that he tried to keep low but which for me only tightened the strain. I was ominously reminded of the night when Warren had become incoherent; and also, as Spike went on, of the hysterical and unreal atmosphere which had been generated in Flagler's house by the delirium of the demented visitor the day before Jim Milholland had killed himself. "Well, Fred Pratt worked at anything and everything," Spike Milholland was going on, "and he saved up enough money to put himself through a year of college—at Lehigh University—I'm not sure that Lehigh is a college—or rather, I'm not sure that I should say Lehigh University—but of course it's a very fine place—and Fred Pratt won a scholarship there and he graduated a Phi Beta Kappa. In college he had read Zane Grey and he resolved to become a writer—and he obtusely—he obstinately plugged away and he carried out this resolve. Ten years ago this month, while wiping weather reports for one of the big morning papers, he conceived a creapive dream"— He here made a long and terrible pause; but when he went on again, he seemed suddenly to have got rid of his constraint: he spoke readily and even recklessly, with a kind of glibness and arrogance that he had sometimes used on the air when tearing into some book that he wanted to discredit; and for a moment our tension was slackened —till we caught up with the meaning of his words. "That dream," he said, "was Yale in China. It began with Dick Pratt of the class of '84 saying grace over a bowl of chop suey and it ended with the expulsion from China of the competitive Japanese invader.—And now, folks, I want to say a word about Gluko jelly desserts" —Gluko, Si afterwards explained to me, was not even the right brand: it was a dangerous rival of the jelly which Spike had been engaged to advertize. "I don't believe that the Chinese coolie is getting his Gluko yet, but it is as certain that he is going to get it as that the Chinese people have been liberated by the American Army and Navy—and by the United States Marines. No longer will the Chinese workingman be forced to invite malnutrition diseases by subsisting on a meager dish of rice—he will sit down to a man's-size meal, topped off with a dainty dessert: appetizing and health-building Gluko. There are ten delicious flavors to choose from and special shades to flatter your complexion. A wonderful treat for Baby; the thrill in a lifetime for Sister; a great big kick for Dad—and for me a sharp throbbing pain in—you know: our favorite novelist! I thank you."

"They say the heat's terrific," said Si, as we were walking home after the show. "It's like getting the third degree. Sometimes they come out half dead."

"It sounded," I suggested, "like some comic line that he might have worked up for a college smoker—with a flare-up of his radical ideas, which must have been rankling in his mind all this time. He can't be particularly pleased by the turn our foreign policy has taken."

"They would have cut him off the air," said Si, "long before he got to that point.—Well, I wonder what the Milhollands will do to appease the Old Creditor now."

"It's between Spike and Warren, I guess—and I believe I'd bet on Spike. He's resourceful and quick and he's streamlined himself to navigate the new age— he has youth and hope on his side."

"Yes," said Si, "but W-Warren's c-closer to the real American tradition—as Spike said, he's nourished on its bones. He has that Yankee tenacity and toughness that the younger generation lack. He's as shrewd as Benjamin Franklin and as hard-boiled as Andrew Jackson. He's succeeded in selling wooden nutmegs to the whole American reading public whereas Spike's already gone to pieces and tried to give the show away. And even if the Devil snares him, he may find he's only got a stuffed soul and that Warren's still doing business above-ground."

6.

Mr. and Mrs. Blackburn at Home

I KEPT THINKING all through one summer that there was something about the American landscape which made you feel that it had just been discovered. This was true even in Hecate County, which was so full of gardened and arranged estates and of "developed" suburban roads. *America:* it suggests to us even now a landscape unfamiliar and wild. When I looked out over an inlet from the sea, I would feel, for all the white moored launches and the graded lawns on the opposite side, that we had sailed into some uncharted estuary and weighed anchor in some virgin harbor, with its pale opaque gray-blue waters, brackish and almost tepid, tranquilly rippled with evening; its large birds of which I did not know the names flying slowly by the shore that had bred them; and its wooded and grassy banks that still seemed, though the houses had already been built, such a good place to build a house, to find at one's ready disposal all the best that a rich soil could afford and not to be bothered by neighbors. There were adventures and new forms of life over there beyond the thick summer foliage—there were leisure, refreshment, romance. Even the sailboats against the gold sun seemed just to have alighted here—where there was nothing to prevent them from making themselves as easy and as much at home as the birds that were now, like them, becalmed in the long sweeping-down of the ample sure-bosomed night. . . . Or I would step over a scrawling fence, a mere twist of old gray rails and barbed wire, and wade up through the unmowed grass into an isolated growth of forest that stood on a rise of ground above a swamp where I had gone as a child in March to see the hard mottled helmets of the skunk-cabbage butting up by the squushy hummocks; and I would find there a wilderness of big old trees amid towering seed-tufted ailanthus, a snarl of blackberry bushes and a matting underfoot of vines, that made it rather forbidding in aspect and impossible to penetrate. Here the forces of vegetation were fiercely asserting themselves and were quite able to keep a human at bay. Yet right along the edge of this wood were several acres completely cleared, with a white farmhouse and a neat ploughed field; and for this family, enlivened by their radio and working the earth with the newest tools, the heavy creepers and thickets and branches still stood as a screen and a background, the old uncouth yet somehow comforting tangle of that one spot which had never been cut and that still kept the mysterious solitude, the inexhaustible recesses and shadows, of a land where we were still frontiersmen.

One was brought to a peculiar consciousness of what it meant to be at home in America, to feel the reassurance of America, and yet at the same time to savor the locust trees and wild grapes in the air as they had reached the first navigators, during the years after the accession of Hitler when the exiles from Europe were arriving. These had come to us, not from curiosity, not from the need for a simpler society, but merely because pressures at home had forced them to take up residence elsewhere, and they would try to go on living in the

United States exactly as if they were still in Europe.
Where their surroundings in America did not give them
the nourishment, the support and the responses that
they had been used to having at home, they complained
or they silently suffered; but they rarely made any attempt—many of them, of course, were too old—to
understand the country they had fled to. The least adapt-
able were the French and the Germans; the most flexible
the Austrians and the Russians; but neither class displayed very much interest in finding out what America
meant. The Germans, whether young radical political
workers or elderly and scholastic "doctors," were always
obsessed by programs or projects of which the desir-
ability seemed to them self-evident, and would attempt
to drive them through under conditions which they had
not applied themselves to studying, among a people
whom they hardly knew, with a complacency and a determination which seemed to us almost insane but which
did something to make Hitler comprehensible. The
French, of course, behaved very differently; but they
maintained their cautious bourgeois habits or promoted
their aesthetic movements as if they were still in Parisian
intérieurs—that word that so excludes the outdoors. The
Surrealists would discover the Indian katcinas or the
statues on Easter Island—"Ah, vous savez, c'est formidable! C'est le vrai art américain que les Américains ne
connaissent pas!"—but they could never bring these into
focus with their own synthetic grotesques which had
been made to be seen only in galleries. The Viennese
learned at once all the tricks of their trades and all
the right tones to take with people, but, confident in the
exercise of their subtlety on what seemed to them the
crudeness of the Americans just as they had been with
the Germans, they remained on the outside in America
just as they had been with Germany. The Russian case

was a little different: the Russian émigré intellectuals
had brought to the United States, as they had done to
western Europe, a gift of idiom and a ready intelligence
as well as something of a more general capacity for
natural human relations that one did not find in the
people from countries more constricted and more cramp-
ingly stratified; and, with their incomparable theatrical
sense, they acted the part of guest more brilliantly; but,
with their inveterate snobbishness toward Europe, they
tended to regard the Americans—perhaps too much
like themselves—as a provincial and uninteresting race
whose principal role, after all, was to provide a fairly
comfortable refuge for accomplished cosmopolitan Russians. Only the English—that odd migration which had
given up England on the eve of the war and gravely,
without explanation, had established themselves in the
United States—only the English sometimes took the
trouble to look into American history and to inform
themselves on modern America, rather as if it were a
department of their colonial activity that they had always meant to get up, and which they required only a
bit of reading to master and to set us right about. We,
on our side, were able to profit, for we had specimens,
often very distinguished, of all the principal European
nationalities to examine and converse with at leisure on
our own ground and in our own light—apparently un-
aware, the exiles, of their educative value for us, who,
not without a certain surprise—the pioneers' final surprise at discovering that a traditionless country has cast
them in a definite mold—were finding our national
strength in the course of such contacts and comparisons
at home as well as through our effectiveness abroad with
the mechanical engineering of modern war.

Thus we were stimulated in a sense by the refugees
even when they let us down; and it was but rarely that

we found them fatiguing or were annoyed, after long
conversations, at becoming aware that we were framing
our thoughts in foreign phrases or an inverted word
order, as if, instead of talking English to the visitors,
we had been trying to make ourselves understood abroad.
One house there was, notably, however, which used
sometimes to affect me in this way without my ever being
able to determine of what nationality the inmates were.
They were not refugees from Hitler, for they had been
living in the United States from the early twenties at
least; and when I found the place one weekend full of
Italian professors and editors, who called the host Mr.
Malatesta, I assumed that he was an exiled anti-fascist;
but I later found it full of Russians, who referred to
him as Mr. Chernokhvostov, and I was told by a clever
Russian novelist who seemed to have known him in
Europe but whom I did not necessarily believe, that he
was a fur dealer who traded with the Soviets, that he
belonged to an old Moscow merchant family and had
left after the Revolution, and that his name had to do
with the skins of some kind of Siberian animal on which
the family fortune had been based. On another occasion
I heard him called Swarzkopf by a theatrical director
from Berlin, but I took it for German banter: a joke
about his swarthy complexion. With us the name he
went by was Blackburn, and there were moments when
his hawklike profile and his sly and homely manner
made me think him a typical Yankee—a Yankee, if that
were possible, with a touch of colored blood; but his
appearance, his accent and his manner seemed to vary in
a curious fashion, so that one never carried away, after
seeing him, a clear impression of what he was like. One
Sunday when a Soviet official was there, I absolutely
had the illusion that Ed Blackburn had three gold front
teeth, and with the agents of big German companies

he spoke German as emphatically as they did and showed the same bullying gallantry with their ladies.

In any case, we went to his parties, which were sometimes small dinners on weekends at which we would meet his guests, sometimes enormous evening blowouts to which everybody in the neighborhood was invited. His house was a gigantic affair on top of a moderate-sized hill, with many stables and graveled drives, bowling alleys, greenhouses and wire-fenced fields, not all of which, however, were now kept up. No doubt he had got the place cheap because it was the kind of thing nobody wanted. The house was a great mound of red brick which a traction magnate had had amassed sometime in the early nineteen hundreds, and it combined the many rows of windows of an old-fashioned summer hotel with the square hardness of a new garage. There was a corrugated green copper roof that used to glare in the August sun and make the whole place look uncomfortable and public, like the factories and the railroad stations, the business blocks and the municipal buildings, among which the streetcars of the owner had crawled and scraped and screamed. "They couldn't bother themselves much in those days," Ed Blackburn would say with a laugh, as if the arrogance and crassness of the industrial millionaires gave him some sort of sardonic satisfaction, "about the mere aesthetic aspects of life—they were too busy making people cough up—if you will pardon my using the idiom of that period—to care what they gave them to look at."

That summer—in '34—when I had been feeling the freshness of our landscape and meeting the émigrés— though all those that I have mentioned above had not yet, of course, come over—I drove up to the Blackburns'

one night for one of their periodical routs. I was glad
of the chance to go out, because, in the last few days, I
had been coming to clutch at pretexts for evading an
internal strain. It was a question of whether or not I
ought, finally, to marry Jo. It was now a little less than
a week before she would have to go out to the Coast to
do her six months of the year with her children, and
our relations were now at the point, after a love affair
that had lasted six years, where it seemed the inevitable
thing for us to marry and live together. It was hard on
her, I knew, to have to leave me for so long a time every
year; but, on the other hand, it was difficult for me to
go out to California with her (her former husband had
made it impossible for her to bring her children East):
it would mean giving up my job, and I had feared that
my meager income would not be equal to her standard
of living out there. Besides, she did bore me a little if I
had to be alone with her too long. I could not talk to her
very much about painting: as a child, she had been
taken to Europe, and she had collected picture postcards
of great paintings, which she still preserved in an album,
but, in spite of my efforts to instruct her, I was never
able to see that her interest had progressed very much
beyond this. Nor did I fit into her world very well. She
had become more and more addicted to a migratory
cocktail set who were mostly far too rich for me and by
the thirties had come to disgust me. I could not imagine
myself spending, as she did, evening after evening with
them nor was I able to imagine *her,* though she assured
me she would like nothing better, drinking quietly with
a book every night while I shut myself up in my study.
The old arrangement had had the advantage for me that
it had combined a dependable girl, available half the
year and never left on my hands too long, with six
months of entire freedom—though I was sometimes dis-

organized when she went at finding myself without resources or annoyed by inferior entanglements which I
should not have let myself in for if Jo had been there.
But she had several admirers on the Coast, and there
was one that she had thought seriously of marrying; and
it was unfair for me to prevent her from doing so if I
did not want to marry her myself. Or was I afraid that
she would decide before I was ready to let her go? In
any case, the moment had come. After all, if I gave up
my job, I should have to finish my book; and, as she
had just inherited securities which, even on a shrunken
market, would bring her ten thousand a year, and a
house in Pasadena with a patio that had belonged to
her late uncle, I should not have to worry about living if
I did not mind living on her. But what worried me now
was to know whether the prospect of leisure and a
house of our own was tempting me to do something
that it was wrong for me to do or whether, on the contrary, the fear of being influenced by practical considera-
tions was inhibiting me from doing the right thing. I
kept putting off the decision and was becoming self-
conscious with her, because I felt that she expected me
to speak: to release her or to ask her to marry me; and,
instead of coming to grips with the problem, I found
myself seeking out people and applying myself to tasks,
as if I were hoping that these contacts with the world
would somehow make everything clear. As I approached
the crisis ahead, I continually became more methodical,
more deliberate, more even-tempered: I was managing,
thus, to defer whatever I should have to feel when I
had chosen one course or the other.

So I welcomed the affair at the Blackburns', and I
greeted Ed Blackburn with heartiness when he happened
to come out into the hall just at the moment when I had
entered the door and before I had joined the party. He

looked quite fine in his stiff white shirt, full black
trousers and jaunty dinner jacket, which he always wore
even on occasions when most people no longer dressed;
and it was only when he came up and shook hands with
me that I noticed how somber and haggard he looked:
the skin hanging loose from the aggressive jaw, the
creases deepened from the dark bristling nostrils and
the round shutters of the eyelids drooping over eyes
that, especially now, had some tinge of the oriental. I
felt more than ever, in meeting him tonight, that he was
not really a part of our community, and I was aware of
a curious impression that he did not grow old as we did,
but belonged to some remote time and place, toward
which, in spite of his well-tailored evening clothes, he
was now rather wearily reverting. But he grasped my
hand so vigorously with both of his and flashed me such
a live black-eyed smile that I found he had become with
the years an old friend as well as a neighbor, and a comfortable part of my life. "Hel-*lo!*" he exclaimed. "I was
hoping you'd come. I've just read your very brilliant
article. I know that it's been out for months, but one
gets so little time for such things. I hope you won't
think I'm trying to flatter you when I tell you that it's
given me more to think about than anything I've read
about painting since Taine. You have, if you'll pardon
my saying so, a sense of the historical background and
an aesthetic appreciation that one very rarely finds together. The historians are not artists and the aesthetes
do not see the world in terms of time and space—isn't
it so?" "There are some very good art critics," I said,
"who are not historically-minded." "But such critics are
insufficient," he insisted. "It's not enough to have an
orgasm over beauty. We must be able to understand why
the athlete cut in stone, the Periclean Greek, with every
muscle perfectly developed, is different from the emaci-

ated elongated saint of the Greek that we call El Greco. And it seems to me that you've formulated some general truths that give the clue to these historical differences in a way that is absolutely masterly. I know that it is stupid of me to be reading you only now when you have been writing for so long a time; but really, your article has supplied me with the answers to many questions that have always puzzled me." It seemed to me that his way of phrasing was more than usually foreign tonight, that he had almost an un-English accent, and, in spite of what was perhaps a slight coarseness in his perception of the problems with which I had dealt, I was pleased that a European should have found something new in my article.

"Don't go in right away," he continued, as I was moving toward the door of the big living room. "Once you're in there with that jabbering crowd, conversation will become impossible. You would be doing me a real favor if you would come into the library for a chat." He led the way through a great enclosed court, full of fragments of Roman marbles and an immense display of hothouse flowers. I lingered a moment to look, and he explained, what I already knew, that the traction millionaire and his wife had always had these flowers on show here, and that he, Blackburn, had kept up the custom, employing the same staff of gardeners—the flowers had to be changed every week—and carrying on the same expensive program, which involved always producing special things that would normally be out of season. This seemed to me rather perverse, because the effect of these bouquets and potted plants was almost invariably hideous: they were at once exotic and vulgar. Just at present, since it was early in the summer, the flowers were mostly of species appropriate to early winter. The main element in the pattern was chrysanthemums: tousled balls of maroon and white, egg-yolk yellow and washed-out mauve; frizzy withering pale yellow puffs and rusty reddish-orange blobs; pink rosettes with round bug-eyed centers and drooping pinwheels of white shredded coconut. Remembering this flower as the feminine emblem of the big college football games, I was rather surprised to see that they could be made to look so unattractive. And among the various objects of antiquity: the stone fruit-baskets and garlanded sarcophagi; the scattering of slender plinths that had no longer any function in a building but were set about in utter futility, and the pedestaled torsos and busts so featureless, maimed and gray that one felt they might have been better left buried; the gaping dolphins with twisted tails dripping water into a chipped stone fountain—among these were set waxen begonias as dry as pink potato chips; anthurium with slim phallic fingers sticking out from flesh-pink elephant ears; potted palms that seemed exasperatingly irrelevant and jungle-sized rubber-plants, growing clumsily and sagging over; and varied Brazilian orchids that, purple, pale-green or brown, streamered, snouted, frilled and lipped, looked, now too much like artificial ornaments, now too much like self-contained goblins, to be pleasantly acceptable as flowers, and that had ugly and wrong-sounding names like *Lc. Miranda McGreevyii gigas and B.Lc. Zygopetalum Hearnii.* "A perfect period-piece, isn't it?" said Blackburn. "The bad taste of the early nineteen hundreds which surpasses any other bad taste—especially in the United States. I've thought it was worth preserving. And when you consider that all these outlandish growths were bought at the expense of the public—by making the passengers on streetcars pay extra nickels and pennies over and above the reasonable fares, where the few cents' difference meant food and coal." He chuckled.

"Not tops in its line, but by no means to be scorned, nevertheless. A Renaissance prince, if you like, would have invested in something more seductive. Here the mask is completely distasteful as the sin was essentially mean—and with only a small slice of that fortune, provided one had civilized taste, how delightfully one could always have lived! A courtyard, for example, can be charming, it can provide an aesthetic center in the general composition of a house—though it's better in a sunnier climate, where one does not have to have it roofed in." I thought about the patio that Jo had described in her aunt's Pasadena house, with wicker furniture and clay Zuñi pots. "And yet"—he returned to his original thought—"the thing has a kind of magnificence: how brazen and on what a prodigious scale! There has never been anything like it: 'Ce n'est pas le Parthénon, mais c'est de la beauté,' as Anatole France once said about the art of the Gothic cathedrals."

"And that brings us back to your essay," he went on, as we came into the big library and poured ourselves tall drinks from a tray of ripe bottled liquors. We settled ourselves, I lying back on the ample red-leather couch with the calmness and assurance of authority awaiting a layman's questions, and he throning in a big leather chair. We were lighted by a single large lamp, which seemed to isolate us in the long dark room, as if our conference were important and private. "What interests me particularly," he said, "is your idea that the methods of the Impressionists were essentially the result of their unwillingness to look the contemporary world in the face. They created a veil between themselves and it. They couldn't come to grips with it, in fact—so that their work was unreal and worthless." This was not precisely what I had said; and he spoke, I thought, a little too dogmatically: as if *he* were telling *me*. I ex-

plained that, though it was true that the Impressionists
had sometimes been repelled by their century, their
work could not be said to be worthless: they had made
their own kind of beauty though they had had to create
special conventions under which it could be realized.
"And eventually, of course," I went on, "it did come to
present a reflection of the world from which it had tried
to withdraw. When crystals began to form in the satur-
ated solutions of the atmospheres of painters like Monet
and Seurat, they made the abstract designs of angles that
you get in a modern city and the accidental patterns that
you find in machines. You have Cubism, in other
words." "I have always been assured that Cubism," said
Blackburn, who had listened to my remarks with attention, "was an experiment in pure and fundamental form,
and now you explain it quite comprehensibly as the
product of historical necessity. I shall be interested to see
if you can explain in such terms all the other aberrations
of modern art." I told him that my book would deal
only with the painting of the nineteenth century. "But
you must follow it with another volume—you must
bring the story up to date! And in the meantime you
make us wait too long. Surely your museum work takes
up too much of your time. You should have leisure to
concentrate and complete your work. This is the moment when such a book is needed, when it can help us
to orient ourselves. The stability of the bourgeois order
is crumbling away before us, and we see its disintegration in the chaos of modern painting. The ordinary
critic—whose bread depends on his persuading people
to take his painting seriously—tells us that we must
admire; you tell us we may sometimes admire, but we
must see these deformities and splotches as the symptoms of the rickets and neuroses from which our civilization suffers." "But it's also true"—I tried to insist—

"that what seems to be decadence in art may involve what is really the beginning of a greater creative movement. The artists of the future may be influencing life, through murals and posters and illustrating and other things we haven't imagined, in a way that our gallery painters have never dreamed of doing and pretend that they'd scorn to do, yet they'll probably look back to Picasso and the rest as the pioneers who made their work possible, who rescued art from the photograph and set it free to act directly on the emotions."

"The artists of the future," said Blackburn, with a sudden sardonic dryness, "will perhaps, as Bernard Shaw says, be earning a few poor pennies by drawing with colored chalks on the pavements." "Then you think civilization is going to Hell?" He smiled as if he had been caught off his guard. "Figuratively, perhaps," he said, "but not in the literal sense. If we're in for some catastrophic happenings, they will hardly turn out to the advantage of Hell—le Diable n'y trouvera pas son compte. Le monde européen—permettez que je m'exprime en français—est en train de s'endurcir à toute consideration de moralité à tel point que bientôt on se passera de lui aussi bien que de Celui à qui il est censé s'opposer.—Ça ne vous ferait rien que nous parlions français? Je sais que vous le connaissez très bien. Vous avez été élevé en France?—non? Alors vous avez l'oreille très fine. Il m'est arrivé, dans ces dernières années, d'avoir recours de plus en plus à cette langue si polie et si nette. C'est le seul moyen, je trouve, de donner un semblant de logique à des évènements qui deviennent à tout moment de plus en plus insensés." What he said about my French was not true, but it pleased me to hear him say it. His own French I had always thought that of a Belgian businessman or of an American lawyer who has practiced in Paris; but, as I listened to him talking tonight,

I seemed to note in it a certain flavor, a turn of phrase, of the eighteenth century. Returning to the earlier topic, I asked him whether the Nazis in Germany were doing nothing to gratify the Devil. "Quant à Hitler lui-même," he replied, "il n'est guère intéressant pour le Malin. C'est un saint, quoi, un patriote—un type dans le genre de Jeanne d'Arc. Cet imbécile ne veut pas même faire le mal. Ça ne lui coûte rien, en fait de principe moral, de faire massacrer un Juif ou un Polonais, parce qu'il ne sait pas ce que c'est qu'un homme—lui-même ne l'étant guère. C'est un fou, un paranoïaque—comme la plupart des saints, d'ailleurs. Il croit tout simplement qu'on le persécute, qu'on persécute la patrie en lui, et qu'il faut bien qu'il se défende. Pour ce qui est des autres Nazis, n'est-ce pas—à part Goebbels, qui est un assez bel exemple d'homme de lettres raté et rancunier—ce ne sont que des hommes tarés de troisième ou quatrième ordre ou bien de simples *Schaffköpfe* allemands, qui, du moment qu'ils ne prennent plus au sérieux ni le Souverain Juge ni son Adversaire, se font forts d'une belle découverte: à savoir qu'ils se trouvent parfaitement en état de faire tout ce qu'ils veulent sur cette terre sans courir le risque ni d'être foudroyés sur place par l'un ni d'être malmenés par les agents de l'autre. Je ne voudrais pas, cependant, donner l'impression de ne pas attacher d'importance à cette certitude de l'homme contemporain qu'il est libre de détruire ou de construire, de faire ce qui bon lui semble de lui-même et de ceux qui se soumettent à lui, sans égard pour le Bien et le Mal érigés en pouvoirs surhumains. C'est même, cette révolution sur le plan moral, l'évènement capital de notre temps—évènement à côté duquel les regroupements dont on entend tant parler ou ne se présentent que comme des changements très superficiels, le remplacement d'une bande de fripons par une autre, un tour de passe-passe politique qui reste sans aucune portée parce que les classes sociales qu'on substitue l'une à l'autre éprouvent, toutes les deux, exactement les mêmes désirs et se proposent des buts identiques—ou bien ils doivent leur seul intérêt, ces regroupements, à ce qu'ils se sont mis en branle sous l'impulsion de ce moteur central.

"On voit bien que c'est à peu près la même chose en Russie. Staline, lui, fait ce qu'il veut des Russes parce que, comme marxiste, il n'a pas reculé devant la liquidation de la religion et il se trouve tout de suite, avec une joie sauvage—et un peu d'étonnement, je crois—maître suprême et immuable de cent soixante-dix millions d'êtres humains, qu'il sait conduire exactement comme un grand tracteur agricole dans une de ses fermes collectives. On peut les organiser, n'est-ce pas, sur n'importe quelle échelle pour accomplir n'importe quel travail. On peut même leur faire avaler les mensonges idiots de la *Pravda*—et on peut leur prêter n'importe quelle idée. D'abord on leur parle du Plan Quinquennal et on les attelle aux corvées d'usine et de construction publique—genre de métier que les Russes n'aiment guère; ensuite on leur fera combattre les Allemands au prix de vingt-cinq millions d'hommes, après que le camarade Staline aura lui-même ouvert la porte aux Nazis et, pour ainsi dire, les aura invités exprès à envahir la patrie russe—car cet homme très borné admire Hitler et reste même stupéfié devant lui. Il voudra s'en faire un bon allié la veille même du jour où ce forcené lui démontrera à coup de bombe et de mitrailleuse que, pour admirer un grand pouvoir amoral, il ne faut pas lui donner sa confiance—surtout quand on a la prétention de jouer soi-même un rôle amoral. Je parle de choses qui ne se sont pas encore passées mais qui vont sûrement arriver."

Little enthusiasm though I felt for Stalin, I could not

believe in these fantastic prophecies, which seemed to
me prompted by some spirit of perversity at the same
time philistine and cynical; and I reminded him that it
had been, after all, the idealists Lenin and Trotsky who
had first mobilized and unified the Russians, and that the
Soviet Union had been dedicated to the establishment
of a socialist society. I spoke of the morality of Marxism and of the creative aims of the Marxists. "Je ne mets
pas en doute," he replied, "que Lénine et Trotsky—
comme Marx—avaient bien leur moralité à eux, mais
cette moralité assez élevée n'intéresse que médiocrement
celui que vous connaissez comme le Diable. Sans doute il
y a des restes frappants de la vieille théologie protestante
dans ce système qui s'est tant vanté de s'être dégagé de
toute religiosité, mais c'est assurément le dernier rayon
d'une lumière qui est en train de s'éteindre; et il ne me
paraît d'ailleurs que trop évident que ce système marxiste
va lui-même toujours en se détériorant et que l'epoque
n'est pas très éloignée où Staline le frappera d'interdit
et ne se fera pas même scrupule d'exterminer ceux qui le
professent. En attendant, je vous accorde que les projets
grandioses qu'on s'efforce de réaliser dans l'union
soviétique peuvent très bien se diriger vers un but que
vous caractériseriez comme le Bien, qu'ils peuvent
même y aboutir—encore que les chances me paraissent
au moins égales qu'ils aboutiront à ce que vous appelez
le Mal. Dans l'un et l'autre cas, l'important pour la
personne dont nous parlons, c'est que les Russes aussi
bien que les Allemands n'agissent que pour des motifs
uniquement pratiques et qu'ils ne s'embarrassent pas de
l'ancien prestige de ces pouvoirs du ciel et de l'enfer
auxquels leurs aïeux ont rendu tant d'hommages. Vous
pensez bien que le Malin n'aura garde de rester plus
longtemps dans ces pays athées où l'on ne fait plus cas
de son œuvre et où il ne se trouve plus chez lui. C'est

un personnage—une façon de personnage, comme disait Saint-Simon de Voltaire—avec cette différence importante que l'avenir était bien à Voltaire"—he gave a rueful and ironic smile—"c'est un personnage du vieux monde européen qui s'est adapté de son mieux à la société capitaliste, mais qui ne parle plus la même langue que ces gredins du Kremlin et de la Wilhelmstrasse—ces *khamy,* comme on les aurait appelés autrefois en Russie.

"Vous vous souvenez sans doute de cet agent soviétique, ce délateur professionnel, que vous avez rencontré ici. C'est un homme très habile, très rusé—originaire de la Bessarabie et parlant à merveille toutes les langues. Il a même—chose qui se voit assez rarement chez les diplomates soviétiques—su acquérir, au cours de ses voyages, une certaine connaissance du monde. Jadis je l'aurais très volontiers recruté—mais aujourd'hui je n'ai aucune prise sur lui, je n'ai plus rien à lui offrir. Je vous assure que cet homme me fait peur. C'est lui qui essaye de me tenter! Quand il m'a écrit en me priant de le recevoir, j'aurais aimé pouvoir me bercer de l'espoir qu'il avait quelque besoin de moi, bien que le ton assez péremptoire sur lequel il m'a adressé la parole ne me laissât pas sans inquiétude. Je savais bien qu'on l'avait placé à l'ambassade pour espionner le malheureux ambassadeur, et veiller à ce qu'il ne s'intéresse pas trop au pays auprès duquel il était accredité—et je ne pouvais pas m'empêcher de me demander s'il s'était avisé de venir fouiller dans mes affaires. Eh bien, il a eu le toupet de m'offrir de consacrer une partie de mon temps—a part-time job, as we say—à sa belle organisation. Il m'a expliqué avec une candeur qui ne cherchait nullement à ménager mes susceptibilités comme doyen du Mal—puisque je sais bien qu'il n'y a ni moyen ni besoin de vous cacher mon identité—vous êtes très intelligent et j'ose espérer que ça ne vous gênera pas si je vous parle tout franchement—ce mufle m'a donc démontré avec une logique d'acier que le Bon D—that my Opposite Number—c'est moi cette fois qui ai failli manquer de respect—voilà le vice du siècle, comme je disais tout à l'heure: le mépris des choses sacrées!—that my Opposite Number had been liquidated and that my own occupation was gone. Eh bien, je ne pouvais pas faire mieux que de m'engager au service de l'U.R.S.S. Je me suis efforcé de lui faire avouer qu'il restait encore en Russie des traces réelles et vivantes de malignité humaine consciente. J'ai relevé quelques mensonges publics de la part du gouvernement qui m'avaient l'air aussi gratuit que les inventions tellement passionnantes de l'incomparable roman russe, et je lui ai rappelé des traits de cruauté qui me semblaient absolument dignes des beaux jours d'Ivan le Terrible. Je lui ai cité ce mot russe *chistka*—euphémisme délicieux qui signifie, au sens littéral, tout simplement une légère purgation* mais qui s'emploie pour désigner aussi la condamnation à mort ou aux travaux forcés d'un million d'hommes et de femmes qui n'ont rien fait de plus coupable que de consacrer leur vie entière à appliquer les principes de Lénine et à s'evertuer à consommer son œuvre. 'Toujours ces diminutifs,' lui dis-je,—'ce sont ces façons de parler enfantines qui donnent tant de charme, n'est-ce pas, à l'adorable langue russe.' 'Sans parler d'Ivan IV,' il m'a répondu, disert comme un avocat, hautain et dur comme un juge, 'que nous sommes parvenus à reconnaître comme stabilisateur formidable de la Russie désunie et

* Mr. Blackburn was in error here. In Russian the ending *ka* is not necessarily diminutive. It may have an active force: *vyveska, vystavka,* etc. But it was natural for Mr. Blackburn to think of it the other way, and the official to whom he was talking had not thought about the matter at all.

sauvage aussi bien que comme fondateur de la Russie
docile et forte—je peux vous dire que sous le régime
soviétique tous ces diminutifs de la vieille langue russe
—qui ne sont que des souvenirs avilissants des ma-
nières câlines et serviles de l'esclavage féodal—je peux
vous dire que ces mignons enfantillages sont en train
de disparaître. Nous ne les tolérons, nous hommes de
culture, qu'en vertu de la nécessité qui s'impose de nous
prêter parfois aux penchants ridicules d'un peuple assez
arriéré, en attendant qu'on lui enseigne un langage plus
moderne, tout technique et tranchant, qui ne laissera
aucune place à toutes ces gentillesses fades qui abais-
sent.'

"Il m'a affirmé, du reste, avec beaucoup d'insistence,
qu'il n'y avait point de cruauté consciente dans les
'purges' qu'on administrait en Russie, et je suis obligé,
ma foi, de le croire. Staline lui-même, naturellement
—aussi bien que quelques-uns de ses fonctionnaires—
ne sont pas dans le cas d'Hitler et des vulgaires bour-
reaux allemands: ce sont ou bien des hommes primitifs
auxquels la vengeance procure une vive jouissance
ou bien des êtres timides et ambitieux qui aiment
écraser—en goûtant un âpre plaisir—les âmes plus
courageuses et plus désintéressées. Mais, en general, ce
n'est que trop vrai que dans la Russie stalinienne on
parvient à entraîner les jeunes gens à appliquer ces
procédés meurtriers avec un sans-gêne presque automa-
tique. On fusille le condamné dans le dos, comme vous
savez, en le ramenant du tribunal: le sang coule dans
deux petits canaux pratiqués sur le bord du chemin, et
on le lave à grands jets d'eau qui n'en laissent sub-
sister aucune trace. Le cadavre ne reste guère plus longtemps—on l'enlève, on l'ensevelit, et l'on n'y pense plus.
Dans le cas où la femme doit disparaître aussi, on ne
s'occupe point des enfants, qui, sans y rien comprendre,

se trouvent tout d'un coup orphelins et deviennent des objets de mépris pour leurs camarades d'école et pour leurs instituteurs mêmes—personne n'ose leur venir en aide. Mais, ce qui est embêtant pour moi, on n'éprouvera pas même de plaisir à penser à leurs infortunes. On les laisse simplement tomber comme les pièces qui n'ont pas la bonne taille sur les convoyeurs des usines taylorisées —alors que tout autre peuple que les Russes soviétiques prendraient soin de les ramasser et de leur trouver quelque usage—bien qu'il ne faille pas oublier, bien sûr, que les ressources humaines de la Russie sont aussi illimitées que ses blés et ses minerais. Quant à l'Allemagne hitlérienne—vous pouvez m'en croire sur parole, quoique je doute que vous y parveniez—cela va augmenter encore. On s'appliquera très systématiquement à asphyxier et à incendier les gens en gros dans des espèces de fabriques homicides construites exprès pour ça—on les réduira en cendres avec une célérité étonnante et on les expédiera dans de grands sacs dans les régions agricoles pour servir d'engrais pour les champs. On mobilisera pour ça, d'abord, des criminels pathologiques qu'on libérera de leurs chiourmes à condition qu'ils se prêtent à des crimes plus infâmes encore que ceux pour lesquels on les a enfermés. Mais ce n'est là qu'un expédient provisoire qu'on n'emploiera que jusqu'au jour où l'on aura enseigné aux jeunes gens que tout ce qui n'est pas allemand n'est pas humain, si bien qu'on se trouvera en état de s'acquitter de semblables devoirs sans broncher mais sans y goûter le moindre plaisir. Ce qui, naturellement, n'est guère pour me réjouir.

"Ah, que je regretterai le bon goût des Français le jour où la France se trouvera, comme elle va l'être, terrassée par ces brutes de boches! La cruauté française, n'est-ce pas, c'est un peu une spécialité nationale, comme la cuisine et la critique littéraire. Quel 'jardin des sup-

plices' merveilleux—c'est le beau titre d'un livre de Mir-
beau—que le roman français de Laclos jusqu'à Proust!
François de Sade, quel génie formidable! J'y songeais
tout à l'heure quand je méditais sur la bassesse indicible
de ces types de la Russie soviétique—vous me pardon-
nerez si j'y reviens toujours—qui ne se font pas scrupule
de dénoncer leurs pères et leurs mères, leurs frères et
leurs sœurs, leurs amants, leurs maîtresses et leurs meil-
leurs amis. Vous savez sans doute que le marquis de
Sade a été, sous la Terreur, juge du tribunal révolu-
tionnaire. Il est arrivé par hasard un jour que sa belle-
mère et son beau-père devaient comparaître devant lui.
Or ces parents de sa femme, la belle-mère surtout,
l'avaient persécuté sans relâche et sans pitié lors de son
mariage, l'avaient fait arrêter trois fois, et avaient même
voulu le faire emprisonner pour la vie. Eh bien, cet
homme épatant, qui se trouvait à même de les perdre,
les a sauvés de l'échafaud. 'J'ai eu ma vengeance,' dit-il.
Il savait bien qu'il n'y avait pas de meilleur moyen d'ex-
aspérer sa belle-mère, qui l'avait poursuivi pendant trente
ans d'une haine implacable, le traitant de monstre in-
humain. C'est un trait d'esprit bien français—très fin,
très discret, très pur.—Le malheur pour le marquis,'' he
added, with a sharp pleased and jeering laugh, ''c'est
que ce geste le fit accuser d'un modérantisme suspect. Il
fut aussitôt condamné à mort—ce qui fort égaya la vieille.

''Ah, ce brave dix-huitième siècle!—il croyait encore,
tout en affichant la libre pensée et le dédain de la
moralité. Les blasphèmes et les ironies mêmes prouvaient
que la religion n'avait pas encore perdu son empire.
Moi, je n'ai plus rien à faire dans un monde où il n'y en
a pas, et je n'y peux plus habiter. C'est pourquoi je fais
tout mon possible pour ramener la religion en Europe.
Ça vous surprend?'' It *had* surprised me for a moment,

though I remembered that he had entertained Jacques Maritain, Father D'Arcy and Monsignor Sheen. "Je me suis aperçu très tard que j'avais été coupable d'une grande erreur qui a failli m'être fatale. Je me suis éveillé un beau matin avec le sentiment peu consolant que l'Eglise Catholique du moyen-âge avait suivi le chemin de la bonne politique, aussi bien pour moi que pour elle, quand elle faisait brûler ses hérétiques. Elle savait bien que, dès le moment où l'on mettrait sérieusement en doute un seul de ses articles de foi, dès le moment où l'on s'aviserait de réfléchir sur ces choses par soi-même, c'en serait fait de la religion, il n'y aurait plus qu'une dégringolade complète. Moi, je n'y voyais pas clair jadis, mais ça ne m'est que trop évident à l'heure qu'il est. Tous ces rebelles fort intelligents, sur qui j'ai parfois osé compter pour m'aider dans mes propres affaires—si sympathiques qu'ils vous puissent paraître— l'Eglise savait bien ce qu'elle faisait quand elle les supprimait avec une sévérite impitoyable. Dès l'instant où Luther s'est échappé du troupeau, le glas de l'Eglise a sonné—ça a amené non seulement le démembrement de l'Eglise Catholique, mais l'affaiblissement progressif de la conception d'une église même—et je crains que ça ne continue jusqu'au point où il n'y aura plus de culte, donc plus de religion véritable, parce qu'on ne saurait accepter comme des religions les sectes rationalistes et purement éthiques comme le positivisme en France ou l'unitarianisme chez vous. Je peux vous dire," he added, dropping his indignant tone with the lightness of good taste, "que mon petit culte à moi n'existe presque plus maintenant. Il n'y a que les étudiants frivoles ou les pédérastes ridicules qui veulent bien me faire l'honneur de quelques rites tombés en décadence.

"Comme je vous le disais, je ne me suis pas aperçu tout d'abord où menait le succès de ces beaux prédicateurs. Je les ai vivement encouragés en leur soufflant des paroles plus hardies. Les moralistes m'ont toujours offert de très riches occasions. Les grands se distinguent par un esprit élevé et un caractère ferme et bien discipliné qui tombent quelquefois, par soif du pouvoir, avec une facilité admirable, dans l'orgueil et le fanatisme. La conscience de la vertu, n'est-ce pas, produit quelquefois une espèce d'ivresse, à travers laquelle on arrive à se persuader très volontiers que tous les êtres qui diffèrent de soi n'ont pas le droit de persister dans leurs erreurs; et quand on se permet de devenir féroce en voulant rendre les gens vertueux, on finit par faire mon œuvre—comme votre voisin M. Stryker," he added with a humorous smile, "vrai rejeton, acharné et tenace, de la vieille souche protestante. Donc j'ai commencé par faire mes délices de ce nouveau genre de moralistes qui, bien autrement intéressants que les princes gâteux de l'Eglise, se montraient d'une force si fraîche et si drue et qui disposaient d'un ascendant inouï sur les âmes les plus intraitables de leur temps—les calvinistes du meilleur cru valaient bien Torquemada; et l'aboutissement du mouvement protestant à ce cuistre anthropophage de Robespierre m'a charmé à tel point que je ne me suis pas tout de suite rendu compte que les adorateurs de l'Etre Suprême ne faisaient plus attention à moi. Puis je n'étais pas revenu de ma surprise et de mon chagrin que je me trouvai en présence de Marx, qui—je vous le concède volontiers"—he gave me a sly look—"pouvait se piquer de quelques beaux traits bigots et exterminateurs, mais qui n'apportait aux hommes comme religion que son matérialisme dialectique. Vous pensez bien que je ne trouvai pas beaucoup d'agrément à jouer éternellement le rôle de 'thèse' dans cette théologie tout abstraite qui m'impose l'obligation absurde de me faire manger, pour ainsi dire, périodi-

quement par 'l'antithèse' toujours vertueuse—procédé qui
me contraint, forcément, à renoncer à toute individual-
ité. J'ai essayé de m'y prêter et je n'ai pas réussi: me
voici tout de suite embrouillé, empêtré, enlisé, dans des
discussions ennuyeuses et interminables qui rappellent
la casuistique chrétienne mais qui n'en possèdent ni la
souplesse ni l'élégance. Le pire c'est que ces protagonistes
de la moralité marxiste ne la prennent même pas au
sérieux: ils n'aiment et ne recherchent que le pouvoir,
un pouvoir tout séculier, qui, soit qu'il rêve pour l'hu-
manité future une vie plus riche ou l'asservissement total,
ne me laisse plus aucune raison d'être.

"En somme, j'ai émigré chez vous, où ces tendances
ne sont pas encore développées jusqu'à ce point funeste.
Vous avez fait de si belles choses, n'est-ce pas, en fait
de forte moralité. The Mathers and Jonathan Edwards
—dont il me semble vous avoir entendu parler avec
beaucoup de perspicacité l'été dernier—c'étaient de
vrais titans. Et penser que Aaron Burr a été petit-fils
d'Edwards!—à mon avis, c'est la famille intellectuelle la
plus remarquable des Etats-Unis. 'My friend Hamilton,
whom I shot,'—je ne connais pas dans tout le dix-
huitième siècle de trait d'esprit plus fort que celui-là—
bien que je croie que cela a été dit un peu après dix-
huit cent. Il m'a beaucoup fréquenté, Burr, lorsqu'il
résidait en Europe. Il est dévenu, dans ses dernières années, un véritable Européen."

I had been listening with mounting impatience. I did
not believe in the horrors he predicted. I had never
been able to take Hitler seriously and I was all for giving Soviet Russia the benefit of every doubt. Now I
found that it annoyed and disturbed me to hear him
talk about American history in French and from that
point of view; and I told him in English that I wondered, none the less, at his coming to the United States,

since the Protestant disintegration had gone farther here than anywhere in Europe. "That's quite true," he admitted promptly, "but the Puritan sense of sin, the respect for my Distinguished Opponent and, I may say, a certain awareness of myself, is still pervasive in American society. The Catholics, too, you may have noticed, have been particularly active here of late. Some profess to see my hand in that—but I assure you the activities attributed to me were already well under way before I turned my attention to them, and I have often found them crude and distasteful. Nous sommes bien loins de Rome ici.

"I must say that my wife has found a better field. She is in constant demand as a speaker, lecturing to women's clubs, meeting the social leaders, and keeping in touch with the settlement work. She believes that the American women can now claim undisputed first place for initiative, aggressiveness, audacity, resourcefulness and dispassionate intelligence." I asked him whether the rumor were true that she was to be offered a nomination for the Senate. "It's impossible to say anything definite,"—he did not seem to care much to discuss it, and I felt in him a certain embarrassment mingled with a real pride. "But she won't forgive me," he said, "for keeping you from her so long."

We went back through the dining room, where the refreshments were laid out on a lavish scale—white tablecloths, pink hams, gleaming urns; and I remembered the evening in that house when I had had my first talk with Imogen. It seemed to me, in a moment of disquietude, of sudden disgust and doubt—though I hardly knew whether with myself or with the life that these things represented—that I had never really enjoyed those refreshments, that I had never got out of such occasions something I had hoped to get. I had at first, in my session with Blackburn, rather relished his cosmopolitan tone, his range of reference in time and place; but he was a gross enough fellow at best, and I was repelled by his efforts to flatter me.

Still, there was something in what he said about religion: we had to evolve our own morality now, and that applied to my problem about Jo as much as to the behavior of nations. Wasn't it really just an old superstition—the religion of romantic love—that made me feel it was not right to marry her?

II

When we came in through the back doorway of the living room, Kate Blackburn was not far away in the crowd. Smartly dressed in a black organdy evening gown, she stood talking to a tall young lawyer, who was laughing at something shrewd she had just said; but when she saw me, she looked in my direction with so quick an apparent interest that I went over to her. She began, without greeting: "I have a bone to pick with you. I don't agree at all with what you say in your article about Ingres's women. Ingres was a hell of a great painter, and his women are beautiful moon-faced dolls, but they're *not* representative of the period. He's left out something that is always important if you're trying to do a portrait of a woman and that was especially very *very* important in the days of the Directory and Napoleon. Fuseli does it wonderfully—they had just the same gals in England. I think you ought to write about Fuseli." I was surprised at her line of approach and at the definiteness of her opinions. The comparison of Fuseli with Ingres had no artistic point whatever, but I saw that she did mean something. I remembered that Haydon had said that the women Fuseli drew were all "strumpets," but there was also something else about them; and I vividly recalled a face in the background of a picture called *The Débutante:* a woman not young, with dark eyebrows, sharp eyes and a painted immodest mouth, who had a queer long giraffe-like neck, encased in a kind of collar. "No, Ingres's women are all idealized," she went on when I tried to explain that I hadn't necessarily meant that Ingres's portraits covered every kind of woman—"even when they're being coy in the harem.—I liked your article, though—if you only wouldn't try sometimes to put quite so much into one sentence—and would talk about things a little more concretely, keep closer to the actual canvases." She was really quite intelligent, I recognized—much more so than poor old Ed: my writing did sometimes have those faults. I admired her in her well-hung black evening gown that had tricky angular flaps at the shoulders, with the little diamond crescent in her hair. She was tall and rather thin, but quite attractive; her straightness and pale intensity somehow saved from the dryness of the blue-stocking and the tiresome self-assertiveness of the career woman by the presence of something more female—something of what the French call *"du chien,"* a flavor of sensuality and smartness. She had rather a wide mouth, with lips in which I now saw a suggestion of that matron of Fuseli's drawing who had also the look of a procuress. Otherwise—though always keeping this quality—she had reminded me on certain occasions of that type of upper-class German woman, very dignified, emphatic and well informed, who is social in a serious way and shows the military tradition behind her, and, on others, of one of those rich Middle Western girls who expect to be served like queens and have the malignity of a deep solemn selfishness. Yet she had also, like the Slavic women, a habit of half shutting her eyelids when anything flickered in talk to alarm her or put her on guard; and now for a moment she turned on this quick blinking as I continued to insist on the nobility of Ingres's porcelain faces. "We must talk about this more," she said. "I really know a lot about that period. I've got to finish an argument now with Charlie Fields, who's defending the Mangiari machine." "On what grounds?"—I glanced humorously toward Charlie. "He says it's an excellent thing because everybody's satisfied with it and they send people Christmas turkeys and sometimes pay the hospital bills when their jobholders' wives are sick—I say that it's a disgrace to the State and that we've got to get them out of office.—Now don't forget we're going to talk some more! Come back and find me later—promise?—Here's an old friend of yours who's thirsting to see you.—Don't forget, though—don't disappear!" There was a friendliness in her fierce dark eyes which had made me assume on her part some special appreciation, and now she gave me a swift smile and a briefly lingering look which might indicate, I thought, that she meant it—though one could never really tell with such women who were hostesses and politicians.

The old friend was not precisely a friend but a man with whom I had gone to school. His school nickname did come to my lips but I could not remember anything else about him. He was a broad-shouldered blond fellow in light brown tweeds who must have grown very much stouter since our schooldays; he had high cheekbones, a ruddy face, a pug nose and a certain boyish humorous charm. We drank a couple of highballs together, and it turned out in the course of our conversation that he was a watch manufacturer in Waterbury, being now head of his father's business. He was a shade apologetic about it and referred to himself as "one of your hated capitalists," but he talked with a good deal of acuteness about the iniquities of investment banking, which he said he had always thought was cockeyed. I could believe that this was not merely hindsight for I could see that he was a canny New Englander. He told me also that he had been following my writing and that he thought my recent article was swell, and he asked me—as he lit his pipe—whether it wasn't a great satisfaction to know that I had been plugging along at something worth while when everybody else had been going crazy. I, on my side, was reflecting that a businessman like Bud could be a great deal more interesting to talk to than most of the professional intellectuals. He was essentially serious-minded, but he read only what he wanted to read, unaffected by snobberies or cults, and he thought about things for himself, arriving at conclusions which were all the more striking for not being theoretical. And the truth was that, contrary to what I had assumed in the days when I was seeing Anna, I found myself at home with Bud in a way that I had perhaps never been with any of my newer friends. The common experience of school was something one could sit back on so solidly. That was my language that we were speaking, after all—that was my way of thinking. We were men of good will, he and I, and we met the crude and stupid world that we had found when we got out of college like those schoolboys who had laughed at the authorities and yet had wanted to do something high and fine. We talked about John L. Lewis, Charlie Mitchell, Franklin Roosevelt and Henry Ford, characterizing them and speculating about them in the same contemptuous or admiring way that one had done, on one's Sunday walks or lying in bed at night, in going over the masters and the more prominent "fellows"; and we reverted, indeed, now, to those "big men" of our so long dispersed class, and I heard for the

first time from Bud a lot of startling or amusing news
about people that I had not seen for years: their impressive or slightly comic successes, their sudden suicides,
their multiple divorces; and then finally we fell back
on the masters: it was surprising with what gusto we discussed them, comparing notes and each furnishing data
that the other had never known. It was a shock to me
that Mr. Maxton had been suspected of taking dope, and
interesting to hear that "Leif" Ericson had used to slip
away to Philadelphia and sit on a park bench all alone;
and Bud's impression of Mr. Jelliffe had been totally unlike mine, for I had been good at Greek whereas Bud,
as he now told me, had usually sat paralyzed in class,
staring at his book and afraid to stir, as he waited for
his turn to come round. There had always been an element of awe in our relations with the masters at school,
that we had carried all through our careers there from
the days when we had been new boys, and it was as if
it were at last a relief, even after so many years, to
break the spell and talk with perfect freedom. Soon I
was imitating Jelliffe and Bud was imitating McGee. I
remembered that there was something in Thackeray
about dining with certain gentlemen whose time of life
could be guessed from the fact that they amused themselves by mimicking their old headmaster—well, that,
then, was the phase I had got to, and wasn't it, after all,
rather a pleasant one, and one that there was no need to
be ashamed of? Weren't we lucky to have been taught
so well?—it had given us a precious advantage in an
age that seemed increasingly illiterate. Good old Thackeray!—one had perhaps been underrating him—and
good old world of his, too, perhaps, of which, when
one read him in childhood, it had still been possible
to think as connected with one's own world in America:
I had identified myself with Pendennis, during my

solitary rides as a boy, on his excursions between Clavering and Chatteris. And perhaps it was still there, after all, where one could reach it with only a step—Bud had just asked me to visit him in Waterbury, where I imagined there would be comfortable families who had always known one another, who had endured and kept their virtue, as families did not often do in our region. What if one really had been in it all the time and had never quite made connections with anything else one had tried?—what if one really belonged to all that?

Wasn't Hecate County part of it, too? I did of course love the neighbors and the gossip, the going to people's houses. By now I knew the locality minutely, and I explained to Bud that the curious name was merely one of those many classical place-names, like Syracuse, Hannibal and Rome, that the early inhabitants of the country appeared to have picked at random out of Plutarch. I also explained the people who passed or who came up and spoke to me so cordially that I found I was in some way proud of them—proud of knowing them all and being known by them. It took, I told myself, years to get to know them and to be really sympathetic with them—but there was much that was fine about them that you might not have noticed at first—they were even rather interesting in spots; and it was fun to be at home with all the sets, as one got to do in time, and not to be part of any. I told the mothers how good-looking their children were becoming; I asked the boat-lovers about their boats; I discussed whether or not it would be possible for me to take one of a litter of cockers; I promised a bored and boring middle-aged married woman that I would come to see the paintings she had been doing—I had said some pleasant things about her first attempts and I could hear myself saying some more, and it seemed to me that there was no harm in this, since it was all on the kindergarten level and one encouraged her as one did a child. "I hear you found a rare bird the other day," I said to a frail shy high-bridged man who went in for serious bird-watching. He recounted to us with excited pride how he had phoned to the state ornithologist, who had come straight out and shot the specimen; and expounded with distinguished precision the difference between an extinct and an extirpated bird. "He's by way of being an extirpated bird himself," I said smiling to my companion, when he had left us, and told Bud about the bird-watcher's wife, who despised his ornithological activities and had complained, "If he would only shoot something, so that at least we could have it to eat!" "Some pretty terrific women around here!" said Bud. I had not met Bud's wife, but I was sure that he had known her since childhood, and I wondered whether she were the jolly kind who had kept up with the cocktail era or the more provincial kind who did not try to look young and smart—the former, I liked to think.

"I've come to finish our conversation,"—Kate Blackburn was standing beside me. "You may have thought you'd escaped me, but I'm very tenacious!" She took me away to the corner behind the piano, where there were relatively few people. "How did you get along with Charlie?" I asked. "Did you convince him of the need for reform?" "Oh, I like Charlie Fields a lot— he always makes me laugh." At the moment I was hardly conscious that this remark about Charlie Fields was not precisely the kind of thing that one might have expected from Kate—my attention had been drawn in the other direction, toward the piano, where a cluster had gathered and where someone was about to play. "You certainly had a field day," she said, "hashing over school with Bud Webster. I always thought you

scorned Hillside." "This is not going to be so quiet,"
I said. The piano splashed out a passage from *Carmen*
and a high distinct cultivated voice began mincing out
a song about a beautiful cigarette girl at the Stork Club
and a man named Don José Hemingway who wanted
to be a toreador. "Ernie Fay's singing one of his songs,"
she said. "I haven't dared ask him to, because I did once
when I first knew him and he turned sour for the whole
evening." She was shy, I reflected, and had a great deal
of delicacy behind her sometimes too-assertive manner.
Ernie Fay, though she had known him for years, was a
professional night-club performer. "You didn't ask him,
did you?" she said. "No: I didn't know he was here,"—
but of course I had known he was coming: we had talked
over the list together. She was chuckling at all the sly
points in the song, which became more and more risqué,
and Ernie Fay, as he wriggled and twitched, would
sometimes turn all the way round and cock an eyebrow
in her direction. A big crowd had gathered about him. Jo
was immensely pleased. "I wonder whether he'll sing another," she said, when the laughter and applause were
fading. "You know, I think this is the best party we've
ever given together. Maybe it's because I'm tight, but
everybody seems to be having a good time. Even you
and your old Hillside friend!—and you usually complain about too many Babbitts."

It *was* awfully pleasant—we *were* having fun—and Jo,
I thought, looked perfectly lovely in her black organdy
evening gown. I had never seen it before, and it gave her
something clear and classic, somehow imposing reserve
on her smiling California openness and bringing out a
pure forehead, a straight nose, a firm chin and a well-
modeled mouth—almost she might have been painted by
Ingres. I watched her with a new admiration all through
the rather nauseating song. "Come outside a minute," I

said, when everybody was clapping and cheering. "I
want to tell you something." She went with me in silence—I was satisfied and proud, and I also felt really
excited. There would be people in the courtyard, I knew,
so I took her to the terrace at the side of the house. I
kissed her, holding her tight against me, one arm about
her naked shoulders, the other under her soft bare arm-
pit just where the breast begins; and she seemed to me
voracious and hot as I had never known her before. I said
nothing, for the kiss said all. But we couldn't go on, so
at last I stopped and looked away to distract myself.
There above us in the sky where it was always summer
hung the dust of the richly-sprinkled stars that gave the
illusion out here of being both closer-to and more tinselly
than they ever did in the East—the stars of the blissful
Pacific that had the look of festive decorations for people to be gay or to make love by, yet with which I had
never been able to feel myself in any vital relation as I
did with the remote ones at home. I spoke of this and
when I looked back at her face, I saw that she was smiling and gazing up with her lips parted in such a way as
to show great long bare-gummed teeth that stuck out and
yet curved back like tushes and that seemed almost too
large to be contained in her mouth. She looked like a
dog panting when you take it out for a drive, and for a
moment I was sharply repelled; but then, saying, "Yes, I
see what you mean," she closed her lips, and the teeth
disappeared. I saw only her wide wet mouth, and I
pounded kisses against it with summoned determined
passion, tasting her perfume and her flesh. It was precisely those long teeth, I thought, that gave her large
mouth its peculiar attractiveness: it might have been unpleasant, but wasn't.

"We ought to go back," she said softly. "Reggie da
Luze is completely pie-eyed and I'm afraid he'll get out

of hand. If he once gets started singing songs, Ernie Fay will never have another chance." We turned back. "I'll check up on Reggie," I said. "You've been handling things beautifully tonight," I added, as we entered the living room and heard the roar of the conversation. "I've never known you to be so nice about a party," she added with a sincerity that touched me. I reflected that I *had* been pretty wonderful. I had had that fine talk with Bud Webster, when I had so caught and entered into his point of view that he could hardly have known how different my own was, and there had been my brilliant French performance, when I had talked to that young Swiss from the Embassy and improvised a discourse on the demise of religion as blandly subversive as Anatole France.—But I mustn't, I reminded myself, indulge too much in the easy satisfaction of feeling social and intellectual superiority to the people one met on the Coast. Anatole France, indeed! They had only just discovered him in Hollywood and thought it made them "sophisticated" to read him.

We parted inside: she, so friendly and happy, stopped to talk to a new arrival, and I floated among the guests. I made my way with light smiles and host's jokes to the crowd about the piano, and there, just as Jo had feared, was Reggie da Luze at Ernie Fay's elbow, bent over with one arm around his shoulder, singing a song of his own composition, which I felt he had every intention of soon letting the company hear:

> *"Who'll bite your neck, your swan's-down neck,*
> *A-after my tee-eeth are go-one?"*

It wasn't really as dirty as the monologues that Ernie Fay had cooked up in New York, and I thought it was just

as funny, but there seemed to be a general agreement
that Ernie Fay's stuff was clever, whereas Reggie's somewhat decadent version of the old-fashioned rough Western humor was considered by many people distasteful.
Yet I felt that these rather kiddish parodies had seemed
much funnier back in the twenties, when everybody had
been more or less kiddish—especially as I heard him
start a ballad of which the refrain began:

> "So we played a little game of ten toes up,
> And also ten toes down."

When he had finished, I took him by the arm. He
turned around with badly-focussed eyes—he was evidently very tight. He had lost more hair from the front
of his head and was getting a lantern-jawed look. I
told him that I wanted to talk to him, and then when
we had stepped back from the piano, "That song is a
riot," I said. "Is that one of your own, too?" "I wrote
words and music," he answered. "I sing it, and I can
lead the band!"

I steered him back into the pleasant little library.
"Look," I began, "I don't know Hollywood and I wanted
to ask you something. I understand they have people
in the movies who advise them about period furniture
and historical décors and that sort of thing. Now I've
had a certain amount of experience working on those
period rooms in the American Wing at the Metropolitan, and I wondered whether there'd be any use in
my talking to somebody about a job." I was startled by
what I heard myself saying, especially since I had never
really worked in the American Wing at the museum,
but I told myself it was all in the interest of keeping
Reggie away from the piano, and, after all, it might

be worth while to inquire about this matter: in the
long run, it would become impossible to let Jo go on
paying the bills.

"Don't do it!" he urged me. "Don't do it! For a hack
like me, Hollywood's all right—but you've still got
your integrity"—he used this word as if it meant vir-
ginity—"and, by God, you hang on to it! Why, you
wouldn't survive the first conference! You don't know
what those apes are like! You know, the first time Freddie Lonsdale sat in on a discussion with Blumberg,
Blumberg asked him what he thought of the picture
and Freddie said he thought it was appalling. 'Yes,'
said Blumberg, 'but aside from that, what do you think
of it?' Can you imagine yourself up against something
like that? Listen: they got Ted Merriman out and he
didn't last out his first contract. He found at the end of
the second week that he was always skipped over in
conference. It turned out that the trouble was that he'd
been too polite to Danziger's wife. The ironic thing was
that she'd slept with everybody else in Hollywood, but
she hadn't slept yet with Ted. He'd just been giving her
his Baltimore gallantry.—Why, you wouldn't be able
to stand it a month! They're all drugged with making
money—it's disgusting. A friend of mine who's a lawyer at Long Beach came up to see me one week-end,
and I took him to a party where they all sat around and
talked about their options and their salaries. Pretty soon
I noticed that my friend had disappeared and I found
him pacing the floor in the next room. He said, 'All
that kind of talk's damned embarrassing, you know,
when you're trying to make up your mind whether
you're going to have enough money to buy linoleum
for the kitchen floor!' Of course, I'm not up in those
brackets myself—I only make five hundred a week. I
belong to the proletariat and I'm getting pretty damned

red, I'll tell you—since the writers took a 50 per cent cut and the producers saved a million dollars. I don't believe in the Screen Writers' Guild—it doesn't go far enough. But a real hard-boiled Left organization that wasn't afraid of the black list could get those sons-of-bitches on their backs. And the time will be ripe for that when the Guild demonstrates its impotence.—But you—good God, I don't believe you'd have a chance competing with those interior decorators that do most of that kind of work. You're not one of the boys, and I don't think they'd let anybody else in. You might better apply to the Los Angeles museum—not that they've got much there in the way of art: it's mostly prehistoric bones dug out of the Labrea tar-pit.—You know what they mean by culture in Hollywood: Scriabin's Golden Poem in the Hollywood Bowl—they think that Scriabin's some kind of big orange!—Still, you might be able to pick something up—they're impressed as hell with Eastern highbrows, and it's just a question of having an in—if you can bear to play up to those pansies. Some of them are way up in five figures. If you could convince somebody like Danziger or Blumberg that you were a big authority from New York, the top man at the Metropolitan, you might even start off in the big dough. That's the way they do it—they come on with prestige and they get paid a hundred grand for their names and doing practically nothing. There's been more than one case, in fact, of people you thought were sensitive aesthetes soon ending up dripping with annuities and whooping at the producer's jokes. Follansbie Winter, my God!—he's living in a Beverly Hills palace, with a private projection room—a custom-made Ferris wheel— a tennis court that's specially processed so that it's proof against hail, rain and earthquakes—a double-sized bath-tub with a phonograph attachment!—If you can get along with the decorator element—and I don't suppose there's any reason why you shouldn't—I don't mean any unpleasant implications, but I suppose all you period experts more or less speak the same language." His mood had now altered completely and he was eyeing me with hostile suspicion as if I were a dangerous competitor and already in enjoyment of these prizes. "Me, I'm just a plugger in the galleys. I've spent three years writing gags and two doing dialogue for louse-Westerns, and I'm still struggling along on a pittance. But I'm more of a radical at bottom than a lot of you Park Avenue Bolsheviks that have the *Daily Worker* brought up with your breakfast, and I'm enough of a dreamer to believe that the day is now not far distant when the sweated five-hundred-a-week man is going to come into his own!"

"Hell," he said, looking around the library. "Where can I get a drink?—Why did you bring up the subject of Hollywood? I came to your house to forget it." He pulled himself to his feet. We could still hear someone playing the piano. "I must go back," he said, "and make comical for your customers. They're clamoring for that salacious song. I've got another new number, too. Ernie Fay seems to think they're terrific, and I'm hoping he'll let me write some of his stuff. That's one part of my creative life that Hollywood hasn't been able to kill!"

I let him go and I soon became occupied with saying good-by to the guests. I was smiling and cordial and charming. Some I persuaded to stay for a nightcap and then I would pass on to someone else. Coming back through the front door into the hall, after seeing some people into their car, I noticed Bud Webster and Jo standing together in the corner by the coat-closet just underneath the stairs. Bud had his coat and hat on and seemed to be drawing away from Jo. I realized that they

were not talking, and it occurred to me that he must
have kissed her. I closed the door and came over toward them. "It's been a damn swell evening," said
Bud, shaking hands with a firm friendly grip. "We must
get together again and talk about school some more—I
believe that there were one or two points that we didn't
get around to discussing." I seemed to notice an accent of irony. "Yes," I answered, rather coldly. "Good
night." I turned back from the door to Jo and advanced
on her with a certain grimness. She met my sharp searching look with a gaze that might mean the blankness of
innocence or a masked doubt as to whether I knew. I
dimmed this glare after a moment, however: "Well,
they're almost all gone now," I said. "You dying on the
party?" she asked. It was true: I confessed to myself
that I was sleepy and bored and hostile. I shot her an
ironic half-smile, and I saw her smile in return: she
was on the point of saying something. I had the fear
that she would show her teeth and kissed her so that
she could not grin, and she gave me the kisses back with
what seemed to be frank full-lipped affection. "Come
upstairs!" I said, with appetite and deep need.

I had her: on the stairs I was sure of that. That momentary pose had meant nothing. I let her into a room
with twin beds that were covered with ladies' wraps:
velvet cloaks and white flannel coats and yellow camel's-
hair polo-coats, strewn in a confused heap. I saw that
there were still many guests, but I would vindicate my
mastership against them. The night-lamps with maps on
the shades were burning beside the beds; and on the
little green dressing table, painted prettily with pink
and blue posies, guest-size powder-puffs and lipsticks
of various tints lay in front of the gilt-framed mirror.
I turned the keys in the door to the hall and the door
into the neighboring bedroom, and cleared a space

across one of the beds by moving the coats away. There were a gold thing and a peacock-blue thing that I had pleasure in flinging aside. "Tell me," I asked, taking both her hands: "Did Bud Webster kiss you just now?" "He just kissed me good-by," she said. "He always kisses me. I've known him all my life." "I didn't know you had." "Well, I have. He used to come out here when he was a kid. Now don't be jealous—it's perfectly silly. Bud's never made a pass at me in his life. Don't, darling!" she was smiling, being sweet. I put my hand over her mouth. She pulled her face away: "What's the matter? Is my lipstick smeared?" I looked: "Yes, it is, a little. If it was merely a good-night kiss, I don't see why your lipstick should be smeared like that." "You just kissed me yourself, you goof.—Is this what you brought me up here for?"

I clasped her and kissed her with desperate greed, then I made her lie across the bed. She put one arm up over her eyes; her legs dangled, like a child's, from her knees—the dignity of her hostess's gown all going for nothing now. "Move forward," I said, and put her legs up. Her white thighs and her lower buttocks were brutally now laid bare; her feet, in silver openwork sandals, were pointing in opposite directions. What gusto I expected to taste in the coarse enjoyment of Jo in her evening gown—the fierce sense of violating a woman at her most contrivedly attractive, when she is usually beyond our reach; just as my club seemed to burn and exult in liberation from the formality of my evening clothes. But then she suddenly uncovered her face and turned her head toward the door into the hallway. Somebody was working the knob in a determined and vigorous fashion, and immediately a high nasal voice that had the clang of the Philadelphia "main line" came through the locked door so distinctly that I could

recognize, could see, the intruder: her tall awkward figure and her bright black eye that had shrewdness but
no sexuality. "Maybe somebody's passed out or been
sick," she was suggesting to some companion. "I'll go
and get Jo." She was a very good sort, goddam her.
She rattled the knob again.

Jo jumped up, her flushed face embarrassing. "I'll
go out through the other room," I told her, and quickly
and quietly unlocked the door with a hand that fumbled
inflamedly at the keyhole. It was a man's room, and
there was a great leather dressing case full of silver-
backed brushes and silver-topped flasks spread open for
use on the bureau, and on a table a tall silver cup
which I knew had been won in a golf tournament. I
knew also that they belonged to me, yet I felt toward
them the detachment and aversion of a guest toward an
unsympathetic host or a host toward an uncomfortable
guest, I could not have told which. I hurried on through
several more rooms—there was always another one—in
all of which people were staying: there were expensive
clothes lying about. I was afraid someone would come
in and see me—I heard voices outside one door: I had
no right in the rooms of my guests; and they would
know I was running away. In the last room there was
a lady at a dressing table. She had her back to me and
did not turn as I was hurrying through the room. I did
not let my eyes rest on the mirror—I dreaded what I
knew I should see; but I kept my glance fixed on the
back of her head with its fine and sheeny coiffure and I
saw it move as if she had heard me, just as I got out
of the door.

I sped through the hallway—there was a little servants' staircase, and I skimmed down it, just grazing the
steps and steadying myself on the railing by touching it
with the tips of my fingers. It kept on turning, and I

could not see behind to know whether I were being followed.

Below, in a little side hall, I was close to the party again: I could hear their loud guffawing and gabbling. But there was a door there that led out of the house. I opened it very softly and adroitly, slipped out and closed it quickly behind me; and now found myself at last—with what freedom and relief!—in darkness and solitude again.

III

I got hurriedly into a car that looked like mine, but I didn't feel safe till the key had worked. As I pulled out, I was further reassured by recognizing the Blackburns' drive, down the steep curves of which I was coasting. Yet, once out on the main road, I had tremors of doubt, not always sure that I knew where the cross-streets were or which turning I ought to take. I must be awfully drunk, I thought: I should have to watch myself to get home.

That enchanted country of drink that was the world one had been young in, in the twenties! One drank to go back there, where one's friends were, where life was irresponsible and daring, where it was passionate, amusing and frank. One got homesick under the grind of the depression and one could not help slipping away. But then one did not find what one had come for: one's friends were no more their old selves than one was one's old self; one could pick up one's cues for the old clever play, but a moment of alcoholic revelation would show up its essential banality, its superficiality, its falsity, and one would walk out with indignation and rudeness. So this evening, I now concluded, I must first, over my highballs, have been carried away by some fantasy of a

future with Jo, which had quite made me forget the
actual company, some bright vision of rejoining the
twenties in Jo's little house on the Coast—and then of
course I had suffered a revulsion. Had I failed to say
good-night to the Blackburns? Had I done something
more or less awful in that room where the ladies left
their wraps? What had I been doing there? The whole
thing was rather dim in my mind, and my conviction of
triumph at escaping prevailed over misgivings of guilt.
A drink when I got home would sustain me, I should
glory in having fled. I could rejoin there my old solitary
self, the self for which I really lived and which kept
up its austere virtue, the self which had survived
through these trashy years. And here was my drive
through the woods. I turned in past the letter-box on its
post, not even looking to make sure of my name there.

And there was my light through the trees. How stabil-
izing to drive up beside my buried stone house—a
lodge that was almost a castle—and put my car in my
own garage, to open my own front door, to find everything just as I had left it. The single lamp in the living
room was on; my book lay face down on the couch. I
could not really be terribly tight, and I positively could
not be dreaming—for in dreams things were always different and here things were all just the same. I picked
the book up and looked at the pages: it was the big
one-volume edition of Spengler. I checked also on the
Matisse drawing, which I had bought with half the advance for my book and of which I knew every line. I
examined the telephone table, where the colored girl
had scrawled a message to call a Mr. Somebody-or-
Other—I could not make out the name and could not
recognize the number, and had a moment's disgust at
the thought that this unknown person might call again.
But the room was all right, reassuring. Here was my

place in the woods, small but sound, where I had made myself independent and built my own kingdom of thought. I stood in the middle of the room and looked proudly at the big stone fireplace, the door onto the flagged back porch that looked down on the little river, the high ceiling that went up to a peak. And there was the door that led into my study and the door that led into the hallway and into those bedrooms that were almost monastic. It had the dignity, that rude yet snug little house, of everything in my life that was good.

I had just put a mark in the Spengler and was about to turn off the light when the silence of that room which seemed almost my mind was broken by a sharp *clack-clack-clack*. I tried to insist for a second that it was only a noise of the night, the floor cracking or a branch rattling, but it did have the purposive accent of somebody at the little iron knocker, and after a pause it clack-clack-clacked again. I wondered a moment whether I could not ignore it and let the visitor go away, but I was standing in plain view of the front windows and it would be too embarrassing, I felt, to have someone look in and see me. Yet I waited a little time still, immobilized with the book in my hand. The next knock was a pounding that jolted me. The visitor had abandoned the knocker and was using his fist on the door.

I strode over and yanked it open. There, pale, with tie askew and suit unpressed, evidently well soaked in drink, leered out from under an old soft hat Si Banks. "Just thought I'd d-drop in," he said. "I s-saw that you f-fled the party, and it inspired me with the same idea!" There was nothing to do but to have him in. His drunkenness and rascality bore down on me like a messy but not unwelcome doom. In rejecting the big house, after all, I had let myself in for this; and it was good to have a companion in protest. I got out the tray with the whisky and ice and put it down, where it was pleasantly convenient, on the little low table by the couch, and now I found that I rather looked forward to talking things over with Si.

"Well, what did you get out of it tonight?" I asked. "Why, I absolutely got the conviction that Kate Blackburn would be our next President!" "She *is* getting along pretty fast.—The whole thing affected me very unpleasantly." "You know, she's practically bankrupted poor Ed financing her campaign for the Senate—and she won't let him invite his friends any more if they're on the wrong side politically—Bert Mangiari, the local boss, used to be a great pal of Ed's, you know. She only invites people that can do her some good." I saw that Si was going to be at his best: extravagant but essentially serious. "What were we doing there, then?" I asked. I was holding on my open hand a little puppet from a child's Punch-and-Judy show: a toy devil with a black face, a red coat and black spindling wooden legs that dangled. "She thinks we're pinks who will influence the liberals—but I'm against government by women more than anything else in the world. I'd vote against the best bill ever drafted if Kate Blackburn were the person who was sponsoring it. That's one reason I don't like the New Deal: too many women in power.—I tell you the real line-up today is not between the classes any more—and it's not between the democratic and the totalitarian states. It's the war between men and women —Thurber's the great prophet of the time. We guys have got to stick together, if we want to keep it a man's world. The magazines are all written for women; the columnists are getting to be women; and if you turn on the radio, you hear some goddam woman squawking about foreign affairs. If we don't stick together now, they'll get us!" I had put my hand inside the puppet

and made it stand up and wave its arms. Si giggled:
"The horns hurt a little," he said. Where had the little
black devil come from? A suspicion disturbed my mind
that Si might be an agent of the Blackburns, sent to
tempt me again even here.

But he was right, after all, I reflected. I was glad that
I had let Jo go. It would be better to risk losing her
entirely than to run the chance of living her life.
Si Banks, in bad shape though he was, had at least escaped from that sort of fate. He had deserted the strong-
minded girl whom he had married in his early twenties
and who had objected to his friends in the Village, and
now he had to give up part of his salary for the support
of her and her child; but he did have his uninhibited
freedom, and I thought he would write something someday. Here he had staggered in tonight like the jackdaw
of Rheims, cursed by bell and book, his hair sticking up
behind and the two bottom buttons off his vest, but not
merely appealing to compassion; inspiring, also, a certain respect by the purity of his love of letters and his
stubborn insistence on his right to judge the actions
and values of the world. Had I not much more in common with Si than with any of those false-solid people?
—than with that stupid old school-friend, for example,
with whom I had been wasting my time? The only
things that were supremely worth doing had to be put
through outside all that—the way Si and I chose to
live: in Greenwich Village or in the forest.

I told him—and, as I did so, was conscious of my
superior and mocking tone—that he reminded me of the
jackdaw of Rheims. "I haven't s-stolen anything," he
said. "Yes, you have: wherever you are, they feel that
somebody is laughing at them, and that steals some of
their self-respect. I almost got stultified at the Blackburns' tonight, but somewhere there was a leak and a

draught, and it must have been caused by your presence." I was warming, feeling more and more cordial.
Why shouldn't I talk freely with him?—I was thoroughly glad he had come.

"The *Ingoldsby Legends* are marvelous, aren't they?"
he began, with that fine light in his eye that always
woke me to a responsive enthusiasm. "Nobody seems to
know them any more. I discovered them one summer
on the Cape when I'd gone up there to visit my aunt.
I used to read them all afternoon in a hot bedroom up
under the eaves and I'd hear the one train a day from
Boston whistling at three o'clock. Boston seemed a long
way off and there was nothing beyond but Boston. All
the rest of the world, such as New York, was a great
deal more unreal to me then than the world of the
Ingoldsby Legends." "I read them at my aunt's, too,
curiously enough," I answered with a thrill of remem-
brance—"right here in Hecate County. The Cruikshank
illustrations I really liked better than the poems, though.
And I went through the albums of Hogarth and some
big volumes they had of the *Antiquities of Rome.* I used
to hear the whir of the lawnmower and the crack of
people hitting croquet balls." "Everything was so quiet
and dependable," he said. "There was plenty of time
to look at pictures and read long poems in big arm-
chairs. But we can never get back to that now."

I was moved—I found—almost to tears by the
thought of the beauty and pathos of those days when
one had read through the afternoons. It was as if my
own youth sat beside me. He was several years younger
than I, had been a freshman when I was a senior, and,
with his smooth brow, his twinkling eye and his black
Charlie Chaplin mustache, which I imagined he had
originally intended to have a gay cavalier look and
which did preserve a touch of the dashing, he had al-

ways remained boyish. I had been just such a solitary child—silently in love with excellence and unable ever to take quite seriously the respectable pursuits of my elders. And now that childhood was still with me there, it had come to me in dear little Si—to reassure me, entertain me, renew me.

"The character in the *Ingoldsby Legends* that I've really felt most like tonight"—he was picked up by some stimulating and droll idea—"is the man with the severed head. Do you remember that?—Hamilton Tighe?

"And he cries, 'Take away that lubberly chap
That sits there and grins with his head in his lap!'"

I could see the grisly picture, with the bristling hair, the bared teeth and the glaring eyes. "That's really the way I've been all evening. I was thinking tonight at the party that I was like Bertram del Bornio in Dante—you know: he holds his head like a lantern—I was going to do a poem about it. But the grinning old fool is much better. It's curious how frightening that idea is—I suppose it's the split personality. That's just the way I was sitting, that picture—holding my head in my lap like a hat while it went on laughing at everything insanely—and in the meantime the rest of the body is quivering and shaking all over."

This vision did scare me a moment: I wondered again whether *they* could have sent him. "It's still detachable, I think," he said, grinning. "Would you like to have me put it in your lap?" He was raising his arms to his head, as if he were going to lift it off; but I stopped him: I could not stand this—I pulled his hands down and held them. I noticed how fine they were: sensitive, nervous and slim, not practical and knuckled like Jo's. "Don't worry about yourself," I said. "You better have another drink. Why don't you stay here tonight? It's too far to go back to the Point." I was still holding down his hands, and my tenderness seemed overflowing in an emotion uncontrollable, demoralizing, yet too quickly becoming welcome. I looked up at him and he met my glance with a self-conscious half-feminine smile. He was giggling in a way that I did not like: it made a grating disagreeable sound. "That's the ovenbirds," I said. "Don't worry. It's all done by a little brown bird that builds a nest in the underbrush." And I fixed my attention on the bird where it perched on a branch just above us, its tiny body so tense and vibrant as it pumped out its raucous notes. I concentrated on driving it away and I yelled at it again and again, but I couldn't make it stir from the branch: it kept up its harsh reiterated rasping.

"What's the matter?" said Jo. I had waked her up and she looked at me over her shoulder. I saw that her eyes were puffy. "It's those goddam ovenbirds," I cried, with menacing indignation. "They make that damn racket every morning." I lay there a few minutes listening; then leapt up and rather gropingly but determinedly got my feet into my slippers at the bedside and propelled myself out of the house, picking up on my way through the living room a burst tennis racket and some old magazines; and, standing in the damp June morning with the grass about my half-bare feet, I hurled these up at the high tops of the locusts, in which exasperating New Year's Eve rattles seemed hideously to be scratching the dawn. I saw the little birds fly quickly away, and I returned to the house relieved. I started to climb into bed with the bottoms of my pajama pants wet, but I realized that that wouldn't do, and went to the bathroom and dried my ankles and took off the pajama bottom and got back into bed without it. The birds had by this time begun again, having merely withdrawn a short distance. I cursed them more bitterly: "Goddam them!" I said. "They oughtn't to have birds like that in summer!" "Don't be so frantic!" said Jo. There she lay beside me, solid and warm, and always so fundamentally good-natured. We had not made love the night before, as we usually did when she came out to see me. I had worked up a hypocritical quarrel with her about her going away to the Coast: "I'm sorry I was nasty last night," I said. I was glad to see her teeth were all right, and that her lips were clean and straight. In those days, what with revery and alcohol and art, I carried so much of dreaming into real life and so much of my real life into dreams—as I have sometimes done in telling these stories—that I was not always quite sure which was which.

We repaired our omission of the evening before, and it was as if I had been purified and freed from that nightmare that had still hung in my mind like the headache of an asphyxiation. "You've never been in the Southwest, have you?" she asked, as I lay with my arm around her. "You like living in the woods so much, you ought to be crazy about those great big forests that they have in the Jemez Mountains. I've promised to take Billy out there for a month or so sometime this summer. Why don't you come out and join us?"—and suddenly, for the first time in my life, it dramatically flashed upon me that I, too, could climb the mountain trails and ride among the Western cattle and hear the cougar cry. A few weeks on a ranch in New Mexico—"Not a dude ranch at all," she assured me—would rescue me from Hecate County and put me in touch with that heroic America, the America I had sniffed from our inlets and brushed through in the tangled grove, and it would carry along my relations with Jo: there would be no time for anyone else to make an impression on her.

So still we turned West, as our fathers had done, for the new life we could still hope to find—so we sought to regain that new world which seemed still to be just at hand, with its wild forest trails and fresh waters, but from which we now found ourselves divided by a pane of invisible glass. It was not really the new country any more; it was the old country: we had passed it in history; and the loves and achievements of our youth had all taken place somewhere else. When Jo and I, later that summer, came to visit the corn dance at Cociti, the cave-dwellers' canyon of Frijoles, the old mining towns with their overgrown diggings—all those primitive and romantic things—we were to find that the hangover by the cold mountain stream made it hard for us to see the bright morning; that the space of the gigantic pastures turned to boredom before we had crossed them; that the tall intimidating presence of the forests of aspen and pine, with their alien life that excluded ours, only left us the more alone with the strain of our wrong relation. We were to find the fears and suffocations, the drugged energies, of Hecate County; I had packed my bad nights with my baggage, and I was later to look back with more pleasure on the excitement I had felt that morning when I had first had the vision of Jo as an exhilarating Western girl, laughing her open-air laugh in my tight little comfortable house and hungrily devouring my breakfast, as we had planned the exploits before us.

The stars move still, time runs, the clock will strike.